REBEL ACADEMY

WICKEDLY CHARMED BOOK TWO

CRUSH

REBEL ACADEMY: CRUSH

WICKEDLY CHARMED BOOK TWO

Nothing is more seductive than the forbidden...

...and temptation could crush this cursed academy.

As both a witch *and* ghost in an academy for bad boy supernaturals, you would think that I'm at home amongst the monsters. But in this home, I'm a prisoner.

Pleasure and fate bind me to three devastatingly hot Immortals, but our unbridled lust feeds a dangerous power inside me. Will I destroy us all if I lose control?

The perilous trials of the Rebel Cup are only the beginning. The ruthless fae and elf princes are deadlier than even the academy's tests, and their love could shatter me.

When I'm sent on my first assassin mission, will my immortal lovers and I survive?

REBEL ACADEMY CRUSH: WICKEDLY CHARMED BOOK
TWO © copyright 2020 Rosemary A Johns

www.rosemaryajohns.com

Fantasy Rebel Limited

BOOKS IN THE REBEL VERSE

REBEL ANGELS - COMPLETE SERIES

COMPLETE SERIES BOX SET: BOOKS 1-5
VAMPIRE HUNTRESS
VAMPIRE PRINCESS
VAMPIRE DEVIL
VAMPIRE MAGE
VAMPIRE GOD

REBEL WEREWOLVES - COMPLETE SERIES
ONLY PERFECT OMEGAS
ONLY PRETTY BETAS
ONLY PROTECTOR ALPHAS

REBEL VAMPIRES - COMPLETE SERIES

CHAPTER ONE

Prince Willoughby's Diary, Wednesday September 4th 2017

WILLOUGHBY

The cursed silk winds around me, crushing the air from my lungs.

I gasp. I can't breathe, and my magic is trapped.

Brother, please don't betray me.

But then, I killed father.

Another royal blue snake slithers from my younger brother, Darby's, hand and winds around me to create a gossamer light suit.

Round, and round, and round...

It's scented with Darby's magic of winter grasses,

but it makes me shudder, rather than feel safe. It glimmers in the light like the silver shackles at my wrists and the collar at my neck.

My magic screams at the unnatural cage that binds it.

I'm a collared prince dressed in silk. A fallen king. *Deposed.*

Why am I surprised that I'm on my knees before the throne, which I'd been destined to sit on?

Darby sprawls on the frozen throne. He wears the Ice Crown, which is as high as antlers, like he craves to gore me with it.

I shiver because it's like looking at my younger self in the mirror: large sky-blue eyes, which match the cascade of silky sky-blue hair. Yet have I ever been flushed with such hate or ambition? He watches me with a ravenous expression like my every flinch and gasp feeds the darkness within him.

Had I merely missed it before, clouded by love?

Father raised a kingdom, but I raised Darby. I dragged him away from his musty books and out to explore the mountains, rivers, and woods of our Other World. I crouched with him in the mud, as we cupped frogs in our hands. Then we swam under the freezing thunder of waterfalls to explore hidden chambers and dream of dragons. When we clasped hands and blew the fuzzy heads off dandelions, screwing shut our eyes to make a wish, I'd never known that as the seeds scattered on the breeze, I was blowing away my last moments with my brother.

A king who now watches the life in my eyes die.

Yet were Darby's wishes back then different to my own? Had he always desired my crown?

I shudder, and my mind grows hazy. My powers are forced down, dangerously deep inside. Yet aren't *they* what's dangerous? I'm deadly. That's why I'm in chains.

I sway, and my vision blurs.

In the name of the Other World, don't restrain my magic...my mind...my body in this enchanted straightjacket.

Kill me.

Did I scream that out loud or did it only echo inside my mind?

Don't condemn me to this slow death.

My brother's lips curl into a cruel smile. He's always been a talented sorcerer. I'd been proud of his talent. Once, I'd been puffed up about my own skills both as a warrior and a sorcerer. Now I know that I've never been able to control either power.

As the last length of silk slithers around my chest, I choke.

Help me.

But I deserve this: my sentence and salvation. If I can't control myself, then perhaps, this cursed suit can.

I wrench at the shackles, fighting the panic.

3

Don't struggle. You're a prince, act like one.

The palace chamber is dim in the evening light. How long has this curse been woven? How long have I knelt on this sapphire floor as a prisoner, which once I'd played on? I battle to lift my head and look through the arched window out at the palace gardens beyond. The lattice of oaks, which form bowers for fountains, are beaten by a snowstorm.

All around me, servants who I've known since I was a child and would once have bowed and waited on my orders, bustle to their work like I'm invisible. They drop silk banners across the wooden columns.

Why are they hiding my father's palace? They are burying its simple lines under extravagance. Does Darby wish to bind it in his magic as much as he's binding me or to hide it away...?

Will he imprison me in the dungeons?

I press my nails hard into my palms. An elf's life is too long to live without touch, life, and light...

Kill me.

I stare defiantly up at Darby, who glowers back.

"Stop this, brother." I wet my dry lips. "It's enough."

"You think to tell your king when it's *enough*?" Darby arches his elegant brow.

"Since when were you the king? Or *mine*?" I tilt my head. "You're my younger brother. It's *I* who father sat on his knee and told stories of our ancestors.

One day, it'll be my turn to add a sculpture. You know how hard I studied for that skill." When Darby shifts, I raise my shackled hands to point at the frozen ice sculpture of a dragon on the back of the throne. "Every king adds their own legacy. Yet I only cared about the feel of father's fingers between mine, as he'd traced them across each one: warm against the cold."

Sitting on that throne with father, I felt that he could protect me from anything. *But he couldn't protect himself from me.*

Darby clutches the dragon's wing like he wishes that he could break it off. "Well, he's dead now. So, his fingers are only cold, and it's mine that get to hold the throne."

When I flinch, Darby's expression darkens like it's a personal victory.

I swallow. "I didn't mean—"

"*No more lies, traitor.*" Darby leans forward on the throne that I'd been brought up since birth to inherit, wearing the Ice Crown on his head that'd only been meant to grace *mine.*

I clench my jaw. "Where's mother?"

"Weeping."

Who was lying now?

For the first time, rage bubbles through me. The tips of my hair sharpen with ice. The room becomes chilly.

Not again, not again, not again...

"I'm still her son," I hiss.

A sly smile creeps across Darby's face. "Are you so certain, killer?"

The hurt flashes across my face, before I can mask it.

Under my breath, I hum the calming lullaby that mother taught me, when I was plagued with nightmares of Dark Elves and unable to sleep. She's skilled in magic but only to heal, unlike Darby who uses his to harm. I possess merely a spark of her talent. Her songs are like being dragged down into winter waters, sliding into sleep.

When Darby leaps off the throne and prowls towards me with predatory danger, I stare at him in shock.

The throne room falls to a deep hush. The servants huddle together, scared. My hum echoes through the ancient chamber like calm waters beneath the deadly ice of my brother's rage.

The *crack* of Darby's slap across my cheek, silences me.

"Shall I spell your murderous lips unable to sing our blessed songs again?" Darby circles me.

The hairs on my nape rise. I stiffen my shoulders, and my expression becomes shuttered.

Would he truly do that? It broke every elven belief.

Don't take my music.

Still, I don't move.

"Yet that wouldn't solve the problem of the elves outside this palace who hold vigil for their dead king and call for your execution." Does he wish me to beg for my life? *Let him take it.* He blinks. "Won't you say anything?"

"It's hard to be the one with the power," I answer, softly. "I shan't make the decision for you."

Darby's eyes widen. "I wasn't...I mean..." His gaze slides from mine. I can see him then: the boy who climbs trees with me and charms the horses to gallop faster than the fall winds. "I believe mother weeps because she's worked out that you're not a Light Elf at all. In fact, you're nothing but a *Dark Elf* from our nightmares. You're a changeling who was swapped at birth...the reason that my true brother and prince was killed."

How could he shame me like that? He could have my magic, mind, and body but not my heritage.

I birthed with my own hands two foals, Thunder and Lightning, who I raised to be stallions for my brother and me. Their coats gleam midnight black against the snow. They understand me better than any elf. Together, my brother and I have ridden them on missions, as well side by side into battle to protect the kingdom.

Even if the same people who I protected now wish me deposed and executed, I still love these lands.

How could I not be his brother?

"A fairy tale. I'm a Light Elf...I'm *me*..." Yet the uncontrollable power that's been bound is different. It's...*monstrous*. My stomach lurches. I bend over, resting my forehead against the cold floor. "I'm not Dark..."

Darby's sharp heel digs into the back of my neck, holding me to the ground. "You're a *monster*. Be grateful that I love the elf who you once were enough to be honest. As you can't control yourself, it's my duty to leash you. Hereby I judge you banished from the Other World and sentenced to the Rebel Academy, until such time as it's reported that you've repented, paid penance, and have learned to control your power."

Banished? Sentenced to the Rebel Academy?

"Please, brother," I beg, "don't send me away from the Other World. It shall wither my Soul to lose the music of these hills and streams. I've spent centuries defending and loving this kingdom. My magic and Soul are connected to it like ivy. If I'm torn from the Other World, across the Eternal Forest, it'll be like..." My brain's foggy with the cursed silk binding it. "...tearing me apart."

All of a sudden, Darby grabs my hair and wrenches back my head. I cry out, as he pulls me up, until I'm staring into his glittering gaze.

His eyes narrow.

"Do you deserve anything different, changeling? You're royalty and so you must continue with your life — such as it is — but you won't escape the prison of the coven-led academy. The worst supernatural *boys*," I force myself not to wince at his sneer, "of the paranormal world are controlled by the witches. They have the specialized experience to dampen your powers even further than the curse that now binds you. If you ever loved this kingdom as you claim or any of your family," for a moment, his expression softens, before becoming glacial again, "then don't shame us. Serve your penance. Impress me with your achievements. No matter how far apart we are, I control the magic within that suit and I can still crush the rebellion from you."

"Reject, crush, and imprison me," I say like I'm not shattering inside; the blizzard rages outside the palace, smashing against the windows, "but look after Thunder and Lightning when I'm gone. Those stallions are loyal and love us both. They won't understand where I've gone, and I'll..."

...Miss them.

They don't deserve to be left behind.

When Darby's expression transforms to false sympathy, I tense. *By my ears, what has he done?*

9

Not my horses...I can't...anything but... They're innocents...

I'm shivering. I can't stop. Darby rests his hand on my shoulder like he's steadying me but instead, he's dragging in my shivers like they're strengthening him.

Has his magic truly become this dark? *How could I have been so trusting?*

"Don't hurt others because you won't execute me," I whisper. "I'd do anything to gain your forgiveness, but if that's not possible, then kill me."

"Thunder roared when I fired the arrow through his brother's heart." Darby tilts up my chin, so that our gazes meet with a searing intensity. "But he didn't try and run. He's always been obedient like that. So, it appears that he doesn't take after you." A tear chases down my cheek. I can't stop it...stop anything. Don't say it, *no more.* "But he was silent when I wound silk just like this around his neck."

Silk spun in the air and then around my neck above the collar. I scrabble at my neck, but Darby holds my bound hands down like I'm reduced to the younger brother.

I'm powerless against him.

I gasp, dragging in desperate breaths. Darby yanks me off my knees, dangling me in the air as if I'm on the end of a noose.

Then he cups my cheek. "When you fall asleep in your academy, I want you to think about the moment that I killed your horses because *you killed my father*. And how at any moment, I could unwind the silk from your suit and..." His fingers slip down one by one from my cheek to clasp around my throat like a threat. "...choke you in your sleep. Will you behave for your professors now? I expect you to win every tournament, prize, and trial. Sweet dreams, killer."

The silk tightens, my eyes flicker shut, and I fall into darkness...

I'm dying.

AND THAT'S HOW I WOKE UP ON THIS FIRST NIGHT IN the Rebel Academy.

Alone, hurt, and trapped.

Shaking, I gasped for breath. The silk was tight around my throat, as I struggled, still haunted by the nightmare.

I'm writing this in my Crystal Diary. It's the only place that I can be honest.

Who can I trust after the darkness in my brother? After I lost control of myself?

I've been told that I now belong in the Princes Wing. A haughty fae prince has been put in charge of me. He's a Prefect but he's more like my guard. There's also a vampire whipping boy who's beautiful and as lost as me.

Yet what frightens me most about this academy

isn't that I'll be crushed. It's that I'll lose control like I did in my own kingdom. Then *I'll* crush my eternal prison, this *Rebel Academy*.

After all, they've taken in a true monster.

CHAPTER TWO

Rebel Academy,Wednesday September 4th
PRESENT DAY

MAGENTA

When I'd been burned alive over one hundred years ago, it'd appeared *miraculous* that the witches' goddess Hecate had trapped me in her tree as a ghost.

On Sunday, it'd been just as miraculous that my delicious Immortals — a mage, god, and incubus — had risked their lives to free me as a Ghost Witch.

Yet I didn't believe in miracles.

I twisted my tendrils of magenta power around Damelza Crow, the Principal of the Rebel Academy, piggybacking on her magical transportation.

It shouldn't be possible... I'd be torn apart and scattered through the four corners of the grounds.

If I survived though, it wouldn't be a miracle. It'd be *my* magic and the academy, grasping onto me as naturally as a tree holds a bud to its branch against the winter breeze.

The House of Crows never understood nature, but my magic *was* nature.

I hung onto the pathway that should've flown Damelza smoothly from one side of the castle to the other, as she attempted to drag my incubus lover, Bask, to her study. She wished to hand him over to the Duchess, the succubus who'd once been bonded to him.

Well, that wasn't going to happen. *But then, I was wicked.*

I was born the first Blessedly Charmed witch in five hundred years, but when the mage that I loved had been walled up alive because I'd dared to share my first kiss with him, I'd lost control of my powers and cursed the entire academy, becoming Wickedly Charmed.

Cauldrons and candles, everyone had their tipping point, didn't they?

It *was* rather reckless to grab hold of Bask, since I was hexed not to touch him, and that hex was a bitch. It electrocuted both Bask and me, as we fell through the darkness, spinning off course from the study.

14

I coiled my magic around Bask, until he glowed. Then I wrenched, yanking Bask out of Damelza's hold and away from her dark magic.

The air itself crushed me.

I clung to Bask's hard chest; his sweet scent of coco and almonds cocooned me. I longed to kiss his plush lips and taste him. His arms wrapped around my shoulders, stroking my long blond hair, like he'd never let me go.

Don't. Let. Go.

The hex ripped through me, savaging me. I screamed, and my ears rang. The shock shuddered through both of us together, as we shook like we were dancing.

Hecate, please, please, make it stop...

Perhaps, I needed to have **NEVER PRAY TO GODDESSES** tattooed somewhere intimate. My crow familiars, Echo and Flair, would've voted for my bosoms.

They were certainly ample enough.

Keep concentrating on my jiggling bosoms and not the agony...

I bit my tongue to hold in the pleas: *stop the man who I love from being forced into marriage just like I'd almost been to a fae prince, save the mage from death, even if I hadn't been able to save my best friend, and pull me back from the crushing black.*

Yet the last time that I'd prayed to Hecate, I'd been

burned as a sacrifice. So, I rather thought that this time I'd save myself without divine...*anything.*

I'd had enough of being witch slapped by either covens or ancient deities. Life had been breathed back into me, and I was just discovering true belonging amongst the living. Yet Damelza had intended to whisk one of those *living* Immortals who'd introduced me to the sensations, experiences, and love of this new world in the twenty-first century away, and I'd stolen a ride.

It was time to steal him back.

I clutched Bask tighter, as the magic spun out of control, careening us through the veils. My Blessedly Charmed magic pulsed through the castle. The castle's heartbeat *thud — thud — thudded* in time with my own.

I'd created and cursed Rebel Academy. *It was mine.*

Its shadows and secret places, which smelled of white sage and forgotten magic, were opened to us. *We were inside them.*

Don't let us be lost between worlds.

My nerves fried, and my teeth chattered.

Bask and I tore through hidden passageways, chambers, and shrines.

Mage's balls on a stick...make it stop...

There was a darkness like icy blood poisoning the veins of the academy, and it was my own loss and grief. I shook with the realization that only I could heal it.

I might be a wicked witch, but I could bless, as well as curse. My mother and her descendants who ran this academy had their Principal's Motto Book, but I didn't have a rule book.

My stomach lurched, and for a moment, I had the disconcerting sensation that we were hanging upside down. I wasn't cut out to become a bat, even if my billowing black velvet dress could play the part of wings.

How did I land this magical transportation again?

I concentrated on the academy. I could sense the dragon shifters in the stable, the thrumming power in the Dead Wood, the frozen lake, and the wards that trapped all the Rebels inside the grounds.

My magic reached like pink roots beneath the academy and to the ruins outside the castle. I should...*perhaps*...have paid more attention to the professor in Strategy and less to Lysander's unfairly tight behind, but wouldn't the ruins make an excellent position to defend my lover? Although, I was certain that Bask would assume that *he* was defending *me*.

Vanity, your name is an incubus who looks like he was created to tempt witches to sin.

Suddenly, Damelza's magic snapped against mine with the *crack* of a whip.

Bask howled, as Damelza tried to haul him away

from me and back to her...and the inspection by the Duchess, his old bond.

In the name of Hecate, I wouldn't let that happen.

My magenta magic burst from me like a firework in an explosion that burned me out. At the same time, it burst us free from Damelza and the secret heart of the academy.

I rather feared that I was no longer in control of this flight.

My pulse raced. *Why couldn't I move?* Had I truly used up all my energy? I struggled to scrunch up my nose or wiggle my toes.

Nothing.

Like a robin with broken wings, where I crashed would now be total blind luck.

Not the study...

I screwed shut my eyes, holding my breath. Then it was knocked out of me in an *oomph*, as Bask and I landed.

Silence, apart from Bask's heartbeat and my own, which were both wild in our chests.

When my eyes blinked open, I found myself staring straight into Bask's adoring ruby gaze. I shivered at the wordless way in which his gaze said that I was *his world*, and he'd die if I looked away. He caged me between his arms, as he lay above me like a sinful emperor.

Bask's pleasure had summoned me as a ghost, then his love had resurrected me.

I craved to devour him.

Bask's silky black hair veiled my face, tickling my cheeks. His uniform of pink blazer and tie with black pants was as perfect as if he'd been strolling down a corridor rather than tumbling to possible oblivion.

Only the way that he sank closer to me, before resting one shaky hand, which was encased in a long pink glove because incubi could read your deep, dark desires and control you with them through touch, on my cheek told me that I wasn't the only one still tremoring with shocks.

Bask stroked the tip of his finger along my jawline, and I shivered. "I'm touching you, and it doesn't hurt."

"Why, you're quite turning my head with your sweet talk." I smiled, and longed to catch Bask's lower lip between my teeth. "I'm awfully sorry, you meant that the hex has fried itself out on my magic. In the witching heavens, I never wish to stop touching you again."

"Pet me," Bask commanded.

Incubi were only meant to gain power from giving pleasure, but Bask was considered *bad* because he gained it from receiving pleasure as well. He needed touch to survive and he'd been touch deprived for days.

Hand, why aren't you rising to pet my incubus? Stop this witchy laziness at once.

"It would be my pleasure," *hand, I must insist that you behave and start petting,* "if I could only move more than my head and toes... Give me a second... possibly one more... Look, I've conquered my little finger."

"If it pleases you, much fun can be had even with a wee finger like that." Bask slunk down me, only to catch my wiggling finger in his mouth.

Even through my gloves, I jumped at the heat and the way that his tongue curled around my finger, as he looked up teasingly from underneath his butterfly lashes.

Why hadn't I tried this before? And when could I try it again, when I had enough power to vanish my gloves?

Was this why the Rebels sucked each other's pricks? Sleipnir, my gorgeous god and Loki's son, had certainly appeared to enjoy it when I'd experimented on *his*, and I'd loved the power of dragging the same flush to his cheeks and breathy gasps from him that Bask was now dragging from me.

Although, to be fair, Bask was achieving that with only my finger, whereas I'd had a whole prick to play with.

When Bask let go of my finger with a *pop*, he

rested his head on my stomach, and I wished that I could stroke his hair.

"Delightful as that…"

"Finger fellatio…?" Bask offered.

"Kissing with beautiful extras was," I continued, "I've just dragged you away from Damelza's cruel clutches, and she'll be searching for us. I can't even manage a very British *tapping foot of disapproval* in defense, and there's only so much a little finger can achieve in a fight. Where are we?"

Wherever Bask and I had landed it was soft, light, and decidedly *not* Damelza's study. Also, it wasn't anywhere that I recognized, even as I luxuriated in the warmth of the furs beneath me.

Above, stars twinkled from the canopy of an obsidian four-poster bed.

If this was Damelza's bed, then I'd never be able to scrub myself clean, even with one of those magical showers that existed now.

As I stared at the gleaming black, it appeared to swirl and mold into different shapes around the stars like suns were dying and new galaxies were forming.

Whoever slept in this bed apparently believed that they were the center of the universe.

Ah, a *fae* then.

My breath hitched. This couldn't be the forbidden East Wing and the Princes' bedroom, surely?

Bats and cats, was I snuggling in Prince Lysander's bed?

I wanted to hurl...but at least if I vomited, it'd be entertaining to see Lysander's expression when he found out who'd destroyed his bed that was fit for a...*prince*.

Why did the Princes deserve such luxury, when the Immortals' Wing was plain and cold? There weren't even enough pillows for both Bask and Fox to cuddle, and they starved, at the same time as the Princes dined on delicacies sent by their wealthy patrons. Yet on this bed, there were heaps of furry cushions like a gang of cats had claimed it as their territory.

Bask wrinkled his nose, before snatching up one of those fluffy *creatures* and wafting it under *my* nose. "Do you smell cherry blossoms?"

I choked on the intense sweetness. "It's like being smothered by spring." Then I sneezed. A gold feather rested on the end of my nose. "Would you awfully mind not shedding on me."

Bask looked affronted. "Get on with you, I'm not a..." Then he became ashen. He picked up the gold feather between his finger and thumb like he'd discovered a hair on the sheets from a far more private place of the body. "Lysander tastes of cherry blossoms. He was temptingly delicious, until he poisoned me."

"Typical predator behavior," I muttered. "There are frogs like that."

Bask bounced up onto his knees. "Do you know what this means?"

"You shouldn't go around licking fae?"

He nipped my lower lip. "I get to wank on a Prince's bed."

I blinked at him. "Are you awfully certain that's our priority? Lysander shouldn't have suggested that your sword was short in Warrior Training, but there are more constructive ways to prove your manhood. Right now, we could be searching for how to restore my power."

Bask bared the long line of his alabaster throat, sliding his hand down to undo his pants and slipping his hand inside. He bit his plush lip, and his eyes became half-lidded. "I am," he panted. "Let me please and feed you. Marking the arrogant fae's bed is only a brilliant bonus. Tell me what you desire."

Who wouldn't give in to such seductive temptation? *I desired him.*

I circled my little finger. "Push down your pants."

Bask wriggled his pants down in a move that was so sexy, it made me squirm inside. My skin prickled at the way his hand hesitated over his own hard prick. When he glanced at me for permission, I flushed with warmth because he knew that he didn't need it. "Cup your balls with one hand, then stroke yourself, hard and fast. You come in the next minute or you don't come at all."

Sweet Hecate, that hadn't sounded at all as if I'd just copied the script from one of Flair's favorite... and most vocal...fantasies.

Bask's eyes widened.

Could he manage it? Had I set an impossible challenge, just the same as the trials within the academy?

My familiars had kept watch over the Rebels with a Wank Count for decades but they hadn't timed them or at least, they *might've* and simply not told me. It wasn't the type of thing that a lady asked: *Do tell me the length of time that the students took to achieve climax in self-pleasure today...to the second, please.*

Yet if my power was to be recharged, then it was worth a try. Bask set to the task with a determination that teetered on the line between pleasure and pain. His back arched, and I was mesmerized by the slide of his hand up and down his throbbing prick. His thighs trembled.

He groaned in frustration.

Then all at once, I could move again *and touch*.

I clasped my hand over Bask's, uniting us. I pressed my mouth to his, stealing a taste of his coco and almond lips. Bask shuddered like he'd been electrocuted for a second time; he'd never been this sensitive before.

What had it done to him to be deprived of my touch?

Instantly, he came. A pearly arc streamed out, painting the black covers of the bed white.

Fifty-six seconds precisely.

I caught Bask in my arms. Together, we tumbled to the other side of the bed, laughing. His eyes glittered. I was lit with joy, and my magic vibrated through me again.

I caressed down Bask's neck, his collarbone, and along his hip. I touched every inch of exposed skin simply because I *could*.

Bask sighed happily, pulling me closer. "I'm pettable again." Then he smirked. "Especially my arse." When I pinched his behind (which I had to admit was the most splendid example of its kind), he merely grinned. "You can spank me if you like. My sweet behind is at your service."

"*Ehm*, grateful as I am for the offer, I shan't ever wish to thrash you. Why, what have you done wrong? Are you hiding a guilty secret?"

Bask jolted. "I was thinking more erotic fun and less bad boy discipline."

"Excellent because I only want to save you."

I glanced around the room.

At least this was the last place that the witches would think to look for us. Immortals were banned from the Princes' rooms and the Princes from the

Immortals'. The witches kept the academy and the wards that trapped us running by keeping us as rivals.

At the far side was the archway with the *key* emblem above it (just like the Immortals had the torch in their Wing). The three Hecates in the courtyard chose which group each student would belong to on arrival: Princes, Immortals, or Randoms. There were wardrobes and desks just like the Immortals' rooms. Except, these ones were grand with gold gilt and inlaid with mosaic battle scenes. The floors were thickly carpeted, and the ceiling was ornate.

On each wall was a glowing board with scrolling **Privilege** and **Punishment Points** in pink letters.

What would it be like to wake up to that each morning?

Juni Crow, the Princes' Tutor, had terrifyingly organized motivational techniques. I hadn't expected myself to feel grateful that Bacchus, the Immortals' tutor, was into *chaos,* even if that included random Ice Water Punishments.

The other bed in the room, which faced Lysander's on the far wall, was carved out of ice. It glittered like crushed diamonds. It must be Willoughby's.

It was sad that the two princes didn't share a bed. It'd break Echo's heart to lose *that* cherished fantasy. Perhaps, their tutor didn't allow it…? The Immortals slept together because Bask needed the touch as he slept. But didn't fae need it in precisely the same way?

Bask pulled up his pants, tucking himself back into them. "Where's Midnight sleep?"

Midnight was the Princes' vampire whipping boy. I'd witnessed him being forced to kneel naked in corners like he was a bicycle waiting to be ridden.

I truly hoped that wasn't what happened at night. I mean, either the kneeling or the being ridden.

My brow furrowed. "Considering the alternatives, the floor looks tempting."

Bask snorted. "A bed of nails coated in itching powder would be tempting."

He grabbed a pillow, which was silk with a black swan feather sewn on the front, before starting to reach for another one.

After living in Hecates' Tree with two crows, I could tell a nest when I saw one being built. "When an incubus marks a bed, does it mean that the pillows become his?"

Bask froze. He carefully pushed away the pillow, although I noticed that he didn't let go of its corner. "Away with you, I wasn't planning on stealing it."

He assuredly was.

I studied the feather, which had been attached with such care to the front. The pillow was special, worn, and older than the ones around it.

It didn't fit.

"I'd put that back," I warned. "I'd imagine that the

fae lies here at night cuddling and kissing it, just like you do Nile."

Bask gasped, dropping the corner like it'd burned him. "Nile will expect a kiss on his crocodile tooth to make up for that." He shuddered. "I have second-hand Lysander love all over me. Am I less slinky already?"

I struggled not to smile. "You'll never be less slinky, and don't worry, it'll wash off."

Yet as I caught sight of the feather, I suddenly shook with the memory of Robin's *Your Heart's Desire* book, which he'd created for me by plucking his own feathers, while in bird form.

Was this Lysander's version?

Had someone made it for him? Was this a love token, so that Lysander could remember them, while he was trapped in prison?

Who had Lysander loved and lost?

In Hecate's Wood, when I'd passed my fingers over the spelled feathers of the *Your Heart's Desire* Book, they'd sung with Robin's silvery birdsong. It should've meant that he could always be with me, wherever I'd gone. He'd intended to give it to me as a courting present at the Enchanted Ball. But then, mother had arranged my marriage to Lysander's uncle and guardian, Titus.

Lysander wasn't his uncle. If I thought it enough times like a mantra, then I'd believe it.

I gritted my teeth together.

I *knew* that Lysander wasn't the same fae prick, although he was *a* prick. But I couldn't help how he reminded me of the man who controlled the academy as its patron and who'd destroyed both Robin and me.

Robin once told me that to be a ghost was to *eternally crave*. Yet even now, I spent every moment craving Robin. I'd never forget my first love, whose kiss had tangled his soul with mine. Yet I also craved the lovers who'd brought me a second chance at love after death.

Bask was the Rebel who was in danger now. If I didn't find a way to break him free from the Duchess, then she'd break him again.

I swung my legs over the bed, hauling Bask with me. "On Hecates' tit, delightful as touching you was, we have to work out a way to stop *the Duchess* from touching you as well."

I hated the way that Bask's gaze became glazed. He must be remembering something, and I'd guess that it wasn't the Duchess and him playing with puppies.

Unless the Duchess had a disturbing habit of naming her bonded incubi's balls.

Bask wandered to the far side of the room, fiddling with the objects on a marble counter. The Immortals' Wing didn't even *have* a counter.

"Look, wi-fi!" Bask exclaimed.

I hadn't thought that I'd shattered Bask by

29

mentioning the Duchess but apparently, I had. "My apologies, I didn't mean to startle you into baby talk. Do you also perhaps perceive we-fe, wo-fo, and wu-fu?"

Bask turned to blink at me. "Have I told you how sexy I find your Victorian weirdness?"

I flushed. "Do go ahead."

He licked his lips. "I'll prove it later."

Promises...

Then my foot knocked against a large basket, which was lined with a blanket. It was rough and stuck out against the pampered luxury of the rest of the bedroom.

I scuffed my boot against the basket. "Why would they keep such a thing?"

Bask's eyes lit with excitement, before he twirled around like he was looking for something. *In the name of Hecate, were we about to be consumed by carnivorous gargoyles?* "It's a wee dog's bed. I bet that it's an adorable Pomeranian."

"I'd have guessed something more *proving my manliness* like an Alsatian."

Bask snickered. "Bacchus turns students into Pomeranians." A*h, that quaint dog transfiguration tradition.* Perhaps, Bask would get to play with a puppy, after all. "Come on, ex-prince who I want to snuggle and carry around in my satchel, don't hide from the cuddly incubus."

"To be fair, he'll just have witnessed you wanking on Lysander's bed. It wouldn't fill him with trust."

Bask smirked. "That's just like a handshake for an incubus."

I crouched beside the basket. It was worn like whoever slept there had been trapped in the academy for a long time. And there were *feathers* stuck in the blanket, but this time not golden, rather black.

The breath caught in my throat.

It couldn't be...

I slowly stood. "There's no dog. I'd wager that we've discovered Midnight's bed."

"And to think that I was considering giving at least the elf petting privileges," Bask hissed.

When I turned away, however, the exquisite porcelain tea set at the back of the counter, caught my eye like it'd always been waiting for me.

I clapped my hands together in delight. "Why, what do I have to do around here to get the perk of my own personal tea?"

I fingered a cup that was decorated with a black stallion, which galloped across the white of the cup as if across a snowy plain.

Bask eyed me. "Add that to the list of questions never to voice to the witches who run this place."

I arched my brow. "Noted." Then I stared at the seven glass jars of different tealeaves. Their scents mixed like the grasses on a mountainside. It was the

31

fresh earthiness, which took me back to every single morning that I'd sat with my father, Byron, drinking tea together in the Bird Turret. It'd been a quiet ritual, which bound us together. In that moment, we'd been safe and free. "But *seven...?*"

Bask snickered. "Is there something magical in that number? There are seven dwarfs *and* deadly sins, but you don't desire them."

With a last...*admittedly envious*...glance at the tea, I narrowed my eyes at Bask. "How do you know? A wicked witch has needs."

"Kinky." Bask winked. "Let's see if the Princes are kinky too."

He waggled his eyebrows, before dragging out the drawer beneath the counter. When emerald silk panties spilled out, Bask *whooped* in victory like he'd discovered a dragon's hoard.

I *tutted*, but Bask only shrugged.

"An incubus may raid a princes' underwear drawer." He swept the panties back in. "Away with you, if Lysander was shy about it, he'd have found an Immortal-proof hiding place."

"Like his private bedroom in a Wing of the castle, which is both forbidden to and warded against Immortals?" I deadpanned.

Bask tried for the innocent face; he was decidedly good at it. "Exactly."

When he slid the last of the panties back into the

drawer (and I shivered at the thought of next seeing Lysander and not glancing at his behind to imagine him wearing them because surely they rode up under his tight trousers to wedgie in the most uncomfortable of places?), he knocked a button.

To my shock, music blasted out, which sang hauntingly of snowmen and a desire to build them. I recognized it as the song that Prince Willoughby often sang, yet I still had no understanding why he was so intent on playing in the snow.

Did elves miss out on their childhoods, and so still yearn to play?

I'd gladly show Willoughby how to build a snowman because Robin and I had stolen away on many winter days to build snowsquirrels beside the lake. He'd transform into his red squirrel form and sit on top of his snow brother, wrapping his tail around it and chattering.

"Willoughby adores to sing this in the shower," I pointed out. When Bask raised his eyebrow, I flushed. "And I discovered that in some entirely nonperverted way, of course."

"I can't even lie that I'd like to believe you because I wouldn't."

I gasped in mock horror. "For shame! My familiars have simply watched him in the shower. They report that he has a voice, which is as beautiful as his prick."

It was a wonderful sensation to watch the blush creep up Bask's neck. I wished to lick up it and across the blooming pink of his cheeks.

He swallowed. "Not pervy at all."

I smiled. "Thank you."

When Bask slid his finger across the button again, all of a sudden, I couldn't breathe. A love ballad sobbed from the machine like a lament of loss. I'd never heard anything before like the soaring vocal in its despairing loneliness and longing.

Was this Willoughby's or Lysander's music?

Did they choose this because they'd lost a lover like me? How could they stand to listen to something with such flayed grief?

I stumbled at the pulsing mourning in the music. Startled, Bask gripped my elbow, before pulling me to his chest. His breath was hot against my ear.

I'd already lost Robin. I refused to lose Bask as well.

Yet the emotion of what it'd mean if I *did* was lived out in this song beat by beat in its haunting loss.

Not again.

Tears chased down my cheeks, and I paled. I wouldn't ever be over Robin. I never wanted to forget and lose the pain because then I'd lose him too: his memory. He didn't deserve that when as a mage and an orphan, he didn't even have a grave to mark that he'd been alive.

He'd existed and he'd been loved.

But Bask was alive, warm, and in my arms right now. I wouldn't allow the agonizing cycle of grief to begin again.

Bask shook me. "Magenta? Please, please... what do you want me to do? I can be whatever you wish. I'll find a way to stop the Duchess. I won't leave you."

Chills ran through me. He didn't know how dangerous that was. "Don't say *always*. If the Principal or professors ever ask you whether you want to remain with me, then say anything but *always*."

"I don't understand."

"If the question is whether you belong with me, the answer is no," I insisted.

When Bask drew back to study me, his hair fell across his eyes. "But what if it's *yes*?"

I bopped him on the end of the nose. "Then, you remember that I love you, and I've asked you to say *no*."

He scrunched up his nose, offended. "You mean that I lie."

I nodded.

Bask grinned. "As you wish. So, you don't want to just drop me off with my old bond...?"

I sucked hard on his neck, enjoying the taste of his skin and the way that his breath hitched. I believed *that* answered his ridiculous question.

I pulled back, licking over the pretty purple

hickey. His hard-on pressed against my hip, and his pupils were dilated.

I gave his neck one final lick. "Did you imagine that I'd deliver you to the Duchess in a bow?"

Bask's voice was fragile and raw. "Ma presented me wrapped in ribbons."

"I should rather like to kick some succubi ass today." My hands clenched into fists.

"See, here's the thing of it, we're not free to kick the asses that deserve it. If it was done on worth, our own would be petted and there'd be serious kickings all around for professors, princes, and patrons." He kissed the corner of my mouth, curling his hand possessively around the back of my neck. "How do you think the contracts are signed, which condemn us to the academy?"

"With a run up, pirouette, and a flourish to finish?" I ventured.

Bask huffed, sucking on my earlobe in retaliation. "In blood."

"Rather a cliche." I squirmed at the same time as I melted at his continued assault on my ear. "Although Hecate appears big on blood magic. Why not go for champagne or chocolate? Chocolate Magic would be something that I'd never complain about studying."

"It's *your* magic that winds through the academy, demanding blood sacrifices."

"Ah," I licked my lips, "in that case, what a

wicked baby I was. I wonder what sacrificial blood tastes like?" When Bask gave me a sidelong look (I imagine that *had* sounded creepy but then, after over a century trapped with only myself and my familiars, I had a tendency to say what I thought), I smiled at him brightly. "Don't worry, I'm certain that your blood would be the most delicious."

"Of course it would; this incubus is tasty." Then he tore at his lower lip with his teeth. "*Ehm*, just don't drink me, please."

"I shall endeavor not to." I struggled to smother my laughter but then I sobered. There was a contract in blood that bound Bask directly to the Duchess. What could she do to him, even while he was in the academy? What control did she have? "How long have you known about this danger?"

"I've only just learned that you wanted to drink my tasty self..."

"I meant the Duchess arriving today to inspect you with the contract."

When Bask ducked his head, I knew. *He'd been hiding this secret from me all along.*

"I'm sorry," he whispered. "I only wanted one week with you, Slippy, and Fox. I thought if I could feel what true love was, then I could take that back (holding its memory to me like I hold Nile), against what the Duchess will do to me. When I'm ignored in the incubi harem with the other bonded because..." He

37

broke off, and his shoulders shook. "...I'm the freaky *different* incubus who broke, then I'd remember..."

"Wanking on Lysander's bed?" I choked out.

Bask laughed. How could he still sound so free, even though he'd accepted his enslavement? I'd pulled down my entire world to stop my marriage to a fae prince, but then, Bask had already been through this once.

"I'll cherish that and every moment with you. See, the only people who can free any Rebel are the Principal or the person who signs the contract. The Duchess could free me...take me away...whenever she thinks that I've learned my lesson."

"Then how do we break the contract?" I demanded.

"We don't. End of story." Bask gripped my chin, forcing me to look at him. "I swore that I'd protect my whipping boy and I won't let Fox be hurt because of me. I worked with the others to save you from Hecate's Tree because we love you. I'd been an idiot to put you in danger now. I knew that the Duchess would take me back. Just love me, that's all I crave. *Love me.*"

I was losing him and I loved him.

I screamed with a primal rage at the unfairness. Then I slammed Bask back against the wall. My magic exploded around us in a spray of pink sparkles like snowflakes.

He was pleasure, sensation, and love.

I'd told him not to say *always,* but he'd already let go.

My magic spiraled wilder and wilder around us both. I couldn't control it. It bound us together.

Bask's eyes widened, as my lips that were pressed to his tingled with magenta magic.

I was wicked. I was back. And I was out of control...

CHAPTER THREE

Rebel Academy, Wednesday September 4th

MAGENTA

I shivered, as wild magic pulsed through me, lighting the East Wing in a pink blizzard. It was thrilling to have no control and terrifying in equal measure. My power drew its energy from nature, sucking it from the air and questing its roots down to draw it from the earth. Yet it stole nothing because nature couldn't be controlled either; it chose to answer my call.

It was a scream of *no more*: no more loss or loneliness. No more would this academy take my lovers.

It was every buried truth crushed from me.

The Rebels were mine, and our souls were bound both now and after death.

Nobody would take Bask from me.

I wound my arms around Bask's neck, and my skirts dissolved to black mists that coiled around him, binding him even closer.

It appeared that my ghostly side took the whole *possessive* part of me, which had been awoken, literally. Yet by the way that Bask's hard prick rubbed against my thigh, and his wide eyes stared into mine with an aching longing, he didn't mind.

It wasn't only crows and incubi who had nesting impulses, however, but also my Wickedly Charmed magic. It quested around the room, across the desks and counter, searching for a safe place....I hoped, to ravish Bask.

When my magic hesitated like a sniffer dog over Lysander's bed, I yanked at it with a grimace. Wanking was one thing, but I was not making love to the man who I craved more than my next breath in a fae prince's bed. I did not have a fae kink (although, Flair insisted that did indeed exist).

I glanced across the room at Willoughby's bed, which was beside an open window. The carved ice glistened; the ice columns rose high. It looked like it belonged to a true Prince Charming, if Charming was a killer.

An ice bed for an Ice Prince.

41

Perhaps, it'd at least cool down the fever, which was burning through me.

I swallowed; my forehead was damp with sweat. When Bask's gaze caught mine, his tongue darted out to wet his plush lips. I forced myself to look away because it made my fingers ache to reach out and trace down the alabaster line of his throat to the dip of his collar bone, which was definitely clouding my decision-making abilities.

"Do you have any bad associations with Willoughby's bed?" I panted.

For the love of Hecate, say no.

"Only that it'd be a fine thing to be sharing it *with* Willoughby," Bask replied. Then just in case I'd missed his meaning, he continued, "This pettable incubus, that pretty elf, and you...together, here, in this—"

"Let's christen it then." When I grabbed Bask's hand, his eyes widened in surprise.

We fell onto Willoughby's bed, amid the sky-blue velvet covers that swathed the ice and the scent of tea. It was cool and aromatic. The ceiling glistened with ice just like the tips of Willoughby's hair would glisten when he lost control of his anger. Perhaps, he did when he slept? Did he suffer from nightmares, the same as the Immortals?

For a moment, it was like Willoughby truly was in the bed with us, wrapping his arms around us both.

When Bask shuddered and scrambled to the head-board to take refuge amongst the snowflake cushions, I caged him beneath me.

There was dark magic in this bed: *binding magic.*

Yet was it Willoughby's or whoever was controlling *him*?

"You can feel it too?" Bask whispered.

I nodded.

"We must save the elf," Basks voice was steely. "Someone's hurting him. I owe him a touch debt, and he pet me. That means I'll protect him, even though he's a Prince."

I rested my forehead against Bask's, as my magic swirled around us. "But you're leaving us all, are you not?"

Bask drew in his breath, sharply. "It's not my wish."

"Then stay with me." My magic spun above our heads, faster and faster. It clung against the bed's columns. "I came back to life for you."

"It'd please me if you did." When Bask feathered kisses along my jaw, my pulse fluttered in my neck. My nerves were on fire. "But it was Slippy's sacrifice and Fox's blood that resurrected you. Don't you see?"

I drew back in shock. Bask's eyes gleamed with tears but none fell.

Why would he never allow himself to cry?

I froze at the thought that the instinct to weep

could've been trained out of him. Was that why he loved us so fiercely but didn't believe that *I* could venerate *him*?

He didn't need to prove anything to me. I'd just have to prove how much he was adored, instead.

Bask gasped, as my black mists shot out, drawing back his hands and binding him to the bed. Then I slowly loosened his tie.

Bask never broke eye contact with me, and his lips parted. I longed to push my tongue between those sweet lips and kiss away every moment of broken doubt. But first, I had glorious skin to stroke and claim, while he was still here with me: alive and mine.

I'd been forbidden to touch him and now I'd luxuriate in every caress. I was a rebel, after all.

How could I lose this?

When I pushed back Bask's blazer and unbuttoned his shirt, pausing to tease each inch of revealed skin with the tips of my gloved fingers, lips, tongue, and teeth, Bask panted and tugged on my mists that bound his hands. I swiped my thumb over his sensitive nub, and he arched.

So, I did it again.

Then I pulled his shirt out of his pants. When I rested my hand over his crotch, his prick twitched against my hand. I glanced from underneath my eyelashes into his flushed face. His pleasure coiled through me, and he glowed with mine.

Couldn't he see how powerful...*and dangerous*...we were together?

I'd once heard Flair call it a *power couple*.

"Your pleasure is what summoned me from Hecate's Tree. Without your power, I wouldn't have been able to escape in the first place." I slipped my hand into Bask's pants, pulling out his prick, before melting away my own clothing. I loved how efficient it was now to undress. I also loved Bask's appreciative gasp. My bouncy bosoms certainly were perkier for the praise. "I needed all three of you to save me; your pleasure and love combine in a way that no other Rebels' ever has. You're special *together*. I need all three of you."

"*Four* with Willoughby," Bask insisted with a tilt of his chin, which was impressive, as I rubbed my palm over the head of his prick.

I smiled. "Four."

I floated above him — half ghost and half witch — but all wicked. My lips curled into a smile. Even I knew that I couldn't get away with that type of thought, when I sounded like Mary bloody Poppins. Still, I could pull off being a spirit lover.

My lips tingled with a magic that vibrated through the entire academy.

I pulled back Bask's shirt to reveal his sculpted chest, and I was flooded with warmth, despite the coolness of the velvet beneath me. "What a perfectly charming gift to unwrap."

Bask stretched like he was showing himself off with the way that his body bowed and his muscles bulged, glancing at me with half-lidded eyes. My stomach clenched at his sinful beauty.

I'd never believed it possible to come untouched, before. *Until now.*

I traced my hand down his muscles, pausing only to lean forward to lick at his nipples. My hair swept across his skin, and he jumped like he'd been tickled.

"Who wouldn't want to find this incubus underneath their tree?" Bask rolled his hips.

I tightened my hold around his prick, before sitting up and rubbing its silky head along my inner thigh. I gasped at the sensation at the same time as Bask.

"What fun I'd have playing with you." I slid my hand lower to cup his balls.

His beauty burned me, as he murmured, "If you wish, I'm whatever you desire."

Our desires are deadly. But pleasure called to pleasure.

I crushed my mouth to Bask's, curling my tongue around his. My black mists slipped down his body to bind around his prick and balls.

I'd never let him go.

Cresting waves crashed through me. *Again, and again, and...*

As I clenched, caught in the intensity of the spasms wracking me, Bask's prick pulsed in the hold of my mists. His cum fed my pleasure, and in the cycle of our passion, I lost control. My magic spread in pink brambles that grew Sleeping Beauty style out of the castle walls around the bed, until Bask and I were safe inside their thick tangle.

Yet there was no true protection from Damelza, Hecate, or the world outside.

But just for now, sweet Hecate, give me this.

I ripped my mists away from Bask, solidifying back to my human legs again, so that I could wrap them around Bask, as I gripped his cheeks and kissed him. I wanted nothing but the taste of coco and almonds.

Always.

I'd told him not to say it, but my answer was: *always*.

If saving Bask meant that I became Sleeping Beauty to Bask's new Prince in the safety inside the glowing womb of my magic, then I chose always to dream.

Why couldn't I dream just a little longer?

Yet broken broomsticks, even I could see the thorns in the brambles, as they curled around the frosty columns. In truth, was it *I* who trapped the students in the academy, as much as the wards themselves? After all, it was my Blessedly Charmed magic that'd set them, even if I'd been no more than a baby in a cradle.

The room shook, darkened to hazy magenta. Bask and I clung to each other; our pleasure fed each other's. Bask's eyes glowed with predatory power.

Did anything outside our love and this cool, tea scented chamber even exist?

Peck, peck, peck.

When I broke the kiss, Bask was dazed. His skin gleamed with sweat. My brambles drew back, filtering in light that made me blink, as something tore at them with a sharp beak.

"What's wrong?" Bask's voice was slurred like he'd been drugged.

Peck, peck, peck.

The hole in the brambles grew. My magic drew back, shivering.

"*Stop destroying this infernal academy with your Muff of Doom, boss,*" a loud London voice called.

Then a crow's beak poked through, snapping with a loud *click* of disapproval.

My head felt like it was stuffed full of cotton wool, whereas the rest of my body felt filled with something far more pleasurable. I magicked myself back into my clothes. "My...what?"

Why was English so hard to understand all of a sudden? And why was a second beak and two sets of beady eyes now peering through at us, as I slipped

Bask's prick back into his pants. I enjoyed the way that he gasped, as it rubbed against the stiff material.

"*Your Deadly Quim, Dominator Cocklane, Cu-*"

"I assure you that I have it under control, Flair," I said, hastily.

"*You have his _prick_ under control.*" Flair flapped his wings. "*He's been dying for want of a fuck for days.*"

As my magic faded, and the room stopped shaking, my mind cleared. How could I've forgotten (even for a moment), my crow familiars and twins, Echo and Flair? They'd been burned alive with me and had been my only company in Hecates' tree for over a century. Together, we'd gone a little crazy. Even though I was now half witch, they were still all ghost and only visible to me.

That sort of thing tended to bond you.

Flair swooped to settle on my shoulder. I winced, as his scaly claws bit into my skin, even through the velvet of my dress. His brother, however, tumbled into my lap in a magenta feathery bundle. He let out a series of rambling *clicks,* and I stroked over his wings, which were as sensitive as a fae's. Then I cuddled him because despite everything, I never wanted to forget him or the world, again.

"Are those pesky crows here now?" Bask snatched the pillows around himself like he expected the familiars to steal his nest at any moment.

"*I'll show him* pesky *when I peck off his cock and balls and turn them into an ice sculpture for the Princes.*" Flair cawed. "*Ask him if he likes being a crow's bitch.*"

"I most certainly shall not," I hissed.

"*By my blood, are you quite well?*" Echo tilted his head, studying me, anxiously. "*I couldn't sense you like you'd faded again. Don't leave me. I need you.*"

Would Bask give up just one of his pillows for Echo? "Trust me, it's all right."

Bask straightened his tie. ""Away with you, that was better than all right. A screw with an incubus of the Night Lineage is epic."

"*Epic bollocks.*" Flair pointed his wing at Bask. "*Does this idiot know how dangerous a fuckathon between a crazy—*"

"But *ours*," Echo interrupted, fondly.

I wasn't entirely certain that was better.

"*...crazy pleasure Ghost witch (who's ours) and a touch deprived incubus is?*" Flair demanded.

Bask's brow furrowed. "Are they talking about me?"

I wished that I'd paid more attention to my father, Byron's, skill at diplomacy or how to hold two conversations at once. "They believe that you're dangerous."

"Of course I'm *dangerous*." Bask smirked like it was a badge of honor.

I huffed. "By Hecate, that's not awfully helpful.

Look, we didn't...screw...we just..."

"*Screwed like bunnies who've just discovered espressos in their annual spring fuckathon,*" Flair amended. "*We heard you, boss, with the moaning and the* ah, ah, ah..."

I flushed.

When Bask did up the buttons of his shirt. I cursed each one of those buttons that they hid his skin from me. I couldn't help that I took it personally. Perhaps, I understood a little of why Lysander kept his whipping boy naked: all that gorgeous skin to see and touch when he wished.

Except, with Bask it'd be willing. If I suggested he strip and go around naked, I'd never be able to get him back *into* clothes.

Modesty, your name was *not* incubus.

"Here's the thing, I'm grateful that your familiars rescued us, but how did they know that we were here?" Bask did up the last *traitorous* button on his shirt.

"You weren't hoping to discover Willoughby in the showers by any chance?" I raised my eyebrow.

"*I always hope to catch the pretty elf singing in the showers, watch him soaping, or catch a glimpse of his beautiful prick.*" Echo rubbed his head against my hand, innocently. "*When he sings, it's like waterfalls cascading down my spine.*"

"*Apart from my brother's princely darling, we*

heard that you'd gone on the run with one of the Rebels and then lost yourself somewhere in the academy." Flair swooped to the headboard, settling down. His eyes glinted. "*You know that a crow flies faster than these witch bitches. But they'll find you.*"

Unfortunately, I knew that he was right.

Bask slid one of the pillows that he was jealously guarding to the side and pulled out a book. It was bound with crystal. I'd never seen anything like it. It must be elven and ancient.

The book glistened, as Bask moved it side to side, like it'd been coated in ice but also with magic. My own quested around it, afraid to touch.

We should put it back.

The thought punched through me.

Private, private, private....

Whatever this book was, it belonged to Willoughby and the world of the Elven Court before he'd been sent to Rebel Academy. I knew how fiercely I clung to my own memories, before everything had been taken from me, just as Bask clung to Nile. I'd already claimed Willoughby's bed without his knowledge. This book, however, was a step too far.

"Put that down," I whispered.

Bask stared at the book like he couldn't look away. His hand trembled, and his eyes were wide and fearful. "I can't. I desire it. I think it's his diary."

"*I don't give a feathering fuck if it's the Never-*

ending Suck Job Special. Get the incubus to put down the diary. Didn't messing with Hecate's Tree teach you not to play with other people's magic?" Flair *thwapped* his wing across the back of Bask's head, but it only *swooshed* straight through him.

My breath came in ragged gasps. "How'd you even know it was there?"

Bask shrugged. "My head banged against it earlier, but I was distracted."

"And you didn't think to say something startlingly original like *ow*?"

"Would that turn you on because I'm meant to keep quiet. I'm used to pain mixed in with my pleasure. It's brilliant that you don't want that like the Duchess, but I can take it. Suffering is easy if you've been trained how."

My guts roiled. I never wanted Bask to simply *take* anything, just because he thought that I desired it.

I reached forward, dropping Echo sneakily onto the pile of pillows, and gripped Bask's chin. "I don't ever need you to suffer for me, and I'm not the Duchess or like the other witches of the House of Crows. That's why we're going to put the diary back where we found it. Don't you remember how much it destroyed Willoughby earlier to have the letter from his brother read out in class? We can't make it worse by reading his private thoughts as well."

Bask wet his lips. "But what if he talks about us?"

"I rather imagine that he has plenty of impolite things to say on the subject of Immortals."

Bask shook his head. "What if it teaches us his darkest desires and hidden needs? We could use it to convince him to our side. It could be what helps us to break the wards and escape."

My expression hardened. Power thrummed through Bask. This is what made him a dangerous incubus: the thirst to rule through desire. "Almost like you'd gone skin to skin with him," I said. "How much are you hungering for that right now?"

Bask jerked back from me. Hurt flashed through his eyes, before he was able to mask it. "Lay off, you've no idea." He swallowed. "I can control myself. *I will.*"

Reluctantly, he placed down the crystal diary.

I let out a shuddering breath, which I hadn't even known that I'd been holding.

All of a sudden, Echo launched himself forward, however, tearing at the book with his beak. "*I want my pretty elf. Bones and blood, he should be an Immortal. But you have to see him first. Please, please, please...love him.*"

Bask and I cried out, as the book flew open onto crisp white pages that were filled with elegant sky-blue writing.

Then in a glittering explosion, the letters curled out of the diary, spilling Willoughby's hidden secrets.

CHAPTER FOUR

Rebel Academy, Wednesday September 4ᵗʰ

MAGENTA

The words curled out of Willoughby's diary, painting the glistening ceiling above the bed in sky-blue. Despite myself, I stared up at them. Curiosity killed the witch as much as her black cat.

I knew that I shouldn't read these private thoughts but witching heavens, I couldn't look away, and neither could Bask. He clasped my hand, as entranced as me.

The writing was beautiful and flowed like cool streams to read:

By my ears, I'm falling deeper and deeper under my

brother's spell. The suit crushes my magic and soul.
Yet today, I met a witch whose magenta magic
entangled with mine, calling to nature and dragging
me up from the silk's cursed sleep.
She's life.
I never dreamed that I could feel again. Not after what
I've done, and my deserved shame.
But now, she's here, and I'm awake. The flood of
feelings and sensations in this vile academy drown
me. With her, I taste only joy, but that joy freezes
within me to terror as soon as she's gone.
How can I live here, now that I must sense the sadness
even within the walls? There have been murders in
this castle.
But still, all I can think about is a murdered witch.

I startled.

Ah, so I'd discovered not impolite truths about me,
rather obsession.

Had the moment that Willoughby had looked at me across Bacchus' classroom truly meant so much to him? How was it possible? My heart beat rapidly in my chest, and all of a sudden, my mouth was dry.

I didn't want to hear any more, and yet I was desperate to. The elf was so emotionless that a twitch of his lips was the same as Fox's laugh. Yet anguish ran like a raging river beneath his cool exterior. I feared that I'd be swept away.

Willoughby's difficulties with new sensations was like my own after my resurrection; my heart ached for him. Witching heavens, I'd never imagined that I'd have so much in common with a *Prince*.

Then both Bask and I jumped, when the words were spoken like they were breathed from the diary in Willoughby's ethereal but anguished voice:

When I'm around her, the tendrils of her magic and spirit call to the Other World. I can hear the trees, streams, and hills again. I know the taste of my favorite pears, and the smoke on the fall air, and once more, I can feel Thunder's mane under my hands, as I gallop across the planes.
To think of Thunder is to feel the silk around my neck that strangled his. Forgive me, my sweet steed. No innocents should've suffered for my crime.
It haunts me.
Yet why must I struggle against my exile? I deserve this punishment. If you fall, does it not hurt when you hit the ground?
Brother, will you ever forgive me? Please...
But with her...this witch who is yet a ghost...my mind clears, and for a little while, I'm me. At least, I'm the elf who I once was, when the Other World still welcomed me into its arms, rather than turned away from me.

I don't deserve leniency but I yearn for it. I yearn for <u>her</u>. She's all that I can think about.

Will she notice me, when she already has such love surrounding her?

I envy her.

She's part of nature, and I crave it. I long to talk about...every word and look and... But I don't have that right. Lysander made that clear to me tonight. He bid me remain on my bed like I was a child without supper, ranting that Immortals don't talk to Princes. He insisted that I've disgraced our Wing, just as I've disgraced the Light Elves.

I wish I'd been able to tell him that he was wrong, but I'm the Light Elf who's no better than a Dark one. Lysander was once no more than a guard to me, but I must admit, he's become my friend. I don't blame him for his strictness. Lysander's guardian is far harsher with him, than Lysander has ever been to me.

He's never struck me, after all.

If I disobey Lysander, however, then he shall report me to Darby. I shudder at the thought of my brother tightening my suit, as he did when I first arrived at the academy and earned too many Punishment Points.

I had to battle for every breath.

I need to pay penance. I understand that. Every night, Lysander must watch over me as I write the lines that my brother insists upon.

One hundred times, I write: **I am a changeling, Dark Elf, and killer.**

Inside, I'm numb.

Yet those words are the only ones that can still make me smart, and burn my eyes with tears.

Tonight was the first time that those words could not touch me because of the witch.

She does not know me as a killer. Perhaps, she could even see me as I truly am?

I wish that I could sleep in her arms at night, rather than in this cursed bed, alone. I'd be cocooned in her comforting magic, as well as the embraces of her other lovers because the way that the whipping boy and incubus spoke to me (like I was neither prisoner nor deadly), made my soul sing.

I desire them.

Yet I should sleep now because in these pages, I've allowed myself to dream. The Immortals' friendship and the witch's love is only a fantasy fit for the secrecy of my Crystal Diary.

It's as dangerous as I am.

A monster lies within me. One day, a professor or Lysander will reveal my buried self to these new students. Then they won't even wish to look at me. The more that I allow myself to care, then when that day comes, the more that I'll be crushed...

This diary was elven magic and dark grief. I shook, desperate to break the enchantment.

Sweet Hecate, nobody should hear such heart-breaking truths. They belonged to Willoughby alone.

Bubbling cauldrons, *no more...*

My magic wound around the book, battling the blue magic, which glowed from its pages.

Back inside.

I bared my teeth, snarling like I could scare the Crystal Diary into behaving. The cold nipped at me, but I snarled again, forcing the book to close with a *snap*. The words faded, along with the melancholy of Willoughby's voice.

I was desperate to hold him as he wished and tell him that it wasn't a dream. Immortals *could* love Princes; he wasn't alone.

Yet how could I do that without him knowing that I'd read his diary? It'd destroy him to find out that anyone knew his private thoughts.

I'd written a diary when I'd been growing up, which had mostly contained my love of tea, hatred of embroidery, and determination to free Robin (or how much I adored snuggling him in his squirrel Mr. Tailsy form). I'd have died a slow, red-faced death of humiliation if anyone had ever read it, and it'd never contained my fantasies, shame, or desires.

What had happened to Willoughby to destroy him in such a way or to make his brother insist that he write such terrible things about himself? He believed that we'd hate or fear him, when we discovered that he was monstrous.

Sleipnir had thought the same about his shifter form.

I didn't think that either of them were monsters. Yet even if they were, monsters deserved love too.

Willoughby wasn't a slave who had no control over his own mind. Whoever this brother was who'd cursed and controlled him, I hated him with a witching passion. I was quite certain that my thoughts against the so-called elven king ran towards the traitorous.

Why were my cheeks wet?

I reached up to wipe at them with my sleeve. When I glanced at Bask, I saw my own tears reflected in his eyes, although *his* cheeks were dry.

Bask squeezed my fingers. "We're saving that elf."

I nodded. "Most certainly, but first, I have a crow to have serious words with, since he decided to open a book that didn't belong to his feathery self."

I fixed Echo with a stern glare.

"The word you need to say quickly is *sorry*," Bask mock whispered.

"*Sorry, sorry, sorry...*" Echo sang at the top of his tone-deaf voice.

"*Not as sorry as you're going to be,*" Flair snapped. "*Get your feathery arse over here. My wing's itching to spank you, until you caw for mercy."*

Echo lowered his head. *"By my blood, I'd do anything to make Magenta happy, and I know that this will in the end."* He hopped towards me with a hopeful glint in his eye. *"I'm only a familiar. I understand about dreaming that you could want me, when I know that you shouldn't. Every time that he sings, the elf sounds sad. I long for you to kiss that away. Now you've listened to the diary, could you love a Prince?"*

Flair swooped to his brother, but instead of pecking him like I'd feared, Flair threw his wing around his twin consolingly. *"Fuck me, that was quite the speech."*

Could I love a Prince?

I didn't know. It was rather like asking whether I adored pizza. Fox insisted that the strange flat dough was delicious but never having tasted one, I could only say that others *urged* me to adore them.

Except, the difference was that I'd never nearly been forced to marry a pizza.

"You knew," I said, staring at Echo, "what was inside the diary. You assuredly had every notion what I'd hear. Did you watch Willoughby write it?"

Echo ruffled his feathers (I was fairly certain with pride). *"I was sitting on his shoulder. I seized the opportunity, like you always say."*

I narrowed my eyes. "I've never said that."

Echo did the crow equivalent of a shrug. "*You should.*"

When Flair flapped to the window, Echo trailed after him. "*Crows exit stage left. We're not off to do anything suspicious, dangerous, or forbidden.*"

I arched my brow. "How splendidly reassuring."

As he followed his brother out of the room, Echo cast a longing glance at me. "*Be careful with the Principal. Remember, you promised not to leave us.*"

Bask played with my fingers, turning over my palm and tracing his gloved hand in circles over mine. "Willoughby has a crush on you."

I froze. "You mean that he loves me."

Bask shook his head. "It's not the same."

I frowned. "Why's it any different to your obsessive love or how I crave all my Immortals?"

Bask stilled; I instantly missed the soft sensation of his finger. "Because you don't love him back."

He glanced at me carefully from underneath his eyelashes.

I opened my mouth to answer but then closed it with a *snap*.

What could I say? Willoughby's magic called to my own, just as mine did to his. But he wasn't Robin or one of my Immortals.

Yet he could be.

Should I simply trap Willoughby to undo the wards, using his love to free all the Rebels? It was a worthy cause. I'd discovered a rival's weakness that would save Fox. It could end my own curse.

Yet I'd never play with anyone's emotions in such a way.

I leaned closer to Bask, and he pushed towards me to hear my answer. I trembled at the choice.

All of a sudden, the Privilege and Punishment Board blazed on fire.

Crack my broomstick and call me a witch, is that what happened when you broke too many rules in the Princes' bedrooms? Had we literally burned the rule book?

At least Bask and I were lying on a bed made out of ice. Wait, did Willoughby keep it that way for protection against his own spontaneously combusting room? Since I'd already experienced being burned alive, I believed that sensible. The ability to battle fire was an underrated talent in a man.

Bask scrambled out of the sheets, dragging me off the bed. I eyed the window and the door. If I was alone, I could've simply done my *mist thing* and escaped as easily as a bird. But I wasn't, and I'd never leave Bask behind to face...

Wait, *what* precisely? The burning board wasn't turning to ash. The fire must be magical, but what had triggered it?

Then all at once, the wall melted in on itself to reveal a hidden passageway behind.

Sweet Hecate, how many secrets were there in this castle?

When a professor stalked out of the passageway with a scowl on her sharp pointy features, Bask gasped and straightened his shoulders. He edged even further in front of me.

The witches of the House of Crows liked to make an entrance.

Juni, the Prince's Tutor, Professor of Divination and Damelza's daughter, who was alike to her mother, apart from the shortness of her hair that was trapped beneath a woven cap of feathers, hesitated at Lysander's bed, staring down at the sheets with a grimace. Then she scanned the rest of the room; her eyes danced with malice.

I wrapped my arms around Bask's waist. "Fancy seeing you here. Nice weather we're having."

Juni's cheek twitched. "It's the same weather that we've been having for over a hundred years. I believe that it can be counted to the day that you cursed the academy. Are you so fond of snow?"

I reached out, running my hand along the column of Willoughby's bed. "I'm finding myself growing fond of ice."

Juni's eyes flashed, before they narrowed. *She was dangerous and she'd discovered Bask and me.* On Hecate's breath, I wouldn't forget that again. "Music. Unmade beds. Evidence of immoral acts." She scrunched up her nose. "The Princes have earned themselves three Punishment Points each and a Shame Hex."

"Not a chance. It was us who played the music, messed up the beds, and had wicked fun with the immorality," Bask insisted.

Juni shrugged. "This is their room and so their responsibility. I'd suggest that you should have thought of the consequences of your actions before you acted but then, that would be unfair without casting a Self-Restraint Spell." When her gaze darted to Lysander's bed, it lit up with as much curiosity as disgust. "If these were Crown's *stains* then he'd lose his Privacy Privileges for a month."

I winced. Why did I have to feel sympathy for the fae prince again? But the thought of him here, where even privacy was a privilege that could be lost, was agonizing.

Even a haughty prick of a prince didn't deserve that.

Juni swept around to Bask. "But they're not Crown's, are they?"

Bask smirked. "Guilty."

Juni tilted her head, assessing Bask. "Of course you are. I'm just wondering what creature my mother shall turn you into. I can't wait for you Immortals to be tripped up on your own overconfidence. She's been practicing slugs. They leave slimy trails behind as well, so it'd be fitting."

Bask paled.

I glared at her, imagining *her* transformed into a dung beetle with a heightened sense of smell.

Ah, happy dreams.

She stared at me. "Why are you smiling? You've been caught."

"Have I?"

Juni's cheek twitched again. "You don't understand how furious mother is." I shivered. *I had an idea.* She glanced at Bask. "I haven't seen her this angry since the time Crave refused to go on his first mission, and she was forced to hang another Rebel." Bask paled further. "The way that her eyes are blazing is almost as scary as the way Bacchus' went all swirly, when Sleipnir delighted us all by pissing *Loki Rules* in the snow." When she strolled towards the counter, grasping the stallion teapot, I tensed. "Do you see the pattern? Immortals have no *self-restraint.*"

"Still," I rested my head on Bask's shoulder, nibbling on his ear until he sighed, "they make up for it with bonus rebellion and high jinks. Wouldn't you rather we were in human form, rather than slugs? Otherwise, who will you be able to act superior to?"

When Bask snickered, Juni ignored him. She wrapped her hands around the pot, before pouring the now steaming tea into a cup. She'd warmed it with her magic, which was impressive. Although, I was less impressed with her tea making etiquette. She poured the milk in from the porcelain jug *after* the tea. I *tutted*, tapping my foot.

Quite appalling.

"Oh, how kind." I sauntered closer, holding out my hand, hopefully. "One for me…?"

Juni appeared to consider it for a moment, holding out the cup. I grinned. *The Princes' luxury beverages here I come...*

Then she snatched it back, sipping on the drink with a satisfied sigh. "If you'd only heeded my warnings about how to behave, then we could've taken tea together like sisters every day."

I gaped at her. *Was ever there such a mean trick?*

"Is that your Divination talking? I truly hate how those who know the future *pretend* that they, well, know the future," I retorted.

Juni's fingers tightened around the cup. "Just call me Cassandra because nobody listened to her either."

I grasped Bask's hand, sweeping to Juni. "I listened, which is why I snatched my Immortal away from your mother. When I first lived in this academy, I might not have understood its cruelties but I do now. I'm a Prefect." *I deserved a little boast, surely?* "It's my duty to look out for them, just like you look out for the Princes."

Black cats, that was a stretch, unless looking out

for included obsessive regulation of bathroom breaks, revoking Food Privileges, and checking sizes of pricks. She was at least dedicated.

When Juni slammed down the cup with a sharp *crack*, I flinched.

Don't let it break.

Somehow, it felt like if it did, then Bask would too, and right now, I could still feel him alive and unbroken at my shoulder. My heart sped up, and I clutched my arms around my middle to hide how my hands shook.

"You're a Prefect, and I'm a Professor," Juni hissed.

I raised my eyebrow. "Yet which one of us takes better care of our boys?"

"*Hmm*, certainly not the witch who's risked her Immortals in the Rebel Cup, where the stakes are either their whipping boy's life or my one's *wings* to be decided tomorrow on Torment Thursday." Juni pointed at herself and then me. "Which one of us was that again?"

I wound my black mists around her finger, and my eyes sparked pink. "The Immortals are mine, and the Principal set those stakes and not me."

Juni stared down at her finger, dispassionately. "If Bacchus hears you claiming her Rebels, then she'll turn you into a—"

"Pomeranian...?" Bask offered, bouncing on his toes.

"She's favoring rocking chairs today." To my surprise, Juni yanked her finger towards herself, rather than away. I was pulled by my own mists into her embrace with a startled yelp. She stroked my hair, and the feathers on her hat scratched my cheek. "You care about your Immortals, but I also care about my Princes. *You're hurting them*, sister in the House of Crows. Just by being here and existing, you endanger them. By coming to life, you risk all the sweethearts who you pretend to love."

"It's not true." Bask tugged on my shoulder, attempting to pull me away from Juni.

Except, in the name of Hecate, it was.

I shuddered, but I didn't let go of Juni, as if she was holding me up, rather than entrapping me in her arms.

Juni's smile was sly. "It's such a shame that you didn't take part in Divination. Then you'd have seen that you're on a tragic path, just like Crown did. He witnessed the terrors that your return would bring, and it haunts him now."

I remembered Lysander's distress in Juni's class and how he'd screamed, arching off the floor. Juni had taken dark enjoyment in reducing Lysander to such fear that he'd needed her comfort.

She loved to be the predator in the room.

I'd just have to show her that the wicked witch would never become the prey.

I dragged my black mists away from Juni's skin fast enough to give her mist rash, then I straightened, extricating myself from her hold. But I didn't drop my gaze.

"You're lying." My voice was as icy as Willoughby's bed.

"Am I?"

Lysander was a prick of a fae but he'd begged to suffer through the Divination Spell so that I wouldn't have to. *What had he seen?*

My tongue darted out to wet my lips, before I glanced at Bask. I wished that we could simply be caught in each other's arms again, safe within the womb of my magic. "I'm awfully sorry, but as my familiar would say, *we're all out of giving a witching fuck.*"

Juni's eyes gleamed with powerful magic, before she clicked her fingers and the tea set shattered. I jumped, shielding my face against the shards of porcelain. The tea sloshed in a brown sea down the counter.

Never forget that she was one of my descendants.

Bask wailed, then his gaze became steely. "Why would you break Willoughby's tea set? Fix it, before you force him to cry or lose the shine to his hair."

I knew that Bask was imagining the stuffing pulled out of Nile. My nails bit into my palms.

71

Juni studied Bask like she'd never seen him before. "Really, Crave? Do I take orders from students?" Bask dropped his gaze. "My Princes hurt for me, but nobody else *harms* them. Crown cannot fight his guardian and uncle. Prince Titus runs this academy as much as mother. When you rebel, you *harm* us all."

I froze. "I'm grateful for your sisterly guidance. Are you done smashing innocent crockery and imparting your pearls of wisdom?"

Juni sniffed. "If all I'm doing is casting pearls before swine."

"How did you discover us?" I asked. *Why didn't you tell Damelza*? I wanted to add.

Juni prowled to the passageway, but not before repairing Willoughby's tea set with a *click* of her fingers; relief washed through me more powerfully than I'd ever have guessed. "It was amusing to see mother's frantic shock when she couldn't sense you within the academy. It was like — *pop!* — you'd both ceased to exist. Of course, I knew that I'd broken the rules to install a Privacy Spell in these rooms."

I hated to think about why. It couldn't be purely to reward the Princes.

I mock gasped. "Broken the rules? Why, it appears that I'm not the only rebel in this family."

Juni stiffened. "I call it *becoming independent.* I also guessed that you were here because you're forbidden to enter the East Wing. You're the sort to be precisely where you're not meant to be."

I preened. "Thank you."

Her lips thinned. "Get on with that vanishing trick of yours then. Crave, follow me. I don't trust you with magical transportation anymore, so we'll be taking the long route through the hidden passageways of the castle. What a shame that it'll also give you time to ponder the likely punishment from both the Duchess and the Principal."

I blinked. "Vanishing...?"

Juni twirled away from me, snapping her fingers at Bask like he'd already been transformed into a Pomeranian. "Follow or I'll leash you. And you, wickedest Crow, if you were to go invisible and follow us because you wanted to be present in the study for this meeting but undetected, then I'd easily be able to tell mother that I hadn't seen you."

I stared at Juni. *And she called me the Rebel.*

Bask snatched my hand in his, resting it against his cheek in a gesture that held intense intimacy for an incubus. "I wish you to be with me. I have to do this, but I don't need to be alone."

I nodded.

Yet could I truly turn myself back to my ghostly state and stand by like Bask wished as nothing more than a witness? Was I strong enough for that?

I could be for my lover.

73

If Bask thought that I wouldn't find a way to break the hold that the blood contract had over him or the Duchess who'd once forced a bond, however, then he didn't know the strength of my will after so many years trapped in the Dead Wood. I hadn't escaped, only to lose my Rebels now.

I studied the tense line of Juni's back. "Why help us?"

Juni hesitated, and I didn't think that she was going to answer.

At last, she said, "We don't all get to choose who we love, remember? Do you imagine that simply because I'm a witch, I'm free from suffering? I would've thought that your own experience had taught you better than that." My cheeks pinked. "Are professors and students so different?"

I snorted. "Since one can be sent to their death on missions and one can't, I'd say a resounding *yes*."

"I'm offering an olive branch," Juni's voice was deadly. The hairs on the base of my nape rose. "Don't burn it."

"Good advice," I muttered.

I stroked Bask's cheek for one final time. His smile was fragile, and I could see the cracks. But he didn't stop smiling, even as I unwove myself, thread by thread.

I faded, until I was once more invisible.

When Juni gave a final *click* of her fingers at

Bask, he darted after her into the dark mouth of the secret passageway. I floated behind them, keeping close enough not to get lost in the labyrinth within the walls, through the castle towards Damelza's study, the Duchess, and their rage.

CHAPTER FIVE

Rebel Academy, Wednesday September 4th

BASK

A slinky incubus of the ancient Night lineage shouldn't be ignored. It makes his shiny hair go limp. I shuddered because shoved into the corner of Damelza's study and staring at the shadowy wall, I remembered what it was like to belong to the Duchess.

Invisible. Ignored. Unloved.

Beg me to let you burn yourself...

I shivered. Wow, bad time for thoughts of what my bitch ex-bond would do to me when she dragged me back to the Succubi Court.

Unless that was why I'd been stood here in the first place…?

The displeasure radiating from both the women, who prowled behind me talking like I didn't exist, cramped through me in waves. For an incubus, displeasure was more painful than a beating.

The Duchess knew that.

They were brutal pissed that Magenta had snatched me and even more pissed that only *I* had been returned.

Despite the pain, my lips curled into a smile. Magenta was safe and loved my sinfully sexy self (*of course, snicker*). I'd experienced real love and nothing the Duchess did could take my memories from me. I wouldn't let the Duchess break me again because this time, I'd have Magenta's love inside me, keeping me strong.

I scrunched up my nose at the stench of garlic, before glancing down at the Hecate shrine that'd been built under the narrow window. The Hecate statue, which lounged on the stinky garlic, wagged her finger at me.

I pulled my innocent face, even adding in a flutter of eyelashes, but her eyes only narrowed, as she pointed at the corner.

See, it must be the *limp hair effect* already.

Fox would've flicked her off because my snuggly

foxy was a serious Rebel, but I didn't have the same witch vs mage war raging as he had. Instead, I cast a sneaky glance over my shoulder (at least my arse was still pettable), before putting my nose back into the corner.

Although I should warn Damelza about **Rule 23 of the Incubi Night Code**: If somebody puts you in the corner, put them in the ground.

Harsh but fair.

All of a sudden, the scent of wild woods wound around me. I sighed, as cold lips kissed down the back of my neck, prickling my skin with electric magic. *Magenta* was here with me. It was adorable that she was truly invisible and didn't care. Plus, she wouldn't let me suffer this alone like I once had at the palace.

I raised my chin. If I had to stare at a wall, then I could do it with attitude.

A cool breeze blew across my hip, and I fought myself to stay still, as it cooled my cock and balls. So, my Voyeur Ghost was also a Possessive Ghost. But then who wouldn't want to claim the precious jewels of a sexy incubus (come on, who was I kidding, they were already marked with her name).

I let myself sink into the safety of Magenta's ghostly embrace: her scent and touch. She wasn't visible, but I could *feel* her. She was still inside me, and I knew that she always would be.

Once an incubus loved, it was until death, just as it was *like* death to be parted from their lover; it was this whole *thing*. And when I was parted from Magenta and the other Immortals, it'd be a slow death. Except, I'd never let them know that. Ma had taught me that I should think about my own survival first, but I'd do anything to save the other Rebels. They belonged to me and that meant that I'd do anything to protect them.

After all, I'd also been taught to let myself burn.

"Beg me for your inspection," the Duchess whispered into my ear.

The hairs on my nape rose. *When had she moved behind me?* Had I been that deeply lost in my brilliant dream of the Immortals? Silly incubus, didn't I know that safety wasn't real?

Too close, too close, too close...

I shrank against the wall like I could somehow escape her. If I'd still been her bonded incubi back in the palace, I'd have been punished for flinching.

My tongue darted out to wet my dry lips. The scent of yew trees faded. *Where was Magenta?* "P-please inspect me."

Would I be in trouble for hesitating?

I heard the *click click* of the Duchess' footsteps, as she prowled away.

"He's forgotten his training," the Duchess said, coolly.

I winced. *I was off my game.*

"You broke him and then abandoned him in my

academy. Did you expect to find him in perfect shape?" Damelza replied.

Wow, that was brutal. Also, *true.*

Was Damelza defending her own honor or mine?

Still, we had a saying: *Never trust an enemy who looks like a friend.* Seriously, it was an ancient one. Trust me.

"Turn around." The Duchess' voice was quiet but rang through the study like a gunshot.

I swallowed, and my hands clenched into fists. My nails bit crescents into my palms. I forced myself to turn; my pulse roared in my ears.

The study was dark and stacked with books and potions. On the wall opposite me, beneath the academy's **RA** crest, the wall sparkled with pink and black motivational sayings. Underneath this, scrolled the school's motto:

Rebel Academy — Blessing the Wicked Since 1870

The Duchess perched casually on the edge of an obsidian desk that was cobbled with crow skulls. Her hands were crossed in her lap like she was demurely waiting for a prayer book to be placed in them, but I knew that it was Number Three in her Top Ten Positions to Ride an Incubi's Face. Her red hair tumbled around her shoulders and her skin was the type of peachy that the other bonded incubi in the harem had swooned over.

Yet the predatory hunger in her intense gaze made me want to vomit. But then, that would make me even less pettable.

The Duchess' dress was long white satin with a train that coiled around the study, but her red fluffy tail poked out of the back.

Yep, succubi had tails, which had many sexy possibilities, *if* they didn't use those tails to whip you, rather than stroke your dick.

Away with you, it'd be a fine thing to have a fluffy tail wank.

The Duchess arched her brow. "You displease me."

I howled, doubling over. *Why didn't she just boot me in the balls and have done with it?*

The air around me suddenly became electrified. Magenta's rage now joined the mix. The windows frosted over.

Magenta was only here to watch, although there were far kinkier ways that I could enjoy that. How could I get her to step down on the whole *protecting me thing* because if she saw the state of my hair and was *still* about to reveal herself, then didn't it have to be love…?

I drew in a deep breath and straightened.

Damelza *tutted.* "Entertaining though it is to watch your techniques, are you here to inspect his progress or complain all evening? I have other lessons planned, you know. This is still the start of term, and an academy doesn't run itself. Tomorrow's Torment Thursday, which is always thrilling, then there's the Dragon Polo Tournament. These events have to be organized."

I glanced at Damelza from underneath my eyelashes. My guts roiled. *Other lessons?* At this time of evening, that usually meant somebody had earned the Memory Theater as punishment.

Please, not my whipping boy again.

Damelza's feathered dress ruffled up in outrage, as she sat stiffly in the blood-red leather desk chair. Her silver blonde hair glistened, and she fiddled with the feather that was tucked behind her hair. She appeared as stressed by the Duchess' visit as me. If she wasn't such a bad bastard, Head of the House of Crows Coven and Principal, then she'd have been beautiful.

Yuck. Dick, you're getting a smack even for twitching at that thought.

She wasn't as beautiful as Magenta, of course, although she was her descendant (*dick, for the love of the Immortals, stop twitching*).

I hated to think of Magenta as a witch of the House of Crows, but she wasn't like them. She was *my* witch, like Slippy was *my* god, and Fox was *my* whipping boy.

Unfortunately, the Duchess appeared to think that I was *her* incubus. My expression became steely. I'd

82

rather curse myself with forever frizzy hair, than become hers.

In my heart, I never would be again. Yet once, I would've loved her with my every breath.

The Duchess ran her hand along a spine of a book as if to figure out the words inside by touch alone. "He's different. Who's touched him?"

Damelza's eyes glittered pink. "Since you contacted me, *no one*. I cast a Repellent Hex and—"

"You're wrong." The Duchess' voice was calm but so dangerous that my balls shrank in fright. She crooked her finger at me, and I edged closer. Magenta's icy lips latched onto my ear, sucking. I struggled to keep my expression blank. Even my ears were suckable. It was a gift. One that meant, while I slunk closer to the Duchess, supposedly *pure,* Magenta was touching me in the *wickedest* ways. When I stopped in front of the Duchess, I tried to avoid her gaze, but she tipped up my chin with her tail. It was hot and so unlike Magenta's cool skin. In the palace, the Duchess had almost never touched my slinky self, no matter how much the others helped me to primp or dressed me up, which meant that she was making a point. *She could do what she liked to me.* My heart beat faster. "I sent you here to learn your lesson. But instead, I hear that you're rebellious."

The disappointment in her tone was almost enough to send me to my knees. I swayed but managed to stay standing. "Away with you," I gritted out, "I thought that you chose me because you wanted a challenge. Aren't I meant to be the *freak* of an incubus?"

The Duchess drew back like *I'd* burned *her.* "The Principal told me that she's already punished you for your infractions. I'd planned to forgive you or are you acting up because you *need* me to punish you again and reinforce those lessons?"

My breath came in harsh pants, and I shook my head.

Not here...not in front of Magenta...please...

I shook at the memory of the Duchess' last punishment. She didn't need to inflict simple pain. To be untouched was the ultimate penalty for an incubus. She'd turned me into a *Not There,* which meant that everyone in the palace had been ordered to ignore me like I'd become a ghost. I'd started to wonder if I'd become one for a real.

For the first time, I'd ignored the rule about not crying, weeping and dragging on the other incubi's arms, desperate to get them to at least look at me, but they wouldn't. Instead, they'd continued to eat, exercise, or sleep in their casual group like I hadn't been there. If they'd broken the Duchess' rule, even to press their gloved hand to my cheek or brush their arm reassuringly against mine in passing, then they'd also have been condemned to become a *Not There*.

I hadn't simply been unloved: I'd been erased from existence.

It hadn't mattered how pettable, slinky, or how much I'd hurt myself for the Duchess.

In despair, I'd knelt in front of her and burned myself. But she'd simply continued to turn the pages of her book like even my agony hadn't been delicious to her anymore.

That had been when our bond had broken.

It was a serious thing to break a bond.

I've always been greedy for love, however, and if neither my pleasure nor my pain could gain it, then this sweet arse no longer wished to serve. It wasn't that much of a surprise when the Duchess sent me to Rebel Academy, but the shame of never being allowed to see my family again nearly broke me for a second time.

Ma wanted to hide me from women like the Duchess, but you can't hide. You have to face life.

The Duchess tapped the top of the book thoughtfully. "Then what do you say to my mercy?"

Stick it up that place beneath your fluffy tail? "Thank you." *You psycho bond breaker...*

The Duchess must've read something in my *maybe* not quite so innocent expression because she twisted to Damelza. "I'm telling you that the incubus has been altered. He'll take much re-education."

Re-education. Fun.

I grimaced.

Damelza's lips pinched. "You know how it is between students at this age, especially under the pressure and adrenaline of trials and near death. It makes them fancy themselves in love." I bit my tongue hard to keep still at the way the two women shot each other patronizing looks. *What did either of them know about love?* "Crave has a crush on our new Prefect."

The Duchess shrugged. "My bonded incubi are often fiercely protective of each other."

Damelza shuffled the files on her desk. "She's not quite the same as the other bad boys here."

The Duchess stiffened. "*She...?*"

"Crow is an unwelcome and unexpected student." When Damelza's voice hardened, the temperature in the room fell even further. I longed for Magenta to kick my tormentors' arses, as much as I needed her to stay invisible. "She's a witch from this coven, but I assure you, I have the situation under control. The witch is as weak as Crave. Her own first crush on a mage led to her magic corrupting to Wickedly Charmed and cursing this entire academy."

My eyes widened, and I glanced around like I'd actually be able to see Magenta. Is that what'd happened? She'd loved a mage like Fox, and it'd turned her wicked?

An icy wind blew down the back of my neck as if

steadying me or promising to tell me the secret. I'd go with the *secret* because I was optimistic like that.

The Duchess slid off the table, circling me. I fought not to recoil; I'd forgotten how much taller than me she was. I loved that Magenta was my height.

It made kissing sinfully delicious.

"That's not a crush. It's forbidden and reckless love. A crush is much more painful." The Duchess' eyes danced with glee like she was feeding even from the thought of it. "It bubbles beneath the skin. It burns, unrequited. Bask loved me like that once. I delighted in it. It fed me the most mouth-watering flavors of pleasure." She tilted her head. "Does he love the witch in the same way?"

"Not a chance," I snapped, before I could stop myself, "because *Magenta* loves me back."

Crack — the Duchess' tail whipped me across the arse.

I gasped. My arse was made for spanking, stroking, petting...a whole platter of fun things. But whipping rights were denied to succubi who weren't even bonded to me any longer.

"It would please me for you to lie on your back on the desk," the Duchess said.

She glowed with power. She'd already fed on her commands, and my pain. I fought to resist her, but we'd once been bonded, and she was one of the most powerful succubi at Court. There was a reason that she was feared.

When I sprawled on the desk, knocking books and files flying, Damelza squawked in protest. The files that I'd flattened dug painfully into my shoulder blades. I was too aware of the pulse pounding in my ears and fluttering in my throat.

When the Duchess leaned over me, trapping me beneath the red bars of her hair, everything became blurry.

"Thank Hecate, my study hasn't been turned into a pleasure harem for at least a month," Damelza drawled, shoving back her chair. Then she stalked to the door. "How about I allow you some — *brief* — privacy to inspect that he's reforming as promised? When I come back, it'd be ever so kind of you to allow me my own desk back."

I winced, as Damelza slammed the door.

My hands clawed around the crows' skulls on top of the desk. My breathing was too rapid. My mind was hazy insisting that I *please, please, please...*

Alone. Trapped. Compelled.

It didn't matter whether my hair was lank or at perfect shininess levels: The Duchess would make me hurt.

She always had.

"Undo your shirt." Ruby sparkles glittered from the Duchess' mouth, amplifying each command.

I reached up, pushing aside my blazer and tie. I had no modesty (*startling discovery*), because false modesty was banned in my code. I was certain that I'd read it in the small print. But the Duchess stripped away clothes like stripping away part of my Soul.

If you didn't know how to pet an incubus, then it was petting denied. But still, I lay on that desk, and undid my shirt with shaking fingers.

One button, two, three...

The scent of the wild wood cocooned me. It was stronger now. Magenta was here with me, and her magic thrummed hard and bright. Her fury chilled the air, and painted snowflake patterns across the glass. Outside, a storm battered the window.

I drew in my breath. Did she mean to curse the academy for a second time because of me? I thought that I was the obsessively romantic lover here. I almost pouted.

The Duchess stilled my hand, narrowing her eyes like she'd noticed that she didn't have my full attention. Then she slipped her fingers teasingly inside my shirt and across my collarbone. I jumped, shaking. Her fingers were hot and invasive.

I didn't want this. My skin crawled. *Too much...*

The Duchess gave a cool smile. "How sensitive. Perhaps, you're perfect to be retrained, after all. You'll be fun to play with. This is what I'd hoped to achieve with your touch deprivation as a *Not There*, if only you hadn't been so weak as to break." When she swiped her finger across my nipple, I arched. *Just try and twist and reshape me, snaky tail.* I was no longer hers. She thought that she could retrain me, when I had the Immortals' rebel spirit inside me...? *Cute.* Her eyes narrowed. "Why aren't you breaking?"

"You never loved me," I replied, flatly. "But I'm loved now."

The Duchess' eyes glowed with a fire that I'd always desired to see burning through her cool. This mighty incubus had the power to destroy a Frost Bitch's indifference.

I'd add that to my talents along with knotting cherry stems with my tongue and eyebrow dancing.

Seriously, don't knock it until you've seen it.

The Duchess bared her teeth. Ruby sparkles glittered around her like she could no longer contain them. When she crushed me against the desk, I shuddered. The press of her body against mine was too much all at once. I scrabbled against the piles of books, knocking them to the floor with a *crash*.

"Why would I love you?" The Duchess drew her tail down my cheek, and I flinched. "I already *care* for my harem favorites. You're just an amusing oddity. You always were dangerously naive. Don't you see that you're no more than a toy? I didn't bond with you out of love."

"And now we're not bonded at all." When I batted

away her tail, her eyes widened in shock. "So, don't touch me."

I glowed with as much predator strength as the Duchess. I *was* an oddity because I was as powerful as any succubus.

She wanted a challenge, right? Then *she'd found one* because I wouldn't be pushed around anymore.

When I shoved the Duchess away with more strength than I knew I had in me, she stumbled back, falling on her arse.

The Duchess on her arse with wide startled eyes was a fine sight.

My grin was wicked, as I straightened my tie and crossed my arms; Magenta wound around me in icy gusts, thrilling at my victory. "Do you wish this inspection to be over? What a shame that I failed."

In careful movements that set my teeth on edge, the Duchess pushed herself to her feet, brushing down her dress. "What I *wish* is that you think hard about how much you've *displeased* me and how you can do better."

Now that was a punch to the dick.

I swayed, before falling to my knees. Waves of pain washed over me, as my own nature betrayed me.

Bad...failure...need to please... What can I do to bring her pleasure?

I clutched my hands over my ears, trying to force away the looping thoughts as well as the pain. I didn't mean them, and they weren't mine. But incubus training was effective. If my bonded had been kind and loved me, then I'd never even have questioned if my slinky self should've followed their rules.

Being sent to the Rebel Academy, even if I was taken back, had freed my mind. Ma had raised me with the right to think and scheme like a woman, but that'd broken me. Yet I didn't blame her now because the Duchess could return me to the Court, but my mind would always remain with my lovers.

Free, even within these prison walls.

Whoosh — the Duchess exploded a magical fire on the floor in front of me.

I froze. This was too like all those times in the palace, when she'd trained me. She wouldn't try that here?

Yep, she would.

"Beg me to let you burn yourself." The Duchess towered over me; her face was a shuttered mask, but her eyes studied me with hungry intensity.

She craved to feed off my pain.

Obey...obey...obey...

The flames appeared enticing like they'd kiss, rather than burn me. They were the reward and not the punishment.

Please, let me burn myself and prove my love.

My mind was hazy, and the room shimmered.

Where was I? I didn't understand. Hadn't the Duchess rejected me?

My bonded would never reject a beautiful incubus from the Night Lineage. If only I could grant her pleasure...

"Please may I burn myself?" I begged.

The Duchess' lips curled into a smile. *But why were her eyes dancing with such malicious amusement?* Had my hair lost its shine? "Oh, you can do better than that."

My heart raced, and I quivered in dismay that I'd disappointed her. I could do better than this. *I would.* I clenched my jaw. "I desire to bring you pleasure. So, please let me serve you. I've no greater wish than to burn myself for you. Please, I'll do anything, just let me do this."

"Was that a command?" Her voice was dangerous.

I lifted my shaky hand towards the fire. "Never."

Her smile broadened. "Then please me."

I sighed in relief. Yet why was something deep inside screaming at me to s*top, you silly incubus?* Why was the scent of the wild woods so powerful that it was like I was back hugging Hecate's Tree?

Wait, Hecate's Tree... This was the Rebel Academy... and I wasn't bonded to the Duchess...

The Duchess watched me with dark eyes, as the fire seared my palm.

All of a sudden, the study windows cracked. The

winter storm blasted through them, shattering the glass. I ducked from the shards, as the Duchess screamed. Snowflakes like tears rained on the fire, putting it out.

I clutched my palm to myself, as it cooled. Once again, my mind was clear. I knew where I was and that I shouldn't be kneeling at a succubus' feet.

Furious, I leaped up, before prowling around the Duchess, who struggled to pull out the glass from her arms, which had shielded her face. The wind followed me; Magenta was at my back.

She'd saved my pettable arse (and petted it with icy nips).

"I don't think that the academy is *pleased* with you," I hissed. "You should leave. It's dangerous here."

That wasn't a lie.

The Duchess flicked out the final piece of glass, ignoring the way that her white dress had been stained with red. "Empty-headed incubi are always superstitious. It's nothing more than a storm and an old building. A school (unlike a succubus), can't be displeased with you."

I shivered at the threat beneath her words, but I still smiled.

Wrong, bitch.

A flurry of files, books, and potions flew across

the room to crash and shatter against the wall. The Duchess jumped.

"Just the storm," she muttered.

Magenta's frosty tongue licked across my nipple, and I yipped, stumbling against the desk. Then to my surprise, the desk drawers flew open. I grimaced at the ghoulish contents: crow skeletons.

The skeletons rose up in the hold of Magenta's invisible mists like they'd sprung to life in a flock of dead crows.

The Duchess paled.

I smirked. "It's nothing. Just the storm."

The skeleton crows flew across the room, pecking at the Duchess' tits, as she howled, whipping at them with her tail. I laughed. This was the first time that I'd been glad of the Privacy Spell cast on the study.

"It's this cursed academy." The Duchess backed towards the door. "I shouldn't have trusted witches and their magic. This has nothing to do with me."

"Look behind you," I singsonged.

An incubi could have fun at his ex-bond's expense. That wasn't in the code. But it should be.

The motivational sayings on the wall vanished to display in neon pink:

Bitches not welcome. Duchesses are forbidden on academy grounds. This means you. YES YOU!

It was impressive how pale the Duchess could become. She twirled, slamming open the door.

Was she leaving without me? I bit my lip because an incubus with hope was a disappointed incubus.

Still, I clutched hard onto the desk, ducking my head, just in case she'd forget about me. The words disappeared from the wall, and Magenta danced the crows back into the drawer, wiping away the offensive Unwelcome Message.

"Damelza!" The Duchess hollered.

Wow, that was the first time that I'd ever heard the Duchess raise her voice. It was a fine thing.

Damelza swept past the panting Duchess into the study. She eyed my open shirt and then the state of her desk and the heaps of books on the floor.

Damelza smiled slyly. "I heard that you liked it rough with your boys. Well, that certainly appears to have been a thorough inspection. I'd have appreciated a little more consideration for my belongings. This is a place of learning, you know."

Damelza bustled around to her chair, picking up a torn book and *tutting*.

The Duchess opened her mouth to point out the crows, before shutting it with a snap, as she peered around suspiciously to try and find them. She settled on glaring at me, and I settled on giving her the inno-cent look.

"Look at your window..." The Duchess pointed at the smashed glass.

Damelza didn't glance over, as she slid behind her

desk and into her chair. "I'll add it to your bill. You should be more careful; you've cut yourself."

The Duchess flushed, then she swung to the wall. "How do you explain this...?"

At last, Damelza brightened. "Ah, my motivational sayings. I'm quite proud of those. As you can see, the saying for today is: *Academy attitude is a positive attitude.* I don't think that certain students have quite got to grips with it yet. Crown, the Princes' Prefect, struggles with his attitude, despite his excellent grades. Perhaps, I'll talk with his guardian because he's enthusiastic at adjusting Crown's attitude."

I winced. I'd wank in Lysander's bed, but I'd never wish *attitude adjustment* on him. That was my line, despite the fact that he was a haughty prick of a fae (who was so beautiful that I'd bet the hate sex would be hot; come on now, I wasn't blind.)

The Duchess stared at the wall and the blinking words:

Academy attitude is a positive attitude.

I bit the inside of my cheek to stop myself laughing.

Magenta coiled around me. I could sense her mists and her icy breath mingling with mine. She *was* the academy. I understood that now. And she was more powerful than a woman who'd led me by the balls. Yet she didn't use her power against me, however, only to love.

"Your castle is most rude, hostile, and uncomfortable," the Duchess complained.

Damelza stared at her, nonplussed. "There I was thinking that I ran a spa."

The Duchess sniffed, before sweeping back her hair. "Have this, as yet unreformed, incubus ready for Sunday. I'll make my decision then."

I straightened. Fear shot through me, until I couldn't breathe.

She could still take me away from my lovers on Sunday.

Only four days...

What if the Duchess decided to keep me? She'd be even angrier now that I'd defied her. Would she force me back to the palace but leave me as an unpetted member of the harem? Tell me daily how much I displeased her? Keep me as a *Not There,* until I broke over and over and...

I clenched my jaw, narrowing my eyes.

If the Duchess didn't want me as a proper bond, then she didn't deserve any incubi. *She didn't deserve me.*

Magenta taught me that.

"Get on with you, I thought that I was unlovable...?" When I stalked towards the Duchess, I must've been channeling my predator vibes because she backed away. The thrill rushed through me to be the one in charge; power surged. "I'll find a way to break any bond, into which you force me. You already think that I'm not a true incubi, who should be cut off from the rest of the bonded harem and too shamed to be allowed contact with any of my family. I can't sink any lower."

The Duchess' eyes glittered. "But you can be bad..."

I gritted my teeth against the agony roiling through me. I still prowled closer to the Duchess, however, and she still backed up, banging her head against the door. When she winced, I bounced on my toes with joy.

I noticed that Damelza only studied us with interest and didn't stop me.

The Duchess wasn't a professor, so the Charms that dampened my powers and stopped me fighting them, didn't protect her. I treated myself to a dark grin at the thought.

"It's like this, see, you taught me to take pain. It doesn't frighten me now." I tilted my head. "And I'd rather die than return to a bond where I'm despised, when I know what it is to be loved."

"What if it wasn't *you* who'd die?" I turned to Damelza, and she shot me a crafty look. *No, no, no...* She'd better not hurt my whipping boy; I'd sworn to protect my adorable foxy. I'd already lost Hector. I wouldn't allow anyone else to be hurt. She must've read my expression because she relaxed back in her chair. "I'm impressed by your oration skills, however, maybe we should set up a Debating Club. Plus, the only dying that occurs in this academy is strictly by permission or on my schedule."

When Damelza reached into the cabinet behind her and started to set out deep bowls of herbs that smelled of sweet white sage and rich incense, I tensed. The air around me shimmered like Magenta was as nervous as me.

"More witch magic...?" The Duchess spat.

Damelza lit a black candle. The flame flickered spectral in the dark. Dread choked me.

"It must come as a shocking surprise since you're in a coven." Damelza's gaze darted between us. "I've been working on a spell to cast a ghost back where it came from. Yet it needed blood like most serious spells." Magenta's cool fingers traced across mine. I wished that I could take them in mine. What if Damelza truly could cast Magenta back, after everything Sleipnir, Fox, and I had done to bring her to life? "Yet as a descendant to the House of Crows, it appears that *I'm* the magic ingredient."

I watched, mesmerized, as Damelza pulled out a silver knife and slit her thumb, then she held it over the bowl of herbs.

I wouldn't lose my Magenta.

I hurled myself across the desk, knocking the candle rolling to the floor and clattering the herbs over the books. Then I stuffed Damelza's thumb in my mouth and sucked, until there was no trace of her dangerous blood.

When I lifted my gaze to meet Damelza's, I realized that I was lying on my Principal's desk and sucking on her thumb.

Whoops.

The Duchess arched her brow. "He is very good at that."

Damelza coughed. "I'd noticed." I let her thumb go with a humiliating *pop*, before wriggling off her desk as sexily as possible (away with you, I could pull it off). "But as positive attitude is today's motivational saying, I'll offer a choice. Crave can obey and abide by the Duchess' decision on Sunday, or I cast the spell again (without the finger sucking), and I may as well make this official by punishing your whipping boy. Walling up alive is the traditional punishment."

"Please, don't..." I didn't even have to think about my answer. I couldn't let them hurt the other Immortals. I'd never let them suffer for me. "I'll obey, behave, bond... I'll do whatever you wish as long as you leave the Rebels alone."

The Duchess nodded, approvingly. "It appears that I need to offer you an apology, Damelza, your methods of taming are effective." She glanced around the room. "Even your castle is tamed."

This time, when the Duchess' tail curled possessively around my neck, I didn't move away. I knew how to take pain, and if it saved my lovers, then I'd beg to burn.

CHAPTER SIX

Rebel Academy, Wednesday September 4th

SLEIPNIR

As the son of Loki, I've witnessed both the monstrous and the wondrous. Often, they're one and the same. Just as frequently, I've searched them out, despite the fact that dad and I were hunted by witches and the immortal followers of Bacchus.

We should've hidden, frightened of our own shadows. But I kind of don't follow rules. I loved the world, even if the world feared me.

Yet Magenta has never feared me. She believed that I wasn't a monster, and for her sake, I pretended that it was true. Yet she'd been lost somewhere between worlds; I'd been able to feel it tingling through my magic like the veils were blowing across the back of my neck.

Omens and runes, that was never good.

Why couldn't it've been her cool breath instead, which never failed to harden my dick in my pants? My balls had even ached at the thought of thrusting between her thighs, as she rode me like the animal I was.

Thor's cock, it wasn't like I had to hide it anymore.

Even when I'd sensed Magenta return, it was muted like the Rainbow Bridge had been painted gray. I shuddered at Odin's reaction if Loki had ever played *that* trick.

Whatever was happening, I was stuck locked in the Immortals' West Wing bedroom with Fox. I shook my cotton candy pink hair out of my eyes, which fell in gentle spikes. In my anguish about Magenta, my brother Jormungand had risen to the front of my personality tonight. As a triplet, I loved my brothers, but when I was already battling to deal with the fact that Magenta and Bask were missing, it was harder to cope with their struggle over my mind.

I was wearing the academy striped pink and black silk pajamas but I liked to pull off a rebel vibe even in bed, so I rolled up the shirtsleeves to show my muscular forearms; shimmering sea serpents coiled around them like they were alive.

Jormungand was out to kick someone's ass.

I booted a pillow off the bed in frustration and then was glad…just for a moment…that Bask wasn't there to witness my pillow abuse.

This was a chaos moment.

It called out to me, even from the World Tree. The urgency to seize the event that could change everything thrummed through me. But I couldn't even break through the spell that trapped me inside this freezing bedroom.

As if at my thought, the braziers blazed higher with pink fire, warming me. I turned my cheek towards it. Shadows danced across the stone walls and plain wardrobes and desks. My books were strewn in haphazard piles across the floor, mingling with Bask's. The thought of the gorgeous incubus wrecked me.

Valhalla! I couldn't lose him like I'd lost Hector last term.

Mist, the miniature horse with eight legs who Magenta had transfigured in class out of my plectrum and her black mists trotted along my shoulder like it was a balancing bar. He shot out sad flames on each exhale. I couldn't hide my emotions now because they were shown to the world in Mist's reactions.

I'd been connected to death all my life, just like dad. Yet straddling the line between worlds wasn't the same as watching people that you loved die.

I had loved Hector, hadn't I?

I mean, not in the same *I shall love him, even after*

death intensity of Bask. But Bask didn't seem to be able to love in any way that didn't include throwing his heart at someone's feet. It made him almost as vulnerable as Fox, who'd spent his life trapped in an attic by his dick family and aching for someone to even notice him. Fox would throw *himself* at someone's feet to be loved.

I didn't need love...or friendship...like they did. I'd lived with dad and my brothers who existed inside me for so long that my heart was as much mist as Magenta was.

I sprawled on the vast bed in the center of the room, which I should've been sharing with all the Immortals. A satin pillow dug into my back, which also should've been Bask's because he had a freaky obsession with nesting into or hoarding them. I'd once opened the wardrobe to find two stuffed at the bottom. Bask had winked, calling it his *Emergency Pillow Fund*.

When I grabbed my guitar, my pajamas rode up to reveal a pale strip of my stomach. Fox opened one eye like he was checking me out.

By the Norns, a cat could look at a god.

Fox was transformed into his white Birman form with fluffy fur and a long tail. I'd tried to stroke the crooked tip earlier, but Fox had wrapped his tail around himself like I'd overstepped some kind of Cat Code. Perhaps, there was a feline version of the

Incubus one with rules about mice and feathery things, rather than shiny hair and pettable arses.

Huh, I seriously hoped not.

The way that I'd *cooed* at Fox hadn't helped, but then, he was adorable. Now, he was curled up on Nile like it was a Bask substitute. I'd tried to sneakily replace the crocodile with a pillow, but Fox had hissed at me.

On fear of Valkyries, when Bask discovered white fur on his plushie, it wouldn't be my *ass* who was held responsible.

I strummed my guitar, and Mist perked up, sliding down to fit into my pocket. I didn't cope well either with being caged or feeling powerless. Loki had spent my childhood teaching me to scheme because hoping for the best was a fool's hope.

So far, he hadn't been wrong.

Almost like my fingers had found the chords without my knowing it, I played R.E.M's "Everybody Hurts". Fox shot me a sardonic look (I was learning that he had an impressive ability to *communicate* in shifter form, even if his fluffy shifter ass was trash talking). The music was raw and intimate, however, and held hope for me that my lovers weren't lost. It was nothing but emotion...*heart*...and I clenched my jaw, as it washed over me.

Hey, I could do pining and obsessive love the

same as Bask or Emo angst like Fox. It was just that my guitar spoke for me.

I screwed shut my eyes. *Where was Magenta? What had happened?*

Damelza had burst back into the Bird Turret room at the end of Strategy Class without either Magenta or Bask. Ezekiel had been so shocked that he'd raised his angelic wings in an automatic display of dominance and protection, stepping in front of us students.

There was no way that an Addict Angel, ex-Rebel, and male Professor was permitted to act like that towards the witch Principal. I'd shuddered at the thought of her clamping chains to his wings as she had to Ambrose. To my shock, both the Princes had stepped in a protective semicircle around the Professor at the same time as us Immortals. Both sides had eyed each other warily.

Was this a truce?

Prince Lysander humiliated me, but was I wrong to doubt Magenta's plan of winning them to our side?

Luckily, Damelza had been so furious about Magenta stealing Bask (like the awesome warrior she was), that she ignored Ezekiel and slammed Fox and me against the wall with her magic. Then she'd interrogated us like we'd been part of a grand plot to make her look a jackass in front of the Duchess.

It'd made me wish that I *had* been part of a plot.

When Damelza had threatened to beat the truth out

of my whipping boy, it'd been Lysander who'd sidled towards her.

"You could try that," Lysander had said. "But Midnight rarely admits the truth to his mischief under torture. Rather, he'll say anything to stop the lashes falling." I'd instantly glanced at the beautiful curve of Midnight's shoulders, who was Lysander's vampire whipping boy, as he knelt in the corner. Midnight wrapped his ash wings around himself. He ducked his head, and his dark hair fell to his waist in waves. *How could anyone hurt him?* "My royal personage has found that isolation and time alone to think about the consequences of his actions is much more effective."

Damelza had blinked. "You mean time-out?"

Lysander's mouth had twisted. "If one must look at it that way." His gaze had slid to us. "Shall we call it sending them to their room, while the rest of us help in the search attempt?"

I'd have thought that it Lysander's way to humiliate me, but there'd been something in Fox's expression, as he hadn't taken his searching gaze away from Lysander, which made me take a sharp breath. In turn, Lysander had shuffled his feet.

Bor's beard, the fae was saving us. He was as good a liar as Fox. I had to admire that.

Damelza had nodded. "Excellent suggestion. But if the Princes don't manage to retrieve the runaways before the staff do," Damelza's smile had become sharp at the way that Willoughby had stroked his hand along Lysander's arm, "then *your* whipping boy will take the punishment."

Fox had argued, begged, and ranted that he be punished, instead. Midnight hadn't said a word or even raised his gaze.

Once Fox and I had been shoved into the bedroom for our *time-out*, Fox had transformed into a cat like he needed some feline snuggling to bring down his stress. As a shimage, the most hated of mages, he'd been denied the right to choose when he shifted.

Now, I flinched, as Mist nibbled at the inside of my pocket. He neighed, demanding that I get in some *feline snuggling* too.

I pushed my guitar to the side, lifting Fox onto my knee. He put up a fake squirmy struggle, which ended as soon as I nestled him on my lap. Then he purred, kneading at my balls with his paws.

"*Oww*, I'll be needing those, and that's not the type of milk you're looking for, pussy." I carefully extracted Fox's claws and then tickled behind his soft ears.

Fox rubbed his head against my hand. I stroked down the length of his body but was careful to avoid his tail. I wouldn't admit it on pain of death by troll kiss, but his fur was like petting a cloud. It was almost as silky as Bask's hair.

And I'd never admit that, even on pain of death by troll screw.

I shivered. *Trust me, that was a messed-up way to die.*

When I rubbed one finger under Fox's chin, he purred even louder. I loved that he no longer wore a Blood Amulet around his throat that controlled his powers, stopping him from shifting when he chose.

I'd free him. *I'd free all the Rebels.*

He might allow himself to be petted, but he wasn't a pet. He was my lover and a powerful mage, whose only crime was to be born into a witch family as a male with magic.

I'd never owned a real pet.

Only once, when my attempt to kidnap a human and force them to become my friend had proved to me that I'd never be worthy of true friendship, Loki had returned home with something tiny and howling with pitiful *arroos* in his arms.

I'd jolted upright from my lookout outside our tent on the edge of the Alaskan lake. My hands had sunk into the sludgy mud. The dying sun had cast reflections of the snow licked mountains into the water like icicles. Loki and I had been fleeing for months, hunted by a band of the Bacchus cult, who'd almost caught us outside Michigan.

Except, I thought that their allies, the witches, *had*

caught Loki, which was why he hid his tears behind fake smiles.

Loki's smile had been excited and genuine, as he'd dropped to his knees next to me and placed the squirming *thing* into my lap. My hair had spiked to red, and my brother Fenrir had growled out of his werewolf tattoos in greeting at the wolf cub.

The cub's fur had been dove gray. She'd circled around in my lap on wobbly legs, nosing at my hand, as I'd reached with my palm up, like she hadn't been sure whether I'd been a bed or a play-mate. Then she'd gazed up at me with golden eyes, and my tattoos had howled again. My soul had thrilled at discovering another creature that felt like me.

Such wildness.

"A werewolf," I'd breathed.

It was adorable.

Wait, had Fenrir looked like this as a baby?

Loki had grinned. "Kids today and their obsession with vampires and werewolves. She's a normal cub." He'd stroked his thumb across her head like a blessing. "But she's beautiful, right? She's loveable..."

I'd studied dad's face. Like usual, it'd been shuttered in that elegant way of his. But there'd been something in his eyes that I'd only seen flashes of before.

Hope.

He'd worn the same look when he'd gifted me the guitar. Why had he longed for me to like the cub?

He always tried to give me so much, even when he had nothing.

I'd looped my arms around the cub to stop its attempts to squirm free. Fenrir had thrilled at the closeness. He'd been desperate for the cub to become pack, and I'd struggled to keep control.

She wasn't mine...

"Where are her parents? Her brothers and sisters?" I'd asked.

Loki's expression had darkened. "Most of the pack were captured. It was a full moon last night, which means that the witches were harvesting hearts for a spell. I know it sucks, but she was the only one who I could save."

Loki's eyes had widened in shock, as I'd lifted my arms from the cub to around his neck instead, dragging him in to rest my cheek against his.

"You're a dumbass." When I'd banged my forehead against Loki's, he'd merely hugged me tighter around the shoulders.

"It has been pointed out to me before," he'd answered, drily.

"You went out on a full moon, where you knew there'd be witches," I hissed. "What if they'd..."

Caught you...hurt you...and you'd left me alone forever.

113

Loki had run his finger down the cub's snout. "By the norns, I never wished to. Yet doesn't it make your cub more precious for the danger it took to save her? Without us now, she'll die."

I'd glanced down at the cub, and she'd stared back at me. "But isn't it like dying to be tamed? You told me that you could never force anyone to belong to you."

Why did I have to say that?

Loki had become ashen, but he'd still reached out to smooth down my bristling spikes like he always had when I'd been agitated. "Huh, serves me right for lecturing you with my so-called wisdom. On fear of Tyr's wrath, I swear that we shall never cage or collar any creature. Don't we live like wild beings? Then she will too, and when she can survive by herself, then we'll free her."

I'd grasped his hand in mine. "I swear on the World Tree, I'll protect her."

"I know you will, little stallion." I'd flushed at the pride warming through his words. "You've looked after your dad all these years, right?" He'd nudged me with his shoulder, and I'd nudged him back. "Who-ever you decide to protect in your life, they'll be lucky."

My brow had furrowed. "Only you," I'd promised fiercely, "and cub."

Loki had eased himself back to sit cross-legged

next to me, gazing over the lake; his lips had twitched up at one side. "Not forever."

I'd nodded adamantly. "Forever."

My eyes burned at the memory because I was separated from Loki, and he'd known that I'd find someone else to love and protect or he'd hoped that I would.

I wouldn't abandon dad though, like I hadn't abandoned cub. She'd never become my pet. She'd remained wild like me, and then I'd freed her.

I had to do the same for the cat who was snuggled right now on my lap.

When I pushed Fox onto the bed, he arched his back and clambered to his feet in a tangle of claws, fur, and unhappy *meows*. Then he cast me an aggrieved glance over his shoulder.

Tough luck, wild cat.

I snatched up my guitar and bounced to my knees. Magenta was lost somewhere, but Fox and I were alive. Pining wouldn't protect anyone. I needed a kick up my own ass, and so did Fox.

Luckily for my ass, music was just as effective.

I grinned. "Come on, lazy pussy, let's get you into training. You were seriously unfit on the Discipline Run. The Princes will wreck you in Dragon Polo if you can't do better than collapse in a gasping heap at the first whiff of exercise." Fox's tail smacked dangerously against the bed. Valhalla, I looked one more

115

word away from a face full of enraged pussy; in the right context, I could be down with that. "How about some exercise godly style?"

I strummed my guitar, singing Rick James' disco funk "Super Freak". I bounced up and down on the bed to the sexy and ironic music, thrusting with my crotch because if I was going to be a freak, then I should let out my kinky.

For an innocent who'd only just gifted his virginity to Magenta the night before, Fox had no problem letting out his inner kink.

Fox's eyes lit up at the music, and if a cat could laugh, he was rolling with it. Then he waved his fluffy tail to the rhythm of the music, wiggling his ass.

I struggled not to chuckle, as I blasted out the dirty lyrics. Fox batted his long lashes at me, wiping his tail across his face like a veil. This time, I laughed.

Yeah, freak...and not a pet.

Honestly, Willoughby would make an epic backup...all right, duet... singer.

Could he dance?

It was more than fair to imagine that tight behind swaying as he sang.

I sighed, daydreaming my perfect band: Bask on bass, Fox on the drums, and Magenta on keyboards.

At least I already had a cat dancer.

Fox leaped onto his back, cycling his legs in the air. *Was that meant to be sexy in a feline way?* Then in a spray of glitter, Fox transformed back into a man, and my throat dried. I coughed, forcing myself to keep singing.

Yeah, it was seriously sexy.

Fox lay sprawled palely on the bed with his wavy white blond hair tumbling into his eyes and his bright blue eyes sparkling with joy. His pajamas had slipped down to reveal his slender hips. He was still doing that jackass dance move of his that was meant to be hot, but *he* was hot, even though he didn't know it.

He was clueless that he was about five seconds away from me ripping down his pants and showing him *my* own moves.

Four seconds...

I growled, dropping my guitar on the floor.

Three seconds...

Fox looked at me, startled. His arms and legs were still in the air like he was *begging* me to screw him.

Two seconds...

Fox would never have to beg. But my monster inside still wanted to break him.

One...

CHAPTER SEVEN

Rebel Academy, Wednesday September 4th

SLEIPNIR

I bared my teeth, as my balls ached and my dick pulsed against my thigh.

I was going to wreck Fox.

"It's quite the consolation to see that you entertained yourselves without us." Magenta slammed through the door with Bask. "We were concerned that you'd have been weeping in the blackest despair."

I twisted so fast to them that my neck hurt.

Fox's grin was both shy and radiant; it tugged at something buried inside me. It was the same instinct that'd made me swear on the World Tree to protect cub forever

Forever was a hell of a long time for a god. Yet Magenta had proved that death didn't mean the end of a human's need for love.

It was only the beginning.

Fox flung himself off the bed and bounded to Magenta, grabbing her around the waist and melting against her in that breath-taking way of his, as she in turn wrapped her arms just as tightly around his neck. Then he spun her like he could still hear the music, and she laughed.

I'd never heard such a beautiful sound.

"I *was* sunk in despair. I've been making plans to poke out my eyes with a brooch like Oedipus." When Magenta grimaced, Fox peppered kisses down her neck. *There was my hot pathological liar.* Did he even pause for breath? "Okay, okay, I was actually going to drown myself like Ophelia, but then, I thought since walling mages up alive was so popular—"

Magenta dragged Fox to a stop, bopping him on the nose with an accusing finger. "Don't ever talk so lightly of such cruelty."

Fox's face fell, before he nodded. Then he kissed Magenta's forehead in apology. "No killing the cute foxy...or mages...got it."

I attempted to play it cool unlike Fox, as I pushed myself up. I was the son of Loki and not a new student who'd spent as many years trapped in an attic, as I'd spent in the beds of human women. Although, looking back now, I wasn't certain that I'd had the best deal.

I attempted to act my indolent self, however, until Mist betrayed me (the magical asshole, even if he was only reflecting my own asshole emotions). He poked his head out of my pocket, and his eyes were bright with excitement, as he *whinnied,* calling out to his friends in greeting.

Bask grinned. "You *are* pleased to see us. Pet me."

How could I resist Bask?

Magenta appeared composed (and stunning), but Bask's blazer was rumpled. His shirt was also done up wrong and missing a button, like he'd been distracted or somebody else had dressed him.

My hands clenched into fists, and I growled.

Someone had been playing without permission.

I strode to Magenta, dragging her away from Fox. Her eyes widened, as she steadied herself with her palms against my chest. Then I kissed her like I'd longed to in the desperate hours that I hadn't been able to feel her magic: passionate, hard, and savage. She thrummed through me.

I loved her power. She could wreck this academy and everyone in it, if we found a way to unleash it.

That was such a turn-on.

When I pulled back, Magenta was flushed and panting. Her gaze was hazy as it met mine. Then I twisted to Bask whose dick already tented his pants.

He always loved to watch.

But then, Bask reached for me and all of a sudden, his hand was clasping mine.

How had Bask broken the setting in the brands that should've stopped us touching?

I clutched Bask by the neck, pulling him into just as deep a kiss as Magenta's had been. He whined against my mouth. Magenta's hand rested lightly on my ass, tracing circles. I shivered at the scent of the yew trees, as it melded with the taste of coco and almonds.

Then I tore Bask's blazer off his shoulders, tossing it across the room, before ripping away his shirt that somebody else had touched and desecrated.

Bask was mine. I shared him with my lovers but no one else.

Bask's dick hardened further in his pants.

Mine...only mine...

Bask's gloved hand stroked down my cheek. "Magenta and I are safe. Do you want to check my balls too? They still have your name on them in marker pen. You can stop growling now, Slippy."

Was I growling?

I forced myself to calm, shaking the spikes from my hair and slowing my breathing. "Your balls sound good. Take off your pants." Then I glanced over my shoulder at Magenta. "By the runes, what happened? How can I touch him?"

Magenta cocked her head, watching as Bask slipped out of his pants and underwear with a deliberately sexy wiggle. His clothes pooled at his ankles. Without having to ask, he turned around to show off his ass. He loved a petting tribute, so I didn't restrain myself from stroking its smooth perfection.

Incubi had fine asses.

Magenta didn't appear to be able to look away from Bask's ass either. *Well, she wasn't dead.* Huh, look at that, she *was* dead and the incubi power still worked. "I stole Bask from the barbarous Principal. Then we fell through darkness, broke the hex, escaped and got caught again. The end."

"Wow, what a storyteller," Fox smirked.

Magenta inclined her head. "My thanks. Flair and Echo tell me many saucy stories, but it's been a long time since I've heard one that didn't end in cum."

Fox pinked.

Bask arched like *he* was the feline, as my hand continued to circle his ass, inviting me between his legs with a teasing look over his shoulder. When I dipped my hand to rub his balls, he trembled. "This tale *started* with cum. I marked one of the Princes and decided to claim another."

Hold the frost giant by the cock, what…?

Fox froze. "Please tell me that you're talking in metaphors."

I withdrew my hand so quickly from Bask's balls that he almost fell on his face.

Either they'd come across the Princes in the search and in a sudden fit of passion forgotten all rivalries and screwed...

Let there be an *or*.

Why couldn't I think of an *or*...?

On fear of Ragnarok, brain get with working out how my lovers could've ended up spraying cum over Lysander. Dwarf's on a pike, it'd better *be* Lysander because at least then I could forever have *that* image to chuckle at. I'd bet that he wrinkled his nose and muttered about *the affront to his dignity* throughout the whole time his face was splattered.

Bask studied the way that my lips curled into a smile, before giving a knowing wink. "We fell into the Princes' bedroom."

I was relieved *and* disappointed. It was the same mix of angry and weirdly turned-on that I felt around the Princes like I wanted to wreck them in any number of ways. *Yet some of them would be fun for both of us.*

I sighed. "Tell me that you claimed the elf and not the asshole fae."

Bask turned to me with a flourish that made his gorgeous dick bounce in the most distracting way. "Maybe."

Fox crossed his arms. "And the Duchess...? I can

literally tell when you're hiding something, even if you cut your story down to an elevator pitch."

Magenta and Bask exchanged a glance.

Bask's tongue darted out to wet his lips, before he nodded at Magenta like whatever he had to say was too painful.

Magenta answered, crisply, "She'll be back on Sunday. Damelza's villainous threat is to cast me out and wall Fox up alive if Bask doesn't behave."

When Fox paled, Magenta clasped his hand.

"Behave?" My gaze shot to Bask, who'd turned away and was bustling around the bedroom, collecting up the crumpled uniforms from the floor, which I'd discarded earlier in the evening. He smoothed them out, folding them with loving care and putting them on the desk like he couldn't leave Fox and me alone without him and it was his job to care for us. Except, *it was*. He'd cared for me and Hector ever since he'd been sent here by the Duchess last term. Our uniforms fit as neatly on top of each other's, as we fitted together. Bask looked out for us because he loved us but he didn't submit to others. "When has Bask ever behaved?"

Fox flopped to the floor in a dramatic heap. "I'm dead."

Bask turned to me with such predator rage that I took a step back. *I was a jackass.* "Would it please you to get hard every time that you say the word *professor*?"

I blanched; *Odin's cock, he was pissed at me.* "Woah, I must've mistaken *behave* with *misbehave*. You're one good incubus."

Bask preened. "I do have a fine and pettable arse. And..." He held up his finger. *How could he look so serious standing with his dick out?* "...I love both Magenta and Fox. I can behave in any way that the bad bastards desire to save them. If they only let me love them..."

Fox and Magenta swept to Bask, cuddling him, until there was no doubt left how much he was loved.

I hoped that he could believe it. I wished that I could love in their easy way. But I was a monster. I didn't get to love like that.

My eyes smarted with tears, and I forced myself to walk away from something that I longed to join. Instead, I tapped against the far wall. "If you're done cursing me out and cuddling, we need a plan. Honestly, I kind of think that we need to face each task as we reach it. First, we save Fox."

"Why's fox hunting such a popular witch sport?" Fox mumbled with his curly head still rested on Bask's shoulder.

"Because you're the whipping boy...?" Bask pinched Fox's ass, and he yipped.

"If we don't win tomorrow..." I clenched my jaw.

125

Fox burrowed closer onto Bask's shoulder like he truly could protect him. "I die," he whispered.

"Then after the thrills of Torment Thursday, we go on the mission." Magenta gripped Bask's hand tightly. "Lest we forget, this academy nonsense is a front for training us into supernatural assassins."

Bask brightened. "At least we get to ride on our dragons on Saturday."

"Dragons aren't toys," I growled, "or pets. They're shifters."

Bask fluttered his eyelashes at me. "But they're pretty like the elf." His lips curled into a sly smile. "Oh, can I ride him too?"

"Only with his consent, which the dragons haven't given either."

Magenta gave Bask's hand a final squeeze, before strolling to me. When she tipped up my chin, my skin was on fire at every trail of her fingers. I needed her. My searching gaze met hers.

I could've lost her. *Why did she haunt my soul?*

"We have a plan," Magenta murmured, and I could see the insecurity in her eyes. *Was she asking my permission?* "Prince Willoughby is most likely to come to our side. It'll give us a chance to modify the spell, which traps all of us within this academy and the curse."

"You want my consent to screw Pointy Ears?" I snarled. "Perhaps, you'd manage it, but none of the rest could join in because of the stick up his princely ass."

Fox cocked his head. "Hey, are we going with Pointy Ears as his pet name because I don't think that elves are into the whole degrading names kink?"

Smartass.

"It's fine because Willoughby already has a cr-" Bask snapped his mouth shut.

What word had Bask just stopped himself saying? Whatever it was had made him look like he'd hurl.

Fox's brow furrowed. "Crossbow? Crayon? Crick in his neck?"

"He already *loves* Magenta," Bask corrected himself. "And I think that he cares for us."

I snorted, then so did Mist with a toss of his mane thrown in. When Bask's expression hardened, I realized that he meant it.

Magenta nodded.

"I take back my snort of disbelief. But seriously, how'd you know?" I asked.

Bask shuffled his feet. *Way to look shifty.* "We *accidentally* read his diary."

Fox pulled away from Bask, before grabbing him by his hair. Fox vibrated with power and a protective rage, which told me that Willoughby wasn't the only one who cared. "Don't you remember Willoughby's distress at how his letter was read out? When I was stuck in the attic, being able to write to my cousin,

Aquilo, was a privilege that my dad suffered to win for me. I would've been destroyed if anyone had read them. Did you laugh at all his secrets and...?"

"There was no comedy and far more tragedy." Magenta's gaze became frosty. Fox let go of Bask, smoothing over his hair in apologetic motions. "The Crystal Diary flowed with dark magics, just like the silk suit that traps and controls Willoughby." I stiffened. *He was being trapped, just like me?* "How far shall we go for freedom? The Prince is treated like he's bad, but I don't believe it. You were the one who showed me the R.I.P Membership that controls the brands, wards, and missions. If we can win Willoughby to our side, then the academy could awaken from its long winter. This prison will crumble and fall."

"Now that's a story," Fox breathed.

Magenta's lips twitched. "The Membership."

At the magic word, the spell opened the wall and a board that curled with the RA emblem and neon pink writing slotted out.

Rebel Academy Membership

RANDOMS
Confess - Whipping Boy

Curse - Whipping Boy

IMMORTALS
Crow - Prefect

Crave

Cru

Sleipnir

PRINCES
Crown - Prefect

Sh

I stared at the board in shock.

Names had magically appeared and vanished from the board every time that a new student had been admitted to the academy or had died. After Hector's death, Bask had sat on the floor, hugging Nile and staring at the place where Hector's name once had been like if he only looked long enough, it'd bring Hector back or perhaps, like he could make himself believe he truly was gone.

Bor's beard, I missed Hector.

But I'd never seen a student sliced in half like a magic trick before. It was the kind of thing that Loki would pull off.

I raised my eyebrow. "Does everyone see the problem here?"

"We have two new students with the unusual names *Sh* and *Cru...*?" Fox spun around like he was searching for something. "Cru's invisible or another ghost. Wow, we should rename this the *Haunted Academy*. Step back, fellow Immortals, I'm known as the ghost busting shimage."

Magenta whirled to Fox, catching his arm before he could act out his entire paranormal ghost hunter routine. "You would *bust* me as well?"

When Fox's eyes widened, Bask snickered. "Where *bust* means love like a legend."

Magenta's eyes brightened. "What a lucky coincidence. You shall be able to love Willoughby, who the Membership shows is already divided between both Immortal and Prince." When her gaze met mine, it ached with a loneliness and longing that I understood. "It must be confusing and agonizing for him, you know. If we can entice him fully to our side, then we'll weaken this spell."

Fox laughed shakily. "I'll bust the elf like he's never been busted before."

Bask leaped onto the bed, crawling with a sinful shake of his hips to sprawl over Nile. "I want him to be ours. So, I'll bust him with my pettable arse too, right?"

Bask pushed up his ass in a seriously distracting way. When Magenta's gaze became glassy and her pupils dilated, I knew that she thought so too.

I sauntered to the bed, throwing myself down next to Bask. Mist *nickered*, low and breathy. He was going full out horsey dominant (or I was). I plucked him out of my pocket, dropping him onto the headboard. He galloped up and down so quickly that his eight legs were a blur. He balanced dangerously along the edge with his tail raised in excitement.

He might as well have been proclaiming *dick for hire*.

I rolled my eyes. "If you're asking me if Mr. Dick is an elf buster, then I haven't decided yet. He usually draws the line at touching Princes."

Magenta's expression softened. "No one touches anyone without both love and respect. I was almost forced into marriage. This may be our only way to escape, but force is decidedly *not* to be used on Princes as much as on Immortals."

Now there was a witch who deserved my friendship.

I trusted Magenta not to tie me up, unless it was in the kinky negotiated way. *Would Magenta have time for that after the tournament?*

I grinned. "Mr Dick loves and respects you but is seriously hard right now."

"I'm aware," Magenta smirked. "I wouldn't want him to suffer."

Fox ducked his head. "Firstly, stop talking to his prick like it's a puppet. Wow, I actually just said that out loud. Secondly, if you get a chance to shut down this cage of an academy so that no other Rebel gets sent here, then take it. That matters more than saving me."

Son of a troll, I'd never heard Fox sound so sincere. I thought that he'd been stuck on the *Snarky Factory Setting*.

Magenta's eyes blazed, and she tightened her hold on Fox's arm. I couldn't tell whether she'd pull him into a hug or a spanking. When she backed him up towards the bed, and he paled, I was kind of sure that it'd be a spanking.

Was it weird that I envied him?

"Is that so, my precious mage?" Magenta's eyes glittered. Fox shuddered, however, at the *precious*. Magenta was far better at the whole pet name thing than me. *Had he ever been called that before?* "Have you not learned the danger of others' prejudice? Why would you hold onto their belief that your life is worthless, when in this room alone there are three powerful Immortals who love you? Doesn't our grief *matter* to you?"

"*Woah*, hold on, I didn't think…" Fox said, helplessly.

"That our hearts would shatter and never be whole again, if you die?" Magenta whispered.

Fox fell onto the bed, and I banded his chest with my arms. His heart was beating rapidly, and his trembles shook me.

"We're saving you." I tightened my hold on Fox, meeting Magenta's gaze over his shoulder. They both needed to hear this. "No one else is dying."

"Unless it's death by crocodile," Bask hissed, launching himself at Fox. I spun around, covering Fox with my body, as Bask pounced on my back with Nile like the plushie was attempting to drag me into a death roll. "Only one of us around here sheds white hairs on other's plushies. Shall I lick your special book that your da gave you?"

Fox's breath hitched, even though he was pressed into the bed beneath me. "*Don't*. I'm sorry."

I knew that I should've kept Fox's furry ass off Bask's plushie.

Magenta's voice was steely. "No licking and no more shedding. Yet perhaps, our disrespectful Fox needs to be taught a lesson…?"

When I glanced up and met Magenta's gaze, it was playful. Although, my gaze kind of took a detour because she was already naked and the unexpected shock of it meant that the gorgeous curve of her hips

and tits caught me like the beauty of Odin's golden
hall.

I'd never truly stopped to realize how naturally
breath-taking a woman's body was. I wished to trace
every inch of her pale skin with my tongue.

*I wasn't signing up to the no licking rule. The no
shedding was okay.*

"Trust me, you're long overdue this lesson." I
hugged Fox closer, as I sat up, pushing him towards
Bask. Unsure, Fox glanced over his shoulder at me. I
forgot how new he was to even being around people,
let alone these sorts of games. Whatever happened, I'd
make sure that this ended in the best orgasm of his
innocent life. "Bask gets to decide the sentence. He's
the injured party."

Bask gave a wicked grin, running his hand down
Nile like a Bond villain, if they were naked and their
cat had transformed into a crocodile. He slunk towards
Fox, dragging him to the end of the bed.

"Whipping boys who cuddle their patron's toys or
steal their pillows," Bask added, raising his finger in
warning, "don't get to play." He tempered his words
with a kiss, however, which was so gentle but sensual
that I groaned, palming myself through my pants.
Then Magenta hooked her arms around my neck,
pushing me back onto the bed, and all I could think
about was the warm press of her skin against mine.
"Hands behind your back."

Fox nodded, settling onto his knees and clasping his hands behind his back with an unexpected eagerness.

Magenta pushed down my pants, undoing my top and slipping it off my shoulders with far more restraint than I ever had. Was I just as *precious* to her?

Fox glanced across at Magenta, as she ground herself against my crotch. Fox shuddered at the same time as me. Then Bask slipped his hand into Fox's pajamas, and Fox jumped as he slipped out his hard dick. Bask let Fox's dick stand pulsing against his stomach, wanting and abandoned. Fox whined.

Bask smirked. "Watch and don't touch."

"Cruel incubus," I muttered, distracted by the rub of Magenta's clit against the head of my dick.

Round, and round, and round....

Above me, she moaned. Her hair veiled my face. On my oath as a god, *I* wasn't watching and not touching...

I twisted Magenta, tossing her down amongst the sheets. She gasped, and her eyes flew open; her hair coiled around her head along with her black mists. Sparkles lit her, pricking against my skin and magic in sharp bursts of pain that only added to the pleasure. I caged her with my arms.

Bask crawled to join us, teasing at my nipples, until I shivered, before ducking beneath my arms to

135

suck at Magenta's. *He worshiped her.* Since he'd first found her portrait, I'd known that.

When Magenta's nipples peaked, Bask circled one with his tongue, while circling the other with his fingers. It was like winning every trophy already that he could touch us again and that we were united.

I ducked my head to catch Magenta's lips with mine.

She didn't worship me, and I didn't worship her. But I needed and trusted her. *Was that love?*

For a monster like me, I was beginning to believe that it was.

I deepened the kiss, circling her clit with my finger. My dick was even harder than before, pressing against her. She gripped my shoulders like I wasn't the one who was dragging her towards the crest of pleasure. Then her black mists wrapped around my balls, and I grunted and almost came (*huh, that would've been a shaming of the god*s), dragging *me* towards that crest.

When I slipped my finger into her pussy and crooked it, Magenta shook. It was an honor to be the first to push her towards a shuddering orgasm in this way.

Yet something was missing.

Frustrated, I glanced at Bask, who'd paused in his worship of Magenta's tits to gaze up at me.

When Fox whimpered, I glanced over my shoulder. His hair was sweaty, and his balls were so tight and high that they had to ache like a bitch. Yet he still held his hands clasped behind his back.

My gaze softened.

It'd been agony for Bask, when we'd been unable to touch him and he'd been unable to kiss or screw.

I couldn't...*wouldn't*...deny Fox now. We were connected, and for our pleasure to be complete, we needed to be together.

"If you desire it," Bask called to Fox, "I have a free hand to wank you off."

My romantic incubus.

For an unfit mage who collapsed after a single Discipline Run, Fox could move when he was motivated. To my shock, his mouth crashed over mine, as his hand rested against the hollow of my back.

Bask's clever fingers wanked Fox in long strokes. Bask glowed, feeding on our pleasure, now that we were together. Except, it was Magenta who glowed brightest. When I thrust into her, with Fox's lips still crushed to mine and his taste of raspberries mingled with yew trees, the intimate sensation of sinking into her body wrecked me.

Here was home, love, *mine*. Everything worth dying and living eternally for.

The pink braziers burst up at the combined power of our magic. Then they died to darkness, apart from Magenta's confetti sparkles. In the black, the sensations became even more intense, hot and heavy.

When Fox broke his kiss, it was like losing something precious. Then a gloved palm pressed across my face, and I kissed it.

"You're smiling," Magenta murmured.

"You can't tell that."

"My magic can." When Mist *nickered* in the black, she added smugly, "And your horse backs me up." *Traitor.* "I can tell by the particularly tasty pleasure right now that Bask and Fox are about to come. They're sucking each other's pricks, which is enjoyable, I'd imagine."

"That's some skill." My eyes fluttered shut at the thought of the two of them in the dark.

I strained to hear but all I could focus on was the pulse hammering in my ears, and my own thrusts into Magenta, which spiraled her higher.

She was still way too composed for my liking.

"I'm also screwing you. I can multi-task," I gasped.

Magenta gave a breathy laugh. "My talented lover."

Then Magenta arched, quivering with spasms around my dick.

Again and again and...

The sensation made my dick pulse within her. I couldn't hold back. I never could with her.

I was about to...

I came with such shattering intensity that I slumped.

Valhalla, Valhalla, Valhalla...

My forehead rested against hers. Somewhere, too far away for my screwed-out brain to focus on, I heard panting, howling, and coming.

I hoped that Bask accepted the cum tribute as justice for the plushie incident.

When the braziers exploded back to life, I struggled to blink sparks from my eyes and discovered that Magenta had repositioned herself with her head on my chest, while Bask snuggled on my other side.

Fox draped himself over all of us, with his curls tickling my lap, close to my limp but still valiantly twitching dick; his breath gusted across its oversensitive head in agonizing but tempting puffs. Fox wore the softest but happiest expression that I'd ever seen on him.

It looked like the lesson had worked.

Sometimes, I imagined that I was alone again in dark of the woods or caves with only my brothers in my head to save me from the sounds of my dad's weeping. But at times like this, I remembered that I was held, needed, and loved.

I could *feel* my lovers around me and it took away my breath. My lovers who appeared to have a thing for cuddling after sexy times.

All of a sudden, the **I** brand on the back of my hand burned with a cold blast like I'd pressed it against an ice-cube. Temperature play could be fun foreplay, but the witches seriously didn't intend this to be kinky.

At the same time, the other students (apart from Magenta who to my relief had never been branded), clutched their hands.

"Don't tell me, we're being summoned again to battle or danger," Fox gritted out, sitting up. "Which dragon shifter did you liberate this time because one escaping could be a misfortune but two is carelessness."

"It wasn't me this time, hardass," I snarled, reaching for my pajama pants. "And this isn't the same as the other summons, can't you tell?"

Fox stared at me, horrified. "Wait, they use the brands like bat-signals for *lots* of things? Nerves on fire: that's homework. Muscle cramps: A witch wants a backrub..."

"...And ice burn: Time for a student to suffer in the Memory Theater." I squirmed away from Magenta and Bask, pushing myself to the edge of the bed without looking at the others.

The worst behaved student would be punished in the Memory Theater. Fox had already endured it, but in all my time here, I hadn't.

Bacchus had taken me hostage as bait to capture

my dad. I wasn't even an official student. Yet trapped here without my belongings, all I had left was the privacy of my thoughts.

Loki had always taught me that memory was sacred.

I was a monster. These lovers in my bed claimed to accept me, but what would they do if they witnessed my true face?

In the name of the World Tree, don't let this summons to the Memory Theater be for *me*.

Who could truly love a monster?

CHAPTER EIGHT

Rebel Academy, Wednesday September 4th

FOX

I slumped in the corner of the Memory Theater, trying not to remember that the last time I'd been here, I'd transformed into my cat form, almost pooped (in my hedgehog form), and revealed my worst memory to the entire class.

Wow, good times.

Being sent to a coven-run academy...okay, prison...as a magical son born to witch parents, this term had been just as terrifying as I'd expected. Only, I'd also met my first ever friends and the woman who'd kissed and made love to me like I wasn't a shimage and she was a witch — *Magenta.*

Magenta's Soul and magic wound around mine in the same way as her fingers wound around my wrist, stroking across the brand that still burned like it'd been held against a snowman's face, until the snowman had melted.

The murder of a snowman was a tragic crime.

The room was thick with the scent of burning sage. My skin crawled at the oppressively dark magic, which nipped at my throat like it was trying to devour me.

I pushed down the urge to bite back.

Even though the tiered black seats of the Memory Theater were hidden in shadow, I was still wearing my pajamas like the other Immortals. I'd always hoped that my first slumber party would include more pillow fights, a midnight feast, and porn. My cousin Aquilo had once whispered to me about watching his sister through the crack of their interjoining bedroom doors, passing around a stash of porn at a slumber party. As the son in a witch household, he hadn't been invited, although since the porn had run with a Witches Are the Kinkiest theme that was definitely better than Aquilo self-combusting from blushes. His descriptions, however, still provided some of my best Wank Bank Fantasies.

There was nothing like blushes combined with porn.

Bask slouched with his feet up on the seats below. His dark hair fell across his eyes.

How did he make it look like a fashion statement: *sexy night chic...?*

I bit my lip. My feline side struggled inside me to dive across Magenta and snuggle in Bask's lap. Okay, I hold my paws up, *snuggle* was a useful euphemism for the many fun things that'd lead to the Death of a Fox if Damelza swept in and caught us.

When Bask caught me eying his lap and definitely *not* his hard dick in his silk pajamas, his gaze became half-lidded, and he winked.

I expected Sleipnir, who was sprawled in the seat next to him, to laugh, but he appeared frozen. His jaw was clenched. Only Mist's muzzle poked out of his pocket, and Mist was suspiciously silent.

Sleipnir stared at Willoughby who was just as frozen. Willoughby stood in a spotlight on the stage.

By my prickles, I knew what it felt like to be abandoned in that light.

I swallowed, pulling my hand away from Magenta to wrap my arms around my middle. I shook my head to shut out the ghostly memory of "It's a Wonderful World".

Were the witches truly playing the song again or was my mind playing tricks?

Last time, it'd been *me* standing in the same place as Willoughby. I shivered, forcing away the memory of my sister and her cruel friends. I couldn't lose myself in a time when I'd been desperate for someone to *save me.*

Except, they never had.

When I tipped back my head, I blinked up at the words that swirled in and out of focus on the ceiling:

Share our pasts in order to move forward as one together.

I sighed. Was there an Anti-Motivational Hex, which could shove these sayings one word at a time up Damelza's ass?

That'd be brilliant. Although, also paradoxical because to me that'd be super motivational.

Then the words slipped back, as if underneath the waters of a pool, and new ones formed.

Magenta gasped. "Sweet Hecate, have they not hurt him enough?"

My brow furrowed. "Geralt of Rivia? Oscar Wilde? Quasimodo? Wait, please tell me they have those three together trapped in the academy…"

Magenta's black mists flicked me in warning. "Would it be an awful imposition to ask you to *read*?"

I stared up at the ceiling and the curling letters:

Brother,
As much as it pains me to even think of you, I write
this letter to urge you to listen to your professors,

control your murderous urges, and curb your
dangerous impulses.
Every day, the kingdom calls for your execution. You
deserve to die, I'm certain that you believe a killer
should pay for their crime...

I screwed shut my eyes. I didn't want to read any more of the letter from Willoughby's prick of a brother, which Damelza had already used to shame him once.

Who wrote in that way to their own brother?

It was bad enough that Mr. Nosy Incubus had read his diary. I should copy Bask and curse him to blurt out every time *he* had a sexy thought. Except, then he'd never stop talking, and we'd never get any work done.

Actually, that sounded good.

At last, the black mists tapped me again, and I opened my eyes to look down at Willoughby.

I thought that he'd be shaking or furious. Instead, he was pale and shell-shocked. He looked lost in his own world. He'd never seemed small before, but he did alone on that stage in his silk suit. His hair was loose of his ribbons, tumbling around his face.

His eyes were glazed.

Did he know what was happening?

I only just restrained myself from jumping onto the stage with Willoughby. I was one protective kitty when someone was hurt by their family or witches. If my lovers wanted to claim this Prince (who joined in with my banter, which was always a plus), then I didn't care what brand a Hecate statue burned onto him.

After all, she'd branded me with **R** for a Random whipping boy, which was simply rude. Luckily, I didn't have a complex.

"You know this Love an Elf Plan?" Sleipnir hissed, leaning over Bask. Magenta arched her brow. "I'm kind of thinking it'll be more dangerous than the mission on Friday. Look at the letter." When he gestured at the ceiling, I winced. *I'd rather not, cheers.* "How did we all get distracted by his lullabies and hair?"

Bask sighed. "But such pretty hair."

"He's a murderer and a traitor. He tried to take over his own kingdom." Mist's eyes were wide and his ears pinned, as he pawed at Sleipnir's pocket. "Do you know how many centuries my dad and me were hunted by our enemies? But this one," his gaze darted to Willoughby, "is bad like...a pretty Stalin."

Bask stiffened. "Take that back or from tomorrow morning, your socks will be perpetually damp."

I shuddered. Bask's curses were terrifying but also,

if anyone deserved damp socks, it was Sleipnir after calling Willoughby that.

Sleipnir blanched but raised his chin in defiance.

Magenta blinked. "Who?"

Of course, she was a Victorian who'd been burned alive and then trapped as a ghost in a tree. I allowed myself a moment to mentally rub my hands gleefully. What could I convince her had happened in the last century...? *Hmm*, I'd begin with the Third World War that was started by a genetically modified zombie hamster, which would be particularly fun since she didn't even know about the *first* two wars...

"He means a pretty Nero," I explained, polishing my halo for not pulling out the zombie hamster just yet. "Since I was once Nero in a past life (emperor, charioteer, and fiddler as Rome burned), I can tell you that he's wrong."

Bask glared at Sleipnir. "His *kingdom* thinks that he's a monster. *You're* not a monster." Sleipnir flinched. "What if the Prince also isn't?"

When Magenta traced her fingers across her black pearl choker, I wet my lips, wishing that those soft fingers were tracing my skin with such careful deliberation. "He's the Princes' weakest link. Nero or monster, he's also mine."

"Midnight doesn't want to be a whipping boy," I ventured. In fact, neither did I. Whipping didn't exactly sell it, nor did being the guinea pig for testing potions or having hexes thrown at me. "He can be my special project."

Magenta smiled. "I believe that he already is."

I flushed. Yeah, he was my knight, I was his king, and Magenta would be his queen. The vampire had said that to me like wedding vows.

Did that make me a vampire bride?

Sleipnir snorted. "Lysander's haughty ass will never turn."

I glanced across at the pink seats, as the theatre was arranged like a chessboard, and Lysander who sat alone. Midnight knelt on the floor, and I couldn't see more than the curve of his pale back.

Lysander's emerald hair, which hung to his waist, had been caught back. His large eyes gleamed in the dim light. His golden wings were folded back. Just for a moment, I allowed myself to imagine that he wasn't a princely sized prick, and to see just how beautiful his alabaster skin was, as well as how dangerous a warrior he looked even sitting stiffly in his seat.

Perhaps, it wasn't healthy to have a thing for predators. But I couldn't help thinking how much I'd love to hunt alongside him. Then I sighed because he'd be more likely to kick my foxy ass flying into a snowbank.

Lysander was still wearing his smart black trousers and blazer with the **P** crest embroidered in silk to one side. His silk shirt hung open, revealing tantalizing glimpses of his collarbone. Did the Princes sleep in their uniforms? I bet that they lay ram-rod straight in their blazers like they were in the army.

Beetles and slugs, that was depressing.

Despite all the Princes' luxuries (and I swore on my whiskers that I'd find a way to bust open their private larder and lavish the treats on my lovers), I'd rather wake up in the East Wing in the tangled mess of the Immortals' arms, even with Bask half smothering me like a limpet, Magenta's cold breath tickling my neck, and Sleipnir sleep talking.

I'd never known that you could dirty talk in your sleep. I could never look at a banana in the same way…or eat one.

Magenta assessed Lysander. "Maybe there's more to both his haughty self and his ass than his fear of Titus and his search for redemption. When the fae finds himself alone and divided from the other Princes, then he'll know how I felt. It's remarkable how it forces you to grow up. He'll have to choose either to rebel or to run into the arms of his oppressors."

"Since you're here now…?" I cocked my head.

Magenta's grin was wicked. "I rebelled."

In a flurry of feathers, Damelza appeared on the stage. The light glistened off her hair, until it appeared like polished silver. Her dress *swooshed* across the floor, as she swept towards Willoughby. Yet there was a gleam in her eyes like she was a zookeeper circling a witch-eating lion.

That'd be brilliant.

Instead, she was a prick of a Principal, prowling around an elf, who was humming the Lion King's "Circle of Life". Weirdly, none of that struck me as odd anymore or that an elf would find Disney show tunes a comforting retreat from the upcoming violation of his mind.

I knew what it was like to stand shaking in the spotlight because a spell was about to rip open your mind for everyone to see.

I should've tried belting out "Bare Necessities" (okay, so I might also know the dance, since I forced Aquilo to watch it with me one summer...*don't judge this dancing cat*). Except, that would've led the rest of the Immortals to jump on me and not in the sexy way.

Damelza rolled her eyes. "You're playing the *ignore me* game, are you? After your atrocious behavior over your brother, the *king's* letter, you're in dire need of this discipline. Perhaps, I should set the mood."

Then she glanced significantly at the ceiling.

When The Automatic's raucous "Monster" burst out, with its stomping lyrics and screaming guitar, I startled. So, this theater was alive the same as the Rebel Café with its mischievous AI, Serenity.

The only difference was that the Memory Theater was a prick.

When Willoughby broke off humming and flinched, Damelza's eyes glittered with malicious amusement. Yet my hands clenched because Sleipnir had flinched too.

No way on my whiffling nose would Damelza torment Willoughby like she had me.

"Wow, I'd forgotten just how motivational you were," I gritted out. "Do you run self-esteem seminars too? Classes to Boost Confidence? Wait, I was wrong, this is your romantic mood setting, right? Pan knows, I'm feeling pressured in an inappropriate way right now." *Bad mouth...stop talking...that's enough...stop while you're behind.* "Why don't we all just go back to our *separate* beds, before I report you?"

Whoops.

Bask snickered.

Damelza peered at me. So, that was what it felt like to be a mouse, before the bird of prey swoops. I swallowed.

"I'm sorry that mages are so easily turned on by rock music." Her lips pinched. "Please do report me to Bacchus."

I eyed her warily. I'd fallen into this trap before. "Really? She won't transfigure me into a footstool?"

Damelza shook her head.

"Pomeranian?"

"Certainly not."

I started to ease myself out of my seat. *Why were the others not moving?* "Well, good night, sleep tight, and don't let the witches bite…" I cut off on a choked gurgle, as feathered straps shot out, binding each of the Rebels and me to our seats.

I winced, as the straps cut into my thighs.

Damelza adjusted the feather behind her ear. "Bacchus will, however, transfigure you into a wine rack. She's keen to try out the spell. Can you imagine what it'd feel like to have wine bottles inserted into you?"

I paled, and every part of me clenched in sympathy. "Hey, have you been sneaking looks at my Wank Fantasies?"

Damelza's cheek twitched. "Do you know why witches hate boastful mages?"

"Dick envy? Our perfect skin? Institutionalized sexism?"

"Because they're *liars*." When I dropped my gaze, her smile widened. "They wear masks to hide how wicked they are." When she gripped Willoughby by the shoulder, he finally focused on her, panicked. Yet his gaze flicked to me first.

Was that surprised gratitude?

"Remain silent if you wish, Crush. The Memory Theater's most delightful quality is that the student doesn't need to speak to reveal himself. There's no

ROSEMARY A JOHNS

chance of him lying. The spell shows the truth, as every Rebel relives your memory alongside you."

Finally, Willoughby shook his head in distress. His hands curled and uncurled compulsively at his sides. "Let me suffer this, if I must. But alone." His anguished gaze darted to Magenta. Perhaps, she was right that he loved her. "I refuse to play with an audience."

Damelza's grin was dark and dangerous. "Isn't that lucky then because this isn't a game."

Damelza spun Willoughby to face the back wall of the theater, which was lit with a kaleidoscope of projected images. They were the memories of every student who'd faced this trial before.

Great Pan, there I was too, kneeling up on the mattress in the window of the attic.

My palms became sweaty, and my sight blurred. I shook.

I didn't need wine bottles inserted inside me, the Memory Theater had already inserted its claws... tentacles...okay, I didn't know what it'd used, but the experience had *hurt*.

I was going to hurl.

Then Magenta clasped my hand, and her magic sparkled across mine. I leaned into her side. Slowly, my heartbeat slowed.

My shame was trapped in the academy. My nightmare. *But I wasn't trapped in the attic anymore.* I'd got out, and I was with Magenta now.

Us Immortals would crack open this academy, until each Rebel's life, which had been caught in that kaleidoscope for over a century, could bleed out.

Every Rebel would be free.

Yet first, Willoughby had to face *his* nightmare.

CHAPTER NINE

Rebel Academy, Wednesday September 4ᵗʰ

FOX

When Damelza snatched Willoughby's hand, my own fingers cramped in sympathy.

It was Magenta holding my hand; I was safe in the seats of the Memory Theater. This time, it was Willoughby's punishment.

Yeah, actually that didn't make my furry ass feel any better.

My heart thudded faster and faster in my chest again. I forced myself to keep watching the stage. This was the worst theater production that I'd ever seen and I'd never even been inside a *real* theater before.

But I'd watched Andrew Lloyd Webber's *Cats* on

TV. I think dad thought that I'd feel a connection with the singing and dancing creatures. Instead, I felt weirdly traumatized.

When Damelza pressed Willoughby's palm against the back wall, Willoughby attempted to wrench away, but Damelza shoved him stumbling forwards.

Then it was *me* stumbling and sliding on a sheet of ice.

I landed on my knees with a *crack*, catching myself with my hands.

I wasn't in the Memory Theater anymore but an ice cave.

I shivered, staring down at my fingers, which were covered in thick gloves. Then I gaped at the sky-blue hair that swept across the ice.

Willoughby's hair.

I scrambled onto my knees, glancing down at the loose tunic and trousers, which were underneath a flowing woolen coat. It was as different to the tight silk uniform that Willoughby wore in the academy as a dove to a snake.

I counted back from a hundred to control the panic.

100,99,98...

I didn't want to see whatever was in this frozen memory. *On my prickles, don't make me do this.*

I slid my fingers across the ice. It burned me, even through my gloves.

It was so real.

Whatever had happened here was Willoughby's secret truth. It was the moment that he'd become a monster.

Yet I was a witness now.

Had it been just like this for the other Rebels, when I'd been reliving my sister's birthday party in the attic? Even Lysander had felt what it was like to be me. Had each of them walked around inside my body like a demon possession? Wait, that meant that they'd all been *inside* me at the same time.

Was that sextuple penetration? *Oww...*

I shuddered. I wasn't *ever* thinking that again. Still, they'd literally worn my skin, and now I was wearing Willoughby's.

All of a sudden, a rough hand gripped my arm, yanking me to my feet; I struggled not to fall over again. "Watch yourself. By my ears, let us at least pretend that the dance lessons to teach you to become more graceful were a worthy use of a prince's time."

I was twisted to face a warrior. I swallowed. Okay, not simply an elf, but one who was taller, stronger, and a *king* if the crystal crown (like massive antlers on his head), wasn't simply for decoration.

I was guessing that it wasn't and could also be used for goring disrespectful foxes.

When the warrior elf brushed back my hair, I fought not to flinch. He only readjusted the crystals that were woven through my hair, however, instead of poking me with his crown.

Why didn't Willoughby wear his hair like this in the academy? His hair was always coiled with ribbons, instead.

So, this warrior was Willoughby's dad...?

Suddenly, my mind became hazy, melding with Willoughby's memories, until I didn't know where *I* stopped and *he* began.

Then, I *was* him.

I blinked at father, leaning towards him, as he pressed a kiss to the crystals in my hair. I smiled. Mother had given them to me as a gift on the day that I'd been officially announced heir to the throne. I'd been raised to expect to rule but still, it'd only been days since I'd been granted the official right to publicly wear the crystals that marked my right.

I'd never been so proud because it was my parents' and kingdom's will.

When father turned me by the shoulder, the reassuring weight of his hand guided me further into the Sacred Ice Cave. My magic prickled and sparked across the walls.

In the name of the Other World, this was wondrous.

The winding cave was carved out of sheer ice.

Needle-sharp icicles, which looked like sabertooth fangs, hung from the roof. It glowed with ancient blue magic. I craved to add my own ice sculptures.

I reached out, touching my finger to the wall and dancing ice horses across it.

Did I truly deserve such honor? To walk the path that so few had done before? In the way of kings?

Father's fingers squeezed my shoulder, reassuringly. "Your doubts echo off the very walls. They're the reason that you *should* be king." Then his lips twitched. "I was just as nervous."

I feigned shock. "But I thought that the Slayer of Dark Elves was incapable of fear?"

Father let go of my shoulder to pinch my ear. *Why had I forgotten that was his favorite chastisement?* My dancing horses reared up in distress, and I broke off my ice patterns.

I grimaced, glad that none of my friends could see me dragged like a child by the pointy tip of my ear. I truly didn't look like a prince now. "You should be more frightened of the Pincher of Ears."

Then he let me go with a chuckle.

Ruefully, I rubbed my ear, before sweeping father a bow. "I apologize to both Slayer and Pincher."

Then I laughed, dashing in front of him through the caves. Yet I stopped short, when the tunnel flared out into a vast cavern. A chill seeped into my bones. It felt like this place deep underground was frozen in time.

"Every prince who will sit on our kingdom's throne must first visit this cavern." Father marched to the far wall, which was streaked like the ice had been struck by lightning. "Step forward and discover your magical gift."

I took a deep breath, flushing. *Why was my chest tight and my breathing ragged?* I should be puffed up like Darby was whenever he was the center of father's attention. Yet I felt like transforming myself into one of my own sculptures, so that I didn't have to put on a performance as the *prince* like I did whenever father took time away from running the kingdom, sitting at council, or fighting battles to notice me.

I wished that I could be outside with Darby riding beside him on Thunder or challenging him to climb the oaks in the palace gardens. Yet now I had these crystals in my hair and a sacred gift to receive. The crown would be on my head soon.

Yet what if I wasn't strong enough to wear it?

Listen to me.

"What if I can't protect this kingdom?" I ducked my head, and my hair swung into my eyes. "What if I can't protect Darby, mother...you?"

Father frowned. "I'm going somewhere, am I? You'll get this new gift, and I'll just vanish?"

Listen to me.

"I meant simply that I've been arrogant about my powers as a warrior. But I know Darby possesses the true strength as a sorcerer..."

Father snorted.

I arched my brow in surprise. "I sometimes believe that he thinks I'm weak. Yet I'm frightened I have more power than I can control. I feel it's frozen claws inside me..."

Listen to me.

Father's eyes flashed dangerously. "Do you think your mother *weak* or her magic *frightening*?"

I hurriedly shook my head. *On every oath, she was my light.*

Father beckoned me closer. "Your mother would sooth you to sleep with her lullabies because her healing powers are in her song. You've inherited the same powers. Your brother..." He sighed. "I wish that his powers didn't inflict hurt, rather than heal. Yet he'll stand at your right-hand. He'll be the reason that you'll win every battle and this kingdom shall stand strong."

I straightened my shoulders. Why had I been scared to take up my birthright? I'd have Darby beside me, just like I always had. Once, we'd battled imaginary enemies with wooden swords, but now, we'd fight true battles with my steel and his magic.

I was blessed.

When father nodded at the wall, I gasped.

A glittering book was trapped in the ice. Its magic

was ancient and dark, but it sang to mine a song so beautiful that I ached.

Save me...claim me...forever...

"The Crystal Diary," father's voice was hushed. "If it bonds with you, and you write in it every day, then a part of your soul will live forever in its pages. It's magical immortality."

I licked my dry lips. *I wanted it, or the diary wanted me.*

When I reached out and my fingers grazed the wall, my magic shattered the ice with a sharp *crack*. The wall broke in a jagged line, and I covered my face as it fell on top of me like an icy waterfall.

Then I peered between my hands at the diary at my feet.

It was mine, mine, mine...

"You're my worthy successor." Father's pride wound through me like warm honey; I glowed. "How about I take the next few days off so that we can celebrate together? Would you like a feast in your honor?"

Father would take days away from his duties for *me*...? I felt dizzy. He'd *never* done that before, even when I'd broken my arm or Darby had achieved every accomplishment there was in sorcery.

Darby would love a feast.

He'd always been excited when the palace had been decorated for events, the bustle of important visitors, and the pomp and spectacle. I hated the attention that he swallowed like sweets. I'd rather have been hiding out under the quiet branches of the oaks. Of course, I'd tried that several times, only to be dragged inside by scolding servants.

They always seemed to bow more swiftly to Darby than to me.

I nodded. "Darby as well?"

Father's mouth twisted. "If it'd make you happy."

When I bent to pick up the diary, however, the magic stung me. I jerked back in shock.

I was unworthy. A warrior but no sorcerer. A rejected prince.

I sucked in my breath. *Need me. Want me. Let me be strong.*

Yet as I turned away, I caught movement out of the corner of my eye. Dark shadows slunk at the entrance to the cavern, and my ears twitched at the sound of echoing footfalls.

My eyes widened, and I moved in front of father, at the same time as his hand fell to the hilt of his sword, and he pushed *me* behind him.

"Assassins," he grunted. "Traitors."

The traitors were swaddled in tight black clothes that made them look like true shadows swarming monstrously across the walls of the cavern.

How many were there? *Too many...far too many...*

My eyes widened, and my throat became tight. I'd fought in battles, galloping at their front on Thunder like war itself. I'd faced death, destruction, and danger.

But no one ever attacked the king. To do so in the Sacred Cave was like cleaving open the heart of the Other World.

Who would dare...?

I shook with rage and then I paled because if they'd entered the cave, it meant that they'd killed the guards outside: my friends who I'd trained and fought alongside.

Had they also hurt our horses?

No, no, no... not Thunder...

I wouldn't also let them take father.

"Leave this place," I didn't even know that I was speaking, until the words had rung from my lips like the regal peal of a bell. "I swear on the ancient ice that holds the power of my birthright that I shall kill you if you don't."

Was that me speaking? Where had such words wound from...within my soul or magic? Father stared at me; his brow furrowed.

I expected pride but instead, there was only concern.

My eyes burned that even now, we didn't stand side by side. But he still thought that he had to protect me. He'd told me that I wasn't weak. Yet I knew that Darby would've been attacking these traitors already for daring to threaten the royal family.

And father would've allowed him to.

When I drew my dagger, baring my teeth, why did father shake his head at me?

I clenched my jaw, deliberately ignoring his gaze.

Inside, I was as chilly as the cavern. Something dangerous clawed to be free. My frozen magic surged in a way that I'd always feared, but nobody had ever believed me.

Why had they never listened?

I couldn't control it. The tips of my hair became icy.

Then my shoulders stiffened, as the shadows converged on us in a black silent wave.

They were almost here. *Any moment...* My palm was sweaty around my curved dagger. *Almost here...* My pulse raced. *Too late...*

Dark magic shot in a bolt at father, and he howled, as it seared his leg. He stumbled, falling to his knees. He lost his grip on his sword, and it skittered across the ice.

No, no, no...

A powerful force inside me, which had listened to my oath on the ice, burst out. The roaring in my ears blocked out everything but the winding tale of a song that linked me back to every ancestor who'd ever stood in this chamber, and it was their strength that I channeled.

I lost control.

There was nothing but the tempting dark freeze and the sweet song of my ancestors.

I swayed, before blinking open my eyes.

Where there'd been shadows, now there was frozen death. I gasped, stumbling onto my behind. I clutched my arms over my eyes because if I couldn't see it, then it wasn't true.

I hadn't murdered more men in a single moment than I'd ever killed on a battlefield.

I swallowed, slowly lowering my arms again. The traitors had been frozen into grotesque statues.

Was my legacy to be such an ice sculpture?

I twisted to the side and vomited. Then I pulled back my hair and wiped my mouth, grimacing.

What was I? What was wrong with me?

I stroked over the crystals in my hair. Would they be taken from me and given to Darby now that I'd been shown to be...unstable?

Yet I *had* defeated the traitors, saved the kingdom, and father. Perhaps, my honor could be restored.

I brushed my arm across my eyes, turning to father. "I kept my oath! See, I can fight too. I saved us..."

Then I keened, launching myself towards my father's corpse.

Please, Sacred Other World, take anything from me but this.

I shook father by his icy shoulders, before dragging him to my chest like I could bring him to life again through my warmth. Tears streamed down my cheeks, and I howled.

I take it back, I take it back, I take it back...

He was dead.

Please, no...

On my ears, what had I done? How would I explain this to Darby or mother? Anything that they did to me or sentenced as punishment, I'd deserve.

I was a king-slayer and killer.

Monstrous.

Desperately, I reached to the songs of my ancestors, but they were silent. So, I called to the mountains and woods for healing songs to bring him back, but they merely wept. There were no songs, but the streams screamed at me.

They knew what I'd done, and even they rejected me. Numb, I rocked, cradling my dead father.

More guards would come for us soon.

Come to shackle the monster, monster, monster...

Monster.

All of a sudden, the world spun.

I shook my head and found that I was back in my own foxy body, rocking in the seats of the Memory Theater. The feathered straps opened, releasing me.

Wow, that'd been a bad trip. I mean, I'd been locked in an attic for most of my life, where the highlights of my week were a whipping, wank starring

Tinker Bell, and a Harry Potter comedy routine. But Willoughby's life made mine look like a pampered sultan who had a harem of jinn.

Willoughby rocked in the center of the stage...alone...with his arms clutched over his head. He was ashen, and his cheeks were streaked with tears. He'd never been anything but distant and composed before, except when his brother's letter arrived.

I understood why now.

My dad's funeral had been on the day that I'd arrived at this academy. It was less than a week ago. I'd loved my dad and everything that he'd suffered for me. He'd protected me the best he could. It squirmed inside me that the effort could've killed him. But Willoughby's magic *had* killed his own dad, while he'd been trying to protect him.

No wonder Willoughby believed all those lies about being a monster. But he wouldn't suffer alone. If us Immortals were claiming him, then he'd never be alone again.

When Damelza's eyes glittered with a predatory delight at Willoughby's distress, I stiffened. I glanced at Magenta, and she nodded. I should've known that the witch who could love a mage would never let something as small as *the power to decimate whole armies* stand in the way of her love.

After all, Magenta was a wicked witch with the

power to curse into winter this entire academy. My whiffling nose smelled the perfect match.

When I dived across the seats onto the stage, Damelza let out a squawk of protest, which I ignored. Sleipnir and Bask followed me. Magenta transformed into mist and rematerialized next to Willoughby on the floor. He looked up with hazy, confused eyes, as she wound her arms around him. Then he rested his head against her chest, and she carded her fingers through his hair, until his breathing steadied.

I sat cross-legged next to him, as Bask and Sleipnir stood over him, guarding him from Damelza's special brand of cruelty.

Lysander stood up, pointing at us in outrage. "Get away from his royal personage! Don't sully a Prince with your Immortal—"

I tilted my head. "Brilliance? Wit? Cum?"

Lysander reddened. "Who knows where any of you have been." He glowered. "Let me comfort him."

I snorted. "You mean, manhandle him and then lock him in his room."

Lysander at least had some decency in his fae ass (okay, that was a guess because it could've been in his fae prick, balls, or little toe), because he looked down, chastened.

Wow, that was a weird look on him. *I liked it.*

When I caressed Willoughby's cheek, wiping away

his tears with the pad of my thumb, finally his gaze focused. "You're here now. In the academy."

When I leaned forward, Willoughby's lips pressed to mine like he was desperate for me to prove it. I was up for that challenge. My skin tingled. Willoughby's lips were as soft as I'd imagined and as cold. They opened on a soft gasp, and my tongue pushed inside, twining with his. Instantly, everything faded but the taste of him.

I needed more. *More of him.*

Willoughby's magic was dark and sang to mine. A sorcerer and a mage, we could be powerful together alongside Magenta. His magic was meant to bond with Magenta's and mine because he was death as surely as we were, and Sleipnir too.

Pleasure and death: I'd never forget the essential incubus ingredient.

Sleipnir wrenched back Willoughby's head, pulling him away from the kiss. I let out a whimper of protest.

It wasn't fair to take away a cat treat. Did he want me to bring out *Master Claws*? Because I was close to transforming and using Sleipnir's dick as a scratching post.

Never piss off a pussy.

"We've seen your wicked secret now. And you know what? Who cares." Sleipnir lowered his face closer to Willoughby's. "We're all monsters. The question is whether you want to take control of your story."

Willoughby raised a shaky hand to cup Sleipnir's face. "I have a choice…?"

Bask eased Sleipnir's hand out of Willoughby's hair, smoothing it over.

He knelt behind Willoughby, wrapping his arms around his neck and nuzzling happily against him. "You're not alone, if you wish it. Can you feel me?"

Willoughby arched his brow. "You're the most endowed of the Immortals. I can feel your impressive dick against my hip."

Bask flushed. "I'll take the compliment."

Magenta's voice was low; it made me shudder. "Is there truly any way that you can ever achieve redemption for your past?"

Wait, *what...?* I attempted to *hush* her, but she batted me away.

Willoughby bit his lip, shaking his head. Tears hung like dew drops on the tips of his eyelashes.

"Then we must all of us move forward and show who we truly are in our actions. Believe me, I've had over a century to work that out for myself. I don't recommend taking that long. But you're not alone." Magenta leaned forward, whispering, "If you choose to be, you're a Rebel Immortal like me."

Willoughby shivered, leaning into Magenta like she was his salvation.

Damelza coughed, tapping her foot. *Pissed off Principal alert.* "Disgusting PDA and angsty declarations: I'll have to record these as side effects of the Memory Theater. How fascinating. This academy isn't about *choice*, however, you follow the rules that I set down as your Principal. Why can't you understand that the magical training within these walls offers up secrets like nowhere else in the world. If you survive, you'll experience adventures and realms that are beyond imagination. What's a little danger compared to that? Talking of danger..." Her lips curled into a malicious smile. "Tomorrow is Torment Thursday. I've cast a Celibacy Hex on you all." Her grin widened, as we groaned. "You need your sleep. Torment Thursday will be exciting but dangerous. The mage's life and the vampire's wings are the stake, as you've drawn every day this week. Tomorrow will decide whether the mage dies."

CHAPTER TEN

Rebel Academy, Thursday September 5th

MAGENTA

Torment Thursday didn't feel too *tormenting*, as I sunned myself on the stone window seat in the Conqueror's Gym. This was my first class, after the Immortals and I had been woken up at the punishment hour of 5 a.m. and then had forced down the barely edible slop that Sleipnir had sworn was *porridge*.

Sweet Hecate, I'd bet that the Princes had dined in Crow Hall on poached eggs, kippers, bacon, sausages, muffins and strawberry jam.

Oh, and delicious English tea.

I sighed, and my mouth watered. I couldn't forget

the seven different types of tea, which had been stacked in the Prince's bedroom. Was it greedy to wish to taste each one, passed from Willoughby's lips to mine?

At least Ezekiel hadn't arrived yet to start the lesson and neither had Lysander (so the witching heavens did sometimes favor me). If it wasn't for the fact that my sweet mage would die if the Immortals lost the three classes today to our rivals the Princes, I'd have been able to sneak in a quick rest. Sleipnir had woken me up last night with a sleep talking outburst about *bananas*, which had been followed by Fox's snicker.

I missed Fox with an intense ache that made my magic wish to reach out and burst flowers from the ground to spell out his name.

FOX.

...or perhaps...

MINE.

Flower magic was possessive. Certainly, that was my excuse.

Only, whipping boys weren't allowed in warrior training, which meant that right now Fox was snuggled in bed again. He'd shot me a smug smile, burrowing back under the covers for an extra snooze.

Ah, witchy prejudice defeated by cat naps.

I leaned my head against the stone wall. Perhaps, I'd survive today with all my limbs and even my

175

bosom in one piece. I ran my hand across those ample but perky bosoms just to be certain that I was truly here and looking out at the frozen river, which divided the academy from the domes and spires of Oxford.

It almost appeared that I could reach out and pick up the non-magical world. Could I control it with my magic in the same way as I did the grounds of the academy?

Now, wasn't *that* a thought?

Did the wards keep us hidden and secret from the rest of the world, or keep the rest of the world hidden, secret, and *safe*, from *me*?

Cauldrons and black cats, it was thrilling to be wicked.

I glanced across at Sleipnir and Bask, who'd thrown off their blazers and ties and slouched in the shadows. Sleipnir pushed back his mop of aquamarine hair, licking over his lip piercing like a promise to lick something far more pleasurable. In the far corner, which was painted with the grand battles that'd been fought by previous Rebels, they kissed like it was a battle as well.

Was this Kissing Practice?

That was what Fox had claimed was part of his curriculum this morning. It didn't look to me like either Bask or Sleipnir needed the lesson. In fact, they could be Professors in Kissing.

Yet they needed to take out their frustration, since

last night Damelza's Celibacy Hex had been effective at keeping our lips, hands, and naughty bits regrettably to ourselves.

They clutched hard onto each other's shoulders; their bodies melded as if into one. First one way and then the other, they fought each other for dominance, but neither gave an inch. Bask humped against Sleipnir's leg, but he glanced over his shoulder at *me* with half-lidded eyes.

My lips twitched. They knew that I was watching. Did they wish me to rate them out of ten or politely applaud? Their pleasure fed me, until I had to battle *myself* to hold back the groan.

Was it appropriate ladylike behavior in class to slide your hand up underneath your skirts and...?

In a flurry of feathers and loud *cawing*, Flair and Echo flew through the window and landed on the seat. Echo overbalanced in his excitement and tumbled into my lap. I snatched my hand away from my naughty bits, and Echo flapped around, wrapping his wings around me in greeting.

Flair tilted his head. "*Don't let us stop you, boss, if your cock lane needs a good—*"

"My flower is none of your business." I flushed. "And it's watered enough right now, thank you for your interest."

"*Any time.*" Flair hopped closer. "*I don't know why*

our fuckable backsides were worried, since you're sitting here happy as a pig in shit."

I scrunched up my nose. "More like a ghost witch in sun."

Echo rubbed his head against my chin. "*More like a beautiful witch in love.*"

I smiled, stroking Echo's wings. "Now, why the panicked crash landing? Are the dragons after you or have the witchy bitches developed a taste for crow on toast?"

Flair cawed in outrage.

"*Bones and blood, it's Torment Thursday.*" Echo stared up at me, and his gentle voice became suffused with fear *for me*. "*You love these Rebels, so I'll do anything to save them for you. But today could hurt or kill them.*"

Flair flapped his wings. "*If I had my way, I'd peck off the Rebels' balls, and make them my bitches. But as you'd never stop moaning about it, I'll save them, instead.*"

What kind of vampire had Flair been before he and his twin had been transformed into my familiars? I'd imagine that he'd been fierce. I found it both admirable and hot.

"How restrained of you." I tapped Flair on the beak. "Now on those mage's balls that you swear not to castrate, tell me what's so important?"

"*As I have Fallen, promise not to abandon us.*"

Echo wrapped his wings even more tightly around me; I loved the feel of their feathery softness. "*Please, please, promise me. The next few days...*"

I blinked. "What am I promising?"

"*You're not a ghost anymore.*" Flair assessed me, shrewdly. "*But we are. Do you want to go back to being trapped in Hecate's Tree?*"

I bristled. "What a ludicrous question."

"*Bollocks to that, wrapped in a shiny* <u>Torment Thursday</u> *sized extra dose of bollocks. The werewolf says that today can be deadly, but the mission* <u>tomorrow</u> *is worse. You may not even come back, boss.*"

My guts churned, and my pulse raced. I cuddled Echo like he was Nile, and rather wished that I hadn't already guessed that Flair was right.

"What werewolf?" I asked.

It seemed like the safest question.

That was, until Echo bumped his head against my bosom reprovingly. "*The beautiful Omega who lives here. On my fangs, don't tell me that you missed the cages?*"

I gasped, remembering the cage in the corner of Juni's classroom. During Divination Class, however, I'd been rather taken up with Sleipnir's lips kissing up my neck, until my toes had curled. Of course, also Fox swinging upside down next to a naked vampire.

The cage had been for a werewolf...? Wait, wasn't

there also one by Hecate's shrine in the castle court-yard? That was certainly a new addition, which hadn't been there, during the time that I'd been growing up in the academy.

"I rather hoped that it was for when the Princes handed in their homework late." I shrugged.

Flair shook his head. "*The Omega's collared, caged, and without the kinky fun. He's only allowed to transform on the full moon and at that bitch's command.*"

"But wolves are shifters. They should be able to transform at will. How do you know that he's being controlled like the dragons?"

Echo cocked his head. "*Flair's stalking, stalking, stalking him.*"

"*Following him,*" Flair corrected.

"*Just sleeping on—*"

"*Next to—*"

"*Him at night.*"

I glanced between them, narrowing my eyes. "Uh-huh. Entirely normal crow behavior. But why's he even in the academy? He's not on the Membership list."

"*Juni owns him like you own us,*" Echo replied.

I winced. I opened my mouth to deny it, but Flair shot me a warning look. Last time that I'd tried to assure them of their freedom, Echo had freaked out, until I'd claimed him again. I couldn't tell if it was a vampire thing or a uniquely Echo thing. But since we'd spent over a century as ghosts alone together in Hecate's Tree, we belonged together.

Plus, Echo was technically right. His twin and him had been given to me on my twenty-first birthday, just as the cat familiar, Pocus, must've been given to Professor Bacchus.

They'd all been made property against their will.

Yet the wolves were wild and free. Their civilization was fascinating. Most of it was peaceful or not more war-like than any other paranormal.

How had Juni collared an Omega?

"It turns out that there was a Wolf War," Flair's voice was more anguished than I'd expected. What terrible things had Echo and he learned on their missions around the academy? *"The bastard witches won and enslaved the wolves. From what I can tell, most of the werewolves were freed by some glittery god, a Wolf Charmer and her wolves, and our mage's cousin."* I straightened, staring at him in shock. Fox's cousin had saved an entire race? He'd been brave enough to battle against witches? Wait, that explained the courage of *my* mage and why the magic inside him was so powerful. *"But the witches here in the academy don't give a flying monkeys' fuck about witch law or tradition. They're outside all that shit. The academy's Omega is still a slave."*

"Not if I can help it," I muttered.

When Flair hopped forward, patting his wing on my knee in gratitude, I smiled. Flair must have a crush on this Omega. Now I was truly desperate to see him.

I glanced up at Sleipnir and Bask and I realized that they'd stopped kissing, although they were still wound around each other. They both stared at me with impatiently raised eyebrows.

Ah yes, I should've been watching their sexy show. Instead, I'd been...*talking to myself.*

Sometimes, I forgot that my familiars were invisible to others.

I grinned sheepishly, gesturing *go on.*

Bask shrugged, before clasping his hand around Sleipnir's neck and rubbing his knee across his prick. Sleipnir arched into him.

I wished that I could get back to enjoying the delightful sight. Instead...

"Why are you telling me about your wolfie crush?" I demanded.

Flair *thwapped* my knee with his wing. "*That wolfie crush has something to do with Torment Thursday. I was sleeping...okay, rolling around sniffing his bed...and I heard him talking to the witch. He fears this day.*"

The hairs on my nape rose, and I pressed my nails into my palms. As long as we won to save Fox, I could endure anything.

"*Forgive, forgive, forgive,*" Echo's gentle voice wove up to me like a prayer.

"I'd forgive you anything." Then I bit my lip. When would I learn the danger of such sweeping promises? Yet I'd never take it back because Echo's eyes gleamed with joy like I'd sworn him my eternal love.

Although, I supposed that was true as well.

"*You warm my very heart of pain,*" Echo murmured. "*But I meant please forgive the elf. I'm certain that he's sorry, if he's been bad. The song that he sang in the shower this morning was like a stream weeping down the melting snows of a mountain. I barely remembered to glance at his beautiful prick. Why don't you spank me in his place?*"

When Echo threw himself dramatically across my lap, as if his behind was a sacrifice to save Willoughby's (although I still didn't understand why he believed the elf at risk of my fury more than the fae because my hand truly did itch to give *him* a witch smacking), I startled. When I merely stroked over Echo's feathery behind, he rumbled low in his throat.

"I'm not punishing the Prince," I promised.

Flair cocked his head. "*So, the blue-haired bastard just put himself in the corner then?*"

When I twisted around, my eyes widened.

While I'd been distracted both by my familiars and the delicious pleasure winding to my magenta magic from Sleipnir and Bask putting on a hot show for me, I hadn't seen Willoughby enter the Conqueror Gym.

He never went anywhere without Lysander, as if the other Prince was his guard.

Where was Lysander?

Now, Willoughby stood in the corner with his palms pressed hard against the wall. His back was stiff with tension.

My brow furrowed. *What was wrong with him?*

"I assure you, I'll look after the elf, until he no longer hides himself or sings anything but the merriest songs in the shower." I *shooed* Echo, and he hopped off my lap. "I hope that you'll then remember to take a thorough look at his beautiful prick."

Echo flapped his wings, as he murmured, "*Beautiful prick.*"

Flair and Echo took off, circling above my head.

"*What you need to do,*" Flair called down, "*is to fuck him hard and dirty, until he's seeing icicle shaped stars. That'll do it.*"

The crow twins flew out of the window.

"Thanks for the advice," I called after them, "most helpful."

I almost meant it.

I took a final glance at my Immortals (I'd have to remember to ask Sleipnir to repeat the trick of trailing kisses and marking bruises up and down Bask's neck on mine later), before strolling behind Willoughby's tense back.

I studied his lean muscles and perfectly sculptured figure in the silk suit that was tighter than any clothes I'd ever seen. Witching heavens, the *fuck him hard and dirty plan* deserved definite consideration.

And I understood Echo's obsession with his pretty hair.

I stared at the back of Willoughby's head. "*Ehm*, have you put yourself in the naughty corner? Are you waiting for further chastisement? What happened over your luxury breakfast? Did you complain that there weren't quite enough flavors of tea for you to choose from?"

On a witch's tit, I admit that I *might've* been a little bitter on the tea issue.

For a moment, I thought that Willoughby wouldn't answer. Then his fingers curled against the wall, and he rested his forehead against it.

Perhaps, I'd been a little cruel with the tea jibe?

I shifted from foot to foot, reaching out my hand but not quite touching his stiff shoulder. "I'd understand about the tea, by the way. There's no such thing as too many flavors..."

"I can't fight today," Willoughby's voice was low.

I tilted my head. Screw a mage, he needed me, and I needed him to break the wards. When I wrapped my fingers around his shoulder, he stiffened in shock like he'd never expected that I'd touch him. But then he sighed, relaxing.

"Are we playing hide and seek instead, then?" I asked.

Willoughby raised his head, straightening. "I don't know how to play that. How about Silent Elf? Then nobody would need hear me for the rest of the lesson and I hope, ever."

Now that was quite enough.

I clutched him tighter, twisting him around. He gasped; his eyes were frosty blue pools.

"I battle every day not to fade away again. I know what it is to be invisible and trapped. You shall not let yourself disappear because of your grief or shame. You'll hold on."

I gripped onto him like I could reach into his mind, even though he felt such a long way from me. He was buried beneath dark magic. It burned me. I ached to save him. I didn't care whether it was a crush or love, but it no longer mattered. "You shall stay with me."

His breath caught, and his gaze was suddenly desperate and searching.

I flushed.

Then Willoughby stroked the back of his hand down my cheek, and it was *me* flushing. Even though his kiss was butterfly light on my forehead, it settled hot in my stomach, furling out warmth through me and lighting me up with sparkling magic.

"Even though I'm a Prince, I would obey," he replied. "But this is warrior training, and I *can't* fight."

I raised my eyebrow. "After what I saw last night..."

Ah, someone kick my witchy ass.

Willoughby reddened, trying to pull back, but my mists reached out and dragged him even closer. "I can't control myself."

"Stuff and nonsense." I wrapped his arm through mine, dragging his bewildered behind (and the rest of his cute self) to the middle of the gym. "I claim you as my sparring partner. Do you imagine that I'm ever fully in control? Hexes and curses, how naive. Why don't we be the storm together? It's much more fun that way."

Willoughby's amazed face would've been comical if it didn't show how little anyone had trusted him before. "But you saw..."

"Do you not also see the entire academy covered in ice?" I pointed out of the window with my chin. A chill breeze swept through the window, but I didn't shiver; I welcomed the thrill of nature. "I rather trump you on the whole *they're dangerous* threat level. You shan't have my Ice Witch Crown, but we could always be frozen royalty together."

Say yes...

Willoughby gasped, and his cool face lit with sudden joy. He leaned closer into my side; and the feel of his arm through mine was solid, safe, and right.

Like he'd always meant to fit there.

Witches above, I was taking that as a yes.

Then the door to the gym slammed open, and Lysander burst inside. His black blazer and pink silk shirt were as perfect as always; it was Lysander who wasn't. His alabaster skin was pallid; and there were shadows under his large emerald eyes.

Had he slept at all last night?

His equally emerald hair hung between his drooping golden wings. Why did I wish him to beat them in that arrogant way of his like fae could buy up everything within the academy (even me), just like his guardian Prince Titus, rather than the fake pretense of being *fine.*

I'd watched the Rebels from the window of the Bird Turret as a girl many decades ago. So many had worn masks to hide their fear, pain, or grief. Yet I'd been a hidden witness to the truth. And I could see it now in Lysander.

Was he also limping?

Lysander stared first in amazement at the way that Willoughby's arm was hooked through mine and then at Bask, whose *legs* were hooked around Sleipnir's waist, as Sleipnir ground against him.

It was indeed a charming sight.

Lysander's jaw clenched, before he marched, as if onto a battlefield, towards Bask.

For a moment, I had the disconcerting feeling that he intended to join in their fun to add a dash of fae for my pleasure. Well, that killed all the lightning spark tingles that'd been warming my happy places.

I couldn't quite help the tilt of my head, imagining Lysander's tight behind added into the mix of my lovers. It was simply a shame that it was attached to the rest of him.

Lysander pointed a quivering finger at Bask. "My royal personage received your *message*." He glanced darkly over his shoulder at me. "And of course, your cursed witch's."

Sleipnir casually dropped Bask to the ground, but there was nothing casual about the way that he twisted to Lysander. His muscles bunched, and his hair bristled to red. "I'll show you *cursed*, asshole, if you disrespect Magenta again."

Lysander's wings beat, as he stared intently at Bask. "One merely meant..." His cheeks reddened. Where was the witty insult? Perhaps, he was ill? Was that why he looked like he might even apologize? Mage's balls, let's not go entirely crazy. "Have you not marked me? Were you not both claiming me as yours with...?"

Bask's eyes widened, and he desperately sought

out my gaze. *Lysander thought that we'd been claiming him?*

Sweet Hecate, who knew that fae even had social etiquette for coming on someone's bed? I hadn't been trained on coming misunderstandings.

My education had been sorely lacking.

The silence had gone on too long.

Lysander's eyes flashed with hurt and a desperate insecurity. "Who would wish to be claimed by such pitiable Immortals anyway?"

Wait...*had he*?

Bask blinked, reaching out. "If you wish..."

Lysander sneered, turning on his heel and marching towards the opposite wall. He clicked his fingers at Willoughby. "Here."

I stiffened, just as much as Willoughby. "I wasn't aware that he was your dog."

"But are you aware that he bites?" Lysander tossed his hair, unbuttoning his shirt like all of a sudden, he was too hot. I couldn't help the way that I watched his nimble fingers, and the sudden pale strip tease of his skin. "One has already suffered this morning at the hands of Juni because she believes that I've lost control of my fellow Prince. While you've played at friends with this witch, I've been played with by our Tutor."

Willoughby flinched. "I'm sorry. May I heal you?"

I hadn't expected the concern or the way that

Lysander's expression gentled. *Perhaps, it'd be harder to win Willoughby away from the Princes than I'd thought.*

"You know that's cheating. Punishment Points must be endured and not magically healed. Now...*here*." Lysander snapped his fingers again.

I tightened my grip on Willoughby. "Today, he's playing at being *my friend*, remember?"

Lysander's eyes glittered dangerously.

Suddenly, the angelic Professor of Dueling, Ezekiel, swooped through the open window with a *swoosh* that blew my hair back from my face. The sun shone off his violet wings and his bronzed muscles. Truly, had I imagined an angel...*he would've looked nothing like Ezekiel*. But had I imagined a man who I wanted to lick all over and suck his wings, then *that* would be Ezekiel.

By the way that Bask was biting his lip and attempting to hold back breathy moans, I wondered if he felt the same. But then again, that could be because of Sleipnir's hand, which had slipped down the back of Bask's trousers.

Ezekiel landed with an intimidating *thud*. He folded his wings and his arms at the same time. Even in only the ash harem pants of an Addict Angel, he was unmistakably a warrior. Luckily, he was also kinder than the other Professors, as long as you didn't forget that he was just as ruthless. He'd never have been the sole survivor of his year of Rebels otherwise. There was no escape from the academy, I'd learned. There was only death or the offer of a professorship.

I'd yet to decide which was worse.

"I'm glad to see that you're already partnered up and ready to go. Yesterday was..." His gaze settled on Willoughby, whose expression became shuttered. "...difficult for us all. Let's start today with a clean slate. The others will want you fighting between yourselves, but I don't. I'm glad to see that you listened to me."

Lysander raised his hand. "One appears to be lacking a partner."

"It's not all he's lacking," Sleipnir muttered.

Lysander affected not to notice.

Ezekiel cocked his head. "Then ask yourself why that is."

"I was late," Lysander gritted out.

Ezekiel *tutted*. "Then you don't get to train today." He pointed with his wing to the corner, which Willoughby had been standing in earlier. "No moving and think about why you're missing out."

Sleipnir chuckled.

"B-but this is an outrage," Lysander spluttered. "It's essential that I train. My uncle will know if I don't."

"Disobedience as well." Ezekiel swept towards Lysander, guiding him firmly into the corner. My stomach squirmed. Was Ezekiel helping us Immortals to save Fox? Helping *me*? Yet why didn't it feel fair because Lysander couldn't help being late, and despite everything, I hated to see him in trouble for that. Wait, I couldn't be under a Fae Lover spell because I should be enjoying this torment. Only, I *wasn't*. "I'll have to write to Prince Titus now."

"*Don't*," I called at the same time as Bask.

Ezekiel turned, raising his brow at both of us. Then he smiled. "You're lucky that you have some brave defenders, Crown." Lysander only snorted. *Impolite.* "Keep your nose pressed into the corner in total silence through the lesson, and I won't have to inform your uncle."

Lysander nodded; his wings quivered with anxiety.

Then Ezekiel marched into the center of the gym. His wings outstretched in a display of dominance. "Today is Torment Thursday. Sometimes, we all have to face our nightmares." *Not if I could help it.* "And when we do, it's unfortunate but we can't always rely on those around us. We could be alone with our weapon lost. So, I'll teach you to defend yourself hand-to-hand. But this is about the defensive. I've seen more than enough how you can attack."

Sleipnir lounged against the wall. "You want one to attack and the other to defend. Then how will you know who wins this lesson because hey, that's our nightmare right now."

Ezekiel sighed. "You have more nightmares than that." I jolted with fear. Black cats, what a motivational teacher he was. He swooped to Willoughby and me, wrapping us in the feathery softness of his wings that smelled tangy but sweet like citrus creams. *Would he notice if I just nibbled a single feather?* I sucked one into my mouth, before I caught his amused expression, and hastily spat it out. Then he ran his hand down Willoughby's neck. "Crow, you're defending against Crush's attack."

Willoughby shook his head. "I won't attack—"

"You're a worthy partner for me," I insisted. "I need an equal to my power." His breath hitched on the *partner*. "Don't fear the cold."

Willoughby's lips twitched like he was desperate to smile but couldn't quite remember how. "I've always admired strong women."

"Ah, such a charmer."

"But what do you fear?" Ezekiel demanded. Magic sparked across his wings: he was casting a spell. "What's your nightmare?"

"Don't do this..." I hissed.

Would it be dark elves, the traitors who'd attacked him and his father, clowns juggling snakes...?

I trusted Willoughby to control himself when he

fought me but could he when he was under an enchantment?

I saw Lysander glance worriedly over his shoulder from his corner. I shook my head at him. There was no point him getting in even more trouble. This was Torment Thursday, after all, it was filled with our nightmares.

"Myself," Willoughby whispered.

I drew in my breath, and my pulse was loud in my ears. I wished to draw Willoughby into an embrace, rather than being forced apart from him by Ezekiel. Willoughby's expression was blank like he no longer knew where he was.

He'd think that he was fighting himself because he feared and hated himself that much.

I'd told him that we'd be the storm. We truly were now twin Ice Princes.

When Ezekiel swept to Sleipnir and Bask, Sleipnir stood protectively in front of Bask.

"Lay those nightmares on me." Sleipnir boldly met Ezekiel's gaze.

Ezekiel shrugged apologetically. "Crave isn't a god or a warrior. I have a feeling that your nightmares would lead to the dismemberment of one of my students, and I don't have time for the paperwork."

Sleipnir paled, almost as much as Bask.

"I call for the non-dismemberment option," I said.

Bask slunk around Sleipnir, patting his shoulder.

"Don't underestimate an incubus. You should tremble before me."

Ezekiel smiled indulgently. "We'll see." Then he wrapped his wings around Bask, who settled his hand on the angel's chest like he didn't blame him for putting him under a spell. Then I realized: this wasn't Ezekiel's fault. He was a prisoner here at the academy too and always had been. He was trying to save each of us in his own way. Had he also saved Lysander from suffering this spell by putting him in the corner? Did he know how terrible *his* fear would've been? "What's your nightmare?"

"The Duchess," Bask breathed.

My witchy behind was entirely unsurprised. It was also, however, furious.

I clenched my hands into fists and concentrated on remembering that my role was merely to defend.

My magic snapped within me, desperate to *attack, attack, attack*...

Pink tendrils streamed through the window and into the sky. They burrowed into the earth. Nature screamed along with me to unleash my Wickedly Charmed magic and protect my Rebels.

Because this time, they were still alive.

Ezekiel's smile was grim, as his wings beat down like the shot of a starting pistol. "Nightmares begin!"

CHAPTER ELEVEN

Rebel Academy, Thursday September 5th

MAGENTA

I've grown accustomed to being thought wicked. It was disconcerting, however, to be hated as a monster because your sparring partner believed that you'd transformed into their *own* monstrous self.

Ezekiel's Nightmare Spell was *truly* wicked.

It'd brought alive whoever haunted both Willoughby and Bask. And it appeared that Willoughby feared himself.

Ah, the wonders of an academy education.

When Willoughby narrowed his eyes and stalked towards me, I backed towards the wide window, which streamed sun across the dusty floor of Conqueror Gym.

Mage's balls, how did I fuck him hard and dirty, when he looked like he wished to choke me?

Although, Flair had told me some interesting things about how that could be quite arousing in the right circumstances. I didn't imagine those were under an enchantment, however, where Willoughby believed me to be his Evil Mirror Twin, or did that merely make it *more* kinky?

Willoughby and his dark twin would look delectable together.

Damelza had said that I should be open to new opportunities, and I'd never been someone's Evil Mirror Twin before. As long as I didn't die, this could be an interesting chance to work out whether Willoughby truly could become one of my Immortals.

Witch's tit, I wasn't even kidding myself. *He already was.*

That still didn't hold back the wave of sparkling magic that struggled to burst out of me and crash over his pretty head in retaliation.

Defend, defend, defend...

I shook, struggling to hold my power inside.

Willoughby crouched, ready to attack. His gaze was intent and predatory. I shivered at how deliciously dangerous he was.

When he leaped at me with a flurry of blows, I

spun and deflected, vibrating with joy in the fight. My legs melted into mists, just before he attempted to hook my legs out from under me. I hooted in delight at his huff of frustration.

I'd never been allowed to join in with such sparring, when mother, Henrietta, had kept me isolated in the Bird Turret. I found that I rather enjoyed the sweaty *hand to mist* battle, from which she'd been protecting me.

My magic wasn't delicate, after all. And I was just as capable of a magical education as the Rebel boys.

The need to fight back zinged through me at the thought. My magenta trailed out, winding around Willoughby like ivy.

Don't you dare... I dragged it back with a yank.

Ezekiel paced with controlled but coiled energy, crossing his arms.

"Remember that restraining ourselves is as important as facing our fears," Ezekiel's voice was soft with compassion, as he met my gaze. *Had this been hard for him as well?* "Isn't allowing yourself to be attacked...vulnerable...hurt and *not* attacking back, *your* nightmare?"

I hissed a breath sharply through my teeth.

I'd always found being *seen* the most seductive thing in the world, but Ezekiel also saw my darkness.

When Robin had been murdered by Henrietta, my magic had reacted on instinct to the grief blasting through me. I'd lashed out and cursed the academy. Would it've been better to have meekly followed Henrietta's orders and married Prince Titus? To have remained Blessedly, rather than Wickedly, Charmed? To have failed to avenge Robin's death, remaining powerless in the face of cruelty?

Indeed, that *was* my nightmare.

I swallowed, forcing my magic back down. Would Robin have wanted me to turn the academy to perpetual winter so that every Rebel had to freeze in its cold? I had a feeling that he'd have pecked my behind for making that his legacy.

At the thought, my pink faded into sparkles, which caressed (rather than hurt), Willoughby.

Robin's legacy would be to help and free every Rebel. He was my first love and he'd died because of me. Blessed be, there could be no better way to honor him.

Unfortunately, Willoughby hadn't appreciated the teasing strokes of my magic or the quite beautiful (if I said so myself) dedication to Robin. To be fair, that'd only been inside my head.

When the Prince circled me, I could imagine every battle that he'd fought against the Dark Elves.

Against the far wall, Bask was attacking his Evil Twin Duchess (or my hot god, Sleipnir) with a string of curses that I'd never have guessed he knew, a flurry of slaps, and the power of a deadly incubus glare.

Casually, Sleipnir lounged against the wall, holding Bask back with one hand. It was like an adorable kitten, smacking the nose of a lion. Sleipnir's control impressed me; I knew that he'd never hurt Bask.

Sleipnir's genuine worry about whether any of the curses about *never-ending glitter* on his clothes or *stepping on a Lego every time that he walked through a door* would come true, however, was shown in Mist's frantic tossing of his mane. The tiny eight-legged horse wildly galloped laps around Bask like he was running a race all by himself.

All of a sudden, Willoughby spun towards me with a series of kicks, which were beautiful, elegant, and deadly. I *eeped*, floating to the side and slamming into the wall.

Only defend...

When the tip of Willoughby's foot caught my bosoms, I gasped in outrage, grabbing his ankle and twisting him away. He sprawled onto his front, quickly catching himself and bouncing back to his feet.

"Watch the bosoms." I patted them like comforting a pussy or Fox. "You menfolk have no idea how difficult it is to fight with these large things."

Yet Willoughby saw me as his Evil Mirror Twin and *he* had nothing but a flat chest. I forgave him the lack of manners, therefore, with his high kick.

I dematerialized, reappearing behind Willoughby. When he turned on his heel with military precision, I fought not to flinch. My pulse thundered in my ears because his sky-blue eyes were clouded.

He didn't see me...*he saw himself.*

"Have you no shame?" Willoughby's voice was ice-cold; it cut me. "Will you not even stand still for punishment?"

I jiggled my bosoms to readjust them. "You're not the one having to battle in a corset."

He cocked his head in confusion. "What nonsense is this? You're guilty. Why won't you let me kill you?"

Such pain...

His anguish howled through me. I'd felt it myself on Robin's death. Except, then I *had* died, burned to death by my own mother.

Yet did this mean that Willoughby wished to die?

My hands fluttered at my sides, desperate to pull him to me and then stroke away the pain furrowed on his brow. My mouth was dry, and my heart clenched.

I wouldn't let him die. He needed to be shown that he was more than a nightmare. He could be loved and discover a new family. There was always a way out.

Yet right now, if I tried to tell him any of that, he'd only boot me in the chest again. And once in a day was more than enough for that, thank you very much.

"I do not wish to be burned," Bask snarled. "How

about I curse *you* to *beg* to be used as an ash tray every time that you see a cigarette?"

He was on a roll.

Distracted, I didn't notice the sudden drop in temperature, until my breath came out like white ghosts and my skin ghost bumped.

Dizzy with awe at the startling beauty, I stared at the blue ice that streaked from Willoughby's skin like the roots and branches of a tree, as natural as my frozen breath itself.

Willoughby was death and life and everything that matched my own frosty magic. He was my equal partner in wickedness, just as I'd said, and I wanted him as hard and dirty as I could have him in that moment.

The ice crackled across the gym, coating it in a slippery skin like an ice-rink. Delicate icicles hung from the ceiling, transforming it into a glimmering cave that sparkled in the sun.

It was as beautiful as Willoughby, whose hair had frozen to ice. Yet he hated this side of himself, enough to wish to destroy it.

I would never allow him to.

Ezekiel yelped, as his bare feet burned on the freezing ice. He hopped up and down, before flapping his wings and swooping up to the roof of the gym.

"Stop this travesty at once." Lysander didn't dare leave his corner, but he twisted to glare over his shoulder at the professor. He hugged his wings around himself for warmth. "If you do not, then I shall be the one writing to my uncle. One is under strict instructions not to lie, and I can only spin the truth so far. How would you suggest I creatively hide the fact that you broke the killer loose?"

My eyes narrowed. "Fae may tremble at a little cold, but I don't. I love it."

I strolled towards Willoughby, resting the back of my glove against his cheek. "We don't fear the cold, remember?"

For a moment, Willoughby's eyes cleared, and he blinked. "Magenta...?"

He moved closer; his breath was rapid and his skin was frozen. I brushed my lips against his forehead to warm him up.

But then, his eyes became clouded again and filled with such hate that I recoiled. His lips twisted into a snarl, and his hair coiled like ice snakes.

A shard of ice snapped off the end, accidentally whipping off his long hair and slashing across my throat.

"Valhalla!" Sleipnir hollered. "Stop the spell."

I reached up to my neck: *crimson*. I stared at my fingers in shock.

Ezekiel stormed towards me, catching me in the sweet fragranced safety of his wings. Yet he'd been the one to cast the spell. It wasn't Willoughby's fault. It never had been. "Nightmares end!"

When Bask collapsed, Sleipnir caught him. Willoughby groaned, clutching his head, as he stumbled to his knees. Instantly, the room warmed, and the ice melted to puddles, dripping onto my head and sliding in icy trails down my neck, washing away the streams of blood as if I'd never been cut.

Yet the fiery line, which still stung, told me that I had.

I pressed my palm across my throat like I could hide the evidence. I was an optimistic witch, when I wasn't being forced into marriage, burned alive, or trapped by goddesses.

Ezekiel's wings tightened around me. "Let me see. I can heal you."

"Shouldn't you rather be worrying about the students who you spelled to suffer nightmares?" I shrugged myself out of Ezekiel's embrace, even though I missed his wings' softness and the hardness of his chest, which he'd held me against like he was a lover and not a professor.

I nudged Ezekiel towards Willoughby, whose eyes were still dazed.

Willoughby shook his head like he was trying to clear it. "Magenta...?"

"She's *our* Magenta," Sleipnir growled. "The *monsters* who'd never hurt her."

Sleipnir swept Bask into a bridal carry, ignoring his *squeak* of protest, before storming towards me and dropping down beside me with Bask on his lap.

Immediately, Bask's mouth was on mine. It was as tender as if it was our first kiss. Bask's lips pressed to mine, before his tongue swept to encourage my mouth to open to ruby sparkles, which wove his incubus magic thrilling through my blood to heal me. After his passionate Kissing Practice with Sleipnir, which had teased pleasure through all three of us, his magic was powerful.

I shuddered, as Bask's fingers carded through my hair, before he clutched the back of my head and pulled me into a deeper kiss.

My skin knit, until there was nothing left but a trail of crimson over fresh skin. Then I shivered, as Sleipnir leaned down and licked away the blood. His tongue worked between the pearls to the sensitive skin, and the pulse in my neck fluttered.

"My apologies," Willoughby's voice was tentative and strained. "I warned you that I couldn't control..."

"You *could* but you chose not to." Ezekiel's voice was harder than I'd yet heard it. "There are no excuses for harming another student. You must be deadly to those who you assassinate, but never to fellow Rebels, even if you believe them to be *yourself*."

Ezekiel stood, yanking Willoughby with him.

"Now see here..." I leaped up as well, regretfully

breaking away from the delicious combination of Bask's lips and Sleipnir's talented tongue.

I tried to catch Willoughby's eye, but his head was ducked and his hair (which had now returned to silky sky-blue), covered his face.

Lysander twirled out of the corner, throwing up his hands. "My royal personage demands to be allowed out of your childish punishment to deal with *this*." He pointed at Willoughby like he was an out of control troll, rather than an introverted elf (was he playing the Silent Elf game now?), who was standing obediently next to his professor. "Do you wish to line up to allow him to slit your throats or perhaps, to blast us all to ice?"

Lysander stormed to Willoughby, despite the fact that his limp was even worse now, manhandling him to the window; his fingers dug into Willoughby's arms.

Was it wrong that I wished Willoughby's hair to turn to ice and for him to become the storm again? Sweet Hecate, at least long enough to burn Lysander's fingers for daring to touch him like he was his personal prisoner.

"Enough." My magenta lit up the room in my fury. "Stop acting like he's—"

"Dangerous? A killer? The elf who just cut you?" Lysander raised his eyebrow. Yet it was Willoughby who I watched, and he flinched on each word. He didn't, however, defend himself. Instead, his shoulders slumped, and he curled in on himself. I knew that there was no way to hide or disappear. Such things had to be faced. "One would almost believe that you were keen to end up like his father."

Lysander pulled tight a length of silk, which had fallen loose at the neck of Willoughby's suit, during the fight. Willoughby winced, then the life in his eyes died. All of a sudden, he became lost and confused again.

I would not lose him.

I straightened my shoulders, marching up to Lysander, whose eyes widened in alarm. "I shall not allow Willoughby to hurt himself anymore, and I shall not allow anyone else to hurt him either."

Lysander's face paled, before his expression hardened. "You always think so little of me. You forgive and cuddle a killer. But for the sins of my uncle, do I deserve nothing but your contempt and hate?"

Sleipnir sprawled on the floor, running his hand through Bask's hair. "Sounds about right. Oh, and because you're an elitist asshole."

I blinked. Once, that was true. As patron of the academy, Titus had been and still was the reason for the oppression of the Rebels. By trying to force me into marriage with him, he'd caused Robin's death and my own. As trauma went, I believed it perfectly understandable that I'd despised fae.

But not anymore.

"I don't hate you." I patted Lysander on the arm. "I just don't like you."

Bask snickered.

Lysander glared at me. "Was that supposed to make me feel better, witch?"

"Not particularly. Is the way that you're holding Willoughby's arm hard enough to bruise making him feel better?" Lysander dropped Willoughby's arm like it *had* burned him. *Snap my broomstick, I was good.* I nodded, with a smile. "See, now I dislike you a little less. I won't stand by, whilst those I..." Mage's balls, had I just been about to say *love*? "...have responsibility for are shown cruelty."

"*My royal personage* is his Prefect," Lysander sneered. Then he waved at the Immortals. "Go and be all *responsible* for those creatures over there. I have my orders for my Wing. I'm taking him outside for some air."

What was that code for? Take Willoughby for a refreshing walk, back to the Princes Wing and tuck him into bed, or hang him up by his thumbs?

Ezekiel beat his wings together in agitation. "As the actual professor in the room, I'll have to insist, not yet." Lysander flushed. "I don't understand why you get out of hand every lesson. I've never had such a rebellious class." He ran his hand over his face in frustration. "Together, your magic is volatile but powerful.

209

You need to learn to use it to work for you and not against you. I had intended to declare today a draw, so that you wouldn't have to play the Punish and Reward game."

My heart thudded, and my chest was tight.

We had to win. Fox's life depended on the outcome of the three lessons today.

I wet my dry lips, staring at Ezekiel. Lysander had gone very still. *Was he even breathing?*

"The one who draws blood in my lesson will always lose." Ezekiel shrugged. "And that means that the Immortals win."

Bask bounced to his feet with a *whoop*, holding out his hands to drag Sleipnir with him. Mist whinnied, raising his tail and prancing around the gym in delight.

To my surprise, it was Willoughby who patted Lysander's arm reassuringly. Lysander carefully didn't look at us, fixing his stare at the far wall.

I found that I hated that as much as Willoughby's lost look.

"We choose Punish." Sleipnir's grin was dark.

Bask slunk to me, winding his arms around my neck. "Would the Princes posing for a sexy calendar please you? It could be the Hot Rebel Princes 2020. Naked, oiled, and pinned in our bedroom."

Lysander made a low, choked sound, and Sleipnir chuckled.

"As Willoughby loves the cold," when Sleipnir's eyes narrowed, it reminded me of how dangerously protective he was, "why don't we send them for a night tied by the frozen lake?"

I cocked my head. "Well, that doesn't sound too bad."

"Also, naked and oiled." Sleipnir smirked.

"I detest this game. No one's to be punished," I declared. Bask pouted; he'd truly been looking forward to that Rebel Prince Calendar. To be fair, I was flushed with warmth myself at the thought of it. "I choose Reward."

Sleipnir's jaw clenched. "Why would you reward them?"

"Because it's what they need." For the first time, Willoughby looked up, and I met his anguished gaze. "Both of them." I took a deep breath, as Lysander shot me a startled look. "I choose for Willoughby to heal Lysander."

"Your concern for me is touching." Lysander sniffed. "But I'm in no need of..."

I prickled my magic across his back, and even at the light touch, he yelped.

I raised my eyebrow, and he reddened. "I believe that it's my choice of reward."

Ezekiel's lips curled into a smile. He nodded at Willoughby, who rested his forehead against Lysander's. Then Willoughby hummed a lullaby that made me tingle with its beauty. It was like being drawn beneath dark waters into the Other World. My magic stilled, lulled into the calm.

It was magic with the power to heal and more powerful than even my own.

I could've died and been happy in that moment. It was magic like nothing in my world. When Willoughby stopped, I couldn't help the sense that I'd lost something special.

On Torment Thursday, nightmares were made real, but not the kind that children conjured. Instead, the type that lurked deep in our Souls. Fox had been saved in this lesson, but we had to win the next class to save his life.

Yet now we had Spells, Hexes, and Potions with Professor Bacchus. She was a witch from Sleipnir's nightmares, and her enchantments were terrors.

CHAPTER TWELVE

Rebel Academy, Thursday September 5th

FOX

It was becoming a familiar feeling to start a lesson tied up next to a naked vampire. Since this was also Spells, Hexes, and Potions, the class held the added bonus that as the whipping boy, I'd become the test dummy for one of those three fun options.

Wow, I just couldn't choose if I preferred that Midnight and I be used as the guinea pigs to try out the classes' potions or their dodgy spells. Let's just pretend that Hexes had been wiped from **SHP** because I didn't want to imagine the *crucio* level curses that Lysander would direct at my prickles.

Who said that a coven-run academy education had to suck for a mage?

Wait, *everybody* did...

I sighed, settling back into my chair, which was a tangle of vines that rubbed at my wrists and ankles. I gritted my teeth against the pain. The chair grew out of the roots, which burst from the floor and curled up and around the mossy walls. I scrunched my nose at the earthy scent. Ancient magic bloomed out of every spore; I choked on it. It was like Hecate and Bacchus were hand in hand to smack a mage.

Perhaps, sister witch and goddess played that as a fun game to bond over, bitch slapping male gods like Pan (and why did that get my fur fluffing up in his defense?), and holding slumber parties where they braided each other's hair.

Okay, I was erasing that *braiding hair* part forever from my mind because the image of Professor Bacchus and Hecate all cozy together and choosing matching glittery clips, set off my Mage Shivers.

Pan help me.

I clutched the arms of the vine chair more tightly, struggling to count back from a hundred to calm myself. I'd done bondage in a lesson before and last time, I'd been swinging upside down.

Slugs and snails, I was even feeling grateful now not to be hanging from my ankles like a snared fox.

Yet Bacchus' classroom wasn't *witchy* like Juni's. It was more like a science lab that'd been grown inside a tree. Not that I'd ever been inside a lab before coming to this academy or inside a tree, unlike Magenta.

Look at that, Rebel Academy truly *did* offer new opportunities.

When I caught Magenta's furious whisper behind me, I struggled to listen...I mean, actively overhear her conversation with Sleipnir...okay, *eavesdrop*. But my chair was turned to face the back wall and Midnight. The vampire, who was also the Prince's whipping boy, was bound in the chair facing me. His gorgeous ash wings were also dragged behind him and bound down by vines.

Whiskers and claws, that looked painful.

Midnight was also naked. He offered me a lopsided smile with a hint of fang like calmly waiting to be used as a *naked guinea pig* was a typical Thursday for him.

I had a feeling that it was.

What if Damelza had handed me over to the Princes to be their whipping boy instead of the Immortals? Would I've ended up looking grateful to be sitting on a chair, rather than kneeling in the corner? I grimaced. Lysander's balls would soon discover what it felt like to have Mr Fierce roll his prickles over them.

I winced. *Was there any way that I could make that sound unkinky?*

Midnight was palely beautiful. His dark hair tumbled in waves to his waist, and I made a valiant effort not to look at Midnight's prick, even if his hair was like a waterfall leading to it, before it twitched *hello*.

I didn't imagine that.

Midnight's smile widened. When he blinked his charcoal eyes with his sinfully long eyelashes, I flushed. Then I squirmed against the ropes again, banging my head back in frustration. If this class was about our ability to remain submissive in bondage or the Pretend to be a Chair game (so far it could go either way), then I was one dead fox because Midnight held himself as still as a statue.

Apart from his rebel prick.

Almost like it knew that it was betraying me, my foot tapped up and down on the floor.

Tap — tap — tap.

I'd been trapped in a single room from the moment that my mum had discovered I'd had magic. I couldn't take being ensnared again. Last time in class, I'd been able to see Magenta, but now I could only hear her whispers.

I needed to smell the sweet scent of her yew trees winding around me and not the earthy scent of Bacchus' magic that suffocated me.

Magenta...

Tap — tap — tap.

I was desperate to call out to her. But what would she think of me if I panicked over something as simple as being tied down? Sleipnir was a bloody god, and Bask was brave and protective.

What was I?

A hedgehog with anger management issues? A cat with more funk than fight?

The Mage who Loved…

Tap — tap — tap.

My breaths became short and fast. Light-headed, I banged my head against the back of the chair again, yanking my ankles against the restraints. Bruises blossomed.

Then Midnight pushed his knees against mine, and my startled gaze shot to his. "I promised to hold on for you, my king," his voice was gentle with a Welsh lilt, "and so you must hold on for me."

Truth: If he's forgotten his promise to me, then I'm worth nothing.

With my Power of Confess, the truth of Midnight's despair hit me in a sticky black wave. I shook with its intensity. I could never allow him to think that I wouldn't help him or my own Magenta shaped meltdown meant that he was worthless.

I'd spent too many years thinking the same.

My breath steadied, and my expression became

steely. I bumped my knuckles against Midnight's because if I couldn't kiss away the crease of concern between his brows, then I could at least soothe him through my wriggling fingers. "Hey, my Memory Palace is better than Sherlock Holmes'; it even has a jacuzzi, private cinema, and an entire wing for my harem of Tinker Bell impersonators." I bit my lip. "*Ehm*, just don't tell Magenta about the harem bit."

Midnight nodded, solemnly. "By my fangs, I'll keep your secret."

"And I'll keep my oath." I lowered my voice, willing Midnight to believe me. He belonged to the Princes. Theoretically, he was a rival. But then, how many theories had been disproved? I could smugly declare that I didn't believe in the crazy theories of being able to write on the moon in blood or that my sexual mojo controlled the universe (although, I wished that it did). Yet today, I'd have to battle against Midnight to win this class and the Rebel Cup. If I did, then my life would be saved, but Midnight's wings would be broken. I shuddered at the thought of a single feather being harmed. "Magenta's brilliant. She has a plan to free us all. But I don't know how long it will take. Can you put some more faith in me? I swear on my prickles that I'm working on saving you."

Midnight ducked his head, and a blush spread across his cheeks. "You don't need to swear on your prickles, see. We're already bound to each other, and I trust you *and* my future queen."

Wow, he truly meant that he saw Magenta and me as his king and queen.

It came of being a pathological liar, but I'd pretended to be royalty more times than I had rooms in my Memory Palace, and no one had ever believed it before. On the other hand, Midnight had chosen me for the role, and that made a grin spread across my face that was as warm as the feeling in my chest.

Until two heavy hands landed in my lap, danger-ously close to my balls, and I yelped, as their nails dug into the sensitive flesh of my inner thighs.

"Why would you trust a mage, especially one with all that curly hair?" Pocus, Bacchus' Halfling and familiar, hissed.

I shivered at Pocus' predatory danger, which was hidden under the softness of his voice. Also, at the insult to my hair. After so many years without the ability to look in a mirror, I was suddenly desperate to run my fingers through my curls. *What was wrong with them?* Bask insisted that they were *pettable*.

Pocus rose up on his knees, shoving his face close to mine. He scrutinized me like I was Midnight's new boyfriend and I had to pass the test before I could take him out. Pocus was a lithe Korean vampire with striking black eyes and equally black ears that poked out of his mop of hair.

He was also naked and way too close.

"How long did you spend grooming *your* hair today?" I raised my eyebrow, and Pocus' tail swished furiously in response. "Why should I trust a cat that looks like K-pop is missing its greatest star? Wait, I saw you perform on TV. Aren't you the cute new member of BTS?"

Pocus' eyes flashed, and his claws extended. I shivered with *claw envy*.

When he lowered his claws towards my crotch, I tried to shrink back. I knew now why I hated being tied down: you couldn't protect your prick from Halfling attack. I should add the policy to health and safety.

"Don't hurt my king." Midnight's voice was hard. "It's not worthy to attack someone who can't fight back."

"What he said," I mumbled.

Pouting, Pocus retracted his claws. Then he rested his head on Midnight's lap, rubbing his ears against his thigh, before offering a single lick across the head of his prick as if in apology.

Hey, it'd been *my* prick that he'd been threatening to slash.

"I'm guarding you." Pocus nuzzled closer.

I'd only been allowed to see my dad, cousin, and family werewolf in my confinement. But none of them had been able to *guard* me. In fact, we'd all been surviving in our own ways together. I was happy that Midnight had found another vampire in the academy, who'd been able to become a friend and protector, even if he *was* a psychopathic cat.

As a fellow cat, I resented his feline villainy. I was classifying him as my *pussy nemesis*.

I couldn't help the grin. I'd never had an animal nemesis before. I'd been missing out.

Midnight's expression softened. "You don't threaten my friends. You wouldn't claw Om just because he's got curly hair, would you?"

I perked up. I'd been wondering about the werewolf, since I'd seen him on my first night in the academy, caged in wolf form beside Hecate's altar in the courtyard. He'd been lonely, and I'd sworn to free him, just like I had Midnight. Plus, the pretty white Omega werewolf had curly blond hair in human form like me.

Now all the cool boys would want it.

I preened, and Midnight's eyes danced with an unexpected fondness.

Pocus blinked up at Midnight, wriggling his ass guiltily. "Om's our friend, and he has silky hair."

"Try out the mage's," Midnight offered like this was one of Aquilo's sister's swingers parties, and I was being offered around as a favor.

"No freebies," I yelped.

Things had become officially weird...okay, weirder...okay, kind of nice. I melted, as Pocus carded his fingers experimentally through my hair.

Pocus cocked his head, sitting back on his heels. "Silky but not as silky as Om's."

Bastard pussy nemesis.

"Whatever. It's not like I haven't won the Silkiest Hair ribbon for the last two years anyway. I normally wear pigtails to show them off, but with it being Torment Thursday, I wanted to give off more of a warrior vibe." I attempted to shrug but then remembered that I was tied down. I pretended that I was simply rolling my shoulders. *I pulled it off.* "Anyway, I'm known as the Wolf Lover, which is kind of like the Wolf Charmer, only it means that all wolves love me. Your Om will become my friend by magical charisma. It's fated."

Pocus' eyes narrowed. "Do all mages talk bullshit?"

"Only the best ones." I tilted my chin. "Plus, Puss in...*Nothing At All*...I wasn't lying about loving wolves. My best mate was a werewolf."

Pocus stuck his nose in the air. "Pocus doesn't believe you. Oms are particular about their packs."

Before Magic, when I'd yet to experience the *Kitten Incident*, when my transformation into a Birman had led to my banishment, the family werewolf had raised me as much as mum. Most witch families collared at least one Omega to use as a slave.

You were only meant to call them Omega (or Om) because in their culture as much as our witch one, they didn't deserve a name. Except, Glow had once told me that he had a twin, at least until they'd been separated and he'd become owned by the House of Jewels. His brother had been brave enough to name them.

I'd always thought that his brother must've been braver than me.

Once as a kid, when I'd been shaken by mum and then sent to the corner for running inside like I hadn't even been trained in suitable *male behavior*, the Om had slunk to sit behind me, whispering to distract me from my disgrace. He'd told me the story of his twin, even trusting me by telling me his secret name: Glow.

There were many treasures in the House of Jewels (mum had worn so many blue diamonds every day that she'd glittered like a magpie's wet dream), but Glow's name was priceless.

He didn't possess anything else, and no secret had ever been worth more.

To repay Glow, I'd helped him...okay, *lied*...to save him from whippings. I'd found that I had a talent at being inventive with the truth, but also, that lies were safer than the truth. When Glow had found out, however, he'd pulled me into my bedroom and closed the door.

"You're only a cub." Glow's soft Scottish voice had washed over me, calming me. He'd hugged me in a way that no one else, even dad, ever had. It was like he'd needed the gentle touch as much as me. "You don't risk yourself for a wolf. What kind of big brother would I be, if I didn't protect you?"

My breath had hitched.

Big brother?

Glow's eyes had widened at his own daring. A werewolf who saw themselves as part of a witch's family and not a *savage beast* could be flayed. *And that wasn't metaphorical.* After all, I had a white wolf fur rug across my bed.

Glow had drawn back like he'd expected me to reject him, but I'd only wound my arms more tightly around his neck.

I'd never wanted to let go; he was my safety.

Yet after that, Glow had helped...*lied*...for me. Except, when he was found guilty in my place of breaking a vase or being at fault for my lateness, he wasn't put into the corner but whipped.

I'd beg Glow to stop taking the blame, but he'd only smile and pat me on the head.

"Wee brother," Glow would say, "you're pack. You'll understand one day."

I understood now.

"My king is pack too," Midnight said with a certainty that made my heart beat faster. "He's a fellow whipping boy. We must look out for each other."

"*Pfft*, don't worry about it. He's just checking out

the new boyfriend." I smirked, as Pocus' ears flattened to his head. "How about we all get to know each other? Like, are you a cat or a dog person?"

What was I turning this into, *Interview with the Vampire*?

Midnight's laugh was delighted and surprised even him. I wished to kiss the joy from the corners of his lips and down his throat. Then make him laugh again, as I sucked every one of his feathers.

"He's a *cat* person," Pocus hissed.

Truth: I will find you alone and make a pincushion of your balls.

I paled, before clearing my throat. "Okay, how about: What was the best kiss you ever had?"

Midnight's tongue darted to wet his lips, before his eyes became hooded. "I was hanging upside down, see, next to this mage. Then he kissed me, and it was like for the first time in centuries, the darkness lifted, and I could *breathe* again."

My own breath stopped.

Heat flooded me, and my cheeks pinked. I could feel Midnight in that moment again in Juni's class-room, as cool as moonlight. His lips pressed to mine, and his soft wings wrapped around me.

I needed to touch him.

I brushed the tips of my fingers against Midnight's. "Wow, the mage was that good…?"

Midnight's longing gaze met mine.

All of a sudden, my chair was yanked backwards and twisted around. Disorientated, I gasped.

Then I had a lapful of incubus.

Bask straddled me, pushing his crotch against mine. I wasn't sending back the lapful of incubus, even if I didn't remember ordering it, nor the way that Magenta's arms wound around my neck from behind, and her head rested on my shoulder. The scent of the wild woods blew away the trapped earthy stench of Bacchus' classroom, and *I* could breathe again.

Magenta pressed a kiss to the fluttering pulse in my neck. "We need you to settle an argument."

"You know, I don't think anyone has ever said that to me before."

Now I truly wished that I'd been able to brush my hair for the occasion.

"Pocus is not surprised." The Halfling flounced back to his corner, swishing his tail.

His attempt at the haughty exit, however, was ruined by the way that his balls swung on each *flounce* of his hips.

I tore my gaze away from Pocus with difficulty, studying Sleipnir, instead. Sleipnir strolled to slouch against the wall with a pretend indolence that wasn't tricking me, since his hair was spiked to red and Mist snorted flickering smoke from his pocket.

They'd been arguing about something, and now I was the idiot caught in the middle...*literally*...while bound to a chair. I had an overwhelming urge to transform into Mr Fierce and roll into a ball.

I coughed, nervously. "Lay it on me. After all, I'm known as King Solomon, the Wise."

Bask snickered.

Magenta's hot breath gusted against my neck, and I shivered. "I'm certain that we're lucky to have such a wise man as our lover. So, please *help in our lively* debate. I believe that we should forgive Willoughby for his actions within the gym and love him. I made it more than clear that *no one* would be allowed to hurt him." Okay, there was her *wicked* voice; my prick took a healthy interest. "He's dangerous, I'll admit. But so are all of us."

"Now I have the floor." Sleipnir's eyes flashed with protectiveness. "I'm a monster, and in the gym, I recognized another. It doesn't matter whether we could love Willoughby. I don't want him to dirty Magenta. If we take the killer elf, we're wrecking him, the same as the fae."

"So, I may be King Solomon but since I wasn't allowed in Warrior Dueling, why do I get the sense that I missed something important?" I demanded.

"The elf hurt Magenta," Bask explained.

Bask wriggled his ass against me like he could win the argument by his slinkiness alone.

"You won't convince me by the power of your ass.

But you will give me an embarrassing hard-on just before the professor arrives."

Bask shot me a sly smile and wriggled again.

I groaned.

Was this the incubus form of ass torture? Although, I had a feeling that was a whole different kind of thing. Whatever it was, it was working.

"Away with you, the power of my arse could convince you into anything." When Bask's eyes glittered ruby, I gasped. *He wasn't wrong.* "Don't you desire the Princes — both of them — wrecked but not in the bad way, only all the *best* ways? I *want* to love them, Fox, but they're not like you."

My throat was suddenly too thick to speak.

What was I like? Virginal? Ignorant? Needy?

Panicked, I reddened because the memory of meeting Bask in the courtyard and the easy way that both Magenta as a ghost and he had kissed me (which had been my first ever kisses), and I'd melted into their love were the best of my life.

But what if I'd made a fool of myself? *What was wrong with me?*

Bask pressed his lips hurriedly to mine as if in apology. "You're perfect. But the thing of it is that they need to be…"

"Awakened," Magenta added, quietly.

Bask's eyes brightened. "The Stop Game!" He reached across to poke Midnight's chest. "Tell the

Princes that we're challenging them to a game tonight. If they refuse, then…"

"We'll inform Damelza about their dumb plan to prank their tutor," Sleipnir drawled. "I honestly can't wait to find out what Juni does when she hears about their plans to melt her with a bucket of water above their bedroom door."

Midnight drew in a shocked intake of breath. "You'd lie!"

Sleipnir shrugged. "Hello, I'm the son of Loki, god of mischief and mayhem."

And Sleipnir called *me* a hardass.

Bask stroked one hand along Midnight's tense shoulder. "Trust my slinky ass, it's fun. Stop Game will bring out their hidden desires. Let us please them. I played it all the time in the incubi harem. Well, the other bonded did."

I eyed Bask. "I'm filled with excitement to play it now."

"Of course you are."

Okay, that was a fail on my sarcasm.

"Sweet Pan, how about we stop all the talk of *wrecking*?" I pointed my chin at Sleipnir. "You're all bristled up like a hedgehog impersonation," Sleipnir flushed, "but you'd never follow through with it. Since I arrived, you've done nothing but help, comfort, and protect. Even Bask has attacked the Princes more than you."

Bask puffed up his chest. "Fear the mighty incubus."

I gentled my expression. "Of course, if Willoughby hurt Magenta, then how about I boot him in the balls? See, I'm the master of wise compromise. Just as soon as I can move my feet…"

Magenta's arms tightened around my neck. "Was I unclear about the not hurting the Prince?"

"Just a little kick…?" I hazarded.

This was the problem with whipping boys being banned from lessons. It led to inequalities like not knowing whose bollocks to boot.

"You won't damage my Princes," Midnight's voice was steely.

I twisted to look at him. *Whoops*. Why was he so loyal to Princes who forced him to crawl across snow or kneel for hours like a piece of school equipment?

Magenta met his gaze levelly. "I promise, we're only trying to help everybody."

Midnight ducked his head, and his despair blasted through my *Confess* in a sheet of black.

Truth*:* I no longer believe in promises.

"Hey," I called to Midnight, who looked up, "do you still believe in oaths?"

To my surprise, he perked up with a shy nod.

I smiled back. "Then I, the great shimage of the House of Jewels, give you my oath—"

"Careful," Magenta hissed.

I'd spent too many years being careful.

"…my oath to try to save even the dickish Princes of Rebel Academy, as well as you." I raised my eyebrow. "Will that do, my knight?"

Midnight's breath caught on *my knight*. I really should've learned more about vampire culture. Was that sort of like exchanging pet names or more like marriage vows?

Could I help the way that my heart leaped at the *marriage vows*?

"Thank you for bestowing your wisdom upon us." Magenta feathered kisses down my neck.

Bask ground his ass against me like he was a snake and I was his prey. His version of thanking me would've been epic, if I hadn't been trying to will down the hard-on tenting my pants.

I'd be *bestowing more than wisdom upon him* in a minute.

Prick, ignore the delicious incubus bouncing up and down on top of you…and the gorgeous witch…we will not be broken… At ease, prick, that's an order!

Sleipnir crossed his arms. "My brother, Fenrir, says that if you compare him to a hedgehog again, he'll put you over his knee."

I flushed, and my pupils dilated.

"Call him *Sonic*, I dare you." Bask brushed the back of his hand across my cheek.

Sleipnir's eyes danced with mischief.

Sleipnir wasn't my family, and this wasn't the attic. He'd never whip me. *I was safe.*

Plus, I was tied to a chair. *Good luck Sleipnir getting to my ass.*

I balled my hands "Son—"

Sleipnir's growl was cut off at the deep rumble that shook the room. There was the sudden aroma of mulled wine. I battled the panic that made my throat tighten, until I could only drag in quick, too rapid breaths.

Bound, I couldn't even crouch under the lab tables like my feline side craved to. Next to me, Midnight stilled.

Out of the wall, branches of purple ivy coiled like sinuous vines to tangle into the outline of Bacchus. Then she stepped forward, and the vines formed fully into the shape of the Immortals' Tutor of the East Wing, who was also the most brilliant American witch, who'd been hired by the academy to teach Spells, Hexes, and Potions.

I was at the professor's mercy for the lesson, and as she strode towards me, her eyes flashed with fury.

CHAPTER THIRTEEN

Rebel Academy, Thursday September 5th

FOX

Wⁿhen Bacchus stalked towards me like the unholy mix of an eruption of magma and an avalanche, my heart thudded in my chest.

100, 99, 98...

I forced myself to count back from a hundred to calm myself. I was the whipping boy guinea pig in Bacchus' lesson. Magenta had made me soft. The way that her arms curled around my neck to protect me, rather than to hurt, had confused my Mage Radar.

Some witches were *truly* wicked. They also made me want to wet my pants.

Bacchus' purple dress, which was pinned at her

shoulder by a moth brooch, swept across the floor. Her midnight hair fell to her waist in a silky veil. My breath stuttered, as she raised her arm, and a short iron spear appeared in her hand, which was covered in ivy and topped with a pine cone.

Magenta stood up, clapping her hands. "Ah, how charming. You wish to show off your wand again."

Magenta appeared to enjoy playing with both magma and snow.

I winced, but didn't take my gaze off Bacchus, whose cat-like hazel eyes swirled amber.

"Shall we see just what my bacchal thyrsus can do?" She waved her thyrsus at me

I was glad that wasn't a euphemism.

Then I yelped, as my chair spun around to face the front of the classroom, at the same time as Midnight's. The breath was knocked out of me. Bask tumbled off my lap and into a sexy heap on the floor. I'd never even known that heaps *could* be sexy.

"You've bruised my arse," Bask wailed. Then his eyes narrowed. "No one reduces the pettability of an incubi's arse."

Magenta crouched next to Bask, helping him onto his feet and circling his hip in a way that made the skin of my own hip tingle like I could feel her phantom touch; *I longed to*. "I assure you that you'll always be pettable to me. Bruises and all."

Bacchus' smile was beautiful but wilted my prick,

until there was no longer any risk of me embarrassing myself with tented pants.

Look at that, the witch equivalent of Anti-Viagra. Maybe I could bottle it.

"Calm your cutie pie ass down. Such angst over mere marking!" When she stalked closer, Sleipnir stepped protectively in front of Bask. "I should delight in such power over you, Crave, because you hand it to me like you give away power to your Duchess." Bask became ashen, and Magenta linked her arm around him like she could protect him from Bacchus' words or his own memories. *Could any of us protect him from the Duchess?* "You're a panther and panthers don't need others to acknowledge their beauty. Do you want to be as wild, free, and dark as I know all my Immortals to be or a tamed cat?"

She clicked her fingers. "Here, Pet 9."

I flinched. I hated that witches only called their familiars by numbers, stealing their names, just like werewolves were only called *Omega*.

Pocus crawled to Bacchus. His tail hung between his legs, however, and his ears were flattened to his head. Even if he was my *pussy nemesis*, I still cringed at his humiliation.

And had Bacchus just complimented Bask?

Bask appeared caught between preening and wanting to dash to Pocus and scratch behind his ears.

My feline side, which was clawing at me to step

235

up in solidarity even for my nemesis, forced me to insist, "But look at that adorable tail." Pocus' ears perked up. "I mean, sure the jungle sounds fun, but where are all the feathery things to chase or the belly rubs? And then you'd miss out on the pillow nests and the drugs..." Sleipnir raised a censorious eyebrow at me. "Catnip takes you on a serious trip. How many panthers ever get high on catnip or...?"

"All students to their seats." Bacchus' gaze was fixed on me so intently that I shivered. Yet Midnight's fingers swept across mine, and when I glanced at him out of the corner of my eye, his smile made drawing her attention worth it. *My shivering mage balls hoped.* "Or do I need to tie you all down to your stools? Although, I do adore that my chaos has caught on."

"It was *my dad's* chaos moment first," Sleipnir muttered.

Bacchus' lips twitched, but she turned away as if she hadn't heard him. She carded her fingers through Pocus' mop of hair, allowing him to rest his head against her leg.

Sleipnir and Magenta sat on stools at the lab table at the back, which was beside a window that looked out over the courtyard. Bask slipped behind the table at the front. He winked at me, and I relaxed.

All of a sudden, roots exploded up, curling over the windows and blacking them out. The classroom was cast into twilight.

"I don't want the Princes moaning that I haven't catered for the special needs of their vampire whipping boy." Bacchus twirled around, before her eyes flashed amber. Her ancient magic scented the air. My pulse raced at the sudden threat like fire had sparked. Her voice was deceptively soft but this kitty wasn't deceived. "Where are the Princes, darlings?"

Sleipnir straightened. *Why was he looking so smug?* "Hey, the room could do with a couch. I vote for a silk one with love heart patterns."

I blinked. Was transfiguration Bacchus' punishment for lateness?

Bask bounced on his seat. "If it pleases you, I vote for Lysander to be transformed into a Pomeranian and Willoughby to be a satchel. Then I can carry the dog around with me."

I imagined Lysander's outraged little face all yappy and peering out of a satchel.

Please go with the Pomeranian...please, please, please.

I brightened. "Do I get a vote?"

Midnight kicked his foot against mine. *Oww.* "Do I?" He snapped.

"No one is getting transfigured into anything," Magenta declared. "Black cats, you'd imagine that England had become a democracy with votes for all."

I forgot that as a Victorian witch she'd missed out on some pretty important news.

Should I tell her that the non-magical in this country had also banned child labor, closed the work-houses, and stopped corporal punishment?

Except that much advancement in one go might explode her mind.

The door banged open, and Lysander rushed into the room, dragging Willoughby after him. Lysander leaned against the table, panting and out of breath.

Willoughby straightened like he was on parade, deliberately stepping closer to Bacchus. Yet his gaze was dazed like he'd been pushed deep inside.

When Lysander looked up and met Bacchus' unimpressed expression, he paled. "E-excuse our l-lateness, but it's n-not my f-fault," he gasped, struggling to let go of the table. Had they run the whole way here across the castle? *Where had they been?* Lysander usually looked composed, but now his hair was dampened to his forehead with sweat, and his blazer looked creased like he'd been in a fight *or punished.* Unfortunately, corporal punishment hadn't been stopped within the magical world, which meant that amusingly, we hadn't advanced as much since Victorian times as the humans that we thought ourselves superior to. "Our T-tutor wished to...talk...with us after Prince Willoughby—"

Bacchus held up her long-nailed finger to silence him. "Am I ever interested in excuses?"

Numbly, Lysander shook his head.

Bacchus pointed her thyrsus (to my shock), not at Lysander, but rather at Willoughby. Instantly, Willoughby transformed in a golden swirl of glitter into a sky-blue silk throne.

Lysander looked like he was about to hurl, and so did Magenta.

"What right do you have to talk of power when you so misuse it?" Magenta whispered.

"I have true immortality, girl, and true power, which is neither used nor misused. It simply *is*. I exist the same as the night, and just as that can't misuse the dark, neither can I." Bacchus shot a glance at Sleipnir. "You requested silk."

"I take it back," Sleipnir muttered. "I know what it feels like to have your ass on me all lesson, and even a Prince doesn't deserve that."

Bacchus arched her brow. "Men have begged to feel my ass on their faces."

Okay, now it was *me* about to hurl.

Lysander ran his shaky hand along the arm of the Willoughby Throne. *Could Willoughby feel what had happened to him?*

Lysander cast a horror filled glance at Bacchus. "But it was my fault that we were late."

"No, it wasn't." Bacchus sauntered to the throne, sweeping her dress around her. Pocus prowled at her side. Then she threw herself down on the Willoughby Throne, which let out a yelp. Pocus leaped onto her lap and circled, before he sprawled across her. He pawed at the silk. I itched to rub his fur the wrong way to see how he liked being messed with. "You were about to pin the blame on this one." She booted the leg of the throne, and it howled. "So, now he can make himself useful, and you can think about the consequences of *not* taking responsibility."

Lysander was ashen. "One is truly sorry."

"Hey, there it is." Bacchus leaned forward; her eyes glinted. "Isn't it a shame that you didn't open with that?"

Lysander flushed, looking down. His wings drooped, and he hugged them around himself. I had the sudden urge to hug him as well.

I wonder if *fae kink* was catching.

When Lysander attempted to slink to a seat at the back of the classroom, Bacchus stopped him. "Park your princely ass down in the front next to my Immortals, where I can keep an eye on you. I guess that you'd better not be late next time."

Lysander bristled. "I prefer to sit—"

"In the shadows because you're all mysterious…?" Bask asked, teasingly. He patted the stool next to him.

Lysander huffed, slamming down onto the stool next to Bask. It was weird how different it was to look out at the classroom and see the Immortals and Princes sitting together, just like Midnight and I were next to each other as whipping boys. It didn't matter what rival Wing we'd been forced into; we'd still face this together. When I saw Lysander sitting next to Bask, they no longer seemed different.

The academy forced us to wear different uniforms, eat and sleep separately, and compete in trials against each other. But we were all students and prisoners here. *We were the same.*

By the way that the other Immortals were eying Lysander, I had the feeling that they sensed the same thing. Had Bacchus placed him there on purpose?

Bacchus' long nails rapped on the Willoughby Throne. "As today is Torment Thursday, we'll be studying hexes." *Of course, we would.* "Other academies have to study from books, but magic doesn't come from dried up pages. It's in our hearts, souls, and the connections between everything living and the dead. This academy has always been lucky enough to have whipping boys. You can create your own hexes and test them out on your whipping boy."

"It's funny how you see me as a girl," Magenta's voice was tight and clipped, but her mists swirled around her at the same time as her magic sparkled, "but I'll still hex *your* immortal behind if you suggest such harm to my lover. It's charming that you forget I've traveled through the veils and defeated death. How great do you believe my magic to be?"

Bacchus laughed. "Not as great as *mine*. I've made the homes of creatures across *all* veils my bitches. I've journeyed to realms that you don't even know exist. Your magic is linked to nature, but mine is linked to worlds *beyond* nature. We can battle over who has the biggest broomstick later, but this lesson is to learn to hex. So, Lysander and you have the strongest magic. Step forward and start throwing your best hexes. Let me see what I have to work with."

When Lysander sidled to stand in front of me, I tensed. He wouldn't meet my eye. Only Midnight's fingers, still stroking mine, steadied me.

This was going to hurt.

Would it be the *Poison Ivy Penis Hex*? *Nerd Social Awkwardness Curse*? *Please, not the Justin Bieber on a Perpetual Loop Hex…*

Magenta glared at Bacchus, storming to join Lysander. To my shock, Lysander smiled reassuringly at Midnight.

Then Lysander shook his head. "My royal personage failed to take responsibility for Willoughby. It's a lesson about leadership that I already know, and I'm ashamed that I forgot it. One won't fail again. My apologies, but I won't be partaking in this lesson." He tilted up his chin. "My noble self refuses."

Well, blow me down with his golden feathers.

Magenta stared at Lysander with wide eyes. "Well said. I refuse too."

"*Ehm*, thanks for not hexing me," I ventured.

I didn't think that they heard me. They were too

242

busy staring into each other's eyes. Perhaps, I could play some violin music for them...if my hands weren't tied down...or I knew how to play the violin. Who knew that not torturing my foxy ass would be what united them or brought out Lysander's very, very, *very* deeply buried nobility.

"Mutiny, huh?" Bacchus examined her nails. "Will you hold to this defiance, even if I inform your guardian?"

Fear flickered across Lysander's face, before he was able to hide it. "Better that I suffer than my whip-ping boy."

Bacchus' lips quirked. "You do know that you were given a *whipping boy* precisely so that *he* could suffer for *you*?"

Lysander stiffened. "One wouldn't like to be boringly conventional."

Wow, he was a Rebel Fae.

"I take back at least fifty percent of the rude things that I've said about you." Sleipnir gave an approving nod, and his hair transformed to aquamarine at the same time as Mist's mane. "Hey, let's not go crazy: forty percent."

"You're too kind," Lysander deadpanned.

Bacchus trailed her hand down Pocus' spine, and he purred, arching. "Of course, rebellion can be as conventional as obedience, and in this case, twice as stupid. I won't force you into anything. I can taste the ancient paths of fate winding through this castle and tugging on all our tails. So, all I'll do is point out that if you refuse to take part in my class, then you'll lose it. Who won Warrior Dueling?"

"The Immortals," Magenta said, softly.

Lysander's hands balled into fists. *Uh oh, the Rebel Fae was about to wave the white flag.* I knew that I'd jinxed it by imagining the feel of his golden wings on my prick. Wait, I hadn't said that out loud, right?

I peeked up at Lysander. He still looked furious but less like he wanted to kick my furry ass and more like he wanted to save it.

No more daydreams about fae's feathers circling my balls.

"Then it'll be *your* fault that the Princes lose the Rebel Cup." Baccus scrutinized Lysander, whose shoulders slumped. *She'd wrecked him.* I understood now that he cared in his own way for the Princes like Magenta did for us, although his way included more manhandling and kneeling than kisses and love. "Curse will have his wings broken because those are the stakes." I linked my pinkie with Midnight's at his whimper. Why did it boot me in the balls worse to think about his beautiful wings being broken than my own death? "And at the Dragon Tournament, Prince Titus will witness the Rebel Cup being presented to the Immortals for the first time in a decade. Do you honestly think he'll believe you redeemed or wish to bring you home after that shame?"

"Stop this cruelty," Magenta hissed. Her magic sparkled around her. "Why in Hecate's name are you crushing him?"

"It's called motivation, darling." Bacchus sighed. "After all, this is your chance to save the mage. *You're* the reason that the original mage died a slow death, walled up alive. I kind of thought that you'd care more about saving this one. My mistake."

Magenta's gaze shot to mine like she was pleading for something. Her scent of yew trees cocooned me like she could protect me even now.

My chest was tight, and my breath was raspy. I'd known about the original mage, but the idea of being walled up alive had been theoretical. Now it was as real as Magenta. When she'd been first alive, there'd been a mage and because of her, he'd died in the walls of this castle.

Would I be executed in the same way?

How was it that the fact I only had two lessons left to save my life had only just truly sunk in?

"You must breathe," Midnight murmured. "You're paler than a ghost, see."

My bark of laughter was close to a sob. Bask shot me a concerned glance. I'd known a ghost, and I wasn't one yet: I was just a dead fox walking.

"Are you both motivated yet?" Bacchus leaned back in the Willoughby Throne.

Lysander's gaze was intent on Magenta's. "I shall win the Rebel Cup. No one is breaking my vampire's wings."

A slow smile spread across Bacchus' face. "Now that's the kind of Rebel Academy spirit that I'm looking for! I adore battles between Prefects."

Magenta paced closer to Lysander. "Look at that, *my* motivation has just been set alight as well. I'm quite aflame with hate for a certain fae right now."

Lysander's wings burst out in a display of dominance, cradling around Magenta. "And my blue-blooded self feels something quite the opposite of love for a certain witch."

They were so close that their lips were almost touching. I bit my own lip. They were either going to kiss or...

Wait, why was I hoping that the kissing option was even possible?

I tightened my pinkie around Midnight's, sneaking a glance at his expression. He was watching Lysander and Magenta with as much rapt shock and delight as me.

"Well," Bacchus said, "the winding paths of fate are unexpected." She guided Pocus by his collar onto the floor, before striding to stand behind the two Prefects. Pocus huddled by the leg of the throne. "I delight in the frenzy. Do you know what I can do with this?"

Why did witches always gift me these opportunities? *Bad mouth, don't you dare say it...*

"Stick it where the sun don't shine?" *Bad, bad mouth, no sugary treats for you.*

"Conduct a light orchestra?" Bask fluttered his eyelashes.

Sleipnir cocked his head. "Role play the good witch in the *Wizard of Oz?* Hey, does glitter explode out of the end of your wand when you're excited?"

Bacchus' eyes swirled with amber; her ancient magic spelled the air with the aroma of mulled wine. *Bad mouth look what you've done: you've driven her to drink.* "It whips men and women into a frenzy. I've been inciting true fervor for thousands of years. You've seriously no idea about true love or hate. In frenzy, there's nothing but the freedom of wild emotion. Once, I belonged to a cult where we could give in to every urge. There'll never be anything so liberating. I could tear you limb from limb or screw you until you scream."

"Could I go with the tearing limb from limb option?" I asked.

Was this appropriate from a professor?

Yet I had a sense that Bacchus was no longer herself. It was like the power of her own thyrsus had possessed her. I stared at the thyrsus with more respect than before.

Sleipnir slipped out of his seat, approaching her with his hand raised like she was a stallion that hadn't been broken yet. "Yeah, we're all scared of your frenzy and screw wand now. So, why don't you sit your ass back down on the comfy elf throne?"

"The son of Loki would dare speak to me? *You sit down.* Loki's the one who destroyed the frenzy," Bacchus snarled. Reluctantly, Sleipnir stalked back to his stool. "He made the music and the dancing stop. We shall break him, just as he broke everything of ours." Sleipnir stilled; his breathing was too rapid. "Justice comes to everyone, even to gods." Her gaze swept across Lysander and Magenta. "As well as Princes and Immortals."

When Bacchus raised the thyrsus, I attempted a watery smile at Bask who looked ready to vault the lab table to protect me. I didn't want anyone to suffer for me. I also didn't want to be hit by some crazy Frenzy Hex but if I could take it instead of the other Immortals, then I'd beg for it.

After all, I was the whipping boy.

"Visual aids are honestly way more effective than words. You choose: which whipping boy will demonstrate The Frenzy?" Bacchus swung her thyrsus like a pendulum between Midnight and me.

Me, me, me...

Lysander and Magenta shook their heads at the same time, but I noticed that they both took a step away from each other. To me, that was one point to Bacchus.

Then to my shock, Midnight said, "As I have Fallen, it's all right, my prince. Pick me."

"Hold your tongue," Lysander sneered, but I didn't miss how his voice shook more with fear than anger. "Do you presume to tell me what to do? One should've known that this new ill-disciplined whipping boy would corrupt you. You've earned a punishment after class."

Fae. Kink. Officially. Dead.

Midnight's wings trembled, until his chair rattled, but he still begged, "Please, choose me."

Lysander stared hard at the floor, clasping his hands behind his back like he was on parade. Had he been trained in the military? "Cast The Frenzy on the Immortal."

When Bacchus stalked towards me with amber magic swirling from the end like a promise of loss of control over even my own mind, I couldn't help the undignified squeak. I wrenched my ankles against the restraints. Sweat slipped down the back of my neck.

At least it was me and not Midnight.

Magenta stepped in front of me, blocking Bacchus like she was simply claiming the first dance with me. "I regret to inform you that no one is harming my lovers. Do test your little fervor on me, instead. I'd love to see the explosive possibilities when combined with my Wickedly Charmed magic, and your explanations to the Principal."

Bacchus shook her head.

Magenta's eyes narrowed at Lysander. "It appears that I wasn't clear enough with you about the *not hurting* rule."

Lysander's wings beat angrily. "But if you don't choose, then you're forcing me to shoulder this responsibility alone. Why does everyone always expect that of me?" *Wait, were we still talking about throwing hexes or The Frenzy?* "If I must become the villain to save my...save Curse...then I shall." He hung his head. "Haven't I played that role long enough?"

When Magenta's gaze met mine, it was anguished. I understood because if both Lysander and her didn't play along, then the stakes were Midnight's wings and my life. Yet she was still waiting for my permission like Midnight had given his.

Weirdly, I'd expected her to know that she already had it. I trusted her in a way that I never had any other woman and definitely not any witch.

I'd resurrected her, but she'd brought me to life.

I bit my lip. "Come on, I'm ready to win this today with my spectacular demonstration of fervor. I spent my teenage weekends running around naked in the woods in a frenzy. My bare ass was a terror to the local non-magicals."

Bask snickered, which was better than the pale anguish for me that'd been on his face a moment before.

Lysander's tongue darted out to wet his dry lips. "Exciting as it would be to witness Confess' *bare ass* in a frenzy, I request permission to discipline him by my own method. I'm well-trained with a—"

"Whip...?" The thyrsus transformed into a thin riding whip; it was the type that would slash across the thick hide of a horse.

And my hide was pale and soft.

There'd been stables attached to the House of Jewels. My sister, Hartley, had been given her own pony at the age of three. I'd been desperate to ride as well but as son to a witch family, I'd been forbidden. They hadn't wanted me to injure myself and so reduce my value.

Before I'd been locked away, Hartley had sneaked me out one night to sit on her pony, leading me into the paddock behind the stables. We'd laughed together at the adventure, and I'd thought that my sister would never allow me to be traded to a wife who treated me like mum did dad.

I'd been innocent enough to believe that she wouldn't become like the other witches.

It'd been worth the month's grounding to the house

for me, when we'd been discovered, and the lecture on Husband Management for Hartley. I'd never ridden again. But I recognized the whip. Ironic, as a shifter, that I'd now been transformed into the horse.

Irony sucked.

Yet still, Lysander hesitated.

Perhaps, he was deciding whether to stripe my thigh, shoulder, or balls... *Decisions, decisions.*

I let go of Midnight's pinkie. Instead, I clenched my hands, digging my nails into my palms. It always helped to focus on a small amount of pain that you'd created, rather than the large amount of pain that someone else was about to visit on your balls.

I pushed my nails harder into my palms.

"Amusing that you believe I shall allow you to whip him anymore than hex him." Magenta's gaze was steadying.

I'd never had anyone who refused to allow my whipping before. Dad, Glow, or even Aquilo would beg for mercy on my behalf. Yet that was different to someone who stated that it wasn't *allowed.*

It was almost like Magenta believed that it wasn't right that a mage was disciplined.

I could be strong with her by my side.

Lysander raised the whip above his head; his gaze met mine. Yet I'd suffered enough whippings to know that he should've slashed the implement down by now. So much for his boasting about being well-trained.

Why was he hesitating?

When Bask and Sleipnir both rose out of their seats like they planned to either tear the whip out of Lysander's hand or tear him in half (possibly both), vines grew out of their stools, tying them down. Magenta huffed in protest, swirling out her mists to snatch the end of the riding whip. Lysander's eyes widened, and he snarled, caught in a tug of war with Magenta.

Bacchus smiled. "If you don't complete the assignment, every student shall fall to The Frenzy. I haven't orchestrated an orgy in decades. Honestly, I'm kind of hoping that you go for the orgy. Then all you have to do is let go..."

"Desist," Lysander growled. "My princely personage shall not partake in such debauchery."

Magenta yanked, dragging Lysander sprawling against her. "I knew that you were a virgin!" Lysander pinked, and his jaw clenched. "Don't worry, my lovers showed me some wonderful tricks, and I'm most certainly not one anymore. As soon as we're able to take the stick out of your behind, then I'm certain that they'll show you as well."

"Take your hands off me." Lysander righted himself, batting Magenta away. He shook his whip at her like it was his wand or prick. "There shall be no orgies, taking of virginities, or other...*things*." His wings fluttered. Of course, he didn't yet know about the Stop Game. I had a feeling that Bask had plenty of *things* in store for Lysander. "Just let me beat the mage. I don't understand why you're so outraged. I've been disciplined in such a way since I was too small to fly."

For the first time, Magenta's expression softened, as she assessed Lysander. "I watched too many of the Rebels being beaten when I was a child. I swore that I wouldn't watch it happen again." Lysander blinked at her in confusion. "What was that charming speech you made about responsibility with Willoughby as the example...? I took it to heart, which means that as Prefect, *I* take responsibility for my whipping boy. *Whip me.*"

No, no, no... This was Glow all over again, except without the fur, the collar or... Okay, she wasn't a werewolf slave but she was still about to take my punishment.

I wouldn't be able to bear that.

When Lysander's gaze faltered, shocked, she merely arched her brow.

"On Tyr's cock," Sleipnir growled, "if you even think of raising a hand against Magenta, then you'll discover what it feels like to be destroyed by a god."

I shivered. *Wow, that'd even frightened my balls back into my body.*

Lysander hurled the whip at Bacchus, who caught

it. "Why do you all believe the worst of me? One most certainly would *never* strike a woman."

Thank Pan... I slumped in my seat.

Magenta snorted. "But you'd hit a defenseless man?"

I shifted, attempting to puff out my chest. *Defenseless* stung. I might not have the use of my hands, feet...okay, any of my body...but I still had my lies and the power of Confess.

Lysander shrugged. "Of course, if needs must."

What else had I expected from an Unseelie Fae? They probably taught How to be a Haughty Jerk classes in their nurseries.

Bacchus swished the whip through the air, transforming it back into her thyrsus. "Prepare yourself for The Frenzy..."

Midnight gasped, and Pocus wound around his legs comfortingly. I cringed, waiting to be overtaken by the desperate need to rip off Magenta's clothes and screw. Although, I always felt like that, which I put down to her gorgeousness, being locked alone since before puberty, and being a bloke.

"This is all *your* fault..." Lysander spat.

"What a truly mature fae you are," Magenta spat back.

Bacchus rapped the thyrsus against the floor, and I jumped. "There it is. Now you're ready for the lesson to begin."

I tilted my chin. "I believe I speak for all us...*what*?"

"Hexes or curses aren't created by the power of your magic but the strength of your *intent*. How much do you mean it? For that, you need an emotion, and love and hate are the most potent. Seriously, it all comes down to the connection between the one who casts and the victim. Mild dislike," Bacchus' lips curled, "will create nothing but a smoldering hex. For one that hits like dragon fire, you must have *hate*."

"Not a problem," Lysander sneered.

I glanced over at Midnight. His eyes were creased with concern. He knew as well as me that Bacchus had played the two Prefects against each other to fuel that hate.

I didn't fancy a hex as powerful as *dragon fire* blasted at my face.

"There's no such thing as a hex, which isn't directed at someone specific. They're darkly intimate." Bacchus' eyes became hooded. *I hoped that wasn't her sex face.* "Hexes are fury, hate, and revenge. They're from your imagination and soul. You can't lie to a hex." Bacchus's gaze darted between Magenta and Lysander. "Create a hex in your mind; it doesn't need to be voiced. Imagine your enemy..." By the way that Magenta and Lysander glared at each other, it was clear that they hadn't had to think hard. "Then test it on your rival's whipping boy."

"I said that the mage wouldn't be harmed," Magenta gritted out.

Bacchus' eyes narrowed. "And I gave you the choice that you'd lose the Rebel Cup, and he'll die if you don't."

"It's not like you need it, but you have my permission. Both of you. Hex me up." I forced myself to smile at Magenta, as if getting hexed by a fae in front of the rest of the class was a refreshing start to the day like an extra shot of coffee. "It's not as if the fae has enough darkness or imagination in him to scare me. The pampered prince probably thinks denying me golden spoons to eat off is a curse."

Lysander sidled closer to me, caging me in with his wings. Okay, not intimidating at all...if that means *very* intimidating. "Be assured that there are many deadly things held within my imagination. One could crush your curly head, explode your guts, or tear your magic from you like peeling your very essence from your Soul…"

"My Prince, *don't*," Midnight warned with more steel than I'd been expecting.

Lysander's sharp teeth glinted, as he smiled. "One merely stated that I *could*."

"You're lying," Bacchus snapped. "The hex must come from your truth, which is the line between love and hate. Hey, even I can feel it. Think of your enemy and then imagine what you wish most. The hex will do the rest."

I shook, and my shoulders were tight.

Not the Poison Ivy Penis Hex, not the Poison Ivy Penis...

Lysander leaned closer. His grin was malevolent. Then his eyes opened comically wide, and he stiffened, as if he'd accidentally cast the hex on himself, rather than me. Except, if the hex acted on the truth in your soul, almost like my own power of Confess, maybe that was how it worked.

As if he couldn't stop himself, Lysander leaned down, cupping my cheek with an aching tenderness. Then he kissed my cheek like he was a suitor in a romance novel.

I'd deny to my foxy deathbed both the way that my breath caught and my prick thickened against my thigh.

Lysander's thumb caressed my skin like I was woven glass. When he ducked his head to touch his lips to mine, Magenta dragged him away from me. His gaze was dazed, as he stared at her.

Wait, Lysander hadn't been kissing me. He'd been acting out his desire on his enemy...*on Magenta.* I couldn't help the twinge of regret at that.

"You wish to kiss your enemy...?" Magenta demanded.

Lysander wrenched his arm away from her, stumbling backward and landing on his ass. He reddened. "The s-spell made me d-do it. It must've gone wrong."

I couldn't help the flinch, when he wiped his hand across his mouth.

"I warned you that hexes were intimate or are you as keen as me to start the orgy?" Bacchus threw herself back down in the Willoughby chair. "Shall we see if our wicked witch loves or hates her enemy?"

I didn't miss the way that Midnight straightened and his eyes lit up. *Was he hoping for a kiss from Magenta?*

Unfortunately, I'd imagine that a Posion Ivy Penis hex was more likely.

"I cast the hex, and the Immortals' whipping boy *suffered* the consequences," Lysander pointed out. I grimaced like Lysander's gentle kiss had been a terrible trial, although my perky prick called me a liar. "Surely, the assignment is complete."

I realized that Lysander was frightened to discover the truth: whether Magenta loved or hated him.

I'd bet that it was a mixture of both.

Bacchus rapped her thyrsus against the floor. "You're lucky that I'm so soft. Ezekiel must be rubbing off on me." Now I grimaced for real. I didn't want to hear about the kinkiness between those two in the staffroom. "He sometimes calls draws, right?"

I didn't know whether to sigh with relief or slump

in defeat. We'd neither won nor lost. At least, there'd be no Punish and Reward Game.

Our next class was the Hunt, and nothing good had ever happened to a fox, during a hunt.

Bacchus' eyes glinted with malicious glee. "That means whoever wins the Hunt, wins the Rebel Cup. See how chaos brings everything down to this final crucial moment? On your final class, balances life and death."

CHAPTER FOURTEEN

Rebel Academy, Thursday September 5th

FOX

For a fox (even an Arctic one with pretty cream fur), a Hunt only ended two ways: your blood dying the snow crimson or your fluffy tail waving *goodbye,* as you ran and hid.

Was Saving Your Ass on the lesson plan? I should drop it into Damelza's Suggestion Box.

My heart beat wildly, as I lowered my head in my Arctic fox form, slinking through the trees of the Dead Wood. My fur camouflaged me against the snow. My senses were enhanced, and I sniffed, overwhelmed by the scents of the yew trees and the thrumming magic.

Magenta.

Even though I'd had to leave her behind with Sleipnir at the trees' edges, I could sense her with my every breath. She was in the magic of the wood. As my paws pressed against the cold snow, I could even sense her pulsing through the earth like she was kissing me on each step.

I was safe, despite the fact that if I lost this hunt, I'd be killed.

I wasn't alone.

The woman who I loved would always be with me in the academy because she *was* the academy. I shivered as an icy breeze *whooshed* down my back.

I didn't expect Magenta to save me. I simply needed her to stay with me. Now *I'd* save my own furry ass.

Although, when Magenta had seen the white Omega werewolf at Juni's side, prowling towards Lysander and me with his amber eyes glowing and his teeth bared, she'd rushed forward in protest. Juni's spell had whipped the branches of the trees around her and Sleipnir, trapping them against its trunk.

Why had Magenta paled, as her breath had become ragged? Juni had held *me* upside down by my ankles in her class. Yet the fact that I was rating Tree Trunk Bondage, showed that my education hadn't turned out how I'd always hoped.

Anyway, the Omega was Midnight's friend and a prisoner as well. The witches didn't understand that werewolves didn't intimidate mages because we were on the same side. Except, when they were set on us during a Hunt, of course.

I sniffed, yawning as I turned in a circle. Didn't they know that I was nocturnal in this form? This was cruel and unusual punishment. I should put in a complaint to the *get lost, mage, you're lucky that we didn't throw you to the wolves.*

Wait, I *had* been thrown to the wolves...

Above my head, something golden fluttered. I growled, darting deeper into the shadows.

My only consolation was that Lysander had been thrown to the wolves as well.

I glanced up at Lysander, as he half flew and half leaped from tree to tree. Grudgingly, I admitted that it was a clever tactic. This was a fox and fae hunt. Whoever was caught by the Omega first lost the Hunt.

The stakes were only my life and Midnight's wings. *Brilliant.*

The skill with which Lysander swung between the branches made me wish that I'd taken my own exercise regime more seriously than shaking my feline ass to funk. Lysander would wreck me in a straight race or fight. To be fair, he'd wreck me in most warrior style things but could he recite every line from *Peter Pan*?

I allowed myself to preen on the thought for a single moment (I did an epic impression of Hook... okay, Aquilo had played Hook, Glow had always been cast as Peter, and I'd been...was it confusing to wank over Tinker Bell when you'd been cast as her *every single time*...?), then I padded forward, eying the snow-banks in case the Omega was planning to ambush me.

He was as camouflaged as me with his white coat.

Lysander flew deeper into the wood like a golden hummingbird. *He was breath-taking.* But I was still calling unfair advantage on the wings.

A fox, however, could be sneaky.

I dashed behind the snowbanks towards a stream. The Omega would be hunting by our scents. His was deliciously sweet vanilla, and my nose quivered to catch it on the breeze. I didn't know how *I* smelled in this form, but Juni had allowed the Omega to bury his nose into my fur and then uncomfortably close to Lysander's cock and balls. Lysander had yelped in outrage, reddening. The Omega's touch, however, had made my sensitive fur stand up in pleasure.

Who said that the fox never won the hunt? *Wait, everybody...?*

I smirked (I'm talented enough to pull that off in any animal form, even hedgehog), as I leaped into the stream, only for my eyes to widen, as I remembered that it was frozen.

Mage's balls...

Over a decade stuck inside had sort of destroyed my natural instincts *and my common sense.*

I whined as I hit the ice. My little legs splayed out underneath me, until I looked like a furry clown with a ludicrously long tail. My ears flattened on my head. I slid round and round and...

Landed on my ass.

Mournfully, I struggled up.

Arooo...

My fur stood on end. The howl came from the riverbank behind me. Did I say river? It was more like a stream...okay, trickle of water. It looked large, however, when you were smaller than Hecate's ego but bigger than Pan's cock (which was the new scientific description of all animals, in case you didn't know).

I froze.

The Omega had caught me.

I. Was. Dead.

And not the Magenta type of dead, return as a ghost, and then be resurrected. The dead that you don't come back from.

I yelped, as fangs bit into the back of my neck and lifted me into the air. Yet they were gentle like a mummy cat snatching her naughty kitten by the scruff of the neck.

Wow, that was humiliating.

Bring on the manly savaging.

The Omega growled.

He couldn't hear my thoughts, could he? I swallowed, nervously.

The Omega dropped me onto the snow in a heap, before staring down at me. His fur glittered, and his golden claws looked sharper now that he was free from his cage. Still, he was as beautiful as I remembered.

Was this it? Had I been officially caught?

I whimpered, ducking my head. My heart pounded in my ears. Then I peeked up at the Omega. He cocked his head, nudging me with his nose, before licking my ear.

Woah, personal space. *But then wolves always had a thing about licking.*

I'd failed Magenta and the other Immortals. I let out a desperate *gekkering*. They'd relied on me in this class, and I hadn't been able to outfox a single wolf. If I wasn't going to pay for it with my life anyway, I'd have to give back my fox credentials.

Damelza would be delighted. She hated mages and believed them weak. Why did I have to prove her right?

I didn't know if the Immortals would understand that I'd never expected to experience love, friendship, acceptance, kisses, or the type of connection that I had with them.

I'd give a lifetime in the attic for just this one

week. I couldn't regret being sent to Rebel Academy because I'd spent it with my Immortals.

The Omega rolled his eyes.

***Truth*:** I'm only playing at big, bad wolf.

Embarrassed, I stopped my mournful *gekkering*, twisting to peer up at the wolf. He smiled at me through a mouthful of my fur. Then he spat me out, and I landed on my ass again (which was happening way too often for my ass' liking).

If it wasn't for my Power of Confess, which told me that I had less to fear from the werewolf who loomed above me than from the snowflakes on the tip of my nose, then I'd have been sitting in a puddle by now that wasn't melted water.

I'd embarrassed myself more than enough already than to look like I needed a fox sized diaper.

All of a sudden, in spray of silver glitter, the Omega transformed into a gorgeous...naked...man with bronzed muscles and strawberry blond curls. He shot me a grin, as he crouched in the snow like his changing back into a man was all I'd need to forget that he'd been hunting me, and now I'd die.

My eyes widened. None of that mattered. This gorgeous curly haired werewolf was *Glow*.

So, this was how it happened. Dad had always warned me that if I did nothing but hide curled in a ball (like I had when I'd first been shut away), then I'd go crazy. He'd talk to me, ask me question after question, test me on the subjects that I'd been studying, before I'd been banned from schooling.

He'd told me that if I didn't keep my mind active, then I'd lose myself.

I thought that was why he'd taken so many risks to bring me a TV, books, and allow Aquilo to visit me. In the end, Dad had died so that I could hold onto my mind.

But now, I'd lost it.

I whined, holding my paws over my head.

"By my fur, I'm trying not to terrorize your daft behind. Calm down, wee fox." Glow patted me on the head.

How was my childhood friend comforting me in the middle of the Dead Wood, when he should be in the House of Jewels, having bows tied into his hair by Hartley?

Pan's balls, I didn't care. I was going with it. Perhaps, I'd died or was disassociating with the terror of my imminent death. Whatever, it was better than a savaging.

If I was going to pretend that this was Glow then I wanted a hug.

I transformed back into a mage, who was wearing only my thin black whipping boy outfit. Sleipnir had tried to smuggle me into his woolen coat, but Juni had insisted that I take it off because it broke the rules.

Perhaps, whipping boys were meant to turn into snowmen...?

I shivered, before hurling myself at Glow, who fell onto his back in shock. I hugged him fiercely. There was nothing like a Glow hug.

I'd missed him so much.

I only realized now how it hurt like I'd been booted in the balls that I hadn't even been able to say goodbye to him.

I rested my head on Glow's chest with a happy sigh. Then I tensed.

Glow lay beneath me stiffly. His arms hadn't even raised to loop around me.

This was nothing like a Glow hug. It was as if the Omega beneath me had never even *been* hugged.

I carefully raised my head to study the Omega's confused expression. Now that I looked closely, his hair was shorter than Glow's and his face was harder like he didn't dare show the joy that came to Glow so easily, even if he could be whipped for showing it in front of mum.

Glow's joy was courageous just in itself.

The *Not-Glow* raised his eyebrow at me, but I couldn't quite get myself to let go. He felt too much like the wolf I knew.

"Are all mages this friendly?" His Scottish voice made me shiver because it was like hearing Glow's ghost.

"You're Not-Glow," I accused.

The Not-Glow heaved me away from him like I was still in fox form — Muscle Envy was a definite thing — as his breath caught.

Then his eyes narrowed in suspicion. "You know my twin brother...?"

Twins, of course.

Wolves were sent to Omega Training Centers, before being selected by witches. They must've been separated when they were chosen, despite being twins, which was cruel even by witchy standards.

Okay, that was more likely than me being dead or crazy.

"He lives at the House of Jewels," *because I didn't want to say that he was their slave, even though Not-Glow must realize that he was*, "and he raised me like a big brother. He's safe." Luckily, Not-Glow didn't know that I was lying. Yet Glow wasn't stuck in the Rebel Academy with Juni, so comparatively, he was on top of the world. Not-Glow's shoulders relaxed with relief, and he shot me a grateful smile. Sometimes, white lies were all that kept people going. "I meant what I said to you at Hecate's altar. I'll free us all, and that means Glow as well."

Not-Glow carded his fingers through my curls. "Goddess Moon! I can see why my brother likes you, single skin." I pinked. "But you can't have missed that this is a Hunt, and I've caught you."

I wet my dry lips. "Oh yeah, that."

His lips twitched. "Aye, *that*. But I'd rather take back a fae in my fangs. I'd never catch Glow's wee brother." I shook. *Did he mean...?* He edged closer to me, licking my cheek in reassurance. "There's a cottage beside the lake. Run there now and trust the Groundskeeper. Fur and fangs, he's one of the few who are kind to shifters, as well as animals. He's..." Not-Glow hesitated like he was about to admit a dangerous secret; he looked down, and his sinfully long eyelashes fluttered across his cheeks, "...*my friend.*"

I nodded. "Running and hiding I have down. Who's this Groundskeeper then? Is he another werewolf?"

Not-Glow snorted. "Aye, right. Like they'd give a wolf that type of responsibility. Emerick was adopted by Damelza."

"She walls mages up alive but she adopts one as her son...?" I couldn't help the flinch.

"Emerick's non-magical and strictly to be seen and not heard at all times. Nay, not seen either. That's why he has a cottage in the grounds, rather than living in the castle."

I shuddered. "You know, they went all out on their Cinders remake."

Not-Glow growled. "His name is Emerick." I shivered. Definitely both the dominant brother and not a fan of fairy tale retellings. "I'll set off a firework flare when my quarry is caught." His amber eyes flashed. I wouldn't want to be Lysander. "You, wee brother, stay hidden until then."

I fiddled with the cuff of my shirt to hold in the intense emotion that had coursed through me at the *wee brother*.

It'd sounded so like Glow. Yet it hadn't been him.

Would I ever see Glow again?

Not-Glow noticed, catching my hand between his. "You're the first person to ever talk to me like...flay me, this is hard...to *see* me as more than an Omega and to care that I'm not free. I believe that you can rescue us, but for that, you have to *survive*. Damelza detests your hide."

I shrugged. "And there I was planning our wedding." I might've made myself hurl a little. I brushed one of Not-Glow's curls behind his ear, and he startled like he'd never experienced the tender gesture before. "I can continue thinking of you as Not-Glow, the Anti-Glow, Glow Mark Two, Glow II, or..."

"Snow," the werewolf previously known as Not-Glow said. He glanced around at the shadows between the trees like even here someone would overhear and punish him for using his name, rather than Om. "At the Omega Training Center, it was a reward to be allowed out to work on the gardens, even in winter, clearing the snow because the guards hated the cold and wouldn't oversee us. Moon knows, I loved it because I missed the trees in the Wilds, where I'd been a cub, before..." He paled, and I knew that he was battling to break free of the memory: When he was taken from his home and locked away. It'd happened to me because of my magic, and I struggled too. "My brother and I wanted to sound alike. He was the one who *glowed* like it didn't even matter how crappy our day was, he'd brighten it. I took the name *snow* to remind me of the fun moments we'd steal in the winter gardens, even when I was shut in the dark."

I squeezed his hand because I needed to remind him that he was no longer in the dark. *Yet we were both still trapped.* I had faith that with Magenta by my side, however, we could be freed.

"Not that I'd ever argue against saving my life," I stood, still holding onto Snow's warm hand, "but isn't hiding me in a cottage and chasing only Lysander sort of...just a little bit...cheating?"

Snow's smirk was devilish. "I'd say that it was sort of *rebelling*."

I hid behind the high yew hedge that surrounded the back of the Groundskeeper's cottage. It was like a secret garden with a high oak gate, which was over-grown with ivy.

I whined, scrabbling at my fluffy ears.

Was Emerick a fairy tale giant, luring animals in for his stew? Let's be honest, with a mage's luck in a coven-run academy, I had a good chance of my bones being ground for bread.

I waved my nose in the air defiantly, before pushing on the gate.

Locked.

When I'd skirted the lake, my lungs had burned. My breath had ghosted the cold air. I hadn't dared to look behind me at the thrumming darkness of the wood.

Snow was risking his life to hide me and hunt Lysander. He hadn't admitted it, but the truth had screamed through my mind on every one of his panted breaths.

The cottage had lain in darkness. My heart had thudded painfully fast. How long would I have before Juni checked where I was?

Suddenly, footsteps *crunched* through the snow. I whimpered.

Horn and hoof, Great Pan, let it be Hagrid...

I screwed shut my eyes as the shadow loomed over me. "Poor thing, have you been waiting for me?"

That didn't sound like Hadrid, Britain's last giant Gogmagog (oh yeah, I knew my giant lore), or even the Jolly Green Giant. The voice was as smooth as honey.

Would licking Emerick be a polite greeting? In fox form, I appeared to have some of the same urges as the werewolves or perhaps, Emerick just had that effect on people.

I was about to open my eyes and test out the theory because I mustn't neglect my study of Science, when Emerick grabbed me by the neck and dropped me into a basket.

I yelped. Something pressed uncomfortably into my manly parts. I wriggled around, baring my fangs.

Why did everyone foxhandle me?

Then the basket lurched, as it was picked up.

My eyes snapped open in shock, and I stared up at Emerick. His skin was velvet ebony, and his dark hair was woven with feathers. He was dressed only slightly warmer than my whipping boy clothes, even though his job was based outdoors. He wore heavy boots and leather chocolate brown trousers and shirt that matched his eyes, as if to mark him out from the students.

Yet he was the same age as the Rebels.

His gaze softened, as he studied me. "Are you injured, fox? How about we get you inside and check you over?"

Who was he, witchy Dr Doolittle?

Sweet Pan, if Emerick could talk to the animals, then he'd better keep that trick well hidden, or he'd end up like me. Banished to a comfy cottage in the grounds would turn into banished to the dungeons.

Emerick stroked my head to calm me, as I scrabbled anxiously over the knobbly pears underneath me.

"*Shh*, you're okay." Emerick slipped a rusty key into the gate, and it squeaked open. "Once we're inside, it's charmed so that my family or the other professors can't see or hear us." *So, that was why Snow had chosen this hiding spot.* "You made a mistake hunting on these grounds."

That meant the academy wasn't set up to keep out animals, but I didn't expect that they survived long. Unless, Emerick had set himself the job of helping them.

I liked him already.

I peeked over the lip of the wicker basket at the garden. Then I gasped. The cottage was tiny, ancient, and thatched. It leaned to one side like it was too tired to keep standing. The garden was nothing but a wave of snow, which lapped at the cottage.

Apart from the ice sculptures.

My ears perked, and I balanced on the edge of the basket. A crowd of ice sculptures, which were the most beautiful things that I'd ever seen (apart from Magenta), lived in the garden like they were Emerick's silent family. An elephant blew water playfully at a snarling tiger. An elf climbed the branches of an ice tree, while a vampire waved to him. A sleeping dragon circled the entire garden, even as a family of wolf cubs played on his tail.

It was art, life, and freedom.

They sang *truth* with a piercing violin note that was so pure and perfect that I shivered. I'd never heard anything like it before. I ached inside like I needed to cry and I didn't understand why. But then, I'd never been to an art gallery before. My doodles were epic but nothing like *this*.

Emerick studied me, then he chuckled. "It's like revelation, isn't it? I'm never alone now. My friend makes them for me." His gaze glowed with such warmth that I couldn't help the twinge of jealousy. Who was this friend? *Wait, did he mean Willoughby?* "He's talented." As understatements went, that was up there with calling the Sistine Chapel *pretty*. "And being here with me and creating them makes him feel safe, the same as I'll keep you safe."

That was right, concentrate on the fox.

Emerick laughed, when I puffed out my chest and fell back on my ass amongst the pears.

I needed to leave the flirting to Bask, especially when I was in animal form.

When Emerick pushed open the door to the cottage, I glanced around at the shadowy kitchen. The room was plain, but it was also neat and well-cleaned. I knew what it was like to live a simple life because you were a son of witches.

When I shuddered, Emerick hushed me. He dropped the basket onto his oak kitchen table, before scooping me out and holding me against the hardness of his muscled chest. I sighed, snuggling against his warmth.

This type of holding I could put up with. He reminded me of Magenta because he smelled of the woods, mixed in with leather. I sniffed him again. Then I stiffened.

Magenta and the other Immortals would still be waiting on the edge of the trees. They didn't know that I was safe and being snuggled, rather than savaged.

Magenta...

At once, her pink magic curled from the floor like roots. My eyes widened, as it stroked over me. Had she sensed my call? *Could she feel me?*

Emerick peered down. "Are you okay, fox? I'd better check you over then."

When he tried to drop me onto the table, I swallowed. I knew where vets stuck their fingers.

I mean, at least buy me a drink first.

I snarled, fastening my teeth into his shirt. Surprised, he met my gaze in a staring contest.

Never take on a fox in a staring contest, when his ass was literally on the line.

Emerick sighed. "I guess we can do it your way." He slid onto the seat, still curling me to his chest. Then he eased his hand over me, testing for non-existent hurts. I stilled at the sensation of his fingers brushing through my sensitive hair and then down my tail to its tip. "This is the only shirt I have. I'd rather not explain to mum why it has teethmarks in it, especially since I'm the House of Crow's prize virgin."

I hurriedly let go of his shirt, which was damp with saliva and neat teethmarks. He grimaced. I understood because if I hadn't turned out to be a mage, then I'd have been the prized jewel in my own House. Mum had been giddy about the idea of my own marriage furthering her coven's status.

Emerick was beautiful. It was obvious why Damelza had adopted him.

Emerick smiled. "You pass the exam but you're a long way from the Arctic. I guess you escaped from someone's illegal zoo collection. Are you hungry?" He held up a pear, and I nibbled at it. Then he stood up, strolling to a kettle and one-handedly fixing himself a cup of coffee like it was something that he did every day. If he made a habit of bringing in every stray animal, then perhaps it was. "Just sleep awhile. When it's dark, I'll take you to the boundary and free you. I won't hand you over to be put back into a cage. Next time, stay away from the strange cursed grounds, okay?"

I nodded, wearily.

It'd been a long day, which had included being tied to a chair, hexed, and hunted.

It wouldn't hurt to close my eyes just for a little bit, right? Especially when it was so comfortable and warm held in Emerick's arms but with Magenta's magic still stroking me in waves.

Bang, bang, bang.

All of a sudden, I was startled awake.

Mage's balls on a stick, what was that? Were we under attack? Had the ice sculptures come alive to take revenge on their creators?

I leaped to my feet. Why was I on a cold table? What'd happened to the warm, snuggly chest?

Bang, bang, bang.

Disorientated after my sleep, I glanced out of the window. It'd become dark.

Night-time already...?

Yet glittering fireworks that exploded into the golden wings of a fae illuminated the sky.

Snow had caught Lysander.

Wow, Lysander had survived this long in the wood. I winced with guilt. I'd never have been able to beat him without Snow's help.

Then it hit me.

I'd won the Hunt. The Immortals had won the Rebel Cup. And I'd won my own life.

Thank Pan...

I danced in a circle with wild *gekkering*, fluffing up my tail in triumph, only to stumble over my paws. Emerick sat in the shadows of the kitchen like a true giant, watching my victory dance. His expression was as frosty as his ice sculptures.

Uh oh...

I eyed the door. Could I make a break for it?

"I guess that you should get back to pretending that you're in the Hunt now, *Fox*." He leaned forward, and his expression was unreadable. *Would he tell Damelza?* "Do you think that as the Principal's son, there's much that goes on that I don't know about?"

I shook my head.

"So," he raised his eyebrow, "you just think that I'm a fool?"

Well, that was trick question. Should I transform? But I had to get back to the Hunt. I lowered my ears and whined, flashing him the best cute expression that I could.

Emerick sighed. "Snow told me about you. We're not that different. You must get what it's like for me in a way that the others can't. You don't need to play tricks or lie to gain that help. I know I'm not a mage, but we should look out for each other. You're safe with me. Go on then."

I was going to live...

I bounded off the table, diving for the door.

Almost free...

Emerick's expression hardened, as he called after me, "But if you ever trick Willoughby or lie to *him*, then I'll wreck you. If you mess with my friend, I'll bring down the power of my family on your tail."

I froze.

I wouldn't be executed over the Rebel Cup, but tonight the Immortals had already challenged the Princes to the Stop Game.

Our entire plan was to trick and mess with Willoughby. My heart clenched. I'd hoped that Emerick would become a new mate, but in order to break free of the academy, we'd create an enemy who'd sworn to wreck me.

CHAPTER FIFTEEN

Rebel Academy, Thursday September 5th

BASK

I slid my fingers through my hair.

Shiny hair...? Check.

I wriggled my arse on the rough wooden beam.

Pettable arse...? Check.

Then I glanced across at Fox who shyly met my smile.

Adorable mage who wasn't going to die tomorrow...? Check.

Joy burst through me that was no pain and all delicious pleasure. We'd won the Rebel Cup. It didn't matter that the Duchess would claim me after the Dragon Polo Tournament.

The adorable whipping boy who I'd promised to love and protect was safe. *He wouldn't be another Hector.*

My chest was tight, as I fluttered my eyelashes at Fox across the small room, which was veiled in cobwebs and tingled with ancient magic. Then I sneezed (in a sexy way, of course), on the dust. The chamber was the highest point of the castle with a low arched ceiling and no windows. It was lit only by Magenta's magic that had curled out like the sparkling branches of a tree to tangle over the beams, along with her aroma of the wild woods.

Magenta called it her *Dreaming Space.*

To an incubus, it was romantic. Away with you, I could do romantic better than Sleipnir's attempt, even if he was kissing down Magenta's neck with the devotion of a worshiper.

He'd worshiped my dick like that (who wouldn't?). Magenta was in for a treat, as soon as he kissed between her thighs. *The godly things that he could do with his tongue...*

I sighed dreamily. Then I crooked my finger at Fox.

Fox rolled his eyes but crawled across the crumbling beams. I gasped, as he gripped my slinky self by the hips, yanking me onto his lap. His scent of raspberries was so sweet that I wanted to lick all over his pale skin.

Yet if he wanted to take his turn at romance and worship with petting tribute, then it was against the most fundamental Incubi Night Code for me to refuse. Plus, my hard-on was twitching happily. My dick and balls had been through some brutally traumatic experiences in the last few days. They deserved a wee bit of stress relief.

I melted against Fox, as he stroked circles against my inner thigh, clasping me around my waist like he was frightened that I'd be stolen from him if he let go.

I knew how he felt; I was possessive like that with Nile. It was this whole *thing*. But then, I was enthralling (*of course, snicker*).

Yet I couldn't slip my own gloved hand down Fox's pants like I was aching to and return the favor (incubi are generous lovers), because any moment the Princes would arrive for the Stop Game.

Why had I suggested it again?

Here's the thing, I'd planned the Stop Game to bring out the Princes' hidden secrets and desires. At first, I'd thought that I wanted to...not wreck...but *break open* Lysander and Willoughby. It was the quickest way that I knew to crack through their haughty princely selves because you couldn't keep up your mask during the game.

If Willoughby truly loved Magenta, then it'd bring him over to our side.

At the Succubus Court, the bonded had played it

as a hidden way to love each other, when that was forbidden. It'd also had a darker side, however, because it'd been used as an extreme hazing of new harem members. I shuddered at the memory of being the youngest and terrified on my first night. I'd been blindfolded and told the consequences if I forfeited by saying *stop* during the Stop Game...

Stop. Stop. Stop.

I shivered but raised my chin. I'd faced down a pissed off Duchess. I wasn't broken anymore. My slinky self knew how to play the game now because I was the one in charge.

Rule 46 of the Incubi Night Code stated: You can never have too much power or too much hair product.

Have you ever seen a king without well-groomed hair?

Only, that was the world, which ma taught me. It was one of intrigue and scheming. I didn't know if I wanted power over the cute elf but I did want to love him.

But power over Lysander sounded brilliant.

Sleipnir paused in his kissing to rub his finger over two initials that'd been carved looping around each other into the wood:

MR

"**MR** who?" Sleipnir asked.

"Is that a new kids' book?" When Fox cocked his

head, his curls fell across his eyes. "Mr. Who and his Tardis, like Mr. Rude or Mr. Nosey, only he ends up getting killed and regenerating as Little Miss Who."

Sleipnir rapped his knuckles against the wood. "Hey, I was just asking who was up here and claiming this Dreaming Space as theirs?"

"That would be *me*." Magenta traced across the initials, following the same path as Sleipnir. When she bit her lip, I wished that I could suck it between mine and take away the sadness that'd settled around her like a shroud. My bones ached with it. "**M** stands for—"

"Magenta." Sleipnir covered her hand with his larger one, catching her surprised gaze with his.

"Who's the **R**?" I demanded.

Not a lover... Don't love the past more than me... Please, I'm not invisible...

"My best friend." I didn't miss her fleeting glance at Fox. "He died because he said *always*, rather than *stop*."

That's why she'd insisted that I promise not to say *always*. Not that I *had* promised. I was getting the hang of battling my own instincts and training.

She'd lost someone like I'd lost Hector: This **R**.

Magenta pulled her finger away from the carved initials of her dead childhood friend. Why could I feel the ghost of him in this tiny room where they must've played as kids?

Magenta smiled like she loved feeling close to him.

No one stole my Magenta, especially not a memory.

"Does it please you to remember that we're still alive?" I stroked my gloved hand down Fox's cheek. His breath stuttered, and he flushed. *Cute.* "We're yours, and we'll please you."

"Sweet Hecate, you already please me, and I'm yours as much as you're mine." Magenta's expression softened.

Pleasure flooded through me at her approval. It fed my power. I shuddered, and my toes curled. But then, not only wasn't my sexy self invisible, but I was the incubus who Magenta scrutinized with such sharpness that I might as well have already been naked.

I furrowed my brow. Should I strip? It was bound to happen in the Stop Game, after all, and why deny the others the view? When I reached for the buttons on my pants, however, Fox batted away my hands with a laugh.

His loss. *Perhaps, mages were masochists?*

I glanced at him from underneath my eyelashes. I could have some fun with that. Fox froze, swallowing like I was the wolf in the hunt and he'd been caught.

Silly foxy...

I squirmed in anticipation of testing out my theory (I could start by treating myself to a squeeze of his sweet nipples, a gentle bite on his pale throat, or quick squeeze of his balls), and see if he deliciously moaned or pinned *me* down inside.

Both were fine options.

I latched my lips to Fox's throat, but before I could do more than press my teeth against his skin, he froze. "Have your turned into a Vampire Incubus? Pan's balls, was this whole thing a ruse to get me up here and eat me? Look, my blood'll taste terrible like an unholy cocktail of vinegar, lemon rind, and gin. Try Sleipnir's, instead. His probably tastes like honey and milk."

Sleipnir snorted. "Huh, at least I know who'd be eaten first if we were stuck on a desert island."

"Admittedly, there's the most meat on you." Magenta assessed him, speculatively.

I drew back from Fox's neck in outrage, licking over the hickey in apology. Incubi were better at sucking than biting (*startling discovery*), but we'd proved in the Dick Contest who had the most *meat* on them.

Fox cleared his throat. "Bitey, *don't say it.* Anyway, my cunning plan would be to eat myself and then let you heal me. Then no one would have to die, even if there was a honeyed god to scoff."

He said the sweetest things.

Magenta grimaced. "Well, I'd wonder where such macabre thoughts came from, if I wasn't a Ghost

Witch, this wasn't a magical academy that imprisoned us, and if tomorrow we weren't likely to all die."

Fox's lips quirked. "And that, ladies and gentle-man, is how a Victorian gets a party started!"

All of a sudden, coughing spluttered from the tunnel.

Then a disgruntled Lysander (*wow, he pulled off disgruntled and cute*), crawled out of the low gap into the Dreaming Space, followed by Willoughby. The Princes' smart uniforms were smeared with dust and cobwebs.

That was a fine sight.

I smirked, as Lysander knelt up. He stared with a disgusted expression at his dirty hands. Then reluc-tantly, he wiped them down his uniform trousers, before shuffling closer to us in the circle.

As an incubus of the ancient Night Lineage, I knew the importance of appearance, as well of being prepared. I'd brought a comb, handheld mirror, and wipes with me. I glanced over my immaculate uniform and shiny hair, licking over my kissable lips.

I was sizzling.

My rivals, on the other hand, were rumpled and stained.

Advantage the Immortals.

Plus, as Lysander's suspicious gaze swept over us, he appeared to know it. Was the Fae Court much different to the Succubus one, even for a prince?

Willoughby edged closer to Magenta. He ducked his head, pulling his knees up under him. Magenta exchanged a glance with Sleipnir, before shuffling closer to Willoughby and sitting next to him, cross-legged. When their knees touched, Willoughby jumped, glancing up.

Please let him be ours...

"One does not know why one is here." Lysander sat stiffly like even the air was contaminating his princely arse (and every other part of his bastard self).

Fox shook his head, sadly. "Fae dementia is a sad thing."

I snickered.

"Why you wanted to force us to this dreadful place, you fool," Lysander curled his hands into fists in his lap. "Why you'd threaten to lie about..."

"Your prank to melt your asshole tutor...?" Sleipnir offered, helpfully.

Lysander clenched his jaw. "Have you no idea the penalty that we'd suffer for that? No doubt you do and would delight in our suffering." *Why was he avoiding looking at Magenta?* Ah, did our haughty fae have a true *crush*? Who'd blame anyone for loving my Magenta? Although, I had almost vomited when he'd kissed Fox in Bacchus' lesson and had looked like he'd kiss Magenta as well at any moment. Unlike Willoughby, I didn't think that Magenta could love him back. She'd been hurt by a fae prince (by Titus, his own family), and I knew enough to see that she'd lost everything because of it. I *almost* felt sorry for Lysander. *Yuck.* Now I felt dirty. "Why would you challenge us to a childish game, when tomorrow afternoon you must risk your lives on a dangerous mission?"

Magenta clapped her hands in delight. "Oh, you do care! How kind."

"We always go to bed early on the night before a mission," Willoughby explained; his gaze was mildly curious.

I examined his silk uniform. It set my Incubus Envy-O-Meter tingling because it was beautiful. Yet tonight, I could see that it was wound too tightly. How could my cute elf breathe? His eyes were glazed. It was like he was struggling to focus on staying here with us.

Where was he being dragged to?

I narrowed my eyes. No one ignored an incubus. I'd just have to try hard to keep his attention on us tonight.

Sleipnir slouched against the wall, and Magenta's magic curled around his shoulders like she was still clasping onto him. His hair sparkled aquamarine. When his tongue darted out, his piercing glittered.

It could do magical things that piercing (just ask my dick).

"By the runes, you're the asshole who lost the

Rebel Cup. If we wanted to delight in your suffering, then we'd just watch Titus' fury over that. After all, the dickhead's coming to watch the Dragon Polo Tournament." Lysander paled, flinching. Why was sympathy washing through me again? Away with you, sympathy for the devil was a *thing*. "So, we're offering you the chance tonight to reclaim some honor by being the team who gets to kick off the Dragon Polo. Whoever wins the Stop Game earns that right."

I'd planned the Stop Game to melt the Ice Prince. But Sleipnir had insisted that Lysander was so competitive that he wouldn't play unless there was a winner, loser, and a prize that meant something to his screwed-up *honor*.

He only did anything if he thought that there was an advantage in it for him. It was almost incubi-worthy.

When Lysander hugged his wings around himself more tightly, I noticed the wolf sized teeth marks in his feathers. It'd been a fine sight yesterday to see him dragged out from the wood, snarling. I'd been terrified that I'd see a limp fox clamped between the Omegas' fangs, instead.

I'd *whooped*, hugging Magenta, unable to let go because Fox was *alive, alive, alive...*

My brave, clever, whipping boy.

Caught in the sudden happiness of the memory, I twisted to Fox, pressing my lips to his. His eyes widened in surprise, then his smile against my lips was delicious in its pleasure.

Lysander coughed behind me. "Sorry to interrupt...whatever this is...and thank you for the reminder that Midnight's wings shall be broken because of my failure, as well as my guardian's impending fury for losing the Rebel Cup."

Fox's pleasure soured. *Was that guilt?* I pulled away from the kiss, but kept my hand possessively curled around his neck, as I twisted back to face the circle.

Sleipnir shrugged. "You're welcome."

"Where's Midnight?" Magenta asked.

Lysander's eyes narrowed. "Shockingly, he didn't feel up to celebrating. Will you punish me for granting him that reprieve?"

Punish? Were fae masochists as well? Wow, I had a lot of theories to test tonight. But as the old incubi saying went: *For every kink there's a season.*

Magenta's mists swirled around Lysander, before he could flinch away. She reached across the circle, clasping his hand.

"Do you believe me so cold and heartless?" Magenta worked her fingers between Lysander's, unballing his fist. "It's the professors who punish and not me. We're all students. Can't you allow yourself one evening of merriment?"

Lysander wrenched away his hand. "One was

raised as an Unseelie fae *prince* at Court. You've no conception of the burdens, which were placed on me from the earliest age. The things that they demanded I do... There was no time for games."

"Well, that sucks." Fox pushed me gently off his lap. I pouted, straightening out my uniform. He should fear my plotted incubi revenge (or snuggles, I was one changeable hottie). "But you're at the Court of Fox now, and I say: *fun for everyone*." Then he shot Willoughby a sideways glance that I didn't understand. "Just theoretically...I mean, in theory...if I accidental-ly...lie to you...or *hypothetically* wreck you...then you wouldn't go around telling everybody, right?"

Willoughby's lips twitched. "*Hypothetically*, it'd be dishonorable to tell on you."

Fox's shoulder's relaxed, and he gave Willoughby a bright smile. "Stop Game here we come."

Lysander held up one finger. "My noble self will take part in this farce, but there must be rules first, whipping boy. Of course, I understand that you struggle with those. What is this filthy place anyway? Couldn't we at least have played somewhere that wasn't—"

"This is the most magical part of the castle. Can't you feel it?" Magenta said, softly. I shivered, as her magic thrummed and sparkled. It tingled across my skin, and pleasure wound through me like her roots were inside me now, hot and pulsing. My dick pulsed in time like a musical beat. "I'd crawl through the tunnels to reach it, when mother was cruel to father or I needed somewhere secret. The magic would hold tight to me like it was kissing away every fear."

Willoughby's eyes fluttered closed, and he whispered. "I can feel it. It's calling me to the Other World."

"Snap out of it." Lysander shook Willoughby, until his eyes opened. "Hiding in magic doesn't work, just like a scared child hiding away from the truth."

Magenta became ashen.

Oh no, he didn't just hurt Magenta...

I wasn't a warrior, but I'd just got into biting. The Omega had already sunk his fangs into Lysander's wing; I'd bet that it'd be sensitive if I latched onto the same place...

Sleipnir shook his head at me, however, and I sat back with a frown.

"The asshole fae doesn't want to *hide*. Let's help him with that." When Sleipnir's gaze met mine, it glittered with mischief.

He was hot when he was dangerous. *Almost as hot as me.*

I grinned. "Two teams — Princes and Immortals — each take it in turns to select one player. Then that player sits in the middle of the circle. It's the rival player's job within a minute to make them forfeit by saying *stop*."

Lysander's wings beat in agitation. "But you could do anything: hexes, torture, or..."

"Lay off! Your mind would go there. This was a game played between incubi bonded who feed on giving pleasure and not pain."

"It's a sex game." Lysander became unnaturally still. "You lured us here for a kinky sex club. My guardian warned me about things like this."

Fox barked with laughter.

Why hadn't we thought of a kinky sex club? *That would've been brilliant.*

Lysander scrambled backwards towards the tunnel. Sleipnir sighed, diving across to snatch Lysander around the middle and drag him back, holding him down by the neck and pressing him to the floor.

My balls ached at the sight (*traitor balls*).

I noticed that Willoughby hadn't attempted to escape our clutches. In fact, his gaze was fixed longingly on Magenta, when he thought that we were all watching his fellow Prince being dominated by Sleipnir.

"Of course it was...kinky...in the harem." My grin widened. "But Magenta boringly has more morals than me and has insisted—"

"No touching," Fox explained, far more gently than I'd been expecting. "Except between those of us who are all into the touching."

He winked at me.

Sleipnir eased off Lysander, who slowly pushed himself back up to his knees, smoothing out his hair like he hadn't just been wrestling on the floor with an Immortal.

"And the moment that you say *stop*...it all stops." Sleipnir's expression was more serious than I'd ever seen it.

"Says the oaf who's just been pinning me to the floor," Lysander muttered.

Sleipnir's eyes flashed. "Valhalla! It's kind of like the game hasn't started yet..."

Sleipnir shuffled out of the circle, and Mist leaped out of his pocket. His eight legs splayed, before he scrambled with a whinny and a snort to the center of the circle like he was claiming the role of the referee.

Lysander narrowed his eyes. "But if you say *stop*, then you lose."

The stubborn fae would never say stop.

Sudden memories of being in the harem flooded over me. I pressed my nails into my palms.

Stop, stop, stop...

But they'd never stopped.

I couldn't play this, if Lysander held those same screams within his head, refusing to say the word. My sexy self wasn't the same as the bonded who'd hazed me.

I crawled across the circle, holding out my hand to Lysander. He stared at it in shock for a moment, before taking it. Then I yanked him into the middle of the circle.

"Would you wish one chance to say *stop* without losing? It needs to be said twice by one team to count as a loss."

Lysander nodded, uncertainly.

"And you're first, prince," I whispered.

Did it make me a bad incubus that I loved how he jumped?

"Why must my royal personage be first?" Lysander demanded.

Mist snorted fiery sparks at him in protest and pawed the floor.

My teeth glinted in the eerie light of Magenta's magic. "New rule: the player who's selected must sit *silently* and *still* or they also lose. If you wish, you can say *stop* at any time."

"I do not have fae dementia." Lysander curled his wings around himself like that would protect him from attack.

Never underestimate an incubus.

Fox glanced at his watch. "One minute...starting...*now*..."

Lysander's eyes were emerald pools. I watched his alabaster throat as he swallowed, struggling to stay still. Then I deliberately and never taking my gaze from his, sucked my thumb (*sucking, see?*), while he blinked at me in confusion.

Then I brought my thumb towards his ear. I expected a screech of *stop*, but Lysander only wrinkled his nose in distaste. I swiped my thumb just above his lips, and his gaze threatened revenge.

And not the fun sort.

I snickered, before drumming my fingers on my knee (always out of rhythm because I wasn't an amateur).

Lysander's cheek twitched.

I was getting to him.

I leaned closer, until my breath ghosted across his throat.

Technically, I wasn't touching.

He bit his lip but didn't move.

It was part of incubi training, however, to always be prepared. I'm sure that it included kinky games. Seriously, it'd be in the bonus material. Look it up.

So, now I'd bring out the big guns. Lysander's eyes widened in fear at the predatory smile that curled my lips. Then I burst into a wild...off-key...version of the Spice Girls' "Wannabe" with added *Girl Power* attitude.

This time, Lysander's eye twitched.

I slung my arms around Sleipnir's neck, before throwing a kiss to Fox, who groaned but still dramatically caught it. After all, as the song preached, if

Lysander wanted a piece of my pettable arse, then he had to become friends with my lovers. Well, that was my take away message.

Nobody could survive a combination of the Spice Girls and my slinky self.

Lysander opened his mouth as if to protest but stopped himself in time. Magenta shot me her best *you're a scheming incubus but with that pettable arse I'd let you off anything* look.

Away with you, that was what it meant.

I wriggled around to straddle Magenta, as she teasingly undid my shirt. I slid my hand down my chest to tweak at my own nipples (there was nothing in the rules about touching myself), and writhed up and down like a snake in a lap dance. Her hands rested lightly on my hips.

Fox glanced at his watch. "Ten seconds."

I had to win this for my incubus pride.

Magenta was flushed, and her eyes were glassy. When I glanced over my shoulder at Lysander, just gearing up for the rap section of "Wannabe" (it was going to be *fierce*), I was shocked that Lysander's eyes were glassy too. His hands were clamped over his knees, and his knuckles were white like he was desperate to move. Yet I didn't know if he was struggling not to grab hold of my sexy arse or Magenta's.

I'd bet that it was both.

Fox bounced onto his knees in excitement. "*Five, four, three, two...*"

"*Stop*, damn you," Lysander hissed.

His hands shot to cover his lap in the universal and time-honored *hiding your hard-on* position.

My mouth snapped shut.

Sleipnir breathed out in relief. "Thank the Valkyries." When I arched my brow dangerously at him, he swallowed. "Hey, I just meant that you've spoiled us enough."

I preened. I was one generous incubus and I'd won the Stop Game for the Immortals. At the same time, I'd cracked open Lysander's mask.

Girl Power was powerful.

Yet I was shocked by the malevolence of Lysander's grin. "My turn, I believe."

Here's the thing, my time at the Succubus Court had taught me that a wounded rival was a deadly one. Never whip your enemy bloody and then pass them the whip. *Unless you were playing a kinky sex game.*

"Not a chance," my voice was hard. "Didn't I mention that if you *stop*, then you don't get to choose the next player?"

Lysander slumped against the wall, curling his wings around himself to hide his *condition*. "It must've slipped your musically challenged mind."

Lysander arched his brow, casting a significant glance at Willoughby and then me.

Yep, no attempt to influence his fellow Prince at all.

Willoughby's gaze darted between Magenta and me. I knew which of us he wanted to choose.

Yet I didn't think that it was only out of fear or respect for Lysander that he shuffled towards me. Only an elven prince could manage to make a shuffle look elegant.

I crawled into the middle of the circle, sitting cross-legged. I'd meditated this way with my ma, and it made me feel closer to a time when I'd been safe.

Stop. Stop. Stop.

Willoughby would listen to me if I said it, right?

Willoughby's brow furrowed. "This game is meant to tease and give pleasure, I believe?"

"As you wish."

His forehead touched mine. "It's as *you* wish. Only then shall I play."

I shuddered. I was meant to be in charge here. *When had I lost control?*

"As *I* wish," I replied.

The words were heavy on my tongue. *Had I ever said them before...?*

How was Willoughby cracking *me* open...?

Willoughby's smile was soft, as he moved back. "Then let us play."

"One minute," Fox called.

Sixty seconds. This was easy. I'd stayed silent and

still, while I'd burned myself. What could an elf do to me?

When Willoughby caged me in with his arms, I almost *eeped*. How had I thought anything about him had been soft? He was lithe, coiled, and dangerous. His scent was like being lost in wintry grasses, just as I was lost in the frozen blue of his eyes.

I remembered the feel of his hard thighs and I regretted the *no touching* rule.

Then he started to hum, and it vibrated through me like my nerves were on fire. Willoughby remained as still as me. We were ice sculptures, trapped in a staring contest (and I'd been the harem champion at those).

But Willoughby was better. He didn't even blink.

My skin heated, and my balls ached and tightened. Willoughby's humming grew in volume, vibrating through my dick. I panted and gasped.

Dick...don't listen to the naughty Pied Piper of Cumlin...he's trying to drown you...in your own cum.

But my dick was only interested in the pretty tune and its own forced orgasmic destruction.

Dicks are idiots.

"Say *stop*, and I shall," Willoughby murmured. "Do you want this?" Then he turned to Magenta, concerned. "Is he allowed to nod?"

"Of course, " she replied.

I nodded, frantically.

"Ten seconds," Fox warned.

I gritted my teeth. *Don't you dare stop, elfie...not now...*

"Five, four, three..." Fox glanced at me. I struggled not to arch and lose at the last moment. I'd win against the Orgasm Whisperer. "...Two, *one...*"

Willoughby leaned closer to my ear, humming a long sweet note that pushed me over the edge.

I hollered, before slumping forward. My dick pulsed and came with such intensity that white sparks blurred my vision. When I could see again, I met Willoughby's amused gaze.

He'd just out-sexed an incubus: he'd earned a moment of smugness.

But then, Lysander yanked Willoughby back by the arm, and he winced.

Sleipnir growled, and Mist galloped across the room to butt his head into Lysander's balls.

Lysander groaned. "Call off your monster. One happens to be Prefect of my Wing, and how I discipline my Princes is my affair."

"If I see you disciplining him again," Magenta's voice was as frosty as her magic that now snowed around us in pink snowflakes, "then I shall take back the non-touching rule just for you."

Lysander blanched, then his gaze became steely. He shook Willoughby. "Amusing how you turned a game of torment into one of pleasure. You saw how the incubus humiliated me."

I frowned. "*Harsh*. If we're talking torment, then I'd at least have chosen Crazy Frog's brilliant novelty song."

"Don't even think about it," Fox warned like I was about to launch into the most annoying song in creation after "Baby Shark".

Ah, it was sweet how well he knew me already.

Lysander pulled Willoughby even closer. "Have you no loyalty, even after what I've suffered to keep you safe from your brother?"

To my surprise, Willoughby's expression softened, and he patted Lysander's shoulder. "Can't I be both Prince *and* wish not to harm Immortals?"

I drew in a sharp breath, darting a glance to Magenta. *This was it*: The plan to break the Membership by bringing over the Princes to our side.

Who wouldn't choose Magenta? But if Willoughby was too shy to come to Magenta, then Magenta would have to go to Willoughby.

Magenta's lips curled into a smile, as she nodded at me. I edged to the wall.

"I choose Willoughby." Magenta pointed at him.

The tips of Willoughby's cute pointy ears reddened, and he clutched Lysander like he'd save him.

Instead, Lysander's eyes glittered, and he shoved

Willoughby tumbling into the center of the circle. "Enjoy this so-called game, when she's humiliating you."

Willoughby's expression shuttered, and he sat with his back military straight.

Sleipnir pulled Fox onto his lap, carding his fingers through his curls, as they both intently watched.

"One minute," Fox called.

Magenta's magic slipped from the walls in a fine mist, settling around Willoughby like pink clouds. He panted, and the tips of his hair iced.

"Can you feel the connection of our magic?" Magenta whispered. "Nothing divides us. Feel it...*and awake...*"

"*Stop*," Willoughby choked out.

Magenta froze. Her magic blasted away from him like it'd been stung. Her eyes gleamed with rejected tears, the same as his.

Shocked, I glanced between them. *What'd gone wrong?*

"Fifty-four seconds," Fox muttered. "Wow, I've won Silver Award Mindfuck, but Magenta must be at Platinum."

"The Immortals have won, which means that we're also kicking off the polo," Sleipnir pointed out.

"One has many talents," Lysander snarled, "but caring about your petty game right now is not one of them." I gaped at him. *The perfect prince wasn't bothered about losing a competition...?* Instead, he scrambled to Willoughby, sliding his hand across the prince's arms and legs as if Magenta had broken him. *Except, she had.* "Look what you've done."

Although he glared at us, Lysander still appeared bewildered.

Yet it was clear to my slinky self that we'd wrecked Willoughby. The glimpse of her true self and magic...everything that he'd yearned for in his diary...had been wrong.

I was a bad incubus.

Something squirmed inside, and I didn't like the sensation. Willoughby's feelings for Magenta wasn't a crush; it was true love. He'd join us, but we couldn't play with him anymore.

It had to be real.

"Next time you wish to make someone feel," Lysander said, coldly, "how about feeling yourself?"

I was certain Lysander hadn't meant that to sound so kinky.

Lysander turned, pulling Willoughby after him. Willoughby's head was ducked, and his shoulders shook. It was Magenta's cheeks, however, which were streaked with tears.

Where had the game gone so wrong? My currently sticky pants were evidence that this had been a fun evening...*until it hadn't.*

That squirming feeling was back. Incubi didn't do guilt; it made your hair limp. But the squirming feeling had to be because the game had been my idea.

"Follow Willoughby in your sexy Voyeur ghost form," I urged Magenta, fiercely. "Please, I can't go on the mission tomorrow, leaving behind someone who loves you...*us*...and who's in pain." My temples throbbed. Hector had never truly believed that I'd loved him because he'd been told too many times by bad bastards that he was *unlovable*. I dived forward, catching Magenta's hands between mine. Her magic sparked. "Love Willoughby. *Save him*."

CHAPTER SIXTEEN

Rebel Academy, Thursday September 5th

MAGENTA

Invisible, I sprawled on the thick carpet of the Prince's floor in the East Wing, resting against a grand wardrobe, which was picked out with a mosaic battle scene between Immortals and Princes. I'd been concerned that the wards would stop me from following Willoughby into this forbidden part of the castle, but it appeared that in my ghostly form, I could trick them.

Number 77 in the Advantages to being Undead.

I had to admit that the title Voyeur Ghost did rather fit, as I remained ladylike and only peeked...twice...as Lysander and Midnight changed into pink silk pajamas. I couldn't decide whether the curve of Midnight's ash wings next to his alabaster shoulder blades or Lysander's emerald wings were more beautiful.

Lucky me, I didn't have to choose.

To my surprise, Willoughby perched on the edge of his ice bed, which glittered like crushed diamonds, without changing.

Did he wear that military style uniform even to bed?

Willoughby was pale, and I was decidedly certain that it was my fault. My goodness, that hurt.

To my even greater surprise, Lysander shot Willoughby a glance that was tender, as he strolled to the marble counter at the far side of the room and fingered the stallion cup as reverentially as I had. Then he unscrewed one of the seven jars of tea.

Why, I most certainly would like a cup, how kind.

I bit hard on my lip not to let the words tumble out, even as I eagerly sniffed the scent of fresh earthiness, which took me back to my morning ritual of tea with my father in the Bird Turret.

If *I* asked Lysander to serve me, he'd most likely spit in it...or faint. Unlike the Immortals, he wasn't used to ghosts making demands of him.

So, tempting...

Yet it was even more tempting to watch how the Princes were around each other, when they weren't puffing themselves up like they had to play at being the Immortals' rivals. Lysander's expression was soft in a way that I'd never seen before, and Willoughby's was more broken.

Sweet Hecate, I didn't know them at all.

When Lysander smiled at Midnight, the vampire crawled with a confident swagger towards the basket next to the counter, which was lined by a blanket. The basket was rough and nothing like the rest of the luxurious bedroom. Midnight climbed in, turning around and tucking his wings close to his body...*wings that would be broken tomorrow.*

I winced. I'd saved my mage, yet Lysander had failed his whipping boy. I'd mocked the fact that Lysander could care for him.

Well, didn't I feel the foolish one now?

Midnight stretched out one arm and then the other, wriggling around to fit his long limbs into the basket. *Cauldrons and broomsticks, that must be uncomfortable.*

As Lysander poured the hot water onto the aromatic leaves, he absentmindedly patted Midnight's head.

Ah, so the princes did have their own dog after all.

Perhaps, Bask would get to play with a puppy, just not quite in the way that he'd imagined. I shivered, as Midnight licked Lysander's hand, between each finger, and then sucked his thumb into his mouth.

I held my breath, waiting for Lysander's hex or crisp slap.

Instead, Lysander laughed.

I'd never heard him like that. It felt like he'd slapped *me*.

All of a sudden, I knew what I wanted even more than the tea that he was preparing. And I never wanted *anything* more than a decent cup of tea.

Lysander disentangled himself from Midnight, who let his hand go with a reluctant *pop*. "Tasty as I am, restrain yourself. You may feed from my royal personage in the morning."

My eyes widened. *Feed?* Did a Prince truly sacrifice his blood to a vampire whipping boy?

Lysander glanced at Willoughby, who was curled against the headboard of his bed with his arms around his knees. "You're not still worrying about that witch? She's beneath a Prince's notice."

It shouldn't have hurt, but it did.

Lysander carried the black tea over to Willoughby, passing it to him, before he perched next to him on the bed. It looked like the same easy ritual that I'd had with father. In the West Wing, it was more like a mad scrum for the bathroom, dive for pillows, and then cuddle together on the same bed. This was quieter and fitted royalty.

But it was still familiar and relaxed.

I'd been expecting Lysander would act like a guard

313

or with his usual snark. But then, expectation makes an ass of us all, especially a witch who'd been stuck in a tree for a century and had never even seen how the Rebel boys had lived together before that.

Perhaps, a lot of what I'd imagined had been wrong.

I stood up, before floating closer to the bed.

I just needed to touch. *One single touch....*

When Willoughby took a sip of his tea and sighed in satisfaction, I couldn't help my own groan of frustration.

Willoughby looked up, sharply.

I pinched my non-existent self. *Invisible people do not groan.*

Lysander tapped Willoughby on the knee to get his attention. "Drink up. There's no time to get distracted by witches, who as I said, are bene—"

Willoughby slammed the cup onto the bed, and the teeth sloshed out onto the sky-blue velvet covers. Lysander gaped at him.

"She wasn't beneath your guardian's *notice*." Willoughby's eyes narrowed.

Lysander snarled, and his eyes flashed with a sudden predatory danger. I rushed forward to block him, but I'd forgotten that I hadn't materialized.

His hand *whooshed* right through me.

Hecate's tits, that tingled.

Lysander knocked the stallion cup thudding to the carpeted floor. Willoughby became ashen.

"*Thunder, no...*" He scrambled to the edge of the bed after the rolling cup, but Lysander caught him by his long hair and dragged him back.

"Do *not* speak like that about my noble guardian." Lysander leaned over Willoughby, pinning him to the bed. Yet his gaze darted to the glowing board on the wall with the lists of scrolling **Privilege** and **Punishment** Points. Could the magic woven into the room tell if he didn't defend the academy's patron? I knew from Robin that Titus was a narcissist, but was part of him inside the academy as well? My magic shook at the thought. "You don't have the right and you don't know..."

Willoughby cupped Lysander's cheek as gently as his fellow Prince's words were violent. "I beg your pardon."

Lysander slumped against him like that was all he'd needed to hear. He eased off him, before casting an uneasy glance above him at the ceiling of the bed, which glistened with ice for a moment like it too had been enraged by Willoughby.

"Do you imagine that it'd bring me much pleasure if your brother tightened your suit or made your night-mares worse?" Lysander drawled.

Willoughby's lips twitched. "Not *much*."

Lysander chuckled, before pulling the ribbons out

of Willoughby's hair, which swung like a waterfall over his face. "Why would you risk anything for her?"

For me....

Willoughby wet his lips, hesitating. "Because of the way that her magic and she make me feel. Tonight, for the first time in an age, I heard the rivers sing."

My heart clenched. I'd heard it too: beautiful clear notes.

Had it truly been because of me...because we were together...or because of our love?

Lysander had become very still. He scrutinized Willoughby for a moment.

Then he coughed, dragging the covers over Willoughby. "Sleep, stupid elf."

Yet, there was a fondness to it, just like the way that Lysander sauntered past Midnight, ruffling his hair on his way to his own obsidian bed.

It was certainly a shock that the Princes tucked each other in. Of course, so did the Immortals, but Bask was far more creative, using his teeth, tongue, and fingers in ways that I'd never imagined even with my familiars' descriptions of the Rebels' wanking.

You could only do so much by yourself, it would appear.

Sleipnir would never allow Lysander to live it down.

My brow furrowed. Only, I knew that I wouldn't

tell my delicious Immortals. The Princes believed themselves alone and free to be themselves.

This was even more private than a memory.

I'd never sneak a look into their private world, if it wasn't to save Willoughby. I'd hated the stricken look on Bask's face, after the Stop Game had blown up in our faces in such a spectacular fashion. I should've been able to read Willoughby well enough to never hurt him like that. But instead, I'd made him believe that I was playing with his feelings to publicly humiliate him, just as Lysander had warned.

All of us had come to care for Willoughby, and Echo would weep (or peck my tits because he could be volatile when it came to love), if I left him believing that we didn't.

His magic was powerful, and my magic wanted it.

I wanted him.

Black cats, I hadn't truly understood it until that moment.

The lights dimmed, as Lysander slipped under his own covers.

There was an exhilaration that I didn't understand, as I settled to face Willoughby on the bed, who'd turned to the side. His breath was soft and even. I longed to reach out my arms and clasp them around him, resting my head on his chest.

Ah, so this was obsessive romance then.

I adored watching how the lines smoothed from

his face, as his breath evened out to sleep. I realized then that he must be in pain when he was awake.

He was so beautiful.

I stroked a strand of hair out of his face, and he didn't stir.

When I looked up, I caught Midnight's gaze, which was leonine in the dark, from his basket underneath the counter. My breath stuttered. Could he see me? Or did he always stay awake, watching over the Princes, until they were deeply asleep?

I took a solid form (without making myself visible), and leaned closer to Willoughby. I blew against his lips. His face creased in a frown.

Then his eyes fluttered open.

They were so blue like the frozen rivers that he could hear only because of my magic. I gasped, and his eyes widened at the sound. But he didn't move, cry out, or attack me with his ice.

Instead, he shivered like he was holding himself together from breaking, as he murmured, "Magenta...?"

My name rolled from his lips, slow and sensual, like both a prayer and a seduction. Yet there was nothing to seduce because I was already his.

I moved my lips close enough to his, so that he'd feel their touch on each word. "It doesn't matter where you sleep, Prince, you're still one of my Immortals."

"Am I dreaming?" Willoughby's arms banded

around me like steel, stroking the hollow of my ghostly back.

I wasn't even visible, yet he was the one who was making *me* feel. The bed was cold, but warmth coiled through me.

"You're awake." I shivered at the way that his breath was cool against my lips, just as his fingers heated my back in sweeping circles.

He flinched, and his wide eyes were devastatingly hurt. For the first time, I realized the power that I held over him.

I could truly break him.

Willoughby's fingers clawed into my dress. "This is more teasing like in the Stop Game." When he turned away his head, pain lanced through me. "Will you take tales of the stupid elf back to your beloved Immortals? Do I need to say *stop* again?"

"Do you want to?" I slipped mists around Willoughby, twisting his chin, until he faced me again. Reluctantly, he met my gaze. "Sweet Hecate, this is no game or dream. If you love and want me, then I'm yours. Just let us have tonight."

Willoughby's gaze softened. Then his eyes darkened. "Tonight, you're mine alone..."

He caught my lips in a possessive kiss. His frozen magic slipped over mine, until I shivered. I sank beneath his icy depths. I wrapped my hand in his hair, pulling him even more deeply into the kiss. He was delicious. I could lie like this in his arms all night.

There was a world of need and desire in every kiss that he feathered along my jawline and then my neck. I bit my lip not to laugh as he missed, tonguing only air. I directed him by the hair, and his dancing gaze met mine.

Making out with the invisible girl was a challenge.

I was certain that an elf prince was up to it. His prick was decidedly on board; it pressed against my hip. Yet Willoughby appeared not to notice his own excitement, rather he concentrated on *my* pleasure alone. I yanked his hair lightly, when his kisses became too passionate.

Willoughby and I were turned away from Midnight, but Midnight might've become suspicious of kissy sounds during a wanking session. At least, I hoped that Willoughby didn't normally lie in bed conducting make out sessions with the pillow as my substitute.

Perhaps, he did.

I peered over Willoughby's shoulder. Midnight's glowing eyes still watched Willoughby with an edge of both suspicion and hungry excitement.

I swallowed, and the coiling warmth within me flared even higher. There was something alluringly naughty about pulling this off in the Princes' bedroom at night, while Juni believed her charges to be locked up and chaste. Even more so, with Lysander lying in the opposite bed, quietly snoring.

After all, I was a wicked witch, even if it felt more blessed than wicked, the way that Willoughby hooked his leg over mine, pulling me even closer, until his hard body pressed against mine. His suit was so tight that I could feel every muscle, as his chest rose and fell.

I yearned to unwind that silk and free him. I was desperate to kiss over every inch of revealed skin, licking over his nipples and making him *feel*...

But if he wouldn't remove his clothes, then I'd join him beneath them.

I smiled against his lips, as I slipped my mists inch by inch down his trousers. Then I wrapped them around his hard prick.

Ah, so the stories about elves were true: They were as beautifully formed in their manly parts as everywhere else.

Did that mean fae also had as large pricks as they always boasted? After all, they *were* pricks...

When my mists encircled Willoughby's balls, gently playing with them and the soft skin behind, before stroking up and down his prick in love and worship, Willoughby hissed sharply through his teeth.

Lysander turned over in bed, half waking. "What's wrong?" He called, sleepily. "A nightmare again? Do you need me to come sleep with you, Will?"

I froze with my mists still down Willoughby's pants.

Witch's tit, I didn't fancy attempting to stay silent, stuck between the two Princes. My nose scrunched up. Did that also mean that Lysander comforted Willoughby when he had nightmares?

Was Lysander attempting to destroy all my fae prejudice in one night? Also, why couldn't I stop imagining how close my own lips had been to Lysander's in Bacchus' class?

Willoughby's brow furrowed. "No need to concern yourself. It's only..."

"Oh, I understand," Lysander grumbled, plumping his pile of fluffy pillows and settling back down in a disgruntled pile of fae. He folded his golden wings over his ears, as if to block out any more noise. "It was less a nightmare and more a wet dream about your witch...*again*."

Willoughby flushed, and his eyes widened with panic. I smothered my laughter against his shoulder, but Midnight snickered.

I didn't know if I loved the *your witch* part or the fact that he'd desired pleasure with me so badly that he'd had wet dreams about me, where I now lay.

But this was no longer a dream.

I curled my mists more tightly around Willoughby's prick, swirling around its sensitive head, lapping around it like a tongue, and then stroked him hard and insistent.

Willoughby held me like he'd been frozen to ice and without this touch, he'd shatter.

I pumped his silky prick quicker and quicker...

Sweet Hecate, this beautiful, dangerous creature was mine.

Willoughby didn't turn away from me this time. I was lost in his cold gaze, as much as he was lost in mine. There was nothing anymore, but each other. This moment and touch.

I understood now: *my* pleasure didn't matter because this wasn't about lust or touch.

It was love.

Willoughby's breath became ragged, and he shook. My mists licked round and round the ridge of his prick's head, at the same time as stroking faster.

If I shattered Willoughby, could I put him back together?

"Come," I whispered.

I swallowed Willoughby's gasp with a kiss. His prick pulsed and came, and I held him, as his magic flowed through mine. It craved to break free and freeze the room, destroying everything in our passion. Yet I could control him or together, our magic found a new way to cling to life, rather than to death.

As I lay in bed with a deadly prince whose power was as wild as my own, I realized that this was about more than the Membership or freeing us from the academy. I hadn't lied to Willoughby.

This wasn't a game.

Yet I'd awoken the same as Willoughby, and I knew that I was the one who could shatter.

CHAPTER SEVENTEEN

Rebel Academy,Friday September 6th

BASK

I t was typical Damelza to even make our reward of free time sound like a chore. This afternoon, we Immortals would be sent on a deadly mission, so this morning we'd been treated to Compulsory Relaxation.

I was surprised that the bad bastard hadn't included Compulsory Wanking. Away with you, it was a brilliant way to relieve stress, and it strengthened your sperm into wee Supermen...or Spermen.

Seriously, I was taught about that in the harem. Incubi Sex Education was thorough and practical.

I shuddered. Still, I didn't need to be *told* to relax.

Rule 29 of the Incubi Code stated: Relax, you've already done the hard work to look this good.

Wait, if it was a rule, then maybe I *did* need to be told...?

I snorted, running my fingers through my shiny hair.

Yep, I did look this good.

At least Compulsory Relaxation meant that Magenta had been allowed to lead us Immortals out of the castle and into the crisp air of the grounds. Fox was wrapped in Sleipnir's spare woolen coat. There was no Juni around to insist that Fox freeze. Sleipnir's expression softened, every time that Fox sniffed at the collar like Sleipnir's scent made him feel safe.

Inside, it'd felt suffocating, just waiting for the mission to start. Outside, I'd looked up at the gray sky and the spires of non-magical Oxford. It was possible to remember that there was a free world outside the trials, rivalries, and missions.

I'd taken deep lungfuls of air, which smelled fresh and as untamed as the grounds. As I'd settled on my sexy arse beside the lake, and the snow had *crunched* beneath me like a blanket, the ancient magic from the Dead World pulsed. All of a sudden, I'd felt it twisting deep inside me that there was so much more at stake here than my own slinky self, the professors, or the princes (*remarkable, snicker*).

Magenta was the academy, nature, and death. If

we broke the curse, then we'd save her, free all the Rebels forever, and close down the darkest academy in the supernatural world.

I'd bitten my lip to hide its tremble because *I'd* never be free. My place was as an obedient freak of a bonded at the Succubus Court. But here's the thing, love was eternal to an incubus. It was this whole *thing*. So, I'd never stop loving Magenta, and if I died for her this afternoon, then at least the Duchess would never touch me again.

As long as all my Immortals were safe, I'd burn myself to death.

Come on now, what's not romantic about that?

I peeked at Magenta, who lay with her head on Sleipnir's lap. He stroked his fingers through her hair. His own hair was candy pink and longer than normal in soft waves, which must mean that this *relax* thing was working. Perhaps, I should order him around more to bring out this calm side: Compulsory Petting or Compulsory Cuddling.

Didn't I already do that?

Fox shivered next to me, scooping snow up with his bare hands, which were slowly turning blue. I frowned. He needed gloves, a scarf, and proper boots. Whipping Boy Care was harder than it looked. His curls fell over his eyes, as he knelt up with intense concentration, building a snowman.

Wait, a snow*cat*.

Mist was curled sleepily on Magenta's delicious tits (totally wasting sucking opportunities by nuzzling against them with the occasional satisfied snort), with a flamboyant pink tail and mane.

Magenta glowed with a matching pink aura like she couldn't stop her magic overflowing. She'd been the same ever since she'd returned at dawn from sleeping in Willoughby's bed.

Who was I kidding? From kissing, cuddling, and screwing the elf.

I scrunched up my nose, pouting.

Guilt had caused the nasty squirmy sensation in my guts after the Stop Game, and I'd been the incubus who'd insisted that she *save Willoughby*. It was hot to imagine the way that her mists had wrapped around his dick because she'd shared all the details, until Sleipnir had growled and dragged her down between us Immortals like we needed to claim her from the Princes again. Yet she'd refused to tell us anything else that she'd witnessed in the Princes' Wing.

Even the best incubus could only feel *so* guilty, however, and Magenta hadn't just been *wham, bam, thank you prince*.

She'd stayed with Willoughby, until he'd drifted to sleep in her arms. Jealousy was unattractive in an incubus, but I still shook with it because I was jealous of both of them.

I slid my hands down to my slim waist. Magenta

had been insisting on more food for me over the last couple of days. I'd indulged without thought to my trimness.

Had I broken the cardinal Night Code and become less pettable?

I gasped, shooting Magenta another look. *What if I dyed my hair sky-blue…?*

I moistened my plush lips, preparing myself for a seduction. This was my talent. *Time for a Bask Attack.*

If we survived, Magenta would want *me* in her arms tonight.

I crawled towards Magenta with a deliberate swing to my hips. My ruby eyes glittered. I leaned over Magenta like I was going to kiss her, and her breath stuttered. At the last moment, however, I pulled back.

"Prick tease," Sleipnir muttered, fondly.

Away with you, I didn't imagine the fondly.

"But I don't have a prick to tease…" Magenta's brow furrowed.

I peeked at her from underneath my eyelashes, then slinked down, until my lips were closer to an even more tempting part of her. "If it pleases you, I can improvize."

I pressed my mouth along her thigh and then inward, as she quivered. Sleipnir wasn't the only one with a talented tongue.

Suddenly, Magenta squawked, sitting up. Her

magic sparked, prickling my nose. I fell backward onto my arse.

Fox chuckled.

She'd repelled a Bask Attack…? I must've become less pettable. Did she still even want me? Did I not please her anymore?

I whined, as my own biology punished me even at the thought. Well, that was a boot to the balls.

"Stop panicking," Magenta's voice was quiet but commanding. It shot tingles right through me. *I liked that.* I also loved the way that her magic now stroked over me in apology. "You'll forever please me. Forgive my magic, you simply startled me. Your hand went straight through Flair, and his insult was rather colorful."

My eyes widened, and I straightened myself with a toss of my head.

That she was *pleased* with me, sparkled like champagne bubbles, feeding me with pleasure.

"Your familiars are here…?" Sleipnir blinked. "When did Tweedle Dee and Tweele Dum arrive?"

Magenta grimaced. "They were scouting for me to find out about the mission, but Flair has just informed me that if you refer to him as a character from Alice in Wonderland again, then he'll *stick his beak right up your rabbit hole.*"

"He needs his beak washing out with soap," Sleipnir muttered.

I bounced onto my knees. "Go on, call them the Cheshire Crows!"

Magenta fixed me with a stern glare. "Flair says that *your* rabbit hole isn't safe either."

I squeaked but then narrowed my eyes. "You're making it up."

Magenta waved an airy hand. "My familiars flapped across the lake and joined us about half an hour ago. They're snuggling on my lap right now. Flair is creatively universal in his insults."

I arched my brow.

I wouldn't be intimidated by a witch and her invisible familiars. Then my shoulders slumped. Magenta had nothing to fear from me but multiple orgasms, and she knew it.

Magenta's expression gentled. "Echo is too busy to join in the threats because he's been singing his elf victory song. He has a charmingly unique voice." Then she sang so off-key that my ears ached, "*Screw the elf, save the world. Screw the elf, save the world. Screw the el—*"

I winced. "How about *screw the incubus and save our ears?*"

Sleipnir raised his hand. "You have my vote."

I still had it.

Fox glanced up from the snowcat that he was building. He'd used a fallen branch as its tail, pushed a pebble onto its head to be its nose, and drawn on whiskers. Now, he was molding its ears as lovingly as if he expected it to spring to life.

"Seconded. These *screwing to save the world* dilemmas are tough on us superheroes. Just last week, I was faced with screwing Harley Quinn." He smirked at the possessive way Sleipnir's hair bristled to red. That was a fine bit of alpha posturing, when we all knew that *last week*, the most our whipping boy had been doing with his dick was wanking with it. "It's okay, I didn't go through with it. Batman was just bouncing up and down to do the honors. You should've seen his excited little face. I mean, I couldn't actually see his face behind the mask, but he was up for it." Fox smiled at us innocently. "So, what did the familiars find out about the mission?"

Magenta sighed. "Do you know the ruins? Almost five hundred years ago, the first Blessedly Charmed witch was born. I'm the only other one born after her, and it rather appears that I've corrupted the magic. To be kept pure, they built a small house in the grounds for a nanny and her alone." When her hands bunched in her lap, I wondered if she was crushing one of her familiars or if they'd already flapped somewhere else. I wished that she was holding me, even if she crushed me. "Wasn't I lucky to be kept only in the Bird Turret?"

"As lucky as me *only* to be locked in the attic,

rather than thrown to the wolves like my brother," Fox muttered.

"Flair says that there's powerful magic in the ruins that doesn't belong there." Magenta's eyes narrowed. "The House of Crows have stolen it from the angels: A *Gateway*."

Fox froze. "I read the word *Gateway* with my power from Damelza on my first night. She was one pissed off witch."

Sleipnir sprawled on the snow, cradling his head on his hands. "How'd you think we travel from the academy to other realms? The Gateway is both a powerful weapon and a way to walk between worlds. They shouldn't exist outside Angel World, but I'd take a guess that our fae *patron* is asshole enough to steal one. Then he's using the academy students like his personal mercenaries."

"*Expendable* mercenaries," I added.

I remembered the way that Hector had fought the demons in the Eternal Forest because we'd messed up the stealthy plan and been discovered. I was haunted by the look of fear in his eyes, as he'd been snatched away from me. I'd battled to his side, but I wasn't a warrior, and I hadn't been fast enough. I hadn't even seen what'd pulled him up into the air like he'd been wrapped in shadows, but then, he'd been ripped apart. His blood had wept across my face. It'd baptized my cheeks, nose, and lips.

Red, red, red.

I scrubbed my hand across my cheeks frantically. They were wet. But incubi didn't cry.

Please don't let it be blood...

I bit back a horrified gasp, and my breath became ragged.

Fox shot me a concerned glance. Then I noticed the snowflakes resting on his eyelashes. He was beautiful, and he was alive. My breath steadied.

It was snow, resting as gently as petals across my face.

There was no blood. But my slinky self would be going through that Gateway again tomorrow. What if it was the mage's blood coating my face then?

After all, I'd failed to protect Hector.

I squared my shoulders. I was an incubi of the Night Lineage. I'd promised to protect and love Fox *and I would.* I wouldn't let him be drawn into the darkness away from me. An incubus never let go of any of his lovers. Magenta, Fox, and Sleipnir were mine just like my pillows. There was no higher love than Pillow Love. Seriously, check the love poems on it. There must be loads.

Magenta shuddered, wrapping her arms around herself. "Surely, they can't be expecting us to carry out their dirty work...?"

Sleipnir shoved himself to his feet, stalking to the

edge of the lake. "Valhalla! We're assassins who kill. We're not scouts, selling cookies."

Magenta elegantly rose up, floating after him. "Why would an army scout attempt to sell baked goods?"

Sleipnir pulled her to him by her waist and kissed her forehead. "I'm not even attempting to explain boy scouts and cookies."

I grinned. "I often get those two mixed up anyway, which is messy."

Fox drew a smile onto his snowcat with his little finger, then twisted back to us with a smile that was as wide as his creation's. "*Ta da!* Let me introduce you to the Leader of the Abominable Snowcats. Once, there was a whole tribe of them but a couple of years ago, they wouldn't listen and insisted that they swim the river Thames for charity." He bit his trembling lip, and I dived across the snow to curl my hand comfortingly around his neck. *Wait, had he just conned a snuggle out of me for the fictional deaths of the Snowcats?* He rubbed against my cheek, before winking slyly. "It's okay, it's all water under the bridge now."

I batted him away from me, and he laughed.

Should I curse him to have slime fall *out* of everything that he opened or to have slime fall *onto* him every time that he opened anything…?

Delicious decisions.

"Hey, is that Willoughby?" Sleipnir asked in a hushed voice that vibrated with awe.

Surprised, I shuffled to the edge of the lake, as Fox crawled behind me.

Then I gave a shocked intake of breath.

In the center of the frozen lake, Willoughby skated with a beauty and magic that shook me. His power was controlled but it still arched out of him in waves. The skates themselves were glittering ice, the same as the points of his blue hair. He looked like an ice sculpture come to life. Flares of branching patterns sparked out in lightning strikes across the lake on each jump and spin.

In the academy, he appeared stilted and formal, as if he was lost. Lysander dragged him from class to class or shoved him into his seat. But here, he was in charge with a grace and ease that any incubi would envy. My eyes widened, as he jumped dramatically, spinning in the air, round and round...

My heart pounded. No one could jump and spin at that speed. *He was going to fall.*

But he landed and he didn't fall.

Yep, my dick did a jump of its own at that.

Ten points to both Willoughby and my dick.

"The ice will crack," Sleipnir's voice was low; his shoulders were stiff. "Float out there and save his crazy ass."

Magenta stared at Willoughby, transfixed. "Such

grace and *power*." Then she smiled at Sleipnir. "Does he look like he needs our heroic rescue?"

"He looks like he's standing on ice that cracked the moment *I* stood on it. How long would even an Ice Prince survive in that freezing water?"

Magenta's mists curled around Sleipnir. "I sense that we've stumbled on one of Willoughby's princely Rewards. Juni must hold being allowed this time on the ice over him as motivation for *good behavior*. The ice isn't cracking because..."

"Ice prefers elves, everybody knows that," Fox said, then spluttered, as Sleipnir booted snow into his face. "Or the magic of the academy does."

Before Sleipnir could raise his boot to kick more snow onto Fox (*I'd get my own snowfox*), Magenta wound closer around the disgruntled god.

"You resurrected me: all three of you." She stroked Sleipnir's cheek. "There's no greater connection than that between life and death. Yet there's also a coldness in my magic, which recognizes the ice in Willoughby's. Yours is hot. I adore how it warms me."

"Like mountain pebbles in the sun. I'm amazed that you didn't melt straight through the lake and turn into an iced god, which is a type of popsicle." Fox ducked pre-emptively, but Sleipnir only raised his eyebrow.

I bounced onto my knees. "I'd lick one of those."

Magenta nodded. "If you're referring to his dick, hot or cold, it is indeed tasty."

Sleipnir blushed. Now that was a fine sight.

Willoughby took long strides across the ice closer to us. He was humming the swooning melody of Disney's *Someday My Prince Will Come.*

As Magenta told it, he already had last night.

With the way that Willoughby spun in arcing circles to the romantic jazzy song, I *ached* with desire for the same dream as him.

He was talented, beautiful, and kind. Yet his kingdom only thought he was a killer.

I wanted my elf now.

I cupped my hands over my mouth, before I hollered, "Hey, pointy ears, petting opportunities over here. Come and get them! Do you want to build a snowcat with us or..." How could I tempt him? This was what I'd been trained in. I knew how to turn up the incubi charm. You just had to know the right seduction. *What had he fancied about me again...?* "My arse is at your service for stroking or spanking, as I hear that's what you desire."

Willoughby stared wildly over his shoulder, lost his balance, and landed hard on his own arse.

Result.

I threw myself back happily, making a snow incubus with my arms in the snow. Then I pushed myself up, glancing at Willoughby, who was skating towards us with a frightening purpose.

I *eeped.*

"Spanking Service?" Fox smirked.

Willoughby bended his knees and skated to a stop, shearing off a flurry of snow from the ice. When he prowled off the lake, his skates magically melted. His power thrummed under his skin; it was electric.

"Impressive display *and* control," Magenta murmured.

Willoughby inclined his head, glancing between us. "The skating helps..."

I assessed him. He could've forgotten about my offer. But no one forgot an incubus, right?

"You know that I want you." Magenta rested her hand lightly on Willoughby's chest. "I believe that there's an incubus, attempting to escape over there, who wants you as well."

Oh, naughty...gorgeous...perfect...Magenta.

Willoughby's lips twitched, before his expression became shuttered and he dropped to his knees, crawling towards me like a predatory *hungry* blue panther.

When he smartly sat back and patted his lap like it was a cozy invitation, I swallowed.

I knew that one day my mouth would write a check that my arse couldn't pay.

Although, my arse would be the one who *was* paying. But then, when had I ever turned down a petting opportunity? It'd be breaking the most fundamental of Incubi Codes like spitting on my forebears' dicks.

Away with you, that was how they'd feel about it.

I threw myself over Willoughby's lap, not even trying to hide my enthusiasm, and he chuckled. His thighs were all hard muscle, and his strong arms banded around my waist pulling me closer against him. I sighed at his scent of herbal tea like a wintry breeze across wild grasses.

Was it weird to feel that this was where I belonged? I was safer over an elf's lap than I'd ever been in a succubus' harem.

Anyway, an arse demanded what an arse demanded. There was no talking to it.

I wriggled around, and it wasn't only to rub my hardening dick along Willoughby's lean thighs (*promise, snicker*).

"Pet me," I commanded.

When Willoughby rested his hand lightly on the hollow of my lower back, pushing up my blazer, I shivered. "Are you always pushy in this position? I did warn you once that calling a prince *pointy ears* was a serious crime."

His smack landed with such crispness that I jumped, but I bit my lip to stop the cry.

An incubus must take punishment in silence and not affront others with ugly wailing.

Magenta clapped. "I knew that my Rebels would take their thrashings well."

Fox coughed. "You know that you scare me sometimes...?"

I tingled with warmth from where Willoughby had slapped me. It was the delicious type of pain that radiated all the way to my dick and made my mind hazy with desire. I was starting to float. My limbs felt loose, and I let myself relax.

Again...

Instead, Willoughby stroked my arse like it was made of glass and he didn't know how he'd ever dared to smack it.

That was right: treat the incubus with the respect he deserves.

Willoughby continued to massage my arse with tender strokes, rubbing lower onto my thighs. I stretched out in his lap like I was the cat, widening my legs to tempt him to dip his hand between them to my aching balls.

Come on...

"Now you have me for what you desire," I panted, "you don't need to go looking for clone love."

The Rebel Café could produce clones. I had one of Lysander called Andro, who was submissive. I could summon Andro whenever I had the urge be in charge. I loved him, and in his own way, he loved me. It'd devastated me when Lysander had discovered about him.

Okay, it'd been a wee bit devastating for Lysander as well.

Now I was intimate petting buddies with Willoughby I understood because Willoughby had conjured a clone of *me*.

Could I help it if I was jealous of my own clone?

When Willoughby stopped touching me, I forced myself to halt my desperate humping. It was only polite.

"You know about Bas?" He asked with an iciness that made me wonder if this sexy spanking might turn into the type of thrashing that'd end up with Magenta disappointed in my bravery.

At the thought of her displeasure, my dick wilted.

"Lay off, I'm the one over your lap. You're one of us now, and we don't keep secrets." I huffed.

When Willoughby's fingers carded through my hair, I startled. "I beg your forgiveness. I'm truly grateful for your welcome and petting opportunity." I rubbed my head against his hand to show that his apology had been accepted. "But Bas is... I love him, and it matters not that he's a clone. He's not less worthy for it. Andro isn't the same as Lysander to you, surely?"

I snorted. "Would Lysander kneel and suck my dick?"

Magenta laughed. "Only in my wicked dreams."

Willoughby's fingers tightened in my hair. "I know that Bas isn't you." His voice suddenly became anguished, "Please don't think that I want you only because of him or do you wish to make me choose between you?"

I wrenched my hair away from him (*ouch*), and sat up, straddling him. I placed my hands on his cool cheeks, and stared into his eyes.

Wow, they were so blue.

"Listen here, *pointy ears*, there's no choosing because here's the thing, love isn't like punishment and reward points that get shared from one side of the board to the other. It doesn't work in the way that the bad bastards in this academy want you to believe, where you need to pick one side and then that's all you can have: Princes or Immortals, clones or non-clones, Rebels or Magenta..." When I glanced at her, she floated her mists towards Willoughby and me, catching us in their embrace. We clutched onto each other, as she held us, and I shuddered. Now *this* was where I could live forever. "We'll never ask you to choose. You already have us, if you desire?"

Willoughby's gaze caught Magenta's, and his smile was soft. "I desire."

Yet I knew that this couldn't be *forever*. I belonged

to the Duchess. But first, I'd make sure that this Prince escaped with the Immortals.

He was ours now, just as much as our whipping boy.

All of a sudden, Fox let out a wail and dived towards his snowcat, which had fallen over to the side. Its mouth had blurred into a frown, its ears had melted, and its nose had dropped off.

Fox patted it sadly on the shoulder. "Farewell Leader of the Abominable Snowcat and last of your kind. You were once a good mate but soon, you'll be nothing but a puddle and then, I'll enjoy jumping in you."

Sleipnir straightened from his slouch. "Nothing melts here."

Magenta's eyes widened, before she glanced at the way her mists curled around Willoughby and me.

Willoughby's love must be breaking the Membership and the academy's curse.

Would it be enough…?

Yet the rest of the grounds were still deep in snow, and the snowflakes still drifted from the clouds.

"I would say a few words to mourn your friend's passing," Willoughby said (I kissed the tip of his nose just because I loved to hear the easy way that he now bantered without Lysander guarding him), "but we're all meant to be gathering in the Rebel Café."

Magenta cocked her head. "All as in Princes as well as Immortals…?"

"That doesn't sound good," Sleipnir growled.

Willoughby clasped his arms around my middle. "Juni ordered us to join you in a final hour of Compulsory Relaxation before your mission. I was meant to find you and tell you after my skating."

"Why do I feel that *relaxation* is a euphemism for *torment*," Fox said, wiping his damp hands down his coat.

"Oh no, we've already had Torment Thursday," Magenta said merrily. "I'd imagine that this will be more like a terrifying chore with some angst mixed in. After all, Lysander shall be there."

"Midnight as well," Fox added.

There was one Prince and his whipping boy to tempt to our side, and I'd already proven that my arse *was* tempting.

"Giants and dwarves, a whole hour trapped in that crazy café," Sleipnir gritted out, "with the prince who'd win a contest for the Least Relaxed Asshole ever, and I mean that both ways." I snickered. "Honestly, I'm stressed enough about the mission that we'll end up killing each other way before the hour's over."

"Surely we can use the time to learn more about each other." Magenta exchanged a glance with Sleipnir, and his eyes glittered with understanding. Did she mean to discover ways to wreck them or to love them?

345

It wouldn't hurt to treat ourselves to a wee bit of both...? "In case I haven't been clear: we're all surviving."

Yet why did the witches want to lock us together for an hour? My incubi senses prickled that there was something more dangerous planned than hot baths, dancing, or sucked dicks.

When I rested my head against Willoughby's chest, I could hear his heart *thudding* a beat that was as rapid as mine.

What secrets would the next hour reveal and would we survive?

CHAPTER EIGHTEEN

Rebel Academy,Friday September 6th

SLEIPNIR

One thing that the son of Loki didn't do well in the face of danger was *relax*. On Tyr's ass, this hour of Compulsory Relaxation with the princes was going to *suck*.

Jormungand, my brother, was always better at indolence and napping. Fenrir burned with hot-tempered protectiveness. It didn't matter that they both lived inside me because right now, I was myself.

Plus, I feared for my lovers, despite Fenrir's howled excitement for the wild risk of the mission.

The thrill vibrated beneath my skin, but I held it inside because I also ached with grief. I missed

Hector. I hadn't loved him in the same way as Bask because I kind of didn't think that I honestly could *feel* like he did.

Omens and runes, I swear that Bask laid his heart on a silver platter for every monster to devour.

Including me.

Now for the first time I did love, however, and I was terrified that death would claim the other Immortals on this mission.

Yet if it did, I'd break through the veils and resurrect them. After all, my magic had already worked once on Magenta. I wouldn't lose any of them.

Wasn't that love?

Relaxing with the Princes, who'd won the right to send us on this mission in a dickish game of magical Russian Roulette that'd poisoned Bask, wasn't my style.

It was time for Lysander to taste his own medicine. *I'd create my own chaos moment.*

I slipped off my blazer, tossing it over the back of the suede sofa in the Rebel Cafe. Then I slowly rolled up my shirt sleeves over my muscled forearms.

Hey, I took what intimidation tactics I could get.

Except, the way that Magenta's pupils dilated and she scooted closer to me on the sofa, until our thighs were touching (which sent sparks shooting directly to my hardening dick), looked less like intimidation and more like desire.

Huh, I'd have to remember that trick.

Ian Brown's ghostly "Corpses in Their Mouths" boomed from the walls with its thudding beat and seductive harmonica, which only made my dick harden further. Had Serenity, who'd been magically created to run the café, become confused and fixed the settings to Screw rather than Relax?

Please don't let this be her hint that she wanted to play voyeur at an orgy.

What had I ever done to deserve this AI's crush? *On fear of Valkyries, don't answer that.*

Fox leaned against the sofa, and Midnight curled his beautiful ash wings around him. Of course, Midnight was naked. Did the princes ever allow their whipping boy to wear clothes?

Could I help it if I admired the view?

Willoughby sprawled on the floor, which'd soft-ened to carpet, with Bask on his lap. Willoughby's arms were tightly looped around Bask's waist like he was scared that he'd be snatched away from him. Ever since their *moment* beside the lake, the elf hadn't wanted to stop touching *my* incubus.

Lysander paced from one side of the room to the other like a pink and black caged tiger. He cast confused glances at Willoughby and then Midnight. He'd blink, before glancing disbelievingly at the way that his Prince and whipping boy were cuddling Immortals.

I smothered my laugh against Magenta's shoulder, before glancing up into her dancing eyes.

The Membership was breaking down, so it was time to break a fae prince.

I brushed my lips against Magenta's ear, and she shivered. "How about we hunt a prince?"

Her gaze became knowing, and she nodded.

By the Norns, she was wickedly smart. *Loki would approve.*

All of a sudden, the walls swirled with pictures of giant puppies.

"Odin's cock..." I recoiled because it was like being drowned in cuteness. "Serenity, this isn't relaxing."

"You mean that *you're* stressed, godling," Serenity's Welsh voice crooned from the walls. "It's been proved that dogs calm people."

I clenched my jaw. "I'm not calm right now."

"That's right: admit to your emotions!" Serenity said, brightly. "How about a good cry!"

"No dogs," I growled.

Bask pouted, "Don't take away the puppies."

Willoughby stroked Bask's hair in consolation. He already had his own pet.

Fox pointed at Bask. "How can you say *no* to that face?"

I narrowed my eyes. "Practice."

The puppies vanished from the walls, which softened to indigo, and Bask whined.

"Stroke my pussy!" Serenity chirped.

"I beg your pardon?" Magenta spluttered.

"I meant, stroke *a* pussy. As long as you're not allergic to cat hair, mind." Serenity's voice became sly. "Why don't you use your own pussy?"

"How personal." Magenta crossed her arms. "Use your own. Oh yes, you don't have one."

Ouch.

The lights dimmed, and Midnight tightened his wings around Fox.

Could a Stress Counselor go postal on her students' asses?

Fox glanced around with an adorable attempt to look stern. "As the *actual* cat, I veto all talk of playing with pussies."

When Midnight chuckled, Fox silenced him with a kiss.

Lysander's lips pinched like he might be the one to go postal instead.

Time to kick off the chaos moment.

I cracked my knuckles, and Lysander winced. Now *that* was stress relief.

"How about we play a game?" I said as casually as I could. "Princes against Immortals, and not a pussy or puppy in sight, I promise."

Magenta clasped my arm; her glove was cool against my warm skin. "What fun!"

"Your concept of fun has so far not tallied with my own," Lysander said, dryly.

"How do you know?" Magenta arched her brow. "You've never truly had fun with me, or you'd be begging for more."

Lysander stopped pacing and flushed. "A prince does not beg."

What was the bet that Willoughby had begged last night...?

I tilted my head. "Do you want that asshole guardian of yours to be proud of you on Saturday?"

Lysander shot me a wary glance. "Obviously." He hugged his arms around himself. Did he even know that he was doing it? "But he *won't* because the Princes lost the Rebel Cup. How can I show him that I'm reformed, if I don't even have the honor of starting the Dragon Polo Tournament? If I don't achieve well in the academy, then I shan't return to my own kingdom. If I never rule, then I can never overthrow the archaic and cruel rules and save my people." His lips twisted into a sneer. "Sorry, was that nobler than you were expecting from an Unseelie Fae?"

Honestly, yeah...

I steadily met his gaze. "I was only looking for a *yes* or *no*."

Lysander launched himself towards me, but

Willoughby tumbled Bask off his knee, as he leaped up to block him. To my shock, Willoughby gently rested his hands on Lysander's shoulders.

"That's right, massage out the tension," Serenity encouraged. "Really work those shoulders, chest, wings, tight ass, dick and balls..."

Lysander jumped away from Willoughby with a snarl.

Hunting princes *was* fun.

"I'm sorry that I've made you feel that I don't believe you noble," Magenta said. Lysander's eyes widened, and his breath quickened. He looked like he couldn't decide if he wanted to step closer to Magenta or back away. "If starting the Tournament is so important to you, how about we give you another chance to win it back?"

Lysander ducked his head, and his hands clenched into fists. "What else do you wish to strip from me? What more must one lose?"

"Nothing." Magenta's eyes were soft with sadness.

"Chill out," I eased to the edge of the seat, "just play a game with us. As long as you don't back out, then at the end of this hour, you've won the right to start the Tournament, right?"

Bask and Fox nodded.

Lysander took a single pace forward, ensnared. "What's the catch?"

Magenta sprawled back on the sofa. "No catch."

Midnight pushed himself to his knees, dragging Fox with him. His charcoal eyes shone, and his fangs glinted, as he smiled.

"On blood and bones, it'll be a fine thing to play. I haven't in ever so long." Midnight's wings quivered with joy. It was epic that it wasn't with fear for once. His glance at Lysander was achingly hopeful. "May I, my prince?"

Lysander tilted up his chin. "Why are you talking to me? I grant you one leniency and look where my lack of discipline leads." Midnight's hopefulness died, and his wings wilted. "Silence for the rest of this hour. *Of course* whipping boys aren't included."

Asshole.

When Fox rose to his feet, his furious magic prickled across my own. The fae had no idea how close he was to Fox's hedgehog shifter form breaking out, and that'd be embarrassing for all of us, especially if any of the Princes dared to coo. I winced.

Lysander paled, as Fox stalked towards him.

"Our game, our rules," Fox insisted. "*Whipping boys* are here to stay, and if you don't want your *far too beautiful to be fair* wings pricked, then you'll call us *Master* for the next hour."

"Or what?" Lysander sneered.

"Or *ahh, holds wing full of prickles, and wishes that he'd just said Master, as he rolls around in agony.*" Fox's grin even freaked me out.

"He doesn't have to call us that." Midnight prowled to his feet, resting his arms around Fox's neck and grazing his fangs along it; Fox shuddered. The adoring look in his eyes was like *Fox* was his god. "I don't want to be anyone's *Master*, see."

"I told you not to speak," Lysander said, shakily.

To my surprise, Midnight only latched his fangs more firmly onto Fox and glared at Lysander in a way that was dangerous.

"Just once," Fox carefully pulled Midnight away from his neck with a shiver. "A single *Master*, grovel, or bow…?"

Lysander stormed past Fox, throwing himself down in front of the couch. "Fine, my noble self is here and ready to start this ludicrous game of yours."

When Magenta patted him on the head, I barked with laughter. "Now there's the spirit! I'm certain that the importance of enthusiasm is in one of the Principal's Mottos. Although, when I was a girl, we played charades and croquet, rather than—"

"Dirty Truth or Dare." I smirked.

Hector had taught me this game last term, and seriously, it'd been a dangerous game to attempt with someone as wild as him *and* an incubus.

Bask's eyes glittered. He crawled sexily to join the circle around the couch, holding out his hand for Willoughby to join him. "My favorite."

Willoughby elegantly settled on his knees, although his expression was shuttered.

"Do you not know what Professor Crow does to us if we're not immaculate?" Lysander stroked down his blazer, straightening it. "Her hexes are...unpleasant. One shall certainly not be dirtying this uniform."

I winked at him. "I wasn't talking about that type of dirty, *prince*."

When Lysander bristled, I grinned. I'd developed the skill of making titles sound like insults. It was a talent.

Fox led Midnight by the hand to kneel down with him, completing the circle. "Like a dare to change your Facebook status to *I'm coming...I'm coming...just come*."

Magenta scrunched up her nose. "Why would you put your face in a book or is it a picture book of faces, in which case what has it to do with wanking...?"

"Since there's no Wi-Fi here," Fox sighed, unhappily, "you'll never find out."

"Oh, there's that Wu-Fu thingy in the Prince's bedroom."

On the World Tree, I'd never seen someone's jaw fall open in the way that Fox's did. Then Fox stabbed his finger at Lysander like it was a blade. "The larder of treats and silk uniforms I can live with, but your private access to computers...? That's one entitled privilege too far."

"One is deeply apologetic," Lysander said with dripping sarcasm.

Odin's cock, I hoped that it'd choke him.

"Must it be *dirty*?" Willoughby asked.

Magenta arched her brow. "Certainly not. It's your choice."

Willoughby nodded.

The Princes could never turn down a contest. They were walking straight into a trap, which would reveal their secrets *and* fears. Yet they were willing participants.

Loki had trained me to be a formidable hunter.

"We take it in turns to ask either a Truth or Dare," I explained. "You can refuse to answer the Truth but then you have to take a Dare. If you don't, then you lose the whole game and remember, the stakes are the honor to start the Dragon Polo Tournament."

"I understand," Lysander forced out.

Yet his hands twitched on his knees, almost like he was eager to begin. His gaze was fixed intently on Magenta.

"Hey, Serenity," I called, "how about you pick who plays at random. So, no cheating. Pink for the name of the player who sets the Truth or Dare. Black for the player who has to take on the challenge."

"Do I have to point out that every one of your heartbeats are elevated?" Serenity chided. "How about taking off your clothes and taking a long, hot, soapy shower together, instead? Or a cold one...that'll reduce the tension in this room."

"Just play the game and don't pick my name every time."

Silence.

"Serenity..."

"Carry on you, of course not."

"I'm serious."

"Fine."

"Serious as Ragnarok."

"*Meanie*," Serenity sulked.

LYSANDER blazed across the walls in neon pink.

Lysander perked up. "Perhaps, I shall grow to like this game."

Then **SEIPNIR** flashed in black.

"Perhaps, I won't," I muttered.

"I didn't pick you *first*..." Serenity said, slyly.

Lysander was studying me like he couldn't decide if I was the best gift that he'd ever received or a bug for him to dissect.

Then his expression hardened, as his gaze flicked to Magenta. "Truth: What's something that you're afraid to tell Magenta?"

My mind blanked.

So, that's how the hunter became the hunted.

My pulse thundered in my ears. My mind was overloaded with one word: *monster, monster, monster...*

I opened my lips to say it, but nothing came out.

When had I started shaking?

Suddenly, cool fingers closed around mine, squeezing.

"He'll take the Dare." Magenta's voice was tight.

I nodded.

I raised my gaze to meet Lysander's, straightening my shoulders. I wouldn't let him know how he'd wrecked me. Still, I'd wanted secrets revealed.

Karma loved to kick me in the ass.

Lysander's eyes were wide, and he studied how my hand was linked with Magenta's, as he swallowed. "If I played the game wrong..." He whispered.

"I believe that you picked just the right way to play it," Magenta replied, sharply.

Lysander's wings beat, agitatedly. "As you're too coward to answer, I get to set a Dare, which should be dirty. One doesn't wish to disappoint." His eyes gleamed with malevolence. "Dirty talk to your hand."

Asshole.

Yet Bask wriggled sexily, blowing a kiss across the circle to a startled Lysander. "Slippy's dirty talk is a fine thing. I'm claiming you as an honorary incubus."

Lysander blanched. *Now that was how to insult a fae prince.*

Did he think that it'd be humiliating (or even a

challenge), for the son of Loki to use his talented tongue for...*anything*?

I grinned. *This would be fun.*

I pulled my hand away from Magenta's, holding it up in front of me and catching Lysander's gaze. I forced him not to look away, as I pinched my thumb and finger together to create a hole.

If he wanted me to dirty talk to my hand, then I'd also make love to it, and at the same time, *him.*

"You'll forget your name, after I'm done screwing you," I growled, low and seductive. Lysander shivered, curling his arms around himself. "I'm going to ruin your hole." I slowly extended the finger on my opposite hand, moving it towards the hole like it was my prick. After all, he'd wanted *dirty*. I edged my finger in, catching it around the rim. "Valhalla! You're so tight. That's it, clench...work for it." Lysander's eyes were glassy and blown wide. I pushed my finger in and out, in and out. "I love it when you ride me like this. You were made to take my dick. Tell me how much you love feeling me pulse inside you." Lysander gasped. It was my dare, but *he* was imagining it. He was right there, caught in the fantasy. "Beg me to come." My own breathing was ragged; my balls ached. *I was caught with him.* "You look so sexy. I want you to come for me now, *hard.*"

When I pulled my finger out, Lysander groaned, and so did Fox and Bask.

Magenta snatched me by the shoulders, twisting me to kiss her with a passion that was flustered, messy, and *perfect*. I sucked on her lip, and she bit mine back.

Then we both laughed. Her breath gusted across my mouth.

"Well, that was educational." Magenta licked across my lips like she needed to taste me. "Remind me to request that service in bed."

"Yeah, same here." Fox waved his hand, eagerly. "But no *ruining* my hole because I can't simply order a new one. I shudder at how that request would go down with Bacchus."

I chuckled.

Lysander ducked his head, flushed. He stared at the carpet, avoiding my gaze and picking at a fraying thread.

BASK flashed in pink across the walls, followed by **WILLOUGHBY** in black.

Willoughby stiffened.

There was so little time left to discover the truth about the Princes, but this game offered us the chance to reveal their secrets and our own.

Let the hunt of the Princes begin...

CHAPTER NINETEEN

Rebel Academy,Friday September 6th

FOX

The hunt for the truth wasn't as simple as knowing when somebody was lying. My Power of Confess thrummed snatches of music, burst bright lights, or pounded through me at even an *avoidance* of the truth. I should've at least been granted the title of Lie Referee, since I was the one who took the boot to the balls if somebody broke the rules and lied.

Yet it was far more interesting to watch *whether the Princes would even tell us the truth.*

I'd bet my furry tail that Willoughby and Midnight would, and I was attached to my tail. On the other hand, Lysander was still a dick. I wouldn't risk my tail for him.

Yet when I looked up at Magenta, and her scent of yew trees wound around me like love and home, I knew that I'd do anything for her. This game could help us to free Magenta and everybody else in the academy. I'd made promises to Snow, and I wouldn't break them. I'd also promised Midnight, just like he'd sworn oaths to me.

I pressed closer to Midnight, and his wings curled around me. When I slid my hand along his thigh, his skin was as cool as moonlight. I glanced up, catching Lysander's pointed glare at the way that my hand rested on *his* whipping boy.

Wow, I was even thinking in his haughty fae voice.

I smirked, turning to catch Midnight's lips with mine. Then I gasped, as Midnight pushed me back firmly, deepening the kiss. His fang caught my lip, and my mouth was flooded with tangy blood. He groaned, and his hard dick pressed against my hip.

I couldn't help the smug pride that my blood was a turn-on to a vampire.

Then I realized that my dick was also hardening like an eager wolfhound, answering its master's call (*yeah, wolfhound and not chihuahua*).

Down, boy.

I might only have a hazy idea what my kinks were, but why was the way that Midnight now licked over my cut lip with deliberate care making my dick disobediently press against my pants?

I'd have to whack him with a rolled-up newspaper later.

I winced. Then I edged backwards, until I was able to glare down at my lap. *Dick, you won't become a vampire fanboy or they'll be no coming for a month...okay, a week...okay, at least two days, right?*

That should do it.

Magenta's smile was soft. "Our two *whipping boys* appear to have invented games of their own. Perhaps, we could all join in later."

Midnight grinned at the same time as me.

But Lysander's eyes narrowed. "My royal personage should've made it clearer that silence for this hour included good behavior. Your mage has bred such ill-discipline in my whipping boy that he imagines *public kissing* to be decent."

"You should try it," Magenta offered with a sweetness that made Lysander stiffen.

"It's Bask's turn to play," Sleipnir's voice was hard. Mist snorted awake in Sleipnir's blazer pocket, which Sleipnir had slung over the back of the couch. Then Mist slid down the couch like it was a slide. He landed on his rump with an *oomph* and flickers of aquamarine flames. "Truth or Dare?"

Bask wriggled around to face Willoughby, who'd straightened his shoulders as if he was on parade.

Bask considered Willoughby thoughtfully, before reaching out to touch his silk uniform. Yet Willoughby shied away like the suit would taint Bask.

"Your uniform hurts you," Bask said. "I hate it. So, Truth: Why are you always wearing this bastard suit?" Then he shook his head, correcting himself, "Why are you *forced* to wear this uniform?"

Lysander stalked to his feet. "You go too far. No Immortal has a right to demand such—"

"Sit down," Willoughby's voice was as sharp as a whip. Lysander instantly dropped onto his ass. "Would you have me play the coward? It's unworthy to lie no matter the consequences."

So, that was where Willoughby had been hiding his princely side.

The cafe dropped in temperature, and the tips of Willoughby's hair froze to ice.

Would I be turned into a snowcat if I pointed out that he'd been lying by *omission* since the start of term or that *not lying* as a policy was probably why he was locked up in the Rebel Academy?

"I was once cursed with the inability to lie. I ended up speaking in a language that I called *sarcasmese*. For example, I broke the TV, but when dad asked me if I broke it, I replied: Sure, I *totally* broke that TV. I mean, since that's my main form of entertainment, I'd *love* to ruin my only fun. The fact that you'd blame me is *such* a surprise." I glanced around at the raised eyebrows. I wet my lips. "The curse *was* lifted..."

Willoughby ignored me. Instead, he touched the silk that was wound high around his throat. The tips of his fingers caressed it in jerky motions.

"My brother, Darby, denounced me as a Dark Elf." Willoughby stared at the floor, avoiding our gazes. *It was the truth.* Yet his anguish vibrated through me as powerfully as any lie. Lysander's expression was thunderous, but he remained seated. Perhaps, *he* was the puppy prince. "Yet he used dark elven sorcery to bind me." His eyes fluttered closed; his hair hung over his face. "The silk is cursed. The uniform is part of my sentence. It punishes me by magically crushing my magic, body, and mind. It traps me deep inside myself, blocking any access to the Other World. Through it, I'm most thoroughly banished and controlled."

I gasped, and Midnight's wings wrapped around me again. He was shaking, but so was I.

Willoughby's silk uniform was the same as my Blood Amulet, which Sleipnir had freed me from, when I'd first arrived.

When I'd revealed myself to be a mage by transforming into a Birman kitten, mum had forced me to wear an amulet, which had stopped me using my shimage magic.

I knew how wrong it felt to be locked inside. I

shuddered, as the sensation that I'd never escaped swept through me.

Breathe, come on, breathe...

Then Magenta's sparkling magic coiled around mine, and I could *taste* my freedom on every prickling stroke. If I wished, I could transform right now into a fox, cat, or hedgehog with serious attitude.

I was free, but Willoughby was still trapped by the cursed suit. It must be the reason that he often looked like he was lost, crushed beneath the curse. Perhaps, it was also why Lysander manhandled Willoughby into classes and pushed him into seats.

What if sometimes that was the only way that Willoughby could function?

Shuddering, I studied Willoughby, sadly. I was adding him to my Must Free List, which was becoming as long as my Wank Fantasy List. In fact, the two had a fair bit of crossover.

"If we're talking truth," Lysander said, "that's not all the silk does."

Willoughby's head jerked up; his eyes were wild. "Is that not enough?"

Bask slunk to him, running his hand down his side. "If you wish it."

Willoughby tilted up his chin, meeting Magenta's eye. "I swore not to be a coward. The suit also controls my powers. If I took it off..."

"True, but not what one meant." Lysander hugged

his knees to his chest. "Do you not disturb my sleep with your nightmares? Is it not my noble self who suffers to keep you safe from the monstrosity that they force you to wear?"

"It's *his* truth." Magenta leaned forward, catching Lysander's chin and turning him to face her. His startled gaze met hers. "He only needs to share what he chooses. Perhaps, a fae finds it remarkable to believe, but *I* don't wish to force anyone. I'm not the same as my family."

"And neither am I," Lysander whispered.

"Darby can hurt me with this curse even from his kingdom," Willoughby's voice shook. "If I don't play the perfect prince, then at night, it tightens." Hex my balls and call me a witch...that was *brutal*. "And if he truly wishes, he can execute me with a thought."

Mage's balls...

"Are you all feeling relaxed now?" Serenity's voice oozed from the walls like syrup. "How about a burst of scented candles?"

The aroma of lavender flooded the room like Mr. Fierce had decided to roll about in a field of lavender, which come to think of it, did sound relaxing. I choked, holding my sleeve over my nose.

"Just perfect," I forced out between clenched teeth. "I'm totally calm now."

See, sarcasmese.

"You're not, see. In fact, my scans show that your

pulse is too high and so is your body temperature. I can help with that, mind," Serenity purred.

Freezing water splashed magically out of the air over my face.

I spluttered in shock. Now I was a wet hedgehog in a lavender field. When I shivered, my only consolation was that Midnight licked the water from my cheeks. It almost made the cold water worth it.

Almost.

"Although you don't appear to have an ass," Magenta's magic sparked dangerously around the room, as if it was testing the walls for weaknesses, "if you attack my Rebels again, then I shall find a way through to you...*spirit*...and kick it."

Magenta's defense of me *definitely* made the cold water worth it, especially when I shook my curls and Lysander gasped as he was sprayed.

Serenity was suspiciously quiet, but new names flashed on the wall: **MAGENTA** in pink (so, magical AI's *could* be vengeful). Then **LYSANDER** in black.

Mentally, I rubbed my hands together. Okay, I *actually* rubbed my hands together, before ducking my head at Magenta's stern glance.

Great Pan, please get her to ask if he'd ever role played as Tinker Bell.

Lysander's eyes widened, but then his face became an expressionless mask. "Do as you wish with my royal self."

Now that was a statement that rated high in the *Sentences that Princes Would Live to Regret.*

I rubbed my hands together again, simply because it made Lysander's cheek twitch.

"Truth." Magenta assessed Lysander. "Why is there a swan feather sewn into your pillow?"

Lysander became ashen. I edged my feet back, in case he hurled.

Perhaps, he had a swan shifter kink, just like I had a fae one or had he plucked the swan himself, stuffed the feathers in his pillow and it was the equivalent of a serial killer's trophy?

On a kitten's crooked tail, I didn't know which was worse.

"When did you…?" I'd never seen a vein in someone's temple literally throb with rage before. I watched Lysander, fascinated. If he self-combusted, then we'd all be covered in golden feathers. "Oh yes, when you violated the sanctity of our Princes' Wing. You shan't violate me any further. There's nothing that could make me answer that. Nothing…just…*nothing.*"

His chest rose and fell rapidly; he was breathing too hard.

SECRET flashed like lightning through my mind, along with a burst of Little Mix's angsty "Secret Love Song". I'd never expected a fae prince to project a girl pop group, rather than Beethoven or at least the Beatles. More than that, "Secret Love Song" was filled with Romeo and Juliet vibes.

What was Lysander hiding? Why did his secret about the feather shake me like it was connected to a tragic love story?

I rubbed my throbbing forehead. I knew that I should've pushed for the title of Lie Referee.

Lysander hadn't told us the truth.

Magenta leaned forward, concerned. Even though Sleipnir studied Lysander coolly, he couldn't hide his true emotions because Mist trotted to the edge of the couch and nibbled worriedly at Lysander's hair.

When Magenta held out her hand to Lysander, as if to tug him up onto the sofa between Sleipnir and her, I held my breath.

Come on, Prince Who Loves Girl Bands, just lift your hand and...

Lysander shoved himself to his feet, turning away, instead. "What's the dare?"

"I don't care about the dare," Magenta burst out, leaping up. "I care about..."

Lysander turned back to her.

Wow, when silences turn bad.

Lysander arched his brow. "You shall not make me fail this game by forfeiting the dare. Give me a dare this instant."

Magenta's eyes sparkled, and the windows of the

café frosted. I valued my balls, but Lysander clearly wanted to set his up for target practice.

"How foolish of me to imagine that you were, in fact, different to your family, when in truth you seek to command me," Magenta's voice was frosty. Lysander winced. "And how cruel of me to try and spare you. I shall be certain to challenge you now with something memorable."

Lysander's hands balled into fists. "One would have it no other way."

Prickles and worms, now he'd just added his cock as a target too.

Magenta inclined her head.

I bounced onto my knees. "Oh, oh, I have one!" *What was wrong with being helpful?* "He has to crawl around the café twice, sexily."

Lysander's cheek twitched again.

"Too easy." Sleipnir lounged to his feet, sweeping his arms around Magenta.

I tilted my head. "Ice down his pants...? Lap dance...? Wait, I know: he has to beg you to screw him in three different ways and..." Magenta raised her eyebrow at me. I pouted. "Don't judge the sexually frustrated fox."

Lysander's whole body appeared to spasm.

Magenta crossed her arms. "Your dare, Prince, is to strip."

I choked on my own tongue.

Lysander stilled, but he didn't say anything. Perhaps, he hadn't heard her.

Midnight uncurled himself from me, shuffling to sit at Lysander's feet. To my surprise, he worked at Lysander's boots, pulling them off.

Lysander blinked, as if coming back to himself. "Stop." Instantly, Midnight froze. "You cannot expect me to undress here in front of...*you*."

"Why not?" Magenta asked. "You expect Midnight to remain naked in front of us all."

Lysander stared down at the whipping boy at his feet. He opened his mouth like he was about to answer along the lines of *but I'm a Prince and my dangly manly bits are golden and would blind commoners like you*...but then snapped it closed.

With angry motions, which were far hotter than they should be, he undid his tie and tossed it onto the floor. Then he did the same with his blazer, before working on the buttons of his shirt.

Willoughby crawled across the circle, resting his forehead against my cheek. A tremble ran through him. I pushed him back, catching his mouth with mine to chase it away. With a burst of strength that drove the breath from me, he dragged me up, pressing me against the wall. His power thrummed through him, but he controlled it. He pulled me up, until my legs were wrapped around his waist.

It felt right to be held like this by him. Yet I knew

that it was comfort. He didn't want to watch, while Lysander was stripped.

Yet on the other hand, I would've given my prickles not to miss it.

Lysander undid the last button of his shirt, and it hung open over his alabaster chest. That was a good look on him. But then, he hesitated, like he couldn't make himself shrug off the shirt.

"You don't have to complete the dare, remember?" Magenta said; her eyes were soft with concern. "You can say no."

I was one stupid (horny) mage, which wasn't helped by the way that Willoughby was grinding against me. Magenta had never wanted Lysander to take off his clothes.

It'd been a bluff.

She'd simply wanted him to stand up for himself and rebel, even if it was only against her and our competition. If at the same time, it'd made him think about how he treated Midnight, then that was a bonus.

It was just a shame that Lysander was so stubborn...or *epic* because it'd mean that I'd get to see him naked.

Win-win.

Okay, I was a naughty foxy.

"Do not treat me as though I am weak," Lysander hissed.

"Then strip, fae," Sleipnir commanded, surging

forward with predator speed and grasping Lysander by the neck.

Lysander flushed, and his golden wings flapped. His fingers hesitated over the buttons of his pants.

Was he bluffing too?

We were playing a deadly game between Immortals and Princes. Desire, rivalry, and temptation. The game would crush us all...

At last, Lysander ripped off the shirt, hurling it to the floor in a crumpled heap. My feline side was desperate to snuggle down in the silky pile, but my dick was more excited about Lysander's pink nipples and the glimpse of emerald lace panties showing above the line of his uniform pants.

Now I needed definite membership to FKA: Fae Kink Anonymous.

When Sleipnir stepped back, Lysander clasped his hands smartly behind his back like a soldier. It was Midnight who slid his hands up Lysander's thighs, before with startling intimacy, unbuttoning his pants.

On my prickles, this was it...the big (or possibly small) reveal...

"Witching heavens, enough," Magenta's voice was choked. "I only meant for you to strip to your pants. How else would anyone take it?"

Midnight sat back on his heels, and Willoughby tightened his hold on me.

A shirtless Lysander with his golden wings

outstretched in defiance was the most beautiful thing that I'd ever seen, until he spoiled it by opening his mouth.

"That you meant me to strip *naked*," Lysander drawled. "But if my body offends you, then I'm more than happy not to be ogled by a witch."

"What about a mage?" I raised my hand, as Willoughby carried me back to the circle like I was in cat form, rather than human.

"Or an incubus...?" Bask waved his arm in the air as well.

With a huff, Lysander sat down, but I noticed that he settled next to Midnight, absentmindedly stroking his feathers like he'd forgotten that he was meant to be acting the strict Prefect with him.

Being stripped by your whipping boy was a brilliant leveler. If the thought didn't make me gag, maybe we only had to think of a way to trick the professors into stripping.

We could call it Strip Therapy or the Strip Social Policy.

WILLOUGHBY burst in neon pink across the walls, followed by **BASK**.

Pan's prick, Serenity wasn't picking at random. She was playing Revenge Truth or Dare, which actually sounded an exciting but deadly game.

I smiled at Bask, wishing that I was snuggled in his arms right now, rather than his rival's, who held the power. Weirdly though, it no longer felt like we were divided in that way.

Willoughby assessed Bask. "Dare: Dance with the two clones, Andro and Bas."

Was it just me or did that sound like a reward? Yet when my gaze darted to Bask and then Lysander, they were both shifting uncomfortably.

How would I feel if there was another Fox?

Bask narrowed his eyes, pushing himself to his feet with a sinful wriggle of his hips. "Dare accepted."

Why had that sounded like a challenge?

A green mist formed in front of Bask, and Andro stepped out of it with a flutter of his golden wings. The mist bled into his long emerald hair that hung to his waist. Unlike Lysander, he didn't have pants to cover his nakedness. Yet the soft expression was so unlike Lysander that despite the fact they were identical (which meant that it would've been a *big* reveal), there was no doubt that he was the clone, especially when he dropped to his knees.

Andro stared up at Bask adoringly. Bask ran his hand over Andro's head, before tipping up his chin and placing a single kiss on his lips.

Willoughby was watching him intently. "Bas."

Ruby sparkles lit up in front of him, forming into a gorgeous naked clone of Bask, who bounced onto Willoughby's lap, knocking him away from me in a whirlwind.

I chuckled. So, Bas wasn't as submissive as Andro then.

"I've fierce missed you." Bas kissed along Willoughby's neck, straddling him. "What do you desire? My arse is at your service. Let me please you." The words tumbled out of his mouth so fast that I thought he'd hyperventilate. "Pet me."

Willoughby smiled, gently pushing back Bas. "Calm. I'm here now."

A twinge of jealousy shot through me at the familiar way that they rested their foreheads against each other, and Willoughby placed his hand on Bas' shoulder. It was the same genuine closeness, as the way that Bask tucked a strand of Andro's hair behind his ear.

Lysander's mouth twisted, before he pushed himself stiffly to his feet. Before he could attempt his usual storming away trick, however, Magenta jumped up and snatched him around the waist. Her fingers stroked over his skin; I tingled, wishing that she was touching me.

When her mists coiled around him, Lysander stared at them in shock.

"Andro isn't you," Magenta insisted. "Simply because he's loved and part of our group doesn't mean that *you* can't be."

Was she still bluffing?

Lysander stiffened.

Willoughby glanced at Bask. "And Bas isn't you. Do you truly wish that I'd love you?"

He shook with hope.

Great Pan, say yes...because I wasn't bluffing anymore.

To be fair, despite my compulsive liar reputation (would I be given a badge for that like in the scouts?), I'd been the only one in this café who hadn't been bluffing throughout the game.

Bas' gaze darkened. "What kind of bad bastard wouldn't love my Willoughby?"

Willoughby slipped his hand to stroke warning circles on Bas' hip, and Bas fell silent.

Bask gave a shuddering breath. "Please, *love me.*"

Willoughby dragged Bas up with him, before hauling Bask into a crushing kiss.

All of a sudden, Five's energetic "Everybody Get Up" boomed out of the walls.

"The dare was to dance," Serenity explained. "Dancing reduces stress. Let's see those asses move to the beat."

"Yes!" I hollered...okay, *squealed* because I might be the Fox who Loved 90's Boy Bands. This was a safe space without shaming, right? "Come on, not even a Prince can avoid the siren call to the dance floor of this song."

"Sirens?" Willoughby mouthed.

I dragged up a bewildered vampire.

Midnight whispered into my ear, "I've forgotten how to dance. It's been so long..."

"It's easy." Joy rushed through me. I remembered bouncing around the attic to "Everybody Get Up" with my cousin, Aquilo. He'd been just as stiff and awkward, but I'd loved making him let go and *live* because I'd always had the feeling that when he returned to his family in the House of Blood, he'd been just as controlled and crushed as the Princes. "Just get your funk on."

Midnight laughed, and it was so beautiful that I twirled him even more dramatically.

Magenta tightened her hold on Lysander. "Now this popular music I like. It's certainly better than opera. This is our own Rebel Ball!"

"May I have the honor of the first dance?" Lysander murmured, clasping his arms around Magenta's waist like he thought that Sleipnir would snatch her away from him.

Sleipnir growled. "Not without me you won't."

As Mist boogied on the couch, Sleipnir rested his hand on both Magenta and Lysander's shoulders, leading them out to dance. It was strange how right it looked. Just like the breath-taking way Willoughby and Bask were caught between the two naked clones in a sinuous dance that was like screwing standing up,

Wait, they weren't actually...? Because that would be hot.

Unexpectedly, in a flurry of black crows feathers, Damelza and Juni materialized in the center of our makeshift dance floor, between our gyrating and sweaty bodies, and *epic* boy band impersonations.

The music shutoff like it'd been shocked into silence.

We all froze: Princes and Immortals united together by the power of Five.

Juni's eyes glittered, as she scanned the naked clones and then Lysander's bare chest.

Bask carefully pulled his tongue back from licking Willoughby's neck.

Could you have a stroke from shame because Lysander looked like he could manage it? His ass was pressed against Sleipnir, and his hands had been having fun on Magenta's ass. He squirmed to free himself from their sandwich.

Both Bas and Andro vanished in a mingled puff of emerald smoke and ruby sparkles. Midnight let go of me, falling to his knees and clasping his hands behind him. He ducked his head. He was as still as when the Princes had placed him in the corner like he wasn't real.

I hated it, but were all the Princes under the same pressure?

Lysander surged forward, paling. Then he dropped to his knees next to Midnight.

What was going on? Since when did Lysander kneel? He wasn't Andro.

Damelza assessed Lysander with the same contempt that she usually reserved for mages. "Do you know what I do to Princes who wear incorrect uniforms?"

"Make them only wear panties all day?" I asked, hopefully.

And there was the contemptuous glare that I hadn't missed.

"I'm sure that it's a disappointment to you that it's not my chest on display. My bosom is decidedly boun-cy." Magenta jiggled her tits in demonstration.

"Well, I'll have to struggle on with Hecate's help, despite missing that." Damelza didn't look away from Lysander. "Now, I have official academy business to deal with. It's almost time for the Immortals to go to the dragon stables, ready for the mission. But first, the Princes' lost the Rebel Cup. So, I've made room in my busy schedule to hex their whipping boy's wings."

No, no, no...

Magenta stepped forward. Her mists whipped around her.

Lysander glanced sharply over his shoulder at her. "Do not interfere, unless you wish your mage to die, instead."

My pulse pounded, and my throat was too dry. Wait, did that mean that Lysander also *didn't* want me to die? That was the most romantic thing that he'd ever said.

I'd feel all tingly inside, except I didn't want Midnight to be hurt.

I wrapped my shaking arms around myself.

Juni was pale, and her furious gaze met Magenta's. "I warned you not to hurt my Princes, but look..." She tangled her hand in Lysander's hair. "I wished to call you sister. We're family. But you...strip him...and now, they must be disciplined for their failure in the Cup."

"Have you been watching us?" Magenta's eyes flashed.

Juni snorted. "Do you think I've nothing better to do with my time?" *Bad mouth, don't answer that.* "Or that Lysander would ever take off his uniform without my permission? Unlike you, he knows the punishment he'll receive." Lysander winced. *"Of course* it was you who tricked or trapped him into it."

When Damelza tapped Midnight on the head, he spread out his ash wings. They were as beautiful as him...and so sensitive. It'd be like having his dick broken.

I winced. *On my prickles, this wasn't right.*

I'd been the one to fall in love with the ghost who'd been my first kiss. I'd been the one to resurrect her with my blood. Damelza had set those stakes on the Rebel Cup *because of me.*

All week, I'd been fighting to save my own life, but when it came down to it, I couldn't let someone else take my punishment.

And I'd never allow Midnight to suffer for me.

I dived forward, but Magenta caught me in her mists, at the same time as Sleipnir and Bask leaped forward to block me. Desperate, I struggled, but Sleipnir held my arms behind my back.

Magenta clasped me around the neck. "Believe that we love you enough to save you."

"*Fight*," I hissed.

"Stop fussing," Damelza fiddled with the feather behind her ear, "or this will be a double punishment. I'm certain that I can squeeze you in, as you're so eager. The Rebel Cafe will repel all attacks on professors, as will the charms that we wear. Haven't you read your copy of the Rebel's Mottos? It's all helpfully explained for students in the back."

"Is there a section on breaking wings?" I snarled.

Damelza tilted her head. "Excellent point. I should add one."

Lysander's gaze ached like he was dying inside; he touched Juni's knee. "*Juni, please...*"

Since when was he on first name terms with his Tutor? Did he have a sweet nickname that he murmured to her as well like *Witchy Poo*?

Juni's eyes widened at the use of her first name, rather than professor, glancing sideways at her mum.

Then she smoothed Lysander's hair, smartening him up as if out of habit. "How many chances did you waste to win? *Sweet Hecate, you're Princes.* Yet you allowed yourself to become...distracted. The responsibility and guilt for this lies only on you."

Lysander looked like he'd been slapped.

When Damelza reached out her hand towards Midnight's wing and magic crackled like black poison on her palm, it was Magenta who took a step towards her.

"Stop!" Magenta hollered.

"My patience is officially worn out." Damelza snatched Midnight's wing by the wingtip, dragging it up towards her palm.

I wished that I could see Midnight's face, but tremors ran through his shoulders.

Dizzy, my heartbeat raced.

Don't, don't, don't...

Suddenly, Lysander thrust his arm towards Damelza. "Break my arm, instead."

Midnight's head shot up in shock. "You mustn't, my prince."

"Silence." Lysander's arm was steady.

Respect.

"Mother," Juni begged, "he's obviously under that Wickedly Charmed witch's spell. He doesn't know what he's saying."

Damelza ignored her daughter. She raised her

palm with the spitting hex towards Lysander's bare elbow. He didn't lower his arm. I stiffened, dreading the *crack*...

When Damelza pulled away her hand, Lysander's breathing sped up.

She stared at Lysander in shock. "You'd really do it." Then she gave a sly grin. "But you don't own a dog and bark yourself, and you don't own a whipping boy and take his punishment. You're *meant* to care about them, which is why it'll hurt you so much when I do this..."

She snatched Midnight by the wingtips, before running her palms...and the hex...down both his wings at the same time.

I clutched my hands over my ears, but it still didn't block out the *cracking* of bones or Midnight's howls.

When Damelza let go of Midnight, and he curled into a ball with his broken wings quivering to cover himself like a blanket of feathers, Lysander hovered over him, unsure how he could even touch Midnight without causing him more pain.

Would she allow Bask to heal Midnight, after the tournament?

"Good luck on your mission this afternoon, Immortals," Damelza said like she'd just delivered a detention and not a hexing. "If you refuse to complete it, then I won't break your bones, I'll break your necks."

Hexing Midnight and sending us on the deadly mission wasn't enough for Damelza, she also had to threaten us with execution.

So, it looked like I was right: Life's a witch and then you die.

CHAPTER TWENTY

Rebel Academy,Friday September 6th

MAGENTA

When I reached out with my magic, it curled through the academy's wintry grounds. Its roots burrowed beneath the academy and up into the trees of the Dead Wood. Out here, as I marched towards the dragon stables and the mission, I could sense my Wickedly Charmed powers in every *crunching* step, the snowflakes tearing from the leaden sky, and in the trembling of the breezes.

I was wicked, but now, I wasn't merely an explosion of primal rage, grief, and pleasure.

The curse was melting along with the snow, and the wards that trapped us all in the Membership were breaking down. If my dangerous Ice Prince could control himself, then so could I.

I clasped both Fox and Bask's hands, unwilling to let go. Fox shivered in only his whipping boy uniform, since Damelza hadn't considered him deserving of a coat, even though she could be sending him to his death.

Sweet Hecate, never let me lose my Rebels.

Yet was it worse to hold onto them eternally or free them forever?

Sleipnir stormed ahead of me towards the huge stables with barred stalls, which looked more like a prison than the castle. His shoulders were stiff, and his hair was bristled to cinnamon red.

Music tinkled from around the corner. My brow furrowed. It was the same melancholy song about building snowmen (in my first life, I'd never have guessed that it was so hard for people to find play partners in the future), which my crow familiars had told me Willoughby sang with haunting beauty in the shower.

Was this where he'd learned it?

Ah, that made more sense than it being an elven ballad.

Yet I couldn't shake the sound of Midnight's howling, the *crack* as his wings snapped, or Lysander's desperate *Juni, please…*

389

I hated with a witchy passion the sound of another woman's name on Lysander's lips.

One of the things about being burned alive and then trapped as a ghost, who was unable to escape Hecate's Tree, was that it made me rather possessive of what was *mine*. Strangely, that now included Lysander.

One of the other things about being burned alive and so on, was that it clearly had driven me a little crazy because how could I care like my heart was in flames about two Princes and their whipping boy?

Had I captured them to our side or had they captured me?

I followed Slepnir around the corner and into the yard, which was in front of the stables. I wrinkled my nose against the stinging smoke. Then I narrowed my eyes at Professor Ambrose. He hummed along to the music, crouching over ranks of bridles, saddles, and spurs. I'd never ridden a dragon before, and I'd never been ridden before. *Well, only the once.* But losing my virginity to Fox wasn't something that I'd forget.

Inexperienced as I might be, however, I knew that I'd prefer it not to include anything that controlled, hurt, or whipped me.

My gaze fell onto the leather whip, which was coiled at Ambrose's waist.

Ambrose was a delicate, beautiful Seelie fae with emerald eyes that were bright against his alabaster skin and a matching steampunk uniform. His wings were golden like his hair. It didn't look like he'd have had the strength to have survived as a Rebel and then to have been offered the role of professor.

Yet appearances were frequently deceptive.

Most people, for example, couldn't even see my familiars, but Flair and Echo were loyal, brave, and possibly psychopathic.

They were perfect.

But then, *nobody's* perfect, and what's a ghost if not *nobody*?

"You know that I won't touch any of those torture devices," Sleipnir growled, "or are you getting ready for a seriously kinky party?"

Ambrose twirled around, startled. His wings spread out like he was trying to hide something...or someone.

Hecate's tit, did he have a lover saddled up behind him?

Snap my broomstick, let it be Ezekiel.

Then I gagged as I imagined Bacchus being ridden, instead. Although, I rather thought that it'd be karma for her treatment of Pocus.

"You're early, boy." Ambrose snarled in a Scottish accent that thrummed with such dominance that my knees almost buckled.

His gaze darted between us, as we strolled closer.

"*You're* late, Prince Ambrose," Sleipnir threw back.

Ambrose's wings drooped. "Are you ever going to call me *professor*?"

Sleipnir grinned. "Are you ever going to free all the shifters?"

Fox raised his hand. "Is this flirting session open to all of us or do we need to take turns with the sexual tension?"

Ambrose's expression darkened, and he reached for the whip at his belt.

"Da!" A small, pale face peered around Ambrose's legs.

My eyes widened. Ambrose had been trying to hide Ty, his son, a tiny fae boy with golden hair that curled behind his ears and jade eyes. He wore a plain green coat and leggings, but he wasn't a full fae because he had no wings.

Ambrose blanched. Instantly, he reached down to draw Ty, his son, closer against his leg like he needed to protect him against us. His hand shook.

My guts roiled. Byron had attempted to hide Robin throughout his childhood in the same way, every time that he knew Robin was in trouble. It would usually end in the both of them receiving a whipping, but Byron couldn't stop the impulse to step between the mage and the witch professors.

My breath caught. Robin had become my best

friend, but had father seen him as a son?

"Will you report me?" Ambrose said, stiffly.

"Why are you making da sad?" Ty demanded, tightening his fists in Ambrose's pants. "I'll f-fight you, if you h-hurt him."

"Enough of that," Ambrose hissed, swinging his son into his arms and wrapping his wings around him. "These students…" How much had he been struggling not to say rascals? "…Are your kind patrons in the academy. They're good." Ambrose looked like he was trying to force himself to feed his own son poison, and my stomach twisted. "Show them some respect."

Ty blinked away tears. "Aye, da. But I want the elf. *He's* good." I blinked. If only Darby could hear that it was the *killer*, with whom the child felt safest. "I'm s-sorry, sir."

"Chill out, short stuff, we're cool." Sleipnir shot me a troubled glance, before crouching in front of Ty. When he held out his hand to Ty, it was Ambrose who flinched. Sleipnir snorted. "Fae might be asshole enough to hurt kids, but I won't."

Reluctantly, Ambrose loosened his hold on Ty, who crept out from behind his father.

"I'd never report you," I assured Ambrose. "Would it be for the song about snowmen? Is it some type of incantation?"

Ambrose stared at me. "Are you mocking me?" His translucent skin pinked. When I merely arched my brow, he slapped his hand against his thigh with a crisp *smack*. "Nay, unless *Frozen* has enchanted the world, which is admittedly possible. Ty isn't allowed to be seen. But it was my daft self who risked it, which means that if there's punishment…"

"Yeah, it's all on your ass, we get it." Sleipnir held out his hand again to Ty.

When Ty grasped it, Sleipnir's hair softened to candy pink. A serpent tattoo coiled down from beneath his coat, shimmering and alive, to dance along the back of his hand, flickering its tongue at Ty's fingers. Ty giggled.

"Da, look! A snake!" Ty's bright eyes raised to Ambrose's.

Ambrose's lips curled into a smile; it was a good look on him. "Aye, but now it's time to go to your room."

Ty's face scrunched up like he was about to cry, but then he slowly withdrew his hand from Sleipnir's. Just for a moment, I regretted that this resurrected body couldn't bear children. Sleipnir would've made an admirable father.

Our godly ghost children, however, would've been a handful.

Ty turned and ran inside to the stable block. Ambrose watched, until the door banged shut. Then he spun back to us, and his expression hardened. "Fetch your dragons. It's tradition to ride to the ruins."

Bask wandered to the barred stalls. "Rayn, it's petting time."

When Bask stuck his hand through into the darkness, my heart beat so hard against my ribcage that I thought it'd burst. I doubled over, and my mouth became dry.

Don't let the dragon fry his hand, gobble it, or make it into a tasty finger food treat.

Sleipnir merely slouched to his feet, however, as my magic burst out ready to yank Bask to safety.

A dragon pushed its smooth golden head against Bask's hand; its neck was sinuous. I caught a glimpse of its bat-like yellow wings as it shifted closer to the front. Ethereal magic fluttered around it. Then it nuzzled against his hand gently in a dragon kiss.

Ah, this was the Snuggle Dragon who matched Bask, much like Mist did Sleipnir.

Did that mean my crow familiars suited me? Wow, what an awful thought.

Bask stroked Rayn. *How lonely were the shifters?*

When I caught Sleipnir's sad gaze, I finally understood. This could be Fox and him in these barred prison cells.

Ambrose marched to Bask, hauling him away from Rayn. "He's Lysander's dragon."

Bask's eyes narrowed dangerously. "Would you take it easy? Don't I at least get to choose how I ride to my death?"

Ambrose's hand dropped to the hilt of his whip; his knuckles whitened. "How about you rascals listen to me, and then I don't have to lose any more students?"

Bask nodded, avoiding his gaze.

Ambrose glanced between us. "The Gateway in the ruin is both a weapon and like a library's database to other realms and even alternate realities. None of you have seen a fraction of its power."

I crossed my arms. "As the new girl, I haven't *seen* anything. So, we're meant to step through something that'll take us on a mission to do what, precisely?"

Fox bounced on his toes. "New boy here as well. Voldemort won't be waiting for us, hissing our names like the noseless naughty boy that he is, right?" Ambrose simply leveled him with a blank stare. Fox shuffled on his feet. "What?"

"Have you forgotten that I'm your professor or that I can still sentence you to detention?"

Fox licked his dry lips. "I knew that there was something that'd slipped my mind."

When Ambrose prowled to Fox, raising the hilt of his whip to tip up his chin, I stiffened. "Then you'd best not forget this, *whipping boy*, it's your life at stake. If your Wing fail this mission, then *you'll* be executed."

396

My pulse pounded at the threat to Fox. "And what if we simply run?"

Of course, it was a bluff. I'd found that I was rather good at those.

Even if I could escape, I'd never abandon my familiars, Willoughby, Midnight…or Lysander.

Who would've thought that I'd ever protect a fae prince?

Ambrose huffed. "Like the Crows didn't think of that. You only need to imagine you're back in the academy and you will be. But the magic of the Gateway automatically pulls you back within the wards after twenty-four hours, if you don't return yourself. Then your whipping boy will be executed for your escape attempt."

Fox batted the whip away. "Brilliant."

Sleipnir's voice was low and hard. "So, who are we hunting?"

I shivered. *This was real.* Could I become an assassin even to save Fox? When his wide blue eyes met mine in question, I forced myself to smile. I was lost to him and the other Rebels. I'd find a way.

Ambrose reached inside his jacket, pulling out a sparkling black bag, which was tied at the top with a cord. When he stepped towards me, I shied back.

"Stand still, daft witch. I need to hang it around your neck." When I ducked my neck, Ambrose leaned in. He was shivering; I'd forgotten that Seelie Fae didn't cope in the cold. Witching heavens, he must suffer, confined to this stable block. Carefully, he brushed back my hair, ensuring that the cord didn't catch, as he tied a knot. His cheek was temptingly soft as it brushed mine, before he pulled back. "It's a fae trick; Professor Crow would be displeased with me for making unapproved magic like this. You can tell her, but on my wings, I'd rather that you didn't. It's a Sleeping Charm. You only need to crush it between your fingers, and all beasts will fall asleep."

For the first time, Ambrose appeared nervous.

"Why are you helping me?" I asked.

Ambrose shrugged. "When my son fell from the window and you caught him, you saved the most precious thing in the world to me. Ty is the only reason that I keep living. Plus, a fae pays his debts."

To my shock, Sleipnir stalked to Ambrose and swung him around by his collar, tossing him into a snowbank. Then he pinned him down. Ambrose snarled, struggling beneath him.

Hot as their unexpected wrestling was, now wasn't the time or place for it (which involved nakedness and oil).

"Do gods usually respond to gifts with violence because in that case you're on the naughty list for Christmas." I frowned.

Sleipnir glared at Ambrose. "By *beasts* he means *dragons*. Where's the Gateway taking us, *prince*?"

Ambrose's eyes shone with a mix of defiance and apology. "The Gold Court of the Dragons."

Sleipnir gasped, rearing back. "I will *wreck* you."

Ambrose slipped out a black collar from within his coat. I shuddered, stumbling forward like the dark magic within the collar was calling to me. The wretched thing was cursed. It burned through me. The metal was twisted into the shape of crows' feathers.

"You're the swaggering bastard who thought that he could take this off Marcus and free him without consequences." Ambrose shook the collar, and Sleipnir became ashen. "Now Professor Crow demands that you travel to the Archduke's Court and kidnap him back."

Rayn blew a burst of golden fire out of the stall in protest. Perhaps, not a *Snuggle Dragon*, after all.

Bask stumbled away, shielding his face. I choked on the stinging smoke, as the other dragons blasted their protests as well, before covering my ears as Rayn let out an anguished *screech*.

I didn't blame them, since their brother had escaped from the academy and now we were being ordered to imprison him once again.

"Take it from a fae who knows," Ambrose spat, "the taste of freedom you gave my dragon, will only make his suffering worse when he's back here or did you only care about causing mayhem?"

Sleipnir slammed his fist into the snow next to

Ambrose's head, but Ambrose didn't flinch. "We're not dicks like you. I'd never trap another shifter."

Ambrose shoved Sleipnir off him with surprising strength, and Sleipnir tumbled back. Then Ambrose scrambled to his feet, straightening out his uniform. When he tossed the collar to me, I caught it automatically and then almost dropped it. The cursed magic flamed out, searing me.

How agonising must it be for the dragons to wear these collars?

"Then I'll take Fox to be walled up alive. Do you want to watch?" Ambrose snatched Fox by his arm. "After that, Professor Crow will break your necks one at a time."

"Stop!" I called out at the same time as Bask and Sleipnir.

Yet Fox had remained silent. Would he truly die, rather than enslave another shifter?

Ambrose raised his eyebrow. "Don't waste my time. Will you take the mission?"

I bit my lip. There'd never been any doubt. My duty was to protect the Rebels. I'd spent too many years aching, alone, and desperate to save them.

I couldn't fail this new mage like I had Robin.

I clutched the collar to my chest. "Am I the wicked witch with the bounciest bosom?"

Ambrose rolled his eyes. "*Aye* to the bouncy and *nay* to the wicked. But I'll take it that you need this daft boy then." He hurled Fox on top of Sleipnir, who caught him in his arms. "Saddle up the dragons."

Bask's eyes glittered. "Do you wish us to be roasted alive or thrown off their backs mid-air? We're the bad bastards who are going to kidnap their brother. Whose side do you think they're on?"

Ambrose clenched his jaw. "Feathery heavens, then control them!"

Sleipnir prowled to his feet, before helping Fox up. "This isn't happening your asshole way. But will...any...shifter do?"

Ambrose nodded.

When Sleipnir caught my gaze, he flushed. It pinked down his neck in a way that made me wish to lick it and trace down further to his chest and hard nipples. I longed to turn his shame to desire.

Why was my god anxious?

Sleipnir glanced down, playing with his fingers. "*Please*," he murmured, and the aching desperation in his voice cracked my heart so deeply that I thought it might never be whole again, "still love me, when you've seen the monster."

Then he backed away from Fox with faltering steps, until he hit the back of the stable block. He closed his eyes, shaking.

What was happening?

Suddenly, I was both too hot and too cold at the

same time. I wrapped my arms around myself. *Was Sleipnir monstrous?* Yet I didn't care; he was mine.

I hated that he didn't believe he could be loved.

In a blue spray of glitter, Sleipnir transformed into a giant horse with eight-legs. When I gasped, he ducked his head, whinnying sadly like I'd rejected him. He pawed the floor, swinging his head to face the stable roof like he could hide his ugliness.

Yet he was beautiful.

His mane and tail sparkled like crushed precious gems had been brushed through them. His coat was the same gorgeous aquamarine as his hair.

How had I ever called Mist a monster?

I *was* wicked because Sleipnir had been hiding a *real* Mist inside himself, believing that he was a monster, when he was truly divine.

Bask bounced forward like Sleipnir was a special gift just for him, throwing his arms around Sleipnir's huge leg, before jumping up and down to pat his flank. "Bad Slippy, keeping the big Mist hidden from me. Think of all the lost petting opportunities."

Sleipnir's head swiveled around in shock. His ears raised from where they'd been flattened on his head.

Fox laughed, sauntering to raise his hand for Sleipnir to duck his head and nuzzle at. "Sorry I don't have an apple or any industrial sized sugar cubes. Do you know, I was desperate to ride as a kid, but boys weren't allowed that privilege in the House of Jewels.

Mum would have a fit that I was riding you. This is going to be *brilliant*."

Sleipnir let out a low, breathy *nicker* at the attention.

When Sleipnir nudged Fox, Ambrose watched with an inscrutable expression.

"I believe that your new," if Ambrose said *beast*, then I'd cast a Feather Itching Hex, "*ride* wishes you to mount."

We'd played games to strip back to the truth but in his transformation, Sleipnir had shown us the deepest part of himself. He'd risked everything, and trusted that we'd still love him. After Robin, I hadn't believed that I'd discover a love this powerful. Yet these Rebels shook me with their love.

I swallowed, shaking. Then I tied the cursed collar so that it hung from my pearl choker and next to the charm. I paled at the sensation of it touching my skin. Truly, it was a pity that these dresses hadn't been designed with pockets.

Then I dematerialized thread by thread, appearing again in a dizzying rush on Sleipnir's back. I lay low, winding my hands to hold tight in his mane, which was silky soft. His back was hot beneath me like a furnace. He was on fire, and so was I. My pink magic wound out, sparkling around him. He trembled beneath me with excitement.

My body was close to his in a way that it never

had been before. This wasn't like riding the dragons with the collars, whips, and spurs. Sleipnir had offered me this service.

I reached to stroke his ear. "You're a warrior and not a monster," I murmured. "This is a power like mine. I love this side of you because I love all of you."

Witching heavens, didn't I also need to say those words to Willoughby?

Sleipnir's body became tense like he still couldn't believe it.

I laid my cheek against his mane.

Fox hollered, as Ambrose scooped him up under his arms. Then Ambrose flew to settle Fox behind me on Sleipnir's back.

"Fae Airways," Fox smirked. "Always my favorite way to travel, apart from on a giant eight-legged horse." Then he cocked his head. "This academy actually has opened up opportunities for me."

He settled his arms around my waist with a smile; I enjoyed the close feel of him and the way that his crotch pressed against me.

"Indeed," I replied, "like the chance to be walled up alive if we don't kidnap an Archduke dragon from his own Court."

Fox's expression clouded. "Okay, some opportunities are better than others."

Bask yelped as he was dropped behind Fox by

Ambrose. "If it pleases you, it takes work to get an arse this pettable. You've only gone and bruised it."

Fox shoved his behind against Bask in a way that made Bask groan. "Grab hold of me. I'll kiss your ass better later."

Bask still shot a glare at Ambrose that even made him pale.

"It'll be your balls that'll be bruised for not using a saddle," Ambrose pointed out.

Bask cupped his crotch protectively, whispering to his balls, "Your sacrifice won't be forgotten."

Ambrose fluttered in the air beside us; his golden wings glinted in the light. "It'd drain the gold from my wings if you fail this mission. I promise, I won't punish Marcus for escaping and..." His wings beat even faster. "Look, I'll think about how the *dragons* are treated. Now get your daft selves to the ruins and the Gateway. Your twenty-four hours starts...*now*."

Fox glanced at his watch. "It's 1:17. If we don't return by this time tomorrow afternoon, then I'm..."

Don't say dead. Please, don't say it.

"We will," I said, firmly.

Sleipnir neighed, pawing at the ground. Then he turned and started out of the yard at a speed that almost knocked me back. I grinned, grabbing more tightly onto his mane and winding my mists to tie Fox and Bask to both Sleipnir and me. Now they couldn't fall from his back or away from me.

I took a shuddering breath and allowed myself to simply *feel*.

Sleipnir galloped away from the stables and through the wintry grounds. His hooves *crunched* on the snow, churning it up in freezing waves. Bask cried out in excited delight, and Fox laughed. A glimmer of sun broke through the gray clouds, warming my face as I raised it to the sky.

This was freedom.

This. Moment. Now.

No professor could take it from us Immortals. We were united together, riding through the grounds. My pink magic wound out of the floor and sky in a tunnel, guiding us on like life, death, and love.

It was everything that I was, and our connection together through the veil.

My heartbeat thudded against the beat of Sleipnir's and the *thud* of his many hooves.

Yet the Immortals and I rode towards the ruins, where another Blessedly Charmed witch had once been imprisoned, a Gateway to mystery realms, and a deadly mission to kidnap a shifter. I could feel the flaming magic of the collar, which hung from my pearl choker. It'd crush the shifter, trapping him, as much as Willoughby's suit or Sleipnir's shame did.

I urged Sleipnir on even faster, closing my eyes and losing myself in the sensation of my Rebels' love because ahead lay the Dragon Court.

Then all of a sudden, Sleipnir reared back. His eyes were wide and startled.

A stone block crashed down, blocking the path. It was ancient and dangerous. Shocked, my magic faded. I lost my grip on Sleipnir's mane, Fox and Bask tumbled from his back, and I screamed.

TO BE CONTINUED...

Continue Magenta's adventure in the final book of the trilogy **REBEL ACADEMY: CURSE, WICKEDLY CHARMED BOOK THREE HERE NOW**

AUTHOR NOTE

Curse — Book Three in the Wickedly Charmed series — is already written, so you can continue Magenta and her Rebels' adventures! The trilogy is COMPLETE and available to order NOW! I'm SO excited for you to discover the Rebels' dangerous secrets, as well as the thrill of the Gold Court of the Dragons, Dragon Polo Tournament, and the Enchanted Ball in the finale of the trilogy! The cursed past of the academy will either shatter or free them all...

You're total stars for your recommendations, word of mouth, and reviews because it's how my books reach new readers. I'm truly grateful to you. Even a single line review raises the series' visibility.

I love my Rebels. I hope you do too!

Thanks, you're awesome - my Rebel family :)
Rebel here, yeah?
Rosemary A Johns

Thanks for reading **CRUSH.** If you enjoyed reading this book, **please consider leaving a review on Amazon.** Your support is really important to us authors. Plus, I love hearing from my readers! Thanks, you're awesome!

Become a Rebel today by joining Rosemary's Rebels Group on Facebook!

READ REBEL ACADEMY:
CURSE NOW!

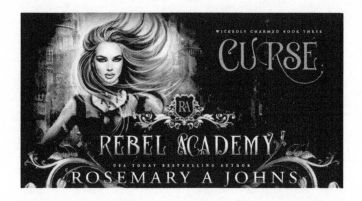

Midnight's fangs grazed my throat, and I shivered. He wrapped his ash wings around me, as I kissed him.

"Let me drink from you, my Queen," Midnight whispered.

My eyes fluttered closed, and his fingers circled my hip. When he licked down my neck, my skin tingled.

All of a sudden, Prince Lysander wrenched Midnight away from me.

"I'll tell you a secret." Lysander's breath was hot against my cheek, and his wings banded around me like he'd never let go. "Midnight is cursed."

"We're all cursed." I pressed Lysander against the wall, brushing my lips against his on each word. "Is the true secret that *you're* the one who desires my forbidden touch...?"

READ CURSE NOW!

READ REBEL: THE HOUSE OF FAE!

Read the standalone complete REBEL and learn the secrets of Prince Lysander's fae Court and Quinn (from Rebel Angel's) fae tribe!

Wicked Reform School, Trial Area

Monday 26ᵗʰ April

LORD SPRING

This morning, I either reformed and graduated or remained wicked and died.

At the Wicked Reform School, once you'd reached the end of your sentence, it was the only choice.

Yet I was Lord Quincey Spring, the leader of the despised *Rebel* Dark Fae tribe from the English forests, who'd walked in the shadow of death my entire life. After a decade exiled and locked up in this American prison of a reform school because my tribe had been sentenced for rebelling against the Unseelie Queen, I wasn't a model student.

This term alone, I'd had to sit a special lesson invented just for me: The Problem Prankster. How to think beyond *What Would Loki Do?*

Let's just say that I hadn't planned a graduation party.

My golden wings fluttered, and I wrinkled my nose at the scent of tangy blood that stained the wooden floor. I edged my foot away from the patch of scarlet (I'd spent ages polishing my boots), and glanced out over the Trial Area that'd been adapted into a stage for the graduation ceremony.

The fae were ranked like an army on parade, if that army were dressed in steam punk military uniforms with slashes in the sweeping coats for their burnished wings. Their emerald eyes were fixed forward, and their pale faces were as emotionless as we'd been taught to be.

Almost like they weren't here to be executed.

My heart clenched at the thought of what was about happen to *my* people.

Why hadn't I been able to save them?

If my older brothers had been here…if they hadn't been killed or exiled…maybe together we'd have led them to freedom. But what did I know about being a leader?

Please, even though I'd die today, let the rest of the fae survive.

When my wings drooped and my shoulders slumped, Radley (or Lord Brooke as I never bothered to call him…okay, as I sometimes *mockingly* called him…more like *Rads* for short), grabbed me by the scruff of the neck and pulled me straighter again.

Radley had a thing for manhandling me but then he had the muscles for it.

I peeked at Radley, as he adjusted my golden scimitar that was slung at my waist and then the swan clips in my hair, which had been digging into my scalp.

Somehow, he always knew what was hurting me.

Radley was my best mate. In fact, since I was a

kid, he'd been like family. The type who were over-protective with a hint of psychopath mixed in. Like me, Radley wore our uniform, which was a long coat with glowing runes on the lapel that stopped us from flying without permission and the swan crest of the House of Fae. The same crest was emblazoned on the belt of our khaki pants, and could be spelled with either restrictions or rewards.

You knew that you were screwed when even your pants could punish you.

Radley was taller than me, and his gleaming emerald eyes were bright against the dark of his ebony skin. His sweeping wings arced over me like he could protect me, despite everything. I'd braided his hair this morning into a warrior style because this was a battle, even if it ended in our deaths.

The other paranormals in the reform school called this day *the culling*, but we fae knew it as the *Day of the Wicked*.

When you reached twenty-five in the reform school, there were only two options: *reform or die.*

The spring sun shone hot across my translucent skin; my eyelashes fluttered against the light. Clouds flew across the cornflower sky like swans. My heart ached at the phoenixes calling to each other, as the bird-like creatures swooped overhead, in haunting melodies.

I wondered if the phoenixes had ever tried to escape through the high invisible barrier, which trapped us in the school. There were rumors that a dragon once had, only to crash. There were always whispers in a prison like this. It was judging between the truth and lies that was hard.

"Brothers in wings," a soft voice said from my other side, as a wing brushed against mine.

I shivered.

Oh yeah, wicked.

"Brothers in wings," Radley and I muttered in response like answering a prayer.

I turned to Felix (or Lord River as I sometime called him…*Lix* for short), and cold gripped me at the way that he forced himself to smile, pushing his tumble of hair out of his light green eyes. His caramel skin glowed in the heat. He was gorgeous but he was always too buried in books and intent on proving that a Forest Fae could be as bright as a Court Fae to realize it.

There were many tribes of fae, but only one Court ruled by a Queen, and she was a despot. The Court Fae were tyrannical and cruel, believing that you mated for life. If tribes rebelled against Court rules, then they were punished.

Like my Forest Fae.

Felix was as close a friend to me as Radley

because the three of us had been sacrificed to the Court Fae as kids. At least we'd always had each other to love.

I scanned the Trial Area. The main campus with its modern buildings was behind, and the school's vast gates in front. Yet the gates were warded and guarded.

There was no escape from this.

"You know," I glanced at Felix, "I'm starting to seriously doubt the claim that you're as magically *lucky* as your name."

Felix grinned. "Hey, Felix does mean *fortunate*, and Fortune Magic is powerful."

Radley grunted. "It also means *fertile*. Is there anything that you want to tell us?"

Felix blushed, and I loved the way that it spread down his chest. He circled around us. "Let's stick with lucky…"

When Felix stumbled, Radley caught his arm and pulled him to his chest.

The other Houses were right to fear the Fae Lords: *we were fierce*.

Felix gave a quiet laugh, scratching the back of his head, which was his tell for when he was nervous. He'd been trying to hide it for my sake like he always did, but I knew him like a brother. We'd spent our childhoods sharing a tiny room that hadn't been much more than a cell.

The Queen had made a mistake when she'd sentenced us to this reform school, which was meant to be for the wickedest paranormals of the supernatural world. How had she thought that it could break us, when we'd already suffered in a prison for most of our lives? Just because that prison had been called the Dark Fae Court, rather than a reform school didn't change the truth.

They'd made us too strong to be *reformed*.

Really, well done on the irony.

I swallowed, steeling myself to look out at the crowds. Staff and students had gathered to watch the ceremony. I avoided looking at the staff members, especially the stern-faced demon, the Dean of Discipline. Vampires, wolf shifters, and witches crowded the stage. I winced at the excited betting on who'd survive and how the execution would take place, which was led by huge shaggy-haired beserkers, (my odds to survive were currently 66:1 *against*, and the most hoped-for execution appeared to be flaying...*bastards*).

Well, this was what we got for making ourselves feared by the other Houses in order to survive. As the only all-male and English House, we'd always been the outsiders.

It took a serious crime to be sentenced here. Most of the other students, whether bear shifters or warlocks, were brutal and deadly. I'd learned to act like I was twice my size, just to stop myself from being torn in half every time that I stood in line for lunch.

A vampire pure blood with his chin tilted up arrogantly, even though he was swathed in dark robes to protect his delicate skin from the sun, sneered at me. His fangs glistened.

I snarled at him because I was having one of those savage moments that broke **Court Dictate 203:** *No snarling or growling.* I took a deep breath and then growled for good measure.

The Court Fae had taken Radley, Felix, and me as Hostage Lords as kids. We'd been the youngest (okay, *dispensable*), sons in our tribe. The Court had demanded that we be handed over and raised away from the forest, fostered at Court, and kept as a guarantee that the Rebel tribe would never raise up against the Queen's Court.

If they did, then we'd be executed.

Of course, my tribe had *still* rebelled in what came to be known as the *Love Rebellion.* Yet the Court Fae had fostered us Forest Lords for so long that they couldn't bring themselves to kill us. Instead, they'd sent us to the Wicked Reform School along with all the other male Forest Fae who weren't yet twenty-five.

But they'd made certain to traumatize us first by slaughtering our brothers in front of us.

I bit my lip hard, struggling to breathe.

In and out, in and out...

My lungs burned with their familiar illness, as I fought for breath. Next to me, Radley stiffened, and Felix swept in front of me to shield me from the view of the ghoulish crowd.

"You're okay," Felix whispered. "We've survived because you're strong. This doesn't make you weak."

Felix never let others see my sickness, which had grown in me since I was a kid. It weighed me down, settling on my chest and stopping me from transforming into my fae form. Something was wrong with my own magic, which attacked itself.

I truly was the worthless youngest son.

Radley pressed his hand gently to my chest, and at the same time, an unfamiliar scent like hot ginger warmed through me. My eyelids fluttered, and I sighed. The pain and tightness eased, and the attack ended.

Yet why did my magic feel more powerful and dangerous, rather than weaker after every attack?

My nose wrinkled. *Where was the aroma of ginger coming from?*

Felix gripped my hand. "We've still got about ten seconds before we're called up to *graduate*, Quince. We can think of some way to escape, right?"

I raised my eyebrow. "It's not as if we're guarded by armed ogres, on a stage surrounded with blood-thirsty witches, shifters, and dwarfs (the dicks), in a warded reform school, so I'm sure that we can make a break for it..."

"Lord of the Sarcasm, you're not cute." Radley gripped me by the neck.

"But *I* am, right?" I leaned closer.

"Do you need a spanking?"

"Does anyone ever *need* a spanking...? Plus, who's the boss here, Rads?" I raised one elegant finger.

Radley's grip on my neck tightened. "Certainly not you, short wings. Has that pulling rank crap ever worked since we were kids?"

I cocked my head. "*Ehm*, nope. But hope springs eternal, and when it does, there are going to be some changes."

"Revenge is a confession of pain," Felix offered with a shrug.

My smile was dark. "But it's fun."

"We could pray to Belenus..." Felix said, thoughtfully.

Belenus, The Shining God, was our Celtic God. He was sacred to the Forest Fae, and hated by the Court.

Would he even recognize a Hostage Lord with my illness as one of his people?

"Never pray to a god for help." I crossed my arms. Quinn had taught me the cautionary stories late at night of the gods who were glorious but terrifying. "They're not there to do what we ask them, and what if we don't like their answer?"

This was our last time together. *Our last chance.*

My breath caught. I wouldn't…*couldn't*…say it. *But we all knew it.* "Whatever happens is the will of the forest. I'm honored that you've stood by my wing. I wish that I alone could die for you."

"Don't you dare say that," Radley growled; his voice was suddenly rough with tears. "I'd burn the world to ash for you."

"I don't doubt it," I said, softly.

Radley smelled of wood and rich leather, as I pressed my lips to his. My heart clenched, as he wrenched away his head.

"I won't say goodbye," he whispered.

My eyes smarted with tears. "I rather thought that I was attempting to say it with my lips instead."

Radley huffed, but Felix snatched my arm, pulling me into a hug.

"I'll find you after death," he murmured against my neck. "They can't part brothers in wings."

I nodded, stroking across his shaking back.

All of a sudden, the ranks of fae began to beat their wings together like a drum roll. My heartbeat sped up — *thud* — *thud* — *thud* — to match its rhythm.

It's here now... any moment Wells, the Head of the House, will call my name...

"The Marquess of Spring, Lord Quincey Spring, step forward. It's time to judge the wicked," announced Wells with a haughty flourish.

I pushed away from Felix, fixing on my Patented Sneer (see, *fearsome fae*), and staring across at the Head of the House, the Duke of Wells.

Wells was a Court Fae, who I'd feared taking my lessons from as a kid because of his dreaded pop quizzes on etiquette, manners, and other things that'd made me want to blow a raspberry in his face just to see his stunned expression. He'd spent the last decade in this school, attempting to reform me.

As usual, Wells appeared as unruffled and elegant as if he was taking tea with the Queen, rather than waiting to find out if today was an execution, rather than a graduation. He was old enough to be our father, and acted like he was merely guiding us out of kindness. His smart military outfit gleamed in all black; his scimitar was neatly at his side. He was tall, pale, and as snootily perfect as a swan.

Was it messed-up that I wanted to wreck his composure, break that cool mask of his, and prove that I was still a Forest Fae?

Around the stage, the school was as elegant and

neat as Wells. Fountains *tinkled* between manicured lawns and trees, as if this was an academy, rather than a prison.

Yet it didn't matter how beautiful the setting, if the reality was your ugly death.

An execution could take place in a palace, as much as in a ditch.

I shuddered, desperate to smell the sweet scent of the wild forest just once more before I died, even though my memory of it had faded after so long away.

I missed the trees and my home like I'd been hollowed out.

If I was going to die today, then it'd be as a Forest Fae, and not a Court one.

I grinned. "You know, I'm not crazy about being labeled."

The fae broke off their drumbeat in shock. Wells' smugness wavered, and the crowd fell silent.

Okay, that wasn't good.

All of a sudden, the spicy ginger scent wrapped around me again, and I stumbled towards it like I was mesmerized. When I looked up, I met the ruby gaze of a succubus.

Who was she?

The succubus was beautiful with golden hair that coiled like snakes, and a white satin dress, which fluttered around her as if she was licked by wisps of frozen flame. But I should've recoiled from her because she also wore the swan badge of both the House of Fae and the Queen's Court. It meant that she was a new staff member, and I *hated* the professors who oppressed and controlled us.

Yet Professor Succubus wasn't watching this spectacle with excitement or dark enjoyment like the other staff. She shook with both rage and grief like it hurt her to witness it. When she offered me a sad smile, the burning inside me flared.

I smiled back, longing to march off the stage and instead, drag Professor Succubus into my arms. My dick twitched, hardening in my pants.

If I was going to die, I needed to hold her at least once. Yet I didn't even understand where those feelings came from, after all, I'd been kept *pure* and *untouched* by female fae for the sake of my future bonded. Except, I *did* know because it was her *smile* that made her truly beautiful. No one had smiled at any of us fae like that since we'd arrived in the Wicked Reform School. We were rebels, and we didn't deserve smiles that spoke of warmth and understanding.

Emotion was a weakness, and we had to mask it.

Bonding to a female was nothing but slavery: I'd soon been taught that at the Fae Court. Brotherhood was the only thing that I could trust.

Yet Professor Succubus' smile was like *hope* in the midst of the despair of this Day of the Wicked. I drew it close into the place that burned inside me. Then I drew in a deep breath. My eyes glittered with a malevolence that blazed through me. Wells had battled to *tame* me. But I was a Dark and wild Fae. I'd prove that I was free even at the end.

When I drew my scimitar, the ogres snarled and circled closer, but Wells waved them back. His cold gaze met mine.

Then I closed my eyes, humming "Don't Fear the Reaper."

How many times would I have to dance to this song and mean it? Although honestly, reapers were dicks.

I raised my scimitar, spinning across the stage and losing myself in the dance of my people. My skin prickled, and I was flushed with warmth. In front of the captive audience, I leapt and pirouetted, slicing my sword through the air in the age-old Forest Dance that Wells despised because it was the tradition of my tribe.

My heart swelled at the grins on the fae's once blank faces, as their feet stomped now in time to my own. I grinned too.

You could take the fae out of the forest, but not the forest out of the fae.

It felt like I was being burned alive from the inside; my legs were like jello. I knew that I was pushing myself too hard but when I was being killed in about...*hey, a minute now*...what did it matter?

Then my knees buckled, and I collapsed at Wells' feet.

Brilliant, I was just where he loved me to be.

I struggled onto my knees.

The fae fell silent.

My ragged breathing was loud, as I gasped after oxygen like a predator chasing prey.

You can do it...just one more breath...in...out... in...come on...

White lights danced in front of my eyes, and I slumped forward. My vision grayed.

Then Felix and Radley were kneeling either side of me, and their wings cradled me. Radley's large hand circled over my chest, as Felix massaged my back, and the pressure eased. When my breathing steadied, I raised my head.

"He only called *my* name," I rasped.

Radley shrugged.

Felix snuggled closer. "When weren't we wing by wing? Sorry, we'll just have to...you know...together."

He meant die together.

I bit my lip to hold back my tears because I wouldn't allow Wells or the other students to see them.

I could act like a Marquess...sometimes.

When Professor Succubus caught my eye again, her jaw clenched. I expected her to look away, rejecting me after my dance. But instead, she determinedly held my gaze like she was saying that she too was with me *wing by wing*, even though she was pale like she was about to hurl.

The staff loved these public punishments. *Why was she different?*

"Now you have your moment of rebellion out of your system," Wells drawled, flicking imaginary fluff off his sleeve, "shall we get on with the ceremony?"

I inclined my head. "Your Grace, the most Noble Duke of Wells." Time for the *pious face*; he loved that one. "I await the will of the House of Fae and our most acclaimed Queen with bated breath." Now *holy face* (another one of Wells' favorites).

Wells scrunched up his nose. "Don't hold it too long, we don't want you passing out on us just yet, *hmm*? Can I be assured that you're not about to burst into a jazz improvisation, rock ballad, or exotic dance? Perhaps, you wish to entertain us with a Shakespearean tragedy before you graduate?"

"Give me another horse! Bind up my wounds! Have mercy," Felix deadpanned. "Shakespeare's kind of *my* thing."

Wells sighed. *It was brilliant to have shattered his perfect mask.*

He rubbed the bridge of his nose. "Lord River,

enough of your tribe's savagery. I know that you were taught better at Court. I've spent years breaking you of such wickedness."

Felix frowned. "S-shakespeare's *c-civilised.*"

I stiffened. When Felix stuttered, I knew that he *was* close to breaking. Lock us in solitary, whip our wings, or threaten to kill us, but *never* insult Felix's Shakespeare.

"It's from the non-magical human world, and you learning it goes against at least five of the Court Dictates," Wells snapped. "When you graduate from here, you'll become Court Fae. What would the Queen think if she heard you spouting nonsense? The fae who choose to bond to you will be much harsher than I, if you can't at least *pretend* to be reformed."

When Wells' cool gaze met mine, I knew what he was pleading for: he knew that I wasn't reformed enough to be married into the Court. Wells had been one of the fae who'd begged the Queen not to execute us after the rebellion and he didn't want to murder us now.

Instead, he was desperate for us to hide our true emotions and act like perfect dolls. If he ever experienced anything as messy as the feeling of being *desperate.*

Why did it matter so much that he save us?

I'd tried Wells' approach as a kid, and I'd still always fallen short. I couldn't manage it for the rest of my bonded life. I didn't have a clue what bonded love was...or if it even existed...but it *couldn't* be that, right?

"On my feathers, I'm just excited about bonding now. The ladies of the Court sound like *keepers*," I gritted out.

Wells stared at me. "Excellent. The Bonding List for the one hundred fae graduating today has already been vetted and decided. There's equal excitement at the Court to welcome you all to your new home...or in your case *home*."

He never had understood my sense of humor.

"It was never our home," Radley growled; his sharp teeth glistened.

Wells ignored him. "Let's just get your graduation officially over with, and then your new life can begin."

I battled to keep myself still.

I was the youngest son of a Duke. I knew that the rest of the tribe didn't respect, know, or want me (*wow, that still smarted*), because I'd grown up away from them at Court. But I was still their leader.

If this was a war, then I'd lead them into battle. *But how could I lead them to their deaths, rather than a new life?*

If I'd known that becoming a grown fae meant decisions like this one, between condemning my tribe to death or forced bonds without love to cruel Court

Fae, then I'd never have envied my older brother so much. I shook because to free them, I'd have to become the disappointment that they'd always thought me.

"That's all fascinating, Your Grace, but I won't make a choice for the rest of the House of Fae." I steeled myself, before I hollered across at the golden ranks words, which I knew would shame me forever, "I relinquish my Claim of Lordship over you. You're free to choose yourselves, whether you wish to graduate or are executed. I'm sorry, I wish more than anything that I could save you but instead, I grant you freedom of choice."

Silence.

Sweat dripped down the back of my neck and between my shoulder blades.

"What are you doing?" Radley hissed.

"You'll be an outcast." Felix shuffled closer; his light eyes were wide with worry and shock.

Amid the sea of disapproving faces in the crowd, however, Professor Succubus' expression flickered for a moment with admiration, before she schooled it to blankness. I blinked. No one but Radley and Felix had *ever* looked at me like that. When Wells wrenched back my head by the hair, agonizingly digging in the clasps, my moment of connection with her gave me the strength to meet his furious gaze.

"Your brother, Quinn, Duke of Spring, was one of

the *best* fae that I've ever known. For his sake, I've tried to help you. Do you not see, wicked boy, how disappointed he'd be that you've abandoned your people?" Wells demanded.

I wet my dry lips. "I'm freeing them." Wells' fingers tightened in my hair, and I winced. "If you love my brother so much, why'd you let the Queen try to force him into a bond?"

Wells stiffened. "The Queen believed that your brother would be a perfect bond, just as you'd be for the Countess Pond."

Where was the Countess? I thanked Belenus that at least she wasn't standing next to Wells like I'd expected.

"Brilliant decision." My eyes narrowed. "Absolute *genius*. If you hadn't tried to force love on him... and me...then the Forest Fae wouldn't have rebelled. You know that we don't believe in a single partner for life, right? We love many fae in different ways. But what does it matter what savage fae like us think? You *forced* my tribe into rebelling. It's your fault that my brothers died, and we're locked up." My pulse was too loud in my ears; and my eyes blurred with tears. "And my fault too," I added in a whisper.

I remembered the night that Quinn and my other brothers had broken into the Court to free me.

Radley, Felix, and I had already been huddled in

the corner of our room, as sounds of battle had raged outside.

"W-what's h-happening? Who'd dare attack the Q-queen and Court?" Felix's hand had stolen into mine.

I'd clasped it to my chest, pulling him onto my lap. "They're stupid, Lix, whoever they are. She'll rip off their wings."

We'd all flinched.

"*I'll* rip off their wings first, if they try and hurt you." Radley had prowled to his feet, standing guard over me.

When the door had banged open, blasted off its hinges by magic, we'd jumped. Then an imperious Forest Fae had swept into our room; his scimitar had glowed in the gloom.

Radley had growled, and his fists had clenched.

Yet to my shock, the Forest Fae had grinned, dashing towards us and holding out his wing in familiar greeting. "I've found you!" *Why was he thrumming with joy? Why did his eyes gleam with tears?* "Come on, we have to go now."

And just for a moment, I'd hesitated. As Radley had refused to budge, I'd recoiled.

The Forest Fae's eyes had widened with a hurt that he couldn't mask, before they'd filled with a compassion that was even harder to take because I'd recognized him then like slowly rising from sleep.

How hadn't I recognized my own brother, Quinn?

I'd never even known our parents, but Quinn had raised me like *he'd* been my dad, until I'd been abandoned at Court. *And I'd hesitated to take his wing...*

"More apologies have wept through me than trees in our forest that I couldn't save you before. But are we not now brothers?" Quinn's sadness had shaken my own tears down my cheeks.

When he'd held out his wing to me again, this time I'd reached for it.

Only, now the soldiers of the Court Fae had been rushing into the room, overpowering Quinn and beating him to the floor. He hadn't taken his gaze from mine, however, like he'd never wanted to forget what I looked like and knew how precious those last moments between us would be.

I'd fought to reach my older brother again, but Wells had pinned me against the wall. Later, Wells had forced me onto my knees to watch as my three older brothers were executed and Quinn was exiled to a land of gods and monsters, so far away that I'd never see him again.

Today, I was on my knees in front of Wells once more, awaiting my own execution.

I slipped my scimitar onto the floor in front of me, caressing my hand across it. It was the only thing that I owned, which had belonged to my dad. In a fit of sentimentality, Wells had allowed Quinn to pass on dad's sword to me. I'd always seen it as a consolation prize for being sent away.

A fae was never parted from their weapon, except by death.

I bowed my head, and next to me, so did my best mates. I should've known that they would've kept their promise to never let go of my wings.

Dizzy, my heartbeat raced. Cold flooded me, as I sensed the green-skinned ogres circling closer with their swords raised. The largest guard caught me looking and winked.

Sadistic bastard.

The ogres' stench of mud and rotting flesh hit me, and I gagged.

Wells pulled out a graduation scroll from his pocket. "You're my flock of hundred wicked boys. I've spent a decade proving to the Court that there are more effective methods to control and curb rebellious impulses of youth than brutality. On the name of the Queen, reform now and graduate. Return as perfect bonded partners and proud members of the Court. Your Forest Fae heritage has been washed clean. You need no longer even remember—"

Radley touched the scroll, and his magic burned it to ash. It disintegrated in Wells' hand.

The crowd snickered.

"Well said," Felix muttered.

"I forgot once who I was," my voice was steadier

than I expected, when all I could see was the memory of Quinn's hurt expression at the moment that I hadn't taken his wing, "and I won't again. I'm a Forest Fae, and I'll die as one."

"Then you'll die," Wells said, icily.

The ogre booted me in the back, holding me down, as he pressed his sword against my neck. I hissed, as its cold iron pressed against my skin.

Iron burned fae. *Didn't they think that decapitation was enough of a punishment?* Tears prickled my eyes at the smarting agony. But then, this was what they'd done to my brothers.

Wells truly was sick to choose this as his method of killing me.

Clack — clack — clack.

Wells' polished boots stepped around me. I hated that his boots would be the last thing that I saw.

"It tires me that you could even ruin my attempt to scare you into behaving. I'm not going to kill you." *Wait…what in Belenus' name did he mean?* When the sword eased at my neck, why did that scare me more than anything so far? "This was just the mock run of your graduation."

I sat up too fast in my outrage, and Radley caught me, before I toppled over.

"Like a mock exam…?" I growled. "Wonderful. Really, I didn't need the practice."

Wells clasped his hands smartly behind his back,

and his smile was so malicious that it made me shiver. "Oh, but *I* did. Now I know that you Lords will sacrifice yourself as long as you're *free*, and your tribe have *choice*. This is your last week in the Wicked Reform School. It's my final chance to break you, and luckily for me, I have some interesting new methods." I groaned: *brilliant*. "Saturday is the first of May, the start of summer, and your *true* Day of the Wicked. You may have given up your Claim of Lordship, but if you're not reformed, then your entire tribe will be judged wicked. Just like you did with your brothers, you'll watch as they're executed. Only after they all lie slaughtered, will you get the chance to die as well."

"Wait, you *can't*." I staggered to stand, but Wells shoved me back onto my knees with a *crack*.

"I'm Head of your House: *I can*. How do you like being pranked for once?" *Did he truly just claim that staging our deaths was karmic prank revenge...?* Wells' lips twitched as he glanced at Felix. "Are you certain that you're not in fact jinxed?"

When Felix launched himself at Wells, Wells stumbled back. Radley caught Felix, pulling him into a tight embrace. I curled my wings around myself.

How had I allowed myself to be tricked?

Court Dictate 307: *Emotions are your curse, and a blessing to your enemy.*

I'd shown Wells just how he could hurt me. He'd tried to teach me for years to mask my true self.

Well, didn't I feel the idiot.

But still, at least a Forest idiot, rather than a Court idiot.

Yet now, I only had a week before the true graduation ceremony, where I'd no longer be merely sacrificing my own life, but risking every Forest Fae's execution...

Discover who will survive the House of Fae now!

USA TODAY BESTSELLING AUTHOR
ROSEMARY A JOHNS

READ REBEL WEREWOLVES THE COMPLETE SERIES NOW!

When Aquilo caught my eye with a grin, I knew that he understood the game.

My shadows thrummed with joy, as Aquilo and I strolled either side of Vala, the Alpha princess. Wind *whooshed* around Aquilo like he was the eye of the storm. His hair whipped across his ice-blue eyes.

I cocked my head, studying the board. This wasn't chess or a fantasy war game: it was battle plans. *Who was Vala intending to conquer?*

"A black hat to represent a witch, seriously?" I tutted. "I resent the witchaphobia."

Vala clacked her golden claws against the table. "What's that? Fear of witches?"

Aquilo leaned over the board. "Then what's fear of mages?"

A breeze shot from the tips of his fingers, sweeping the pieces flying like the wolves who my great-grandmother had controlled in the Wolf War. The mages gaped at him in admiration.

"*Oops*." Aquilo ran his hand through his hair with affected boredom, "My mother always did say that I was deplorably clumsy."

Vala yowled in outrage, raising her claws to swipe across Aquilo's cheek. I blocked her, snatching a bottle off the table and squeezing.

Chocolate sauce squirted over Vala's shocked face. It was almost as satisfying as squirting the sauce onto Moon, my Omega, would've been. If it'd been Moon, however, I'd have been able to fulfil my fantasy of licking it off…

Escape into the world of bad, bad wolves and wicked witches in REBEL WEREWOLVES and discover Fox's mage cousin, Aquilo…

Learn the truth behind the Wolf Wars…

REBEL ANGELS

READ THE COMPLETE SERIES NOW!

"I love you, Violet." The vampire's pupils were blown, and his gaze was desperate. "I know that you don't want my protection." He kissed my neck; his large hands stroked up my spine. "But just once...pretend. I'm not a hero but I could be—"

"I don't need to pretend." I caressed Ash's bare chest, and his wings fluttered.

When my fingers moved towards the waistband of Ash's jeans, however, his breath hitched.

"How can you touch me?" He rested his head on my shoulder. "When you know what I am?"

"You're mine." If Lucifer killed us tonight, at least we died claimed and together. "You're family and the Brigadier. No one can take that away."

I'd show Ash just how much I craved to touch.

I pushed open the button on his jeans, and although his breathing became harsh, he didn't stop me this time.

I slid my hand lower again…

Binge-read the addictive **REBEL ANGELS: THE COMPLETE SERIES** by the USA Today bestselling author Rosemary A Johns TODAY for FREE with Kindle Unlimited.

Discover the secrets of the GATEWAYS, Angel World, and the epic war between vampires and angels!

Click and get this magical, dark, and sizzling hot vampire and angel Romance now!

APPENDIX ONE: ACADEMY MEMBERSHIP

RANDOMS

Confess — Whipping Boy

Curse — Whipping Boy

IMMORTALS

Crow — Prefect

Crave

Sleipnir

PRINCES

Crown — Prefect

Crush

APPENDIX TWO: REBELS

Randoms

Fox, mage and shifter, Immortals' whipping boy (Confess)

Midnight, vampire/Fallen angel and Princes' whipping boy (Curse)

Robin, mage, Princes' whipping boy

Immortals

Magenta, ghost witch of the House of Crows, Immortals Prefect (Crow)

Bask, incubus of the Night lineage (Crave)

Sleipnir, Norse god, son of Loki

Princes

Prince Lysander, Dark Unseelie Fae, Princes Prefect (Crown)

Prince Willoughby, Light Elf (Crush)

WITCHES

Damelza Crow, Head of the House of Crows, Principal

Juni Crow, Damelza's daughter, Tutor of the North Wing and the Princes, Professor of Divination and Hunting

Amber Bacchus, Tutor of the West Wing and the Immortals, Professor of SHP (Spells, Hexes, and Potions).

Henrietta Crow, original Head of the House of Crows and Magenta's mother, Principal

REBELS WHO SURVIVED AND BECAME PROFESSORS

Ezekiel, Addict Angel, Professor of Warrior Training and Duelling

Prince Ambrose, Seelie Fae, Professor of Shifter and Familiar Training

APPENDIX FOUR: CHARACTERS

SUPERNATURALS

Loki, God of Mischief, Sleipnir's father

Andro, clone of Lysander

Bas, clone of Bask

Serenity, magical Rebel Café

Mist, created eight-legged horse that reflects Sleipnir's emotions.

FAMILIARS

Echo and Flair, Magenta's twin crow familiars

Pet 9, Pocus, Bacchus' cat Halfling familiar

SHIFTERS

Glow, Omega werewolf, Fox's friend

Snow, Omega werewolf in the academy, owned by Juni Crow.

Marcus, Archduke and dragon shifter

Rayn, dragon shifter

HOUSE OF CROWS

Magenta Crow, Blessedly/Wickedly Charmed

Henrietta Crow, Magenta's mother and Head of Rebel Academy

Bryon Crow, Magenta's father

Damelza Crow, Principal, Magenta's descendant

Juni Crow, Damelza's daughter

Emerick Crow, Damelza's adopted son and Groundskeeper

HOUSE OF JEWELS

Fox, mage and shifter

Hartley, Fox's sister

HOUSE OF BLOOD

Lux, Head of the Oxford Covens

Aquilo, mage, Lux's twin

SUCCUBI COURT
The Duchess, Bask's first bond.

FAE COURTS
Prince Titus, Guardian and uncle of Prince Lysander

Prince Lysander, deposed prince

Prince Ambrose, Seelie deposed prince

Prince Ty, Ambrose's 'mongrel' son

ABOUT THE AUTHOR

ROSEMARY A JOHNS is a USA Today bestselling and award-winning romance and fantasy author, music fanatic, and paranormal anti-hero addict. She writes sexy shifters, fae, and angels, savage vampires, and epic battles.

Winner of the Silver Award in the National Wishing Shelf Book Awards. Finalist in the IAN Book of the Year Awards. Runner-up in the Best Fantasy Book of the Year, Reality Bites Book Awards. Honorable Mention in the Readers' Favorite Book Awards. Short-listed in the International Rubery Book Awards.

Rosemary is also a traditionally published short story writer. She studied history at Oxford University and ran her own theater company. She's always been a rebel...

THANKS FOR LEAVING A REVIEW. YOU'RE
AWESOME!

**Have you read all the series in the Rebel Verse by
Rosemary A Johns?**

Rebel: House of Fae
Rebel Werewolves
Rebel Angels
Rebel Academy
Rebel Vampires
Rebel Legends

Read More from Rosemary A Johns
Website: https://rosemaryajohns.com
Bookbub: https://www.bookbub.com/authors/
rosemary-a-johns
Facebook: https://www.
facebook.com/RosemaryAnnJohns
Twitter: @RosemaryAJohns

**Become a Rebel here today by joining Rosemary's
Rebels Group on Facebook!**

Made in the USA
Monee, IL
06 September 2021

77413405R00270